Looking Far West

The Search for the American West in History, Myth, and Literature

edited by
Frank Bergon and
Zeese Papanikolas

A MENTOR BOOK
NEW AMERICAN LIBRARY
TIMES MIRROR
NEW YORK AND SCARBOROUGH, ONTARIO
THE NEW ENGLISH LIBRARY LIMITED, LONDON

Library of Congress Catalog Card Number: 78-50713

Permissions and Acknowledgments

Part 1

Hasteen Klah. *Navajo Creation Myth.* Reprinted by permission
of the Wheelright Museum.

Margaret M. Wheat. *Survival Arts of the Primitive Paiutes,* by
Margaret M. Wheat. Copyright © 1967 University of Nevada
Press. All rights reserved. Used by permission of the Uni-
versity of Nevada Press.

J. Alden Mason. "Myths of the Uintah Utes." Reproduced by
permission of the American Folklore Society from the *Journal of American Folklore,* Vol. 23, No. 89, 1910.

Andrew Garcia. *Tough Trip Through Paradise,* by Andrew Garcia. Copyright © 1967 by the Rock Foundation. Reprinted
by permission of Houghton Mifflin Company.

Peter Nabokov. *Two Leggings: The Making of a Crow Warrior,*
by Peter Nabokov. Reprinted by permission of Thomas Y.
Crowell Co., Inc.

Claude Lévi-Strauss. *Tristes Tropiques,* by Claude Lévi-Strauss.
Translated from the French by John and Doreen Weightman.
Copyright © 1955 by Librairie Plon. The English translation
copyright © 1973 by Jonathan Cape, Ltd. Reprinted by permission of Atheneum Publishers and Jonathan Cape, Ltd.

Clara Kern Bayliss. "A Tewa Sun Myth." Reproduced by permission of the American Folklore Society from the *Journal of
American Folklore,* Vol. 22, No. 85, 1909.

Alfred Jacob Miller. *The West of Alfred Jacob Miller,* by Alfred
Jacob Miller, with an account of the artist by Marvin C.
Ross. Courtesy Walters Art Gallery Museum, Baltimore.
Copyright 1951, © 1968 by the University of Oklahoma
Press.

Theodora Kroeber. *Ishi in Two Worlds: A Biography of the Last
Wild Indian in North America,* by Theodora Kroeber. Copy-
right © 1961 by The Regents of the University of California.
Reprinted by permission of the University of California
Press.

Joseph H. Peck. *What Next, Doctor Peck?,* by Joseph H. Peck.
Copyright © 1959 by Prentice-Hall, Inc. Published by
Prentice-Hall, Inc., Englewood Cliffs, New Jersey.

(The following pages constitute an extension of this copyright page.)

Part 7

Cover: "American Progress."
Lithograph by George Crofutt (1873),
based on a painting by John Gast.

 MENTOR TRADEMARK REG. U.S. PAT. OFF. AND FOREIGN COUNTRIES
REGISTERED TRADEMARK—MARCA REGISTRADA
HECHO EN CHICAGO, U.S.A.

SIGNET, SIGNET CLASSICS, MENTOR, PLUME AND MERIDIAN BOOKS are published *in the United States* by The New American Library, Inc., 1301 Avenue of the Americas, New York, New York 10019, *in Canada* by The New American Library of Canada Limited, 81 Mack Avenue, Scarborough, Ontario M1L 1M8, *in the United Kingdom* by The New English Library Limited Barnard's Inn, Holborn, London, E.C. 1, England

First Mentor Printing, April, 1978

1 2 3 4 5 6 7 8 9

PRINTED IN THE UNITED STATES OF AMERICA

Acknowledgments

For some themes and selections in this anthology, we are indebted to the histories of Bernard DeVoto, Howard Mumford Jones, Ray Allen Billington, and particularly Walter Prescott Webb's *The Great Plains* and Henry Nash Smith's *Virgin Land*. We especially would like to thank Wallace Stegner for help and encouragement during the initial stages of this book.

For assistance in securing materials and help in preparing the anthology, we thank Virginia Allison, Don C. Conley, Mary Ellen Luts, Holly St. John Neil, Marian Yim, Ron Shuman and Margaret Cleaver of the San Francisco Art Institute, Shirley Maul and Linda Korber of Vassar College Library, Floyd A. O'Neil of the Western Americana Center of the University of Utah, the considerate librarians and curators of the California Historical Society, Huntington Library, Kansas State Historical Society, Missouri Historical Society, Oakland Museum, and Utah State Historical Society. Finally, we would like to thank the staff of the Bancroft Library of the University of California for their courteous and efficient aid.

*For the Westerners
who are our grandparents*

Prosper and Anna Bergon
Esteban and Petra Mendive
Emmanuel and Georgia Papanikolas
George and Emily Zeese

Contents

General Introduction

"Oh, I don't know, but it seems to me this man has been reading dime-novels, and he thinks he's right out in the middle of it—the shootin' and stabbin' and all."

"But," said the cowboy, deeply scandalized, "this ain't Wyoming, ner none of them places. This is Nebrasker."

"Yes," added Johnnie, "an' why don't he wait till he gits *out West*?"

The traveled Easterner laughed. "It isn't different there even—not in these days. But he thinks he's right in the middle of hell."

—Stephen Crane, "The Blue Hotel"

America has always had a West. To the new republics along the eastern seaboard, the West was an unexplored territory somewhere beyond the Appalachian mountains "inhabited by savage nations . . . almost unknown and without a name." To Daniel Boone, immortalized by Lord Byron as the "happiest amongst mortals anywhere," Kentucky was the West. To many Americans—whether in Pennsylvania or Tennessee or Ohio—the West was a virgin land that was always retreating just beyond the edge of settlement. With the Louisiana Purchase and the Lewis and Clark expedition of 1804–1806, the West became more than merely a direction or receding line of wilderness. It became a region, a vast country extending across the North American continent from the Mississippi River to the Pacific Ocean. A natural division between East and West seemed to fall roughly along the 98th meridian where annual rainfall dropped below 20 inches and the eastern hills and forests leveled into flat, treeless plains inhabited by Indians. But even that boundary was vague. The trans-Mississippi West was not a wilderness inhabited only by Indians, nor was it settled by a gradual pioneering advance westward. Spaniards were already living in Santa Fe before Puritans even reached the Atlantic coastline, and in the same

1

year that colonies in the East were declaring their independence from England, settlement in the West had advanced to
San Francisco. What, then, as George Catlin asked in the
1840s, is the true definition of the term "West"? And where
is its location?

More than other American regions, the West eludes definition because it is as much a dream as a fact, and its locale
was never solely geographical. Before it was a place, it was a
conception. Its characteristics were invented as well as discovered, and its history cannot be separated from its myths. Because the West has become so overlaid with legend, it is
popularly assumed that a stripping of its mythic veneer would
reveal the "real" West. Nothing could be less true. The
American West was an intricate combination of both myth
and reality. The West surely created myths, but myths themselves just as surely created the West. Listen to the voices of
nineteenth-century Westerners, and you hear how the
Western dream, though often debunked, still played a role in
shaping the lives of those who were mocking the dream. The
West and the Westerner were creations of the total American
imagination, and it is for this reason that the real West can be
seen as what Archibald MacLeish called "a country in the
mind." As dream, such a country extends from the early
Spanish image of the West as El Dorado to the contemporary
vision of Marlboro Country. As fact, it exists in the jumble of
assumptions, ideas, expectations, prejudices, and values that
characterize Western speech and shape Western experience.
Both as fact and as dream, the West is more than a history of
westward movement, and the pioneering frontier is only one
aspect of that combination of land, people, experience, and
culture we broadly call the American West.

Before there was a West, the Indians who lived in the land
usually called themselves The People. They lived in a self-
contained visionary world where the distant landscape, far
from being the great unknown that would give impetus to the
white dream of the West as a "yonder," was to them a spiritual and literal home. The whole impulse behind their stories,
their poems, even their economy was to erase the line between what was mythical and what was real. The Coyote of
Indian myth attempts to find his place in the universe so that
its wholeness will not be violated, and a Yuma medicine song
reveals: "The water-bug is drawing the shadows of evening
toward him across the water." Here, in the Indian scheme,
the ephemeral bug "weighs" as much in the scale of nature as

the entire evening. Andrew Garcia, the young Mexican trader in the Montana country of the 1870s, came across the hooves of many deer hanging from the trees along the trail. The Indians had left them there to let the deer people know they had used everything they could of the deer but the unusable hooves. Still, Indians saw no need to be conservationists in our contemporary sense. They caught salmon during the spring spawning season or drove buffalo over a cliff, because as long as respect was shown and the proper ceremonies observed, the animal people would be appeased, harmony would be maintained, and the supply of salmon or buffalo would be inexhaustible. If animals were killed needlessly, or, as the Washo believed, if animal remains, particularly bones, were treated callously, the animals would go away and no longer allow themselves to be killed for the benefit of man. The arrival of the whites would violate this closed Indian world, and the Indian response, after defeat, would be an attempt to replace the old world and the old myths with new ones: the myth of the Ghost Dance and its messianic message.

Since the white newcomers, unlike the Indians, had to make themselves into natives of the West, what most distinctly defines them as Westerners, it has been argued, are those adaptations, habits, and attitudes that evolved out of their encounter with the raw land and the Indians. As a group, the mountain men were the first of these Westerners to find occupations in the trans-Mississippi West and to adopt Indian crafts and skills necessary for survival in the region. "The wilderness masters the colonist," Frederick Jackson Turner claimed in his provocative essay about the significance of the frontier in American history. Walter Prescott Webb pursues the argument in *The Great Plains*, maintaining that the semi-arid plains shaped a distinct character and mode of life, most evident in the world of the open cattle range, where the cowboy, borrowing methods largely from the *vaquero*, became "the first permanent white occupant of the Plains." What must be remembered, to keep the creation of the Westerner in balance, is that newcomers brought with them expectations and preconceptions that molded their reactions to the country. They shaped the West as much as it shaped them. Webb comments that the "memoirs and journals of the Spanish explorers in America reveal few expressions of surprise and astonishment at the nature of the country [or] the aridity or lack of water or the unfitness of the country for human habitation" because the landscape and climate of the West were much like those of the Spaniards' homeland. In contrast, Americans from homes in the wet, timbered East labeled the same area the "Great American Desert," unfit for habitation and comparable to the "sandy deserts of Africa."

The tradition of the "Great American Desert" shows that while the West was being discovered, it was also being invented. Perception of the West was bent to fit various cultural images. The comparison of the Great Plains to the Sahara shows that men like Zebulon M. Pike and Stephen H. Long, who created the image, were products of a time that actively sought what was grand and exotic and romantic. No doubt the Southwest was more like Spain than like Virginia or Pennsylvania, but this similarity does not totally explain the placidity of Pedro de Castaneda's description of the Grand Canyon. He, too, was a man of his times, the early 1600s, when natural scenery was less astonishing to a Catholic European than were events that smacked of the uncanny. When thousands of men and animals could cross the plains without leaving a trace of their passage, this was an event to Castaneda that bordered on the miraculous. But to the Spaniards the rim of the Grand Canyon was merely a "bank of a river [that] was impossible to descend," and there was small surprise in Castaneda's dry report that some of the rocks on the sides of the canyon were "bigger than the great tower of Seville." The Western landscape we have come to know as astonishingly beautiful and sublime was largely a creation of a sensibility that emerged 250 years after Castaneda. It was not until the early nineteenth century that so sober an explorer as Meriwether Lewis could sit in wonderment before two Western waterfalls and comment that one "was *pleasingly beautifull*, while the other was *sublimely grand*." Captain Lewis, like Castaneda, created his own mythical topography.

This creation of a mythological West included people along with the landscape. A good example is California, that island of the West and of the mind. It was named after a mythical island in a popular sixteenth-century romance, an island supposedly near the Terrestrial Paradise and ruled by women. The only metal on the island was said to be gold. The Spanish never found the gold that really was in California, but by the 1800s they did establish communities, presidial towns, and ranchos that many outsiders viewed with disdain. With the exception of some mountain men, most visitors described the early Californians as "lazy" or "idle" or—a favorite word—"indolent." Unable to accept Spanish methods of letting thousands of cattle graze freely through fertile hills, observers condemned *Californios* for not putting the land to efficient and productive agricultural use. Sir George Simpson summed up most reactions in 1841. "Here, on the very threshold of the country was California in a nutshell, Nature doing everything and man doing nothing."

This habit of imposing values on others was typical of the young American nation without an identity of its own. Defining Californians as "lazy" and "wasteful" was of course a way for others to call themselves "industrious" and "virtuous" and later to rationalize seizure of the coveted lands for themselves. Likewise, if Indians could be defined as "barbaric savages," whites could define themselves as "civilized." The other way to avoid taking the Indian on his own terms was to romanticize him out of existence. In the 1820s and 1830s, as Constance Rourke has shown in *American Humor,* a favorite figure of popular theater was the noble and tragic Indian of lofty vision and enviable kinship with nature. Recent sensitivity to the sickening record of the Indians' destruction has brought the stereotype of the superior Indian back into prominence, but stereotypes only obscure our vision of Indians as people, with the virtues and faults of people, and the differences of culture. Today's goal still remains much as Robinson Jeffers expressed it: to be able to look at the rock paintings of Tassajara and hear their makers' message from the past: "Look: we also were human."

Partly because of Indians and partly because of the harsh terrain, the West was seen as forbidding, and we are mistaken in our contemporary tendency to imagine the trans-Mississippi West as a natural magnet, or as a virgin land that inevitably stirred up spontaneous movements of expansion and settlement. The story is told of a Borgian heiress in the 1700s who offered a large sum for the establishment of missions in the most outlandish place in the world. The Jesuits consulted their atlases and announced, "The most outlandish place in all the world is California." To promote missionary work, Father Eusebio Kino had to plead with his superiors and cajole his benefactors to see that the West was not worthless in its apparent lack of gold, but valuable in its rich abundance of souls to be saved. The idea of the West as a wasteland was still prevalent in the 1830s, and this speech, attributed to Daniel Webster, is an example of what was commonly heard in and out of Congress:

What do we want with this vast, worthless area? This region
of savages and wild beasts, of deserts, shifting sands, and
whirlwinds of dust, of cactus and prairie dogs? To what use
could we ever hope to put these great deserts, or those endless mountain ranges, impregnable and covered to their very
base with eternal snow? What can we ever hope to do with the
western coast, a coast of three thousand miles, rockbound,
cheerless, uninviting, and not a harbor on it? What use have
we for such a country? Mr. President, I will never vote one
cent from the public treasury to place the Pacific coast one
inch nearer to Boston than it now is.

One of the West's first promoters was probably the first
European to visit its interior, Cabeza de Vaca, who wandered
through the Southwest between 1528 and 1536 and brought
back an image of a land that "lacks nothing to be regarded as
blest." The stated purpose of the nineteenth-century govern-
ment-funded expedition of Lewis and Clark was to promote
the fur trade; and their reports of fish, timber, minerals, fur-
bearing animals, and other natural riches helped fix the West
as a bonanza open to raid and rape. By the time the West
was largely stripped of beaver, men were rushing to gold
fields where most Forty-niners, as Prentice Mulford said at
the time, expected to stay no more than a couple of years.
"Five years at most was to be given to rifling California of
her treasures, and then that country was to be thrown aside
like a used-up newspaper and the rich adventurers would
spend the remainder of their days in wealth, peace, and prosperity at their Eastern homes." John C. Frémont's description
of vegetation and rainstorms on the plains was his attempt to
undermine the myth of the Great American Desert and to
portray the interior West as a place ripe for settlement. Ini-
tially only the edge of the West, like the lush Northwest,
seemed attractive, but that trek far West was still prohibitive;
at first only those with money, like the Donners and Reeds,
could afford the oxen, wagons, and supplies needed by early
settlers. Even after 1862, when land was free, it took elaborate advertising campaigns by railroads and land speculators
to spur migration West.

Many who came to exploit the West found themselves exploited. Working cattlemen found themselves dependent on
Eastern railroads and markets, and cowboys soon found
themselves working for absentee owners in Edinburgh and
London as well as in the East. Chinese who built railroads
and logging flumes, Scandinavians who cut timber, Basques

who raised sheep, and Greeks, Cornishmen, Finns, Italians, Slavs, and others from Europe and Asia who mined the West's wealth too often labored to make other men wealthy, and aspiring homesteaders too often found themselves busted by land deals or in hock to banks. These new Westerners, along with Latins, Indians, and blacks, did not melt into a homogeneous American society, but they did stamp the West, and by extension America, as a pluralistic society. What brought many of the early pioneers West was not a dream of adapting to the land and creating a new, distinct society of equals, but rather the desire to transfer to the West society as they had known it in the East, with one difference: they would be at the top of the heap. The vision railroads and steamship companies later offered to peasant immigrants was that of proprietorship, but even as railroads promoted a dream of the West as the home of free, independent, classless, self-sufficient tillers of the soil, their presence in the West made that dream impossible. Industrialization transformed the West. Soon individual efforts were subsumed by corporate ones, and the Wild West and the Industrial West interpenetrated, each giving shape to the other. In 1890, the Superintendent of the Census officially announced that the frontier had "closed," and Frederick Jackson Turner added that "with its going was closed the first period of American history."

What is perhaps most remarkable about this period of America's history is its brevity. No doubt the announcement of the frontier's demise was a bit early, and parts of the West ignored it. But even if we extend the date from 1890 to the end of the century, or to 1915, not many more than a hundred years had passed since Lewis and Clark ventured into what was just a vast wilderness. The West of the mountain men and their rendezvous formed a fleeting twenty years of that period, the Forty-niners took up about ten, and the cowboy—that most prominent figure of the Old West—found his world in decline after just twenty years of riding the Chisholm and Western trails. This brief history was also discontinuous. Parts of the Southwest may look back 300 years to when the Spanish first entered the region, but rapid change, not continuity, characterizes the many Wests that followed the Spanish West. The history of the West consists of a history of transitions, and fleeting figures of these brief, broken moments, could not have hardened into legend and endured as myth if there had not been such a longing and a

need for mythic sustenance in America. At the time of the
Louisiana Purchase, the United States was barely ten years
old. There had been no time to develop a mythical center to
the nation, no mystique of the Race or of the State or Empire, no national poem, *Iliad* or *Chanson de Roland* or *Kale-
vala*, to fall back upon. The Constitution and Declaration,
too rational in their underpinnings, were dry substitutes for
an epic, and although hundreds of patriotic plays about the
Revolution were written, few were staged, and even fewer
were popular except as farces. Revolutionary heroes on stage
were not taken seriously as legendary figures and were popular only as comic ones. Noble Indians, though, were taken
seriously. The country had no past, but it did have a West, a
faraway, romantic place that could serve as a basis for myth.
And the West did become an epic, an epic that did not exist
in one poem or in several, or in one historical moment or another, but in a consciousness and a yonder. Americans became a people looking far West.

The nostalgia and regret that color much literature about
the West no doubt spring from a true lament for what was
actually passing with such quickness, but the West was being
mourned as a lost past almost before it began. In 1853, before the era of the cowboys and cattle towns and homesteaders, Edward P. Mitchell wrote an elegy for the West: "In
1820, Missouri was the 'far West,' and Independence the
boundary of civilization. Now, in 1854, there is no 'far West.'
. . . Pioneer life and pioneer progress must soon pass away
for ever, to be remembered only in story." This elegiac tone
was firmly established as early as 1827 when James Fenimore
Cooper published *The Prairie*. As Kevin Starr points out in
Americans and the California Dream, one of the appeals of
Bret Harte's stories was that they imposed on recent events
the charm of antiquity and transformed the Gold Rush, while
it was still warm, into a thing of the distant past. In all of
these instances, the spatial distance of the West was being
translated into the temporal distance of the mythic.

The heroes of this national epic were often the conscious
creations of Eastern dudes and Western promoters. Kit Carson made a brief appearance in the Reverend Samuel
Parker's popular report of a journey across the Rockies in the
1830s, but in the 1840s Carson's reputation was still negligi-
ble, and John C. Frémont went to the trouble of checking
out the man's credentials before accepting him as a scout.
Through Frémont's subsequent reports and memoirs, Carson

gained national attention, and his heroic status rapidly rose to mythic dimensions until, in a biography by Charles Burdett, Carson's exploits were linked to those of the old Danish sea-kings in the age of Canute. A more stunning transformation saw the cowboy change from lout to knight. In *Virgin Land*, Henry Nash Smith charts how the image of the rowdy, dirty cattle drover, denounced by President Chester A. Arthur in a message to Congress in 1881, was replaced by a chivalric hero. Buck Taylor, the first "King of the Cowboys," became a six-foot-five matinee idol of Buffalo Bill's Wild West Show and a dime-novel hero glorified by Prentiss Ingraham. Taylor was largely the creation of William F. Cody, who was himself largely the "Buffalo Bill" creation of Ned Buntline and the Beadle Half-Dime Library. The later literary and film stereotype of the cowboy stems largely from the demigod cooked up between Owen Wister and Frederic Remington. The cowboy emerged as the taciturn gunfighting hero of Wister's *The Virginian* and won the praise of no less respectable an Easterner than Henry James. Letting friendship dictate the tone, James wrote to Wister, "I very heartily congratulate you; you have made [the Virginian] live, with a high, but lucid complexity, from head to foot & from beginning to end; you have not only intensely seen & conceived him, but you have reached with him an admirable objectivity, & I find the whole thing a rare & remarkable feat. . . . Bravo, bravo."

The East wanted the West wild, but not too wild, and Western heroes, like the Virginian, often became embodiments of Victorian virtue. When Henry M. Stanley, of later Dr. Livingstone fame, met Wild Bill Hickok in 1867, he presented him to readers as a handsome man with "wavy, silken curls" who had no "swaggering gait" or "barbaric jargon"; he spoke well, would not perform a "mean action," was "more inclined to be sociable than otherwise," and was "generous, even to extravagance." The only thing Stanley seems to have forgotten were Wild Bill's fondness for children and kindness to dogs. The reverse of such images was also possible, and the West then became the dark side of the East's soul: knives flashed, bullets and arrows flew, and William H. Bonney or William McCarty or Bill Harrigan—whoever he was—became Billy the Kid, and blood flowed like rivers across the plains.

The obvious distortion of this mythic West is not so interesting as is its nearness to the surface of history. Legendary Westerners were not drawn from figures already eternalized

by Arthurian mists of a dim past, they were real men who
confronted their own myths and often helped shape them. Kit
Carson faced himself as a melodramatic hero in 1849 when
he found a sensationalized paperback novel about himself
among the Indian spoils plundered from a wagon train. In his
own autobiography Carson significantly recounts this incident
with Western reticence: he doesn't say whether he is embarrassed or flattered by this sensationalized version of himself.
As the man of the West he simply looks at himself as myth
before he is cold, and he doesn't flinch. Twenty-four years
later, Wild Bill Hickok was appearing on stage playing the
popular role of "Wild Bill Hickok" during an Eastern theater
tour he made in 1873, three years before he was murdered in
Deadwood. With Buffalo Bill, who signed his name to no
fewer than fifteen ghost-written autobiographies and Buffalo
Bill dime novels, we reach that example of Western history
and subsequent American life where fact and publicity blur,
and myth completely overtakes reality. In the West itself, this
overlapping of the mythic and the real gave rise to Westerners' self-conscious tendency to play (or play down) the *role*
of the Westerner. In 1867 a Kansas newspaper reported that
"the story of 'Wild Bill,' as told in Harper's for February is
not easily credited hereabouts. . . . it sounds mythical." Five
years later, the *Kansas Daily Commonwealth* presented the
border-state view of Hickok as "nothing more than a
drunken, restless, murderous coward, who is treated with contempt by true border men, and who should have been hung
years ago for the murder of innocent men." Years earlier,
Charles Preuss, the reluctant cartographer of the Frémont expeditions, found Kit Carson's "butchery" similarly "disgusting," while Frémont found it noble.

The other side of this coin is that these mythic figures offered Westerners something to live up to. When Kit Carson
happened to join a party on the Taos Trail, young Lewis
Garrard, who was there, described him as the "renowned Kit
Carson, so celebrated as the companion and guide of Colonel
Frémont." But Garrard makes no attempt "to detract from
Carson's well-earned fame." He merely comments that "there
are numbers of mountainmen as fearless and expert as he,
though to the reading world little known, whose prowess in
scalptaking and beaver trapping is the theme of many campfires, and the highest admiration of younger mountaineers." It
is easy to understand how the West became a state of mind
for those boys sitting around campfires and aspiring to live

up to the reputations of Jim Bridger and Joe Walker and Tom Fitzpatrick. The later cowboy's pride and sense of self is reflected in his quickness to put on his "woollies" or fancy chaps, draw his pistol, hang a cigarette from his lips, and pose for photographs of himself as a tough swashbuckler of the plains. It is instructive to imagine the state of mind of three bandits who were captured in the Dakotas in the 1880s. Theodore Roosevelt, who was a member of the capturing party, tells us that the outlaws' saddlebags were crammed with dime novels about daring desperadoes. Again and again, the West shows that when a state of mind finds expression in action, myth becomes history, just as history is always aspiring to become myth.

No one was more aware of this phenomenon of Western experience than Stephen Crane, who was twenty-three and already the author of *The Red Badge of Courage* when he came West in 1895. Crane was not alone in his impulse to look at the reality under the Western myth, for unlike the never-never land of Arthurian England, the myth of the West was a myth that *could* be tested: all a homesteader or dime-novel addict had to do was take the train out to where he thought the West began. Even before there were railroads, every season brought some bookish young Easterner or traveling grand duke or painter out to where *he* thought the West began. But unlike many chroniclers who simply spotlighted the tension between their own mythical expectations and the actuality of the West, Crane was quick to recognize the extent to which a mythology was recognized and lived out self-consciously by Westerners themselves. He wrote stories that used the stuff of pulp fiction such as lynchings, gunfights, and last-minute rescues by troopers, but he made them uncharacteristic Westerns in his refusal to follow dime-novel formulas. In a Crane story, a lynching in the name of justice and morality might be seen for what it really was: a "speculation in real estate."

It was the death of a gunfighting hero in another Crane story that caused an offended Teddy Roosevelt to write Crane a letter urging him to stick to the proper myths: "Some day I want you to write another story of the frontiersman and the Mexican greaser in which the frontiersman shall come out on top; it is more normal that way!" In one of the great short stories of American literature, "The Blue Hotel," Crane shows how the mythical Wild West, as a place in the mind, could become a deadly reality in an unlikely town in Nebraska. To the citizens of Fort Romper, their town is on the edge of becoming a metropolis with a second railroad line, a factory, four churches, electric streetcars, a big brick schoolhouse—all the institutions representing the law and civility of the East. To them the Wild West still exists, but it is yonder, *out West*, in Wyoming. When violence erupts in this town, the scene could be in New York or Nebraska or Nevada; geography no longer matters. "The Blue Hotel" reveals a truth that both East and West knew about their churches and theaters and hotels. Culture is a thin and perilous veneer and beneath it lie Crazy Horse and Liver-Eating Johnson and Hangtown and Dodge City.

In the twentieth century, the recent, brief history of the West remains near the skin of the present, and weighted with legend, it remains burdensome, prompting Westerners to spurn it or honor it. The surface of life in the West has changed in the last seventy years, but scattered remnants of an older West survive in corners of the Southwest and Great Basin deserts and in back towns of the Northwest and in stretches of the high plateau cattle-grazing country: John Gregory Dunne in *Delano: The Story of the California Grape Strike* portrays pockets of the agricultural Central Valley of the early 1960s as "largely insulated from what industrial America thinks and does and worries about. . . . The prevailing ethic is that of the nineteenth century frontier."

The heritage of the West most often invoked is that of its code. Often attributed mistakenly to the solitary gunslinger, the real code of the West was communal, a set of unspoken assumptions and unwritten social rules. At the heart of the code was the prescription that when in doubt, one minds his own business and keeps his mouth shut. Pain, for instance, was simply something to be endured, not talked about. The most condemned violaters of the code were self-pitiers, braggarts, complainers, shirkers, and horsethieves. The ethic of fair play commanded that you did not deprive a man of what was most necessary for his survival or livelihood. To a cowboy it was his horse, but to a Basque sheepherder like Robert Laxalt's father in *Sweet Promised Land*, it was his dog. You were expected to be hospitable to a stranger's need, but respectful of his privacy; a man's past was his own business. "Oh, what was your name in the States?" an early song wryly asks, "Was it Thompson or Johnson or Bates?/Did you mur-

der your wife/And fly for your life?/Say, what was your
name in the States?"

There are certain things, according to J. B. Priestley, that a
cowboy "must be able to do well, or it is all up with him, and
they cannot be faked, as politicians and professional men and
directors of companies so often fake things. He cannot pretend to be able to ride and rope, and get away with it." As a
result, the code graced the necessity of competence with the
virtue of pride, but roughhouse practical joking, an important
strain of Western humor, was allowed to keep that pride
within limits. The prohibition against prejudging a person did
not disallow testing or "putting the leggins on" him and
whoever was the object of laughter was also expected to
laugh at himself. The immensity of the West's terrain was the
great equalizer, and the code encouraged assertions of individuality in dress or style, but like the response of the impersonal landscape itself, the code admonished anyone from
taking himself too seriously. Speech was similarly affected. It
could be reckless and extravagant and ebulliant on one hand,
but indirect and laconic on the other. Since a man's word was
binding, words were to be respected, but no restraint was
called for when "puttin the leggins on" someone. As a result,
humor was extreme or understated, often grotesque and even
brutal, but usually oblique. In *Wolf Willow*, Wallace Stegner
points out that cowboys "honored courage, competence, self-
reliance, and they honored them tacitly. They took them for
granted. It was their absence, not their presence, that was
cause for remark. Practicing comradeship in a rough and dangerous job, they lived a life calculated to make a man careless of everything except the few things he really valued."

Like everything else about the West, romanticizing the
code has prettified its vices. Too often invoked to justify impulsive violence and overpraise toughness, the code was crude
in its standards of judgment and narrow in its range of virtues. While much of it might still be valued, much of it is too
limited and callous to meet the complexities of most people's
lives. As Stegner has shown, the code of the West was primarily a response to conditions that were particular to a
"nearly womanless culture, nomadic, harsh, dangerous, essentially romantic." Perhaps the West's most valuable heritage
still stems from what gave rise to the code in the first place,
to what shaped the Indian vision of his world, and to what in
the West remains from its beginning: the land and the sky.
Although diminishing, the immense spaces and lonely terrain

of the West might still let us experience a recovered sense of what Robinson Jeffers says we have lost and of what, even today, is perhaps the West's richest legacy: the dignity of room, the value of rareness.

I

The West Without
A West: The Indians

With beauty before me, I walk,
With beauty behind me, I walk,
With beauty above and about me, I walk,
It is finished in beauty,
It is finished in beauty.

—Navajo Night Chant

Introduction to Part I

The Indians' West was a visionary world, and its boundaries were those of vision. Every hill and bluff and stream was known intimately—with the precision not only of the geographer or the mapmaker, but also of the mystic—and all were associated with tribal legend, with the myths of the creation and the first people, with personal dreams and legends. The animals the Indians lived among and hunted also had their places in the mythical fabric. They spoke to men in medicine dreams and visions and played their parts in a complex mythology which gave order to Indian thought and Indian religion. History, time, and space moved into the endless reaches of legend without interruption. There was no yonder, only one immense here: a West without a West.

It was a hard land, for the most part. Although there were pockets of incredible richness, the Indian way was usually one of lean subsistence. The first Mormon pioneers to enter the Salt Lake Valley found the Indians harvesting crickets. The crickets would prove a scourge to the wheat-growing pioneers, but to the Indians they were not destroyers of food, they were food itself. These same Great Basin Indians gathered eighty-one varieties of seeds and plants in an area that to this day remains one of forbidding hostility. On the Great Plains, Indians followed the vast herds of buffalo, using the meat for food, the skins for clothing and shelter, the sinew, bone, and horn for bow-making and tool-making. The Indians were masters of using without waste the total resources of their environment.

The Indians sought a balance with nature because they were part of it. Out of this sense of balance came their religion and their ethical code. The Paiute woman must travel light in order to survive, so she makes her basket her home, shop and kitchen. Necessity becomes morality and it is considered a bad thing in Paiute society to possess too much. On

17

the fish- and fur-rich coast of the Pacific Northwest, a land of surpassing abundance, elaborate potlatch ceremonies were held where goods were given away or destroyed and immense feasts consumed by tribes who have been seen as proud of their "conspicuous consumption" as any group of Silver Kings. A closer look reveals, beyond the race for status, an attempt to distribute goods which would destroy the delicate tribal balance if allowed to accumulate permanently in such profusion. This same sense of balance is found in Indian myth. Coyote, the trickster figure known to Indians throughout the West, investigates earth, air, water, and fire for his proper element, and is given a rude awakening for his pains. Indians could laugh, and their humor was often obscene: here a risqué story is also part of the timeless attempt to express a world in harmony, a world where coyotes must know their place. The Plains Indian's justice, in the view of the anthropologist Lévi-Strauss, is based on the same principle of a balance of the tribe and all its members: there should be no outsiders. Murder was a crime against the entire tribe for the Cheyennes, and its punishment was a terrible one: banishment.

But if the Indians aspired to a balance with nature and among themselves as a tribe, to their neighbors they could be ferocious. Tribes such as the Hopis were models of peace, but for other Indians warfare was as much a part of life as hunting, and more enjoyable. The warriors of the Great Plains were masters of it. In a sense, the Plains tribes were a creation of the whites, for it was the Spaniard's horse that enabled them to conquer the buffalo and perfect the style of war and long migration that were their characteristics. The plains of the Southwest where Cabeza da Vaca had found only poor, wandering hunters and humble farmers in the 1520s and 1530s had, by the eighteenth century, become the home of Indians of another kind. Mounted on the descendants of the conquistadors' ponies, they had made themselves a formidable war society.

Like other mounted societies, from the Persians to the knights of medieval Europe, the Plains Indians produced a military aristocracy. They were conscious of status and eager to gain it. They were cruel, for cruelty, with lightning raids and ambush, was part of their tactics. But even war was part of the visionary system of the Indian's world. The Crow warrior Two Leggings devoted himself to fasting and self-torture in an attempt to achieve the powerful medicine dream that would give him success in war and make him a chief—an honor he never achieved. But if Two Leggings failed, others succeeded. By the time the whites began to invade the West the Indians of the plains presented a barrier of imposing proportions.

The coming of the whites was not merely a contest of weapons—six-gun and rifle against bow and spear—or of wills, but a collision of cultures, economies, myths. The whites had come to exploit the land, the Indians lived as part of it. Teddy Roosevelt, in his role as a Dakota rancher, could not understand the Indian view. These wandering Indian hunters, since they built no fences, erected no permanent dwellings, could have no possession. They were necessary sacrifices to "civilization." It was a justification for the seizing of Indian lands to be heard again and again. But Roosevelt and his fellow settlers were not the only whites to misunderstand the Indian. Well-meaning Easterners, travelers like the painter A. J. Miller, or stay-at-homes like Longfellow, pasted upon the Indian the literary myth of the noble savage, turning him into a romantic Hellene, or, perhaps worse, sentimentalizing his demise. Others, such as the influential editor-politician Horace Greeley, saw the Indian as a degenerate, unworthy of the land, while Melville found a spokesman in *The Confidence-Man* for the confirmed Indian hater. Protestant America—the sentimentalizers and literary lions, as well as the haters and exterminators—was willing to do what its own missionaries and the Catholic padres before them were not: deny the Indian his soul. But there was another view of the Indian, best expressed by such pioneering observers as George Catlin, the lawyer turned painter who looked at the Indian with an eye to record, without sentimentality or hatred, his rich ceremonial life and the country he inhabited. Catlin's European tours with his museum and his bands of live Indians amused and astonished the curious. His paintings received a mixed reception, but at least one critic—Charles Baudelaire—saw the light of genius. The Iowa medicine man who replies to the moral pretensions of the Temperance Society perhaps speaks for Catlin as well.

The collision of cultures, Indian and white, was as complete as it was brutal. Such lurid massacres as the battle of the Little Big Horn and Wounded Knee have become part of our national consciousness, but as much destruction was done by white undermining of the balanced world of the Indian as by actual warfare. Diseases against which Indians had no resistance exterminated whole tribes. The cheap liquor of the Indian traders devastated the proud warrior societies, and whites, with Indian help, decimated the herds of buffalo and the other animals among which the Indians had lived since the beginning. From using all of the animal they could, and hunting from need, Indians soon learned the value of a pelt or a tongue to a white trader. Catlin heard of one large band of warriors arriving at a fort with the tongues of 1,400 freshly slaughtered buffalo, which they traded for a few gallons of whiskey.

The peace that the whites bought or won from the Indians was neither just nor long in being kept. Treaties, in many ways having no application to loosely organized bands of hunters whose range was where the game trails went, were broken by both Indians and whites. The reservation system was intolerable, with Indians being moved hundreds of miles from their homes to poor land and worse care as dependents of Indian agents. The Ghost Dance was a response to this defeat. It flared up in Nevada in the 1870s and was revived in 1889 by the Paiute messiah Jack Wilson (the name "Wovoka" is preferred by whites). Ghost Dance visions told of the coming again of the buffalo and the rising of the spirits of the dead, who would drive the whites from the land. The movement had a pan-Indian effect in the West (an exception being the Navajos, who feared ghosts), and nothing is sadder—or more Indian—than the Ghost Dance shirts painted with mystical emblems that were to make the wearers invulnerable to the white man's bullets. The Ghost Dance was suppressed with bloodshed, one victim being Sitting Bull himself. By the turn of the century, Indian life had been completely transformed, where it was not annihilated, by the more powerful culture of the whites. An anomaly was Ishi, the Yahi brave who walked into a northern California town after the destruction of the final members of his tribe to become memorialized as the last wild Indian in North America. Theodora Kroeber gives the moving and thought-provoking story of his accommodation with a society so alien to his own.

The West of the Indian will never be recovered, except perhaps in the imagination. The Ghost Dancers of the 1880s had chanted that they would rise again. If they have, it is on a deeper level than they knew. As D. H. Lawrence wrote in 1923, "Not that the Red Indian will ever possess the broad lands of America. At least I presume not. But his ghost will."

BEGINNINGS

A Navajo Creation Song

You say there were no people
    Smoke was spreading [over the earth]
You say there were no people
    Smoke was spreading.

First Man was the very first to emerge, they say,
    Smoke was spreading
He brought with him the various robes and precious things
        they say,
    Smoke was spreading
He brought with him the white corn and the yellow corn,
        they say,
    Smoke was spreading
He brought with him the various animals and the growing things,
    they say,
    Smoke was spreading.

You say there were no people
    Smoke was spreading.

First Woman was the very first to emerge, they say,
    Smoke was spreading
She brought with her the various precious things and robes,
        they say,
    Smoke was spreading
She brought with her the yellow corn and the varicolored corn,
        they say,
    Smoke was spreading
She brought with her the various animals and the growing things,
        they say,
    Smoke was spreading.

You say there were no people
    Smoke was spreading
You say there were no people
    Smoke was spreading.

From Hasteen Klah, *Navajo Creation Myth*, recorded by Mary C.
Wheelwright (Santa Fe: Museum of Navajo Ceremonial Art, 1942),
pp. 135–136. ("There Are No People Song" recorded and translated
by Dr. Harry Hoijer, edited by Dr. George Herzog.)

Margaret M. Wheat

In a Hard Land

The Paiute woman with her willow basket on her back was
the burden bearer of the Indian community until about the
middle of the 19th century when horses, and soon after,
wagons, became common in the western part of the Great
Basin. Since she carried not only the small children and the
food but all the family's belongings as well, it was necessary
that she keep her possessions at a minimum, her domestic objects lightweight and durable. Each woman needed one set of
harvesting baskets; more were a burden. She made no pottery—pottery was heavy and easily broken. To survive the
cold, each person in her family had a rabbitskin blanket. A
second blanket was clumsy and unnecessary. The Paiutes felt
there was no virtue in accumulating excess property. Even
keeping the possessions of the dead came to be regarded as
stealing, and the Indians believed that the ghosts would return to claim what was rightfully theirs.

At moving time, a woman packed the family possessions in
a large basket on her back, which was suspended from her
forehead by a broad tumpline. Only the heavy grinding
stones were left behind. Into the large, coarse-woven conical
basket, a wife first nested a fine-woven basket of the same
shape. Into this she fitted a set of fine and coarse winnowing
trays, the cooking basket, a looped willow stirring stick, and
on top, the rabbitskin blankets. If she owned them, she took
beads, an awl, some fibers for cordage, red and white pig-

ments for decoration and medicine, a bit of buckskin, a few herbs, and some food.

Most importantly, every woman carried bundles of long, slender willows which had been scraped white, and coils of willow sapwood that she had gathered and prepared during the winter months when the leaves were gone. These willows were the raw material necessary for the manufacture of nearly all of the family's household goods. From them she wove the tough little water jugs that she carried in her hand against thirst in the desert. From them she made cradles for the newborn infant, the hat that protected her head, the vessel in which she cooked, the bowl into which she served, and the tray on which she parched seeds, harvested berries, dried meats, cleaned nuts and roots, and with which she seined fish. From the willows she wove the beater with which she gleaned the seeds from the grasses, and the basket on which the seeds were collected. And finally, with these willows she made the basket in which she carried all the other baskets.

From Margaret M. Wheat, *Survival Arts of the Primitive Paiutes* (Reno: University of Nevada Press, 1967), pp. 91–92.

Franz Boas

In a Land of Plenty

The rivalry between chiefs and clans finds its strongest expression in the destruction of property. A chief will burn blankets, a canoe, or break a copper, thus indicating his disregard of the amount of property destroyed and showing that his mind is stronger, his power greater, than that of his rival. If the latter is not able to destroy an equal amount of property without much delay, his name is "broken." He is vanquished by his rival and his influence with his tribe is lost, while the name of the other chief gains correspondingly in renown.

Feasts may also be counted as destruction of property, because the food given can not be returned except by giving another feast. The most expensive sort of feast is the one at which enormous quantities of fish oil (made of the oulachon) are consumed and burnt, the so-called "grease feast." Therefore it also raises the name of the person who can afford to give it, and the neglect to speedily return it entails a severe loss of prestige. . . . When a person gives a grease feast, a great fire is lighted in the center of the house. The flames leap up to the roof and the guests are almost scorched by the heat. Still the etiquette demands that they do not stir, else the host's fire has conquered them. Even when the roof begins to burn and the fire attacks the rafters, they must appear unconcerned. The host alone has the right to send a man up to the roof to put out the fire. While the feast is in progress the host sings a scathing song ridiculing his rival and praising his own clan, the feats of his forefathers and his own. . . .

I thought another one was causing the smoky weather? I am the only one on earth—the only one in the world who makes thick smoke rise from the beginning of the year to the end, for the invited tribes.

What will my rival say again—that "spider woman;" what will he pretend to do next? The words of that "spider woman" do not go a straight way. Will he not brag that he is going to give away canoes, that he is going to break coppers, that he is going to give a grease feast? Such will be the words of the "spider woman," and therefore your face is dry and moldy, you who are standing in front of the stomachs of the chiefs.

Nothing will satisfy you; but sometimes I treated you so roughly that you begged for mercy. Do you know what you will be like? You will be like an old dog, and you will spread your legs before me when I get excited. You did so when I broke the great coppers "Cloud" and "Making Ashamed," my great property and the great coppers, "Chief" and "Killer Whale," and the one named "Point of Island" and "The Feared One" and "Beaver." This I throw into your face, you whom I always tried to vanquish; whom I have maltreated; who does not dare to stand erect when I am eating; the chief whom even every weak man tries to vanquish.

Now my feast! Go to him, the poor one who wants to be fed from the son of the chief whose own name is "Full of Smoke" and "Greatest Smoke." Never mind, give him plenty to eat, make him drink until he will be qualmish and vomits. My feast steps over the fire right up to the chief.

From Franz Boas, "The Social Organization & Secret Societies of the Kwakiutl Indians," in *Reports of the U.S. National Museum under the Direction of the Smithsonian Institution for the Year Ending June 30, 1895* (Washington: U. S. Government Printing Office, 1897), pp. 353–356.

TIMELESS LAUGHTER

Coyote and Doctor Duck

Coyote came one day to a big river. He wanted to be clean,
and not dirty any more, so he jumped in and took a swim,
and washed himself. Then he ate some Indian kamíeris, and
went to sleep in the brush and willows. He dreamt of
birds,—eagles, hawks, geese, and ducks,—and when he
awoke, he saw a number of Geese on the lake. He went
down to the shore of the lake, and asked the Geese how they
flew, how their feathers moved, and how they flew so easily
without falling down. "Yes," said the Geese, "it is just as easy
as walking." Then said Coyote, "Give me some feathers, so I
too can fly."—"No," said the Geese, "maybe you will fall in,
and maybe you will make a noise all the time. You will go
off somewhere and get lost. Geese keep together all the time,
and never stray away."— "But I will go along with you," said
Coyote; "then the Indians will say, 'How nice that looks!' I
will go ahead; I know the way best."

Then the Geese said, "All right," and each Goose gave him
some of its feathers. They stuck the feathers over him, until
he was completely covered; and then they said, "Now try
them!" Coyote tried, and flew easily over the lake without
falling in. He flew easily and lightly. "That is all right," said
the Geese, "now we will go."

They all started up, crying as they went. The Geese cried
only as they rose and descended, but Coyote cried all the time.
He imitated the cry of the Geese, "Ái-i, ái-i, ái-i!" They flew
high in the air, and then descended on the banks of a big
river. When they had all alighted, the Geese said, "Why do
you cry all the time?" And Coyote answered, "I am practicing
the cry. Otherwise I might forget it, so I keep trying it." But

25

the Geese only answered, "Well, we want no more crying. Now we are going again; and if you continue crying, we will pull all your feathers out again."—"All right," said Coyote; so they started again. They all cried as they rose, but Coyote kept on crying. Then they gathered around him and pulled all his feathers out. Down he fell, a great distance to the ground, and was badly hurt. But he got up and said, "Well, my friends, I'll go along on the ground. I see something away over there." The Geese said, "We are going to see the Utes." Then they left Coyote behind. When they arrived, the Utes were engaged in a great fight with the Sioux. Coyote said, "I'll go on the ground; I like it better." He slept and dreamt a little while, and when he came up, the fight was over. The Geese had stayed until the end, and gave Coyote, when he came up, an Indian girl they had rescued. Coyote said, "What's the reason they stopped so soon? Why don't they come back?"

Coyote took the girl to his home. Now a snowstorm began, and she made him a brush house. Coyote carelessly left a pointed stick upright in the ground. The girl came in and sat down on the stick. Then she began to cry, and Coyote said, "Something has hurt my girl. I will hunt for a doctor." He soon found the Duck doctor, and said to him, "My girl is hurt, and I am looking for a doctor." The Duck said, "Go look for another doctor also." So Coyote went. Meanwhile the Duck went to Coyote's home, and said to the girl, "Where are you sick?" She answered. Then the Duck pulled the stick out, and poked it into the bottom of the fire.

Soon Coyote returned home. The Duck did not tell him what the trouble was, but said, "You must go and get water. Get it from the bottom of the lake at the middle." But Coyote thought, "What's the reason he wants me to get water way out there? There is too much water there. I'll get it closer to shore." So he got a jar, and waded into the water up to his knees. Then he reached out and filled the jar with water, and took it to the Duck, who asked, "Where did you get this water?"— "Oh," said Coyote, "I stood so deep in the water. I got it right there."— "I told you in the middle," said the Duck, and he threw the water away. "All right," said Coyote, and he went again. This time he waded in up to his hips and got water; but when he brought it home, the Duck looked at it and said, "This water was too near shore. I told you way out in the middle, in deep water." So Coyote went again. He walked till the water reached his breast, and

brought water from there. But the Duck only said, "No. That
is not deep water. I told you way down in the middle." Coyote answered, "All right, I'll do it," and he went again. He
went in up to his nose, and got the jug full of water. But the
Duck looked at it, and said to him, "No, go far down in deep
water. This water was too close to shore. It is not
good."— "All right," said Coyote, "I'll do it." This time he
walked till the water covered his head, and then kept on much
farther. He filled his jar with water, and waded out again.
But he slipped in the mud on his way out and spilled all the
water. Then he went in again, a long distance after the water
had covered his head. He got a fresh jar of water and carried
it safely home. He entered the house and said, "I got you
water now way down deep in the middle." Then he looked
around. Both Duck and girl were gone.

Then Coyote knew that the Duck had stolen his girl.
"What's the reason," he thought, "that he stole my girl?" He
sat down and thought about it. "Which way did he go?" he
thought. Then far down in the fire he heard a noise,— "psst!"
It was the stick. He thought, "What's the cause of that noise
in there?" Then he poked the fire and pulled the stick out.
"What kind of stuff is that?" he thought. "Maybe it is good to
eat." So he cooled it in the water. "That's my dinner," said
Coyote. Then he began to eat it; but at the first bite he began
to cry, "Wu, wu, wu!" But he kept on till he had eaten it all.
Then he knew all the trouble, and the cause of his girl's
sickness.

—Uintah Ute (slightly emended)

From J. Alden Mason, "Myths of the Uintah Utes," *The Journal of
American Folk Lore*, Vol. 23, No. 89 (July–September, 1910), pp.
310–312.

Edwin James

Indian Wit

The Indians sometimes indulge in pleasantry in their conversation; and Shaumonekusse seemed to be eminently witty—a
quality strongly indicated by his well-marked features of

countenance. Their wit, however, is generally obscene, particularly when in conversation with the squaws.

Washingguhsahba, conversing familiarly with a Frenchman, who had long resided in the Omawhaw village, observed that the white people, being in the habit of reading books with the desire of acquiring knowledge, probably knew the cause of the difference of colour which exists between themselves and the Indian; he therefore requested information from the Frenchman on this subject. The latter, assuming an air of great gravity, assured him that the cause was very well known, and was no other than that the Indian was formed of horse-dung. The chief, with every appearance of candour, which, however, he did not feel, instantly placed his hand on the arm of his companion, and replied that this observation was a convincing proof of the great knowledge of the white people, and that they were perfectly familiar with the early operations of the Master of Life. He had no doubt, he said, that they were equally well informed as to the matter out of which they were themselves formed; but if he, a poor ignorant Indian, with no knowledge but his own, might venture to give his opinion, he would say, that they were formed of the excrement of the dog, baked white in the prairie.

From Edwin James, *Edwin James's Account of an Expedition from Pittsburgh to the Rocky Mountains, performed in the Years 1819–1820* (London: 1823; Cleveland: The Arthur H. Clark Co., Early Western Travels series, ed. Reuben Gold Thwaites, Vol. 15, 1905), p. 121.

Andrew Garcia

Indian Love-Call

I have mentioned this hand-blowing business to you several times and I might as well tell you a word or so about this refined art, a side line of the wild squaw and one of the under workings of the squaw's paradise, for the wild squaw when she made love wanted to be chased over the prairies and through the brush. That would not have been so bad if it was in daytime, but as most of this hand blowing is done by crooked women and young squaws, they chose the night and made the one who was after them do some running when this was going on, for she could, by cupping her hands over her mouth and blowing through them in a way that takes much practice to learn, blow a shrill mournful sound that on a still night could be easily heard a mile away. When the lovely sly little squaw is ready for business, she silently crawls under the edge of the tepee and is now out in the night when all good squaws are supposed to be sleeping so she now goes quietly away from camp and now bugles with her hands, calling for the buck she wants who knows the sound of her call, for each woman has a call of her own for they can make different sounds when blowing by working their fingers like a cornet player, and unless she learns you her call, you cannot tell who the woman is, though you can surely hear her and know that some woman is out for blood and as there may be several of them rutting squaws out at different places at the same time it would be useless to try and there would be a mix-up if you didn't know. But the dusky amourites have taken care of that and each one has a tune of her own to blow, for the wild squaw makes no mistakes and has this down to a science that would make some of their white sisters who play this game in different ways a four-flusher and piker, so when the buck hears this sound of boots and saddle ringing through the air, he silently sneaks off to where the sound is coming from and now thinks she is there; but alas, for the dusky Beau Brummell now hears the bugling coming maybe a quarter of a mile in another direction, for the fairy nymph who is watching him has made a run for it and is off when he gets there and is now encouraging him over there with beautiful bugling that would make a bull elk die of shame and envy, so, as he is no fool and some player at this game himself, he now uses all the stealth and low-down trickery known only to an Injun and soon it is a race o'er vale and dell with her bugling and encouraging him to keep it up when now she may have been only fooling him and quietly slips back into camp leaving him there to ponder on the trickery and deviltry of woman and to get square with her and the next one, but most of the time she takes good care that he will catch her as most of the time this kind of work is only done by crooked squaws who don't like their men and by young squaws who know that any day may bring a warrior who has the horses to buy her, while the one she likes has none.

From Andrew Garcia, *Tough Trip Through Paradise,* edited by Bennett H. Stein (Boston: Houghton Mifflin Co., 1967), pp. 163–165.

A VISIONARY WORLD

Two Leggings

A Warrior's Vision

It was still the moon when the leaves turn yellow. One day a war party led by Arapaho returned with news of Coyote Howls' death. I told Two Belly that I wanted revenge but that first I would visit Sees The Living Bull who was camped in the Hits With The Arrows country. That evening I made a sweat lodge and the next morning rode to his tipi.

When I told him my plans he asked the direction I intended to go. I answered Where The Lightning Strikes, the place I had seen when he had made my medicine. He approved and told me where to camp each night.

I sang many songs as I followed the winding Arrow Creek home, arriving long after sunset at the joining of the two rivers.

That night in my tipi I sang my medicine songs. After purifying my body in a smudge of white pine needles I fell asleep and had a medicine dream. A big hawk flying high in the sky fell to earth and rose again with a man in its claws. It dropped the body at the place in my earlier dream. When I woke I knew that my medicine was with me and prepared to leave. I had told friends that I expected to go out as soon as I returned from Sees The Living Bull's. Eleven joined me; Woman Face, Clear on the Forehead, and High Hawk were about my age but the others were younger. . . .

Toward evening we approached Where The Lightning Strikes where the river banks are cut by a creek bearing the same name. The scouts still reported no enemy signs, but knowing we would meet them here I had my men tie their horses and make camp.

Early the next morning we built a fire, careful again not to use smoking wood. After we ate I ordered my men on their horses, telling them that I was sure we would soon meet enemies. I posted a lookout on a nearby hill and rode carefully up the creek, the others far behind. As I drew near the location in my vision I turned a bend and hid in a willow grove to watch the creek bottom's upper reaches. I was still not certain enemies were in the vicinity, but I had faith in my medicine dream. Then buffalo spilled over the southern bank several rifle shots away, and behind them rode two Sioux.

Singing my medicine song I ran back and met the scout running down the hill. He reported ten more Sioux riding our way. Although we were twelve, two were boys carrying only knives. But I reminded my men that these Sioux were not brave and that as soon as we began shooting some would run off.

I told them to take out their medicines and sing their songs. I told them to be brave. Sees The Living Bull had said there was no reason to be afraid. After opening my medicine bundle I blew my eagle-bone whistle seven times. Then I knelt and held up my eagle medicine with my left hand. As I looked under it I sang: "The bird above is kind to me. There are some Indians. They are easy to me. I want to talk to them. They are easy."

Then I blew my whistle again. Swaying from side to side, I saw two falling enemies underneath my medicine. I was going to kill those Sioux.

The ten other Sioux were a few rifle shots away, but had not yet crossed the spot where I had seen the two men fall. Now the first two hunters disappeared behind the ridge in my vision and I led my men up the other side.

The other Sioux saw us and rushed to join their friends. As the first hunter rode over the ridge I shot him in the leg. Dismounting as soon as he fell I dodged his pistol bullet and killed him with another shot. After I scalped his beautiful hair I held one half up to the sun.

My men were spreading out along the ridge and firing. High Hawk wounded one who escaped. When the ten Sioux saw me kill that man they raced away until they were too far to chase. Also, we feared they might be part of a larger camp.

My first pipeholder's vision had been fulfilled. Although we had only killed one and wounded another I was anxious to bring my men safely back. We traveled all day and reached the river that night, pulling out the skin boats we had hidden under brush. Then I felt safe and, as I swam across, sang one of my medicine songs: "He was just going in front of us."

This time the cold water did not bother me. Once on the other side I remembered that other war parties were out and told my men to hurry. Our celebration would be even better if we were the first to return successfully.

All that night and through the next day we galloped along the Musselshell River. About sunset we came around a bend and saw a Crow camp and recognized several men returning from a buffalo hunt. I took out my new medicine which Sees The Living Bull had given me and we made charcoal and blackened our faces. After everyone had tied on their medicines and the scalp was attached to a long thin pole we rode toward camp, shooting our guns into the air. A moment later the drums began and the women ran out of their tipis singing a scalp song. On all sides people called out my name and pointed to my scalp. They sang my song: "Wherever he is staying, we are going where he is."

They also sang this song: "I want to have another song."

All night long we sang and danced. My ambition had come true and I was a real pipeholder. By dawn we were too tired to celebrate any more and finished by singing a love song: "The one I love, do not go home. You are the only one I love, do not go home."

I gave away half of the scalp and kept the other half to take to our home camp which I learned was on Porcupine Creek. Two days later we left and when we rode into our village, celebrated over again. I sang this medicine song: "Whoever he is, I am going to him."

The whole camp joined in and everyone felt good. I had avenged Coyote Howls and my name was spoken through camp. I never tired of telling about this trip, and visitors returned to hear it again.

From Peter Nabokov, *Two Leggings: The Making of a Crow Warrior*, based on a field manuscript prepared by William Wildschut for the Museum of the American Indian, Heye Foundation (New York: Thomas Y. Crowell Co., 1967), pp. 162–165.

A Pawnee War Song: Testing the Vision

> Let us see, is this real,
> Let us see, is this real,
> Let us see, is this real,
> Let us see, is this real,
> This life I am living?
> Ye gods, who dwell everywhere,
> Let us see, is this real,
> This life I am living?

From Daniel G. Brinton, *Essays of an Americanist* (Philadelphia: David McKay, 1890), p. 292.

Claude Lévi-Strauss

Indian Justice

Societies which seem savage to us in some respects may appear humane and kindly when considered from another angle. Let us take the case of the Plains Indians of North America, who are doubly significant in this connection, because they practised certain moderate forms of cannibalism and at the same time offer one of the rare instances of a primitive community with an organized police system. It would never have occurred to their police (who were also a judicial body) to make the culprit's punishment take the form of a breaking of social ties. If a native had infringed the laws of the tribe, he was punished by having all his possessions destroyed, including his tent and horses. But at the same time, the police contracted a debt towards him: it was their duty to organize collective reparation for the losses sustained by the culprit as his punishment. This put him under an obligation to the group, and he had to show his gratitude to them by means of presents that the whole community—including the police—helped him to assemble, so that this once again reversed the relationships; and so on and so forth until,

33

after a whole series of gifts and counter-gifts, the disorder introduced by the crime was gradually neutralized and there was a return to the pristine state of order. Not only are such customs more humane than ours, they are also more coherent, even if the problem is formulated in terms of modern European psychology; logically, the "infantilization" of the culprit implied by the notion of punishment demands that he should have a corresponding right to a reward, in the absence of which the initial procedure will prove ineffective and may even lead to results contrary to those that were hoped for. Our system is the height of absurdity, since we treat the culprit both as a child, so as to have the right to punish him, and as an adult, in order to deny him consolation; and we believe we have made great spiritual progress because, instead of eating a few of our fellow-men, we subject them to physical and moral mutilation.

From Claude Lévi-Strauss, *Tristes Tropiques*, translated by John and Doreen Weightman (New York: Atheneum, 1974), pp. 388–389.

NEW, STRANGE, WHITE PEOPLE

A Tewa Prophecy: The Coming of the Whites

Montezuma, the Sun-Boy, had for his mother a poor and despised Indian girl. Every fall the people of the pueblo went to the mountains to gather piñon nuts. The girl and her grandmother lagged behind, knowing that they were not welcome among the others. One day, as they traveled, a beautiful vision appeared before the girl, and asked,

— "Why do you make this journey?"

"To gather piñons," she replied.

He gave her a nut, saying, "Here is a piñon worth all the rest."

She took it and swallowed it whole.

"Do not go to the mountains. Turn about and go home," said he.

They did so; and when they arrived at the house, they found it full of new, strange, white-people's food and furniture. From that time all their wants were miraculously supplied, to the great amazement of their neighbors.

In time a baby was born to the girl,—Montezuma, the Sun-Boy. The people paid little attention to the lad; but before he was twelve years old, he had developed great skill—supernatural skill—with his bow; and he was always better dressed and better fed than the others. The men called him to their council meeting, and questioned him about it. He said he did not know whence he got either the food and clothing or the unusual power.

"If you have the power in yourself, perform us a miracle," they said; "bring the buffalo."

"Buffalo will be here tomorrow," he replied.

The people stationed their best hunters at the four corners of the pueblo with bows and arrows. Montezuma stood on the housetop. Just as the sun came over the hilltops, the sunrise was "dirty with buffalo."

The buffalo rushed onward and trampled to death the men stationed to kill them. Regarding this as a punishment for their unbelief in Montezuma, the people elected him chief.

That was in an old pueblo where Ojo Calientè now stands.

Montezuma's rule was so wise that Santa Clara, San Juan, San Ildefonso, Tesuque, Nambé, and Pojoaque put themselves under his dominion. Under him they became rich and powerful.

But at last he began to prophesy changes—the coming of new, noisy conveyances, and of a strange, all-conquering race. The Indians would be subdued by a people coming from the South.

"We will resist them," said the people. "Give us your help to drive them back."

"If you can stand the test I will prepare for you, I will consent to your meeting them with force," said he.

The test took place at San Juan. He gathered all the principal men about him. Then he disappeared. Presently he reappeared, coming through the trap-door in the roof, strangely garbed, booted, and spurred (like a Spanish cavalier). With him came an assemblage of attendants, similarly dressed; and following these came a company of beautiful women, in queer, gay attire. At sight of all this, the Indians were so terrified that they fell over each other in trying to escape from the house.

Then Montezuma came again in his own person.

"I knew beforehand," he said, "that you could not endure the test. If you are so terrified by the mere vision of the conquerors, what will you be by the reality?"

"I must leave you now," said he, "to seek a people greater in strength and numbers. Endure all things, and keep the peace. You will have a long period of trouble and persecution; then will come peace and prosperity. Some time during the latter period I will return."

He went south, taking with him a wife. As they journeyed, the woman was playing with two pebbles, tossing them up and catching them. Near the boundary of Old Mexico, on the Rio Grande, the pebbles went up, and came down huge boulders. They are there yet.

In the South he ruled over a more powerful people, and now and then the Pueblo people used to hear of his greatness. But at last the Spaniards invaded his domain, and though he met them in person, he could not withstand them. They pressed him so closely that he jumped into a lake and escaped through one of its subterranean passages. No one knows where he went; but he will come again, as he said he would. This is the time of peace of which he told them, and he may soon be here.

From Clara Kern Bayliss, "A Tewa Sun Myth," *Journal of American Folklore*, Vol. 22, No. 85 (July–September, 1909), pp. 333–335.

George Catlin

Medicine-man's Reply to an English Temperance Society

After the speech of White Cloud, Mr. J. Cadbury, at the head of a deputation from the *"Temperance Society"* (to which the Indians had sent also the sum of £36 8s), presented himself, and read an address from that association, thanking them for the amount received, and advising the Indians to abstain from the use of *"fire water,"* and to practise *charity*, which was one of the greatest of virtues.

Mr. Cadbury then addressed the Indians, in all the fervency and earnestness of prayer, on the all-important subject of temperance. His words and sentences, selected for their simple understandings, were in the simplicity, and consequently the eloquence of nature, and seemed to win their highest admiration and attention. He painted to them in vivid colours the horrors and vice of intemperance, and its consequences; and also the beauty and loveliness of sobriety, and truth, and charity, which he hoped and should pray that they might practise in the wilderness, with constant prayers to the Great Spirit in the heavens, when they returned to their own country.

When this venerable gentleman's remarks were finished, the old Doctor (or Medicine-man) arose from his seat upon the floor, with his pipe in his lips, and, advancing, shook hands with the two Messrs. Cadbury, and, handing his pipe to the chief, spoke as follows—

"My Friends,—I rise to thank you for the words you have spoken to us: they have been kind, and we are thankful for them.

"My Friends,—When I am at home in the wilderness, as well as when I am amongst you, I always pray to the Great Spirit; and I believe the chiefs and the warriors of my tribe, and even the women also, pray every day to the Great Spirit, and He has therefore been very kind to us.

"My Friends,—We have been this day taken by the hand of friendship, and this gives us great consolation. Your friendly words have opened our ears, and your words of advice will not be forgotten.

"My Friends,—You have advised us to be charitable to the poor, and we have this day handed you 360 dollars to help the poor in your hospitals. We have not time to see those poor people, but we know you will make good use of the money for them; and we shall be happy if, by our coming this way, we shall have made the poor comfortable.

"My Friends,—We Indians are poor, and we cannot do much charity. The Great Spirit has been kind to us though since we came to this country, and we have given altogether more than 200 dollars to the poor people in the streets of London before we came here; and I need not tell you that this is not the first day that we have given to the poor in this city.

"My Friends,—If we were rich, like many white men in this country, the poor people we see around the streets in this cold weather, with their little children barefooted and begging, would soon get enough to eat, and clothes to keep them warm.

"My Friends,—It has made us unhappy to see the poor people begging for something to eat since we came to this country. In our country we are all poor, but the poor all have enough to eat, and clothes to keep them warm. We have seen your poorhouses, and been in them, and we think them very good; but we think there should be more of them, and that the rich men should pay for them.

"My Friends,—We admit that before we left home we all were fond of 'fire-water,' but in this country we have not drunk it. Your words are good, and we know it is a great sin to drink it. Your words to us on that subject, can do but little good, for we are but a few; but if you can tell them to the white people, who make the 'fire-water,' and bring it into our country to sell, and can tell them also to the thousands whom we see drunk with it in this country, then we think you may do a great deal of good; and we believe the Great Spirit will reward you for it.

"My Friends,—It makes us unhappy, in a country where there is so much wealth, to see so many poor and hungry, and so many as we see drunk. We know you are good people, and kind to the poor, and we give you our hands at parting; praying that the Great Spirit will assist you in taking care of the poor, and making people sober.

"My Friends,—I have no more to say."

From George Catlin, *Catlin's Notes of Eight Years' Travels and Residence in Europe, with His North American Indian Collection*, 4th edition, 2 vols. (London: "Published by the author, at his Indian Collection," 1848), Vol. 2, pp. 142–143.

CLAIMING THE LAND

Chief Luther Standing Bear

An Indian's View

Our legends tell us that it was hundreds and perhaps thousands of years ago since the first man sprang from the soil in the midst of the great plains. The story says that one morning long ago a lone man awoke, face to the sun, emerging from the soil. Only his head was visible, the rest of his body not yet being fashioned. The man looked about, but saw no mountains, no rivers, no forests. There was nothing but soft and quaking mud, for the earth itself was still young. Up and up the man drew himself until he freed his body from the clinging soil. At last he stood upon the earth, but it was not solid, and his first few steps were slow and halting. But the sun shone and ever the man kept his face turned toward it. In time the rays of the sun hardened the face of the earth and strengthened the man and he bounded and leaped about, a free and joyous creature. From this man sprang the Lakota nation and, so far as we know, our people have been born and have died upon this plain; and no people have shared it with us until the coming of the European. So this land of the great plains is claimed by the Lakotas as their very own. We are of the soil and the soil is of us.

From Chief [Luther] Standing Bear, *Land of the Spotted Eagle* (Boston: Houghton Mifflin Co., 1933), pp. 44–45.

Theodore Roosevelt

As a Future President Saw It

During the past century a good deal of sentimental nonsense has been talked about our taking the Indians' land. Now, I do not mean to say for a moment that gross wrong has not been done the Indians, both by government and individuals, again and again. The government makes promises impossible to perform, and then fails to do even what it might toward their fulfillment; and where brutal and reckless frontiersmen are brought into contact with a set of treacherous, revengeful, and fiendishly cruel savages a long series of outrages by both sides is sure to follow. But as regards taking the land, at least from the western Indians, the simple truth is that the latter never had any real ownership in it at all. Where the game was plenty, there they hunted; they followed it when it moved away to new hunting-grounds, unless they were prevented by stronger rivals; and to most of the land on which we found them they had no stronger claim than that of having a few years previously butchered the original occupants. When my cattle came to the Little Missouri the region was only inhabited by a score or so of white hunters; their title to it was quite as good as that of most Indian tribes to the lands they claim; yet nobody dreamed of saying that these hunters owned the country. Each could eventually have kept his own claim of 160 acres, and no more. The Indians should be treated in just the same way that we treat the white settlers. Give each his little claim; if, as would generally happen, he declined this, why then let him share the fate of the thousands of white hunters and trappers who have lived on the game that the settlement of the country has exterminated, and let him, like these whites, who will not work, perish from the face of the earth which he cumbers.

The doctrine seems merciless, and so it is; but it is just and rational for all that. It does not do to be merciful to a few, at the cost of justice to the many. The cattle-men at least keep herds and build houses on the land; yet I would not for a moment debar settlers from the right of entry to the cattle country, though their coming in means in the end the destruction of us and our industry.

From Theodore Roosevelt, *Hunting Trips of a Ranchman* (New York and London: G. P. Putnam's Sons, 1885), pp. 18–19.

INVENTING THE INDIAN

Alfred Jacob Miller

Indians as Greeks

American sculptors travel thousands of miles to study Greek statues in the Vatican at Rome, seemingly unaware that in their own country there exists a race of men equal in form and grace (if not superior) to the finest beau ideal ever dreamed of by the Greeks. And it does seem a little extraordinary that up to this time (as far as I am aware) not a single sculptor has thought it worth his while to make a journey among these Indians, who are now sojourning on the Western side of the Rocky mountains, and are rapidly passing away. Most unquestionably, that sculptor who travels here,—and models from what he sees (supposing him to have equal power and genius), will far excel any other who merely depends upon his own conception of what it ought to be.

From Alfred Jacob Miller, *The West of Alfred Jacob Miller*, with an account of the artist by Marvin C. Ross, p. 325. Courtesy Walters Art Gallery, Baltimore.

Henry Wadsworth Longfellow
The Indian as Sentimentalized Victim

Gloomy and dark art thou, O chief of the mighty Omahas;
Gloomy and dark as the driving cloud, whose name thou hast taken!
Wrapped in thy scarlet blanket, I see thee stalk through the city's
Narrow and populous streets, as once by the margin of rivers
Stalked those birds unknown, that have left us only their footprints.
What, in a few short years, will remain of thy race but the footprints?

Hark! What murmurs arise from the heart of those mountainous deserts?
Is it the cry of the Foxes and Crows, or the mighty Behemoth,
Who, unharmed, on his tusks once caught the bolts of the thunder,
And now lurks in his lair to destroy the race of the red man?
Far more fatal to thee and thy race than the Crows and the Foxes,
Far more fatal to thee and thy race than the tread of Behemoth,

Lo, The big thunder-canoe, that steadily breasts the Missouri's

Merciless current! and yonder, afar on the prairies, the campfires

Gleam through the night; and the cloud of dust in the gray of
the daybreak

Marks not the buffalo's track, nor the Mandan's dexterous
horse-race;

It is a caravan, whitening the desert where dwell the Caman-
ches!

Ha! how the breath of these Saxons and Celts, like the blast
of the east-wind,

Drifts evermore to the west the scanty smokes of thy wigwams!

From Henry Wadsworth Longfellow, "To the Driving Cloud," in *Poetical Works*, Vol. 1 (Boston: Houghton Mifflin Co., 1904), pp.
243–245.

Horace Greeley

Indians as Degenerates

But the Indians are children. Their arts, wars, treaties, al-
liances, habitations, crafts, properties, commerce, comforts,
all belong to the very lowest and rudest ages of human existence. Some few of the chiefs have a narrow and short-
sighted shrewdness, and very rarely in their history, a really
great man, like Pontiac or Tecumseh, has arisen among
them; but this does not shake the general truth that they are
utterly incompetent to cope in any way with the European or
Caucasian race. Any band of schoolboys, from ten to fifteen
years of age, are quite as capable of ruling their appetites, devising and upholding a public policy, constituting and conducting a state or community, as an average Indian tribe.
And, unless they shall be treated as a truly Christian community would treat a band of orphan children providentially
thrown on its hands, the aborigines of this country will be
practically extinct within the next fifty years.

I have learned to appreciate better than hitherto, and to
make more allowance for, the dislike, aversion, contempt,

wherewith Indians are usually regarded by their white neighbors, and have been since the days of the Puritans. It needs but little familiarity with the actual, palpable aborigines to convince any one that the poetic Indian—the Indian of Cooper and Longfellow—is only visible to the poet's eye. To the prosaic observer, the average Indian of the woods and prairies is a being who does little credit to human nature—a slave of appetite and sloth, never emancipated from the tyranny of one animal passion save by the more ravenous demands of another. As I passed over those magnificent bottoms of the Kansas which form the reservations of the Delawares, Potawatamies, etc., constituting the very best corn-lands on earth, and saw their owners sitting around the doors of their lodges at the height of the planting season and in as good, bright planting weather as sun and soil ever made, I could not help saying, "These people must die out—there is no help for them. God has given this earth to those who will subdue and cultivate it, and it is vain to struggle against His righteous decree."

From Horace Greeley, *An Overland Journey from New York to San Francisco in the Summer of 1859* (New York and San Francisco: C. M. Saxton, Barker & Co.; H. H. Bancroft & Co., 1860), pp. 151–152.

Herman Melville

The Metaphysics of Indian-Hating

As the child born to a backwoodsman must in turn lead his father's life—a life which, as related to humanity, is related mainly to Indians—it is thought best not to mince matters, out of delicacy; but to tell the boy pretty plainly what an Indian is, and what he must expect from him. For however charitable it may be to view Indians as members of the Society of Friends, yet to affirm them such to one ignorant of Indians, whose lonely path lies a long way through their lands, this, in the event, might prove not only injudicious but cruel. At least something of this kind would seem the maxim upon which backwoods education is based. Accordingly, if in youth the backwoodsman incline to knowledge, as is generally the case, he hears little from his schoolmasters, the old chroniclers of the forest, but histories of Indian lying, Indian theft, Indian double-dealing, Indian fraud and perfidy, Indian want of conscience, Indian blood-thirstiness, Indian diabolism—histories which, though of wild woods, are almost as full of things unangelic as the Newgate Calendar or the Annals of Europe. In these Indian narratives and traditions the lad is thoroughly grounded. "As the twig is bent the tree's inclined." The instinct of antipathy against an Indian grows in the backwoodsman with the sense of good and bad, right and wrong. In one breath he learns that a brother is to be loved, and an Indian to be hated.

From Herman Melville, *The Confidence-Man: His Masquerade* (New York: Dix, Edwards & Co., 1857), p. 227.

HOSTILITIES

Washington Irving

Cleaning Up the Shoshones

The wild and half-desert region through which the travellers were passing, is wandered over by hordes of Shoshokoes, or Root Diggers, the forlorn branch of the Snake tribe. They are a shy people, prone to keep aloof from the stranger. The travellers frequently met with their trails, and saw the smoke of their fires rising in various parts of the vast landscape, so that they knew there were great numbers in the neighborhood, but scarcely ever were any of them to be met with.

After a time, they began to have vexatious proofs that, if the Shoshokoes were quiet by day, they were busy at night. The camp was dogged by these eavesdroppers; scarce a morning, but various articles were missing, yet nothing could be seen of the marauders. What particularly exasperated the hunters, was to have their traps stolen from the streams. One morning, a trapper of a violent and savage character, discovering that his traps had been carried off in the night, took a horrid oath to kill the first Indian he should meet, innocent or guilty. As he was returning with his comrades to camp, he beheld two unfortunate Diggers, seated on the river bank, fishing. Advancing upon them, he levelled his rifle, shot one upon the spot, and flung his bleeding body into the stream. The other Indian fled, and was suffered to escape. Such is the indifference with which such acts of violence are regarded in the wilderness, and such the immunity an armed ruffian enjoys beyond the barriers of the laws, that the only punishment this desperado met with, was a rebuke from the leader of the party.

The trappers now left the scene of this infamous tragedy, and kept on westward, down the course of the river, which wound along with a range of mountains on the right hand, and a sandy, but somewhat fertile plain, on the left. As they proceeded, they beheld columns of smoke rising, as before, in various directions, which their guilty consciences now converted into alarm signals, to arouse the country and collect the scattered bands for vengeance.

After a time, the natives began to make their appearance, and sometimes in considerable numbers, but always pacific; the trappers, however, suspected them of deep-laid plans to draw them into ambuscades; to crowd into and get possession of their camp, and various other crafty and daring conspiracies, which, it is probable, never entered into the heads of the poor savages. In fact, they are a simple, timid, inoffensive race, unpractised in warfare, and scarce provided with any weapons, excepting for the chase. Their lives are passed in the great sand plains and along the adjacent rivers; they subsist sometimes on fish, at other times on roots and the seeds of a plant, called the cat's-tail. They are of the same kind of people that Captain Bonneville found upon Snake River, and whom he found so mild and inoffensive.

The trappers, however, had persuaded themselves that they were making their way through a hostile country, and that implacable foes hung round their camp or beset their path, watching for an opportunity to surprise them. At length, one day they came to the banks of a stream emptying into Ogden's River, which they were obliged to ford. Here a great number of Shoshokoes were posted on the opposite bank. Persuaded they were there with hostile intent, they advanced upon them, levelled their rifles, and killed twenty-five of them upon the spot. The rest fled to a short distance, then halted and turned about, howling and whining like wolves, and uttering the most piteous wailings. The trappers chased them in every direction; the poor wretches made no defence, but fled with terror; neither does it appear from the accounts of the boasted victors, that a weapon had been wielded or a weapon launched by the Indians throughout the affair. We feel perfectly convinced that the poor savages had no hostile intention, but had merely gathered together through motives of curiosity, as others of their tribe had done when Captain Bonneville and his companions passed along Snake River.

From Washington Irving, *The Adventures of Captain Bonneville, U.S.A. in the Rocky Mountains and the Far West* (London: Henry G. Bohn, 1850), pp. 212–214.

Wooden Leg
After the Battle of the Little Big Horn

After the great throng of Indians had crowded upon the little space where had been the last band of fighting soldiers, a strange incident happened: It appeared that all of the white men were dead. But there was one of them who raised himself to a support on his left elbow. He turned and looked over his left shoulder, and then I got a good view of him. His expression was wild, as if his mind was all tangled up and he was wondering what was going on here. In his right hand he held his six-shooter. Many of the Indians near him were scared by what seemed to have been a return from death to life. But a Sioux warrior jumped forward, grabbed the six-shooter and wrenched it from the soldier's grasp. The gun was turned upon the white man, and he was shot through the head. Other Indians struck him or stabbed him. I think he must have been the last man killed in this great battle where not one of the enemy got away. . . .

I took one scalp. As I went walking and leading my horse among the dead I observed one face that interested me. The dead man had a long beard growing from both sides of his face and extending several inches below the chin. He had also a full mustache. All of the beard hair was of a light yellow color, as I now recall it. Most of the soldiers had beard growing, in different lengths, but this was the longest one I saw among them. I think the dead man may have been thirty or more years old. "Here is a new kind of scalp," I said to a companion. I skinned one side of the face and half of the chin, so as to keep the long beard yet on the part removed. I got an arrow shaft and tied the strange scalp to the end of it. This I carried in a hand as I went looking further. . . .

I found a metal bottle, as I was walking among the dead men. It was about half full of some kind of liquid. I opened it and found that the liquid was not water. Soon afterward I got hold of another bottle of the same kind that had in it the same kind of liquid. I showed these to some other Indians. Different ones of them smelled and sniffed. Finally a Sioux said:

"Whisky."

Bottles of this kind were found by several other Indians. Some of them drank the contents. Others tried to drink, but had to spit out their mouthfuls. Bobtail Horse got sick and vomited soon after he had taken a big swallow of it. It became the talk that this whisky explained why the soldiers became crazy and shot each other and themselves instead of shooting us. One old Indian said, though, that there was not enough whisky gone from any of the bottles to make a white man soldier go crazy. We all agreed then that the foolish actions of the soldiers must have been caused by the prayers of our medicine men. I believed this was the true explanation. My belief became changed, though, in later years. I think now it was the whisky. . . .

I slept late that next morning after the great battle. The sun had been up an hour before I awoke. I went to the willow lodge of my father and mother. When I had eaten the breakfast given to me by my mother I got myself ready again to risk death in an effort to kill other white men who had come to kill us. I combed and braided my hair. My braids in those days were full and long, reaching down my breast beyond the waist belt. I painted anew the black circle around my face and the red and yellow space enclosed within the circle. I was in doubt about which clothing to wear, but my father said the soldier clothing looked the best, even though the coat sleeves ended far above my wrists and the legs of the breeches left long bare spots between them and the tops of my moccasins. I put on my big white hat captured at the Rosebud fight. My sister Crooked Nose got my horse for me.

Soon afterward I was on my way up and across the valley
and on through the river to the hill where the first soldiers
were staying. . . .

Some soldiers came to get water from the river, just as our
old men had said they likely would do. The white men crept
down a deep gulch and then ran across an open space to the
water. Each one had a bucket, and each would dip his bucket
for water and run back into the gulch. I put myself, with others, where we could watch for these men. I shot at one of
them just as he straightened up after having dipped his
bucket into the water. He pitched forward into the edge of
the river. He went wallowing along the stream, trying to
swim, but having a hard time at it. I jumped out from my
hiding place and ran toward him. Two Sioux warriors got
ahead of me. One of them waded after the man and struck
him with a rifle barrel. Finally he grabbed the man, hit him
again, and then dragged him dead to the shore, quite a distance down the river. I kept after them, following down the
east bank. Some other Sioux warriors came. I was the only
Cheyenne there. The Sioux agreed that my bullet had been
the first blow upon the white soldier, so they allowed me to
choose whatever I might want of his belongings.

I searched into the man's pockets. In one I found a folding
knife and a plug of chewing tobacco that was soaked and
spoiled. In another pocket was a wad of the same kind of
green paper taken from the soldiers the day before. It too
was wet through. I threw it aside. In this same pocket were
four white metal pieces of money. I knew they were of value
in trading, but I did not know how much was their value. In
later times I have learned they were four silver dollars. A
young Cheyenne there said: "Give the money to me." I did
not care for it, so I gave it to him. He thanked me and said:
"I shall use it to buy for myself a gun." I do not remember
now his name, but he was a son of One Horn. A Sioux
picked up the wad of green paper I had thrown upon the
ground. It was almost falling to pieces, but he began to
spread out some of the wet sheets that still held together.
Pretty soon he said:

"This is money. This is what white men use to buy things
from the traders."

I had seen much other paper like it during the afternoon
before. Wolf Medicine had offered to give me a handful of it.
But I did not take it. I already had thrown away some of it I
had found. But even after I was told it could be used for

buying things from the traders, I did not want it. I was thinking then it would be a long time before I should see or care to see any white man trader. . . .

I went with other Cheyennes along the hills northward to the ground where we had killed all of the soldiers. Lots of women and boys were there. The boys were going about making coups by stabbing or shooting arrows into the dead men. Some of the bodies had many arrows sticking in them. Many hands and feet had been cut off, and the limbs and bodies and heads had many stabs and slashes. Some of this had been done by the warriors, during and immediately after the battle. More was added, though, by enraged and weeping women relatives of the Sioux and Cheyennes who had been killed. The women used sheathknives and hatchets.

From Thomas B. Marquis, *Wooden Leg. A Warrior Who Fought Custer* (Lincoln: University of Nebraska Press, 1957), pp. 238–263 *passim*.

George Catlin

Smallpox Destroys the Mandans

The disease was introduced into the country by the Fur Company's steamer from St. Louis; which had two of their crew sick with the disease when it approached the Upper Missouri, and imprudently stopped to trade at the Mandan village, which was on the bank of the river, where the chiefs and others were allowed to come on board, by which means the disease got ashore.

I am constrained to believe, that the gentlemen in charge of the steamer did not believe it to be the small-pox; for if they had known it to be such, I cannot conceive of such imprudence, as regarded their own interests in the country, as well as the fate of these poor people, by allowing their boat to advance into the country under such circumstances.

It seems that the Mandans were surrounded by several war-parties of their more powerful enemies the Sioux, at that unlucky time, and they could not therefore disperse upon the plains, by which many of them could have been saved; and they were necessarily inclosed within the piquets of their vil-

lage, where the disease in a few days became so very malig-
nant that death ensued in a few hours after its attacks; and so
slight were their hopes when they were attacked, that nearly
half of them destroyed themselves with their knives, with
their guns, and by dashing their brains out by leaping head-
foremost from a thirty foot ledge of rocks in front of their
village. The first symptom of the disease was a rapid swelling
of the body, and so very virulent had it become, that very
many died in two or three hours after their attack, and that
in many cases without the appearance of the disease upon the
skin. Utter dismay seemed to possess all classes and all ages,
and they gave themselves up in despair, as entirely lost. There
was but one continual crying and howling and praying to the
Great Spirit for his protection during the nights and days;
and there being but few living, and those in too appalling
despair, nobody thought of burying the dead, whose bodies,
whole families together, were left in horrid and loathsome
piles in their own wigwams, with a few buffalo robes, &c.
thrown over them, there to decay, and be devoured by their
own dogs. That such a proportion of their community as that
above-mentioned, should have perished in so short a time,
seems yet to the reader, an unaccountable thing; but in addition to the causes just mentioned, it must be borne in mind
that this frightful disease is everywhere far more fatal
amongst the native than in civilized population, which may
be owing to some extraordinary constitutional susceptibility;
or, I think, more probably, to the exposed lives they live,
leading more directly to fatal consequences. In this, as in
most of their diseases, they ignorantly and imprudently
plunge into the coldest water, whilst in the highest state of fever, and often die before they have the power to get
out. . . .

So have perished the friendly and hospitable Mandans,
from the best accounts I could get; and although it may be
possible that some few individuals may yet be remaining, I
think it is not probable; and one thing is certain, even if such
be the case, that, as a nation, the Mandans are extinct, having no longer an existence.

From George Catlin, *Illustrations of the Manners, Customs and Conditions of the North American Indians,* Vol. 2 (1841; London: Henry G.
Bohn, 1848), pp. 257–258.

SURVIVORS

Chief Joseph
Broken Promises

I have heard talk and talk, but nothing is done. Good words do not last long unless they amount to something. Words do not pay for my dead people. They do not pay for my country, now overrun by white men. They do not protect my father's grave. They do not pay for all my horses and cattle. Good words will not give me back my children. Good words will not make good the promise of your War Chief General Miles. Good words will not give my people good health and stop them from dying. Good words will not get my people a home where they can live in peace and take care of themselves. I am tired of talk that comes to nothing. It makes my heart sick when I remember all the good words and all the broken promises. There has been too much talking by men who had no right to talk. Too many misrepresentations have been made, too many misunderstandings have come up between the white men about the Indians. If the white man wants to live in peace with the Indian he can live in peace. There need be no trouble. Treat all men alike. Give them all the same law. Give them all an even chance to live and grow. All men were made by the same Great Spirit Chief. They are all brothers. The earth is the mother of all people, and all people should have equal rights upon it. You might as well expect the rivers to run backward as that any man who was born a free man should be contented when penned up and denied liberty to go where he pleases. If you tie a horse to a stake, do you expect he will grow fat? If you pen an Indian up on a small spot of earth, and compel him to stay there, he will not be contented, nor will he grow and prosper. I have asked some of the great white chiefs where they get their authority to say to the Indian that he shall stay in one place, while he sees white men going where they please. They can not tell me.

I only ask of the Government to be treated as all other men are treated. If I can not go to my own home, let me have a home in some country where my people will not die so fast. I would like to go to Bitter Root Valley. There my people would be healthy; where they are now they are dying. Three have died since I left my camp to come to Washington.

When I think of our condition my heart is heavy. I see men of my race treated as outlaws and driven from country to country, or shot down like animals.

I know that my race must change. We can not hold our own with the white men as we are. We only ask an even chance to live as other men live. We ask to be recognized as men. We ask that the same law shall work alike on all men. If the Indian breaks the law, punish him by the law. If the white man breaks the law, punish him also.

Let me be a free man—free to travel, free to stop, free to work, free to trade where I choose, free to choose my own teachers, free to follow the religion of my fathers, free to think and talk and act for myself—and I will obey every law, or submit to the penalty.

Whenever the white man treats the Indian as they treat each other, then we will have no more wars. We shall all be alike—brothers of one father and one mother, with one sky above us and one country around us, and one government for all. Then the Great Spirit Chief who rules above will smile upon this land, and send rain to wash out the bloody spots made by brothers' hands from the face of the earth. For this time the Indian race are waiting and praying. I hope that no more groans of wounded men and women will ever go to the ear of the Great Spirit Chief above, and that all people may be one people.

In-mut-too-yah-lat-lat has spoken for his people.

From Chief Joseph, "An Indian's View of Indian Affairs." *The North American Review*, No. 269, Vol. 128 (New York: D. Appleton and Co., 1879), pp. 432–433.

A Messianic Movement: Four Ghost-Dance Songs

I.

My children, when at first I liked the whites,
My children, when at first I liked the whites,
I gave them fruits,
I gave them fruits.

II.

Father, have pity on me,
Father, have pity on me;
I am crying for thirst,
I am crying for thirst;
All is gone—I have nothing to eat,
All is gone—I have nothing to eat.

III.

The spirit host is advancing, they say,
The spirit host is advancing, they say.
They are coming with the buffalo, they say,
They are coming with the new earth, they say.

IV.

We shall live again,
We shall live again.

From James Mooney, *The Ghost-Dance Religion and Sioux Outbreak of 1890*, 14th Annual Report of the Bureau of Ethnology to the Secretary of the Smithsonian Institution 1892–93, part 2 (Washington: U.S. Government Printing Office, 1896), pp. 961, 977, 1086, 1047.

Theodora Kroeber

The Last Wild Indian in North America

There were the gadgets, tools, and amenities of civilization which impressed Ishi as desirable or ingenious or delightful, as there were those which left him indifferent or which he rejected.

53

Ishi and his people built winter houses against rain and cold, summer houses against heat, and storage houses. He found the houses of civilization good. They gave protection against both heat and cold, were comfortable, and provided much space for storing food and clothes and tools. He liked chairs and beds and tables and chests and towels and blankets. Running water and flush toilets were not only good, they were very, very clever, as were electric lights, switches, and gas stoves. The telephone was amusing, but less intriguing and genuinely interesting than the penny whistle and the kaleidoscope. Matches were one of civilization's true delights, rated far above gas and electricity.

Someone gave Ishi a watch, which he wore and kept wound but not set. He could "tell time" after his own system. He knew midday, and any hour which was pointed out, keeping his appointments punctually and without strain by some sun sense plus his simplified reading of museum and hospital clocks. His own watch was an article of pride and beauty to be worn with chain and pendant, not a thing of utility.

Automobiles interested Ishi far less than trolley cars. He could watch trolley cars endlessly. They ran on tracks like the train-demon, their gongs were superior to automobile horns, and they were equipped with air brakes which released a cloud of sand and dust with a satisfying "phoosh" whenever the brakes were applied.

To see Harry Fowler take off from Golden Gate Park on a flight across the continent was an event, in 1911, exciting and novel enough to draw a crowd to the park, Waterman and Ishi among them, Ishi the coolest of the lot. He was most interested when the propeller blades began to whir and the engine started with a roar. But when the plane rose, circling over their heads, he nodded in its direction, asking, *Saltu*? "White man up there?" He raised his eyebrows at the funny ways of the civilized: a building is not so much compared with a mountain, and an aeroplane is not so much of a performer in the air as the hawk or the eagle. Birds fly so high in the air that you cannot follow their flight, animals run on the ground more swiftly than man, and fish swim in the sea and rivers, the salmon climbing rapids no boat can make. The white man showed his true cleverness when he harnessed a demon to metal tracks.

From Theodora Kroeber, *Ishi in Two Worlds* (Berkeley and Los Angeles: University of California Press, 1961), pp. 164–166.

Joseph H. Peck

Why Should the Gosiutes Fight the Germans?

In the summer of 1917, when the draft was first put into effect, I had enlisted, but because the training camps for doctors were limited I had to wait a year before I was called. Being located in the middle of the desert, I was directed to examine all the draftees of the region, and I made several trips to various points to accommodate them. I was also under contract to care for the Gosiute Indians. When the three or four boys of draft age at the Reservation received greetings from the Draft Board, I was ordered to go over there and examine them.

These Indians had never achieved citizenship. They were carried as wards of the Indian Department. Probably they never would have been disturbed if the agent had not developed a patriotic brainstorm and insisted to the Department that these boys be called to serve the country to which they owed so little.

This turn of events was just what old Doc Annie Tommy wanted. He left hurriedly for the Blackfoot Reservation in Idaho, and reported everything to the Indian Grievance Committee. They wired the Indian Rights Society in New York, and Uncle Sam had another war on his hands. . . .

The first skirmish was my responsibility. Frankly I thought it all nonsense and believed the Indians were right in refusing to help the U.S.A. out of its difficulties with the Germans. But fifty dollars was fifty dollars, and I went over to examine the youth of Ibapah.

Just as I expected, none of them showed up. It was reported that they were all out sheepherding, an activity that was foreign to a Gosiute's nature and not a very likely story. The agent was raving about calling the sheriff and stomping around so much that I left him to boil and went to call upon my old friend and tribal wise man, Antelope Jake.

Jake was about eighty years old. He smoked a bag of Bull Durham per day in homemade cigarettes, always wore a vest made out of antelope skin with the hair outside, and was the spokesman and leader of the tribal council. He welcomed me graciously for an Indian, and came to the point at once by acknowledging that he was greatly worried.

I tried to bring him up to date on events and explain why the boys must go, but he just shook his head. "Jake no savvy why Americans have to go so far to fight. How come you know Germans well enough to get mad at them? Who are they and where do they live?"

I explained that we were mad because they sunk our ships in the ocean.

Jake replied, "Whose ocean is it anyhow?"

I said it belongs to everybody.

"Well," said Jake, "why not keep our boats at home until the war quiets down? What did the people on the other side have that we needed?"

That one floored me. I fell back on analogies. "Suppose the Paiutes chased your men off the mountains down around Delta when they went there to hunt, how would you feel?"

"But our boys know better than to hunt down there. That is Paiute country and nobody has gone there since Jake was a little boy and we got licked when we did. So we stay home and have no trouble with anybody. What does German look like? You ever see one?"

I explained that Germans look like other white people and that because of his name I was sure the agent was of German parentage,

Jake brightened up. "You tell white father we kill him for free and any other Germans that come around here too. You go fight your war. Gosiutes will stand behind you and keep Germans from capturing Ibapah valley."

It was good to know that we had such a staunch ally to fall back upon if things got real bad, but I got no place in my argument that the boys should come in and be examined.

Jake dismissed me with the promise: "We keep boys at home. Anybody come here you want killed we do it—Germans, Paiutes or Indian agents."

From Joseph H. Peck, *What Next, Doctor Peck?* (Englewood Cliffs, N.J.: Prentice-Hall, 1959), pp. 189–191.

Robinson Jeffers

Hands

Inside a cave in a narrow canyon near Tassajara
The vault of rock is painted with hands,
A multitude of hands in the twilight, a cloud of men's palms,
no more,
No other picture. There's no one to say
Whether the brown shy quiet people who are dead intended
Religion or magic, or made their tracings
In the idleness of art; but over the division of years these
careful
Signs-manual are now like a sealed message
Saying: "Look: we also were humans; we had hands, not
paws. All hail
You people with the cleverer hands, our supplanters
In the beautiful country; enjoy her a season, her beauty, and
come down
And be supplanted; for you also are human."

From Robinson Jeffers, *Dear Judas and Other Poems* (New York: Liveright, 1929), p. 128.

II

The West as Mythical Topography

Few people even know the true definition of the term "West"; and where is its location? —phantom-like it flies before us as we travel.

—George Catlin

Introduction to Part II

The West has always consisted of many "Wests"—each as different in meaning as in topography. What came to be called the Great West in the nineteenth century—that region from the Great Plains to the Pacific Ocean—was a country whose landscape struck newcomers as beautiful, hideous, abundant, desolate, exotic, and drab. It was both paradise and hell on earth. It became a theater of dreams and horrors where people found themselves enacting their truest desires and deepest fears. It offered endless opportunity and relentless frustration; it was the land of adventure and boredom. Its topography was extreme, contradictory, and inconsistent; and its silence was huge.

The first European to describe such a "West" was the sixteenth-century Spaniard Cabeza de Vaca, who came there by accident. He and three others were the only survivors of a 300-man land expedition into Spanish Florida in 1528. During eight years of wandering "to the sunset," Cabeza de Vaca entered what is now Texas, New Mexico, and Arizona. His account of his travels is the first narrative of the interior West, and it is remarkable in its anticipation of Western experience during the next 300 years. It is a story of hardship, danger, and disappointment. It describes a land where Indians as children of nature are seen as either murdering brutes who eat worms and deer dung or noble people capable of great compassion and kindness. It is a story of survival through adaptation, resourcefulness, trade, religious perseverance, and cannibalism. Cabeza de Vaca reminds us of how much early Western experience was bound up with slavery. Indians kept slaves, and he became one of them. One of the three men who crossed the West with him was a Moorish slave himself, and all four of the wanderers were finally rescued by Spanish slave-catchers in pursuit of Indians.

One question always was asked about this new land: What

good is it? Cabeza de Vaca reported, "Over all the region we saw vast lands and beautiful plains that would make good pasture." But the Spaniards grew more excited by hints of abundant emeralds, turquoise, gold, and silver. Coronado's search for the Seven Cities of Cíbola, which probably took him into what is now Kansas, is characteristic of such journeys into the West. Perhaps disappointment is so extreme in much Western writing only because, as with the Coronado expedition, expectations were always so high. When hopes for finding an Eldorado faded, Spanish settlements, such as Santa Fe in 1610, were established as frontier outposts, and trails were later blazed by missionaries such as Father Kino to harvest souls for God and the King.

In the seventeenth and eighteenth centuries, the West was a political object of international rivalry, and its immediate value was judged in terms of possible trade routes, especially as a passage to India. The search for a Northwest Passage by water or a land route to the Western Sea motivated French exploration, including that of the Vérendryes, who traveled as far West as the present Black Hills of South Dakota. Their journey, like other "explorations" of the West, followed Indian trails and would have been impossible without Indian guidance. The dream of a western route to India and the Orient began with Columbus but dominated imaginations into the nineteenth century. Thomas Hart Benton was able to urge adoption of a transcontinental railroad to "vindicate the glory of Columbus by realizing his divine idea of arriving in the east by going to the west."

Attention turned to the abundant riches of the West itself after the Lewis and Clark expedition returned in 1806. They revealed a wild, lush land filled with animals and wider than earlier explorers imagined. This image appealed not only to economic interests, but to the nineteenth-century romantic sensibility that delighted in sublimities promised by virgin wilderness. Edgar Allen Poe's unfinished novel about the West presents a typical response to the new land when he celebrates the spiritual exhilaration of a man in communion with nature. Another response, even more common than Poe's imagined delight, is the awesome fright that Meriwether Lewis records in his journals. Not at all benevolent, nature at times seemed actually demonic in its hostility to man's intrusion.

While painters such as A. J. Miller and later Albert Bierstadt would portray the West as abundant and fertile, exotic and sublime, another common conception in the minds of mid-nineteenth-century Americans was of the West as an uninhabitable wasteland. Until the Civil War, maps of the continent continued to label the region between the Missouri and the Rockies as the "Great American Desert." Acting appropriately to this image of the desert, Jefferson Davis, the U.S. Minister of War in the 1850s, shipped camels to Texas to provide transportation for the army. A common attitude expressed in Congress was that of a senator from North Carolina who said, "I would not give a pinch of snuff for the whole territory." The plains were clearly flat, treeless, and arid, nothing like the country east of the Mississippi to which Americans were accustomed. The value of the West was not apparent until it became actively promoted on a national scale by men like Senator Thomas Hart Benton of Missouri.

Another major promoter of Western expansion was John C. Frémont, Benton's son-in-law and a second lieutenant of the Army Corps of Topographical Engineers. The ostensible purpose of his government-sponsored expeditions of the 1840s was exploratory and scientific, but his promotional purpose is evident in his description of the American Desert as a potential garden. By portraying the movement West as an exciting, patriotic adventure, Frémont furthered the notion of Manifest Destiny. The idea that it was the patriotic duty of Americans to fulfill their destiny by subduing the continent and creating an American empire was so much in the air that even Zenas Leonard, a mountain trapper, was aware of the political implications of his westward travels. William Gilpin, who went with Frémont to Oregon in 1843, became a notable prophet of the West's significance in global terms. In contrast to the rhetoric of Benton, Gilpin, and Frémont, the diaries of Charles Preuss, Frémont's official cartographer, record daily realities that quickly transform the great Western adventure into a drab affair. Read in conjunction with Frémont's *Report*, Preuss's diaries give a glimpse of how the topography of the American West was simultaneously discovered and invented.

Images of Eden color Frémont's and Preuss's impressions of the Sacramento and San Joaquin valleys, just as they colored other accounts of the West. But of all the Edenic dreams to be associated with the West—from universal brotherhood to spiritual rejuvenation—perhaps the most stubbornly rooted was that of individual freedom. People went West to be free, to rid themselves of ill health or economic destitution or religious persecution or social constraint or personal discontent. On a national level, the free lands of the West came to be seen as a great "safety valve" for the unemployed and poor of the East. Some did find truth in their dreams; most did not. "The most unfree souls go west, and shout of freedom," D. H. Lawrence wrote. "Men are freest when they are most unconscious of freedom. The shout is a rattling of chains, always was."

With the passing of the frontier at the end of the nineteenth-century, much of what we identify with the West also became part of the past, but one thing that did remain was the physical fact of the landscape itself. This is the West of extremes, the country of Yosemite and Death Valley and the Grand Canyon and Colter's Hell and the Great Salt Lake and the Dakota Badlands and the Grand Tetons. It is the hottest and coldest, the wettest and driest of regions. It both enhances man's sense of himself and simultaneously diminishes him. This landscape, as noted earlier, can produce excitement and terror, but in its inhuman vastness and silence, it can also breed what the painter John Noble called "the loneliness." Perhaps the writing about the West that now speaks most directly to us is by men like Clarence King and John Wesley Powell, scientists who led two of the Great Surveys during the 1860s and 1870s. Along with others like John Muir, they combined geology and aesthetics to produce a literature that celebrated the West on its own terms. Its value for Powell and Muir was not translatable into trade routes or minerals or furs. Like Thoreau, they knew "that in Wildness is the preservation of the World."

FIRST ACROSS THE WEST:
1528–1536

Álvar Núñez Cabeza de Vaca

Naked Among Indians

I had to stay with the Capoques more than a year. Because of the hard work they put me to, and their harsh treatment, I resolved to flee to the people of Charruco in the forests of the main. My life had become unbearable. In addition to much other work, I had to grub roots in the water or from underground in the canebrakes. My fingers got so raw that if a straw touched them they would bleed. The broken canes often slashed my flesh; I had to work amidst them without benefit of clothes.

So I set to contriving how I might transfer to the forest-dwellers, who looked more propitious. My solution was to turn to trade. . . .

My principal wares were cones and other pieces of sea-snail, conchs used for cutting, sea-beads, and a fruit like a bean [from mesquite trees] which the Indians value very highly, using it for a medicine and for a ritual beverage in their dances and festivities. This is the sort of thing I carried inland. By barter I got and brought back to the coast skins, red ochre which they rub on their faces, hard canes for arrows, flint for arrowheads, with sinews and cement to attach them, and tassels of deer hair which they dye red.

This occupation suited me; I could travel where I wished, was not obliged to work, and was not a slave. Wherever I went, the Indians treated me honorably and gave me food, because they liked my commodites. They were glad to see me when I came and delighted to be brought what they wanted. I became well known; those who did not know me personally knew me by reputation and sought my acquaintance. This served my main purpose, which all the while was to determine an eventual road out.

The hardships I endured in this journeying business were long to tell—peril and privation, storms and frost, which often overtook me alone in the wilderness. By the unfailing grace of God our Lord I came forth from them all. Because of them, however, I avoided the pursuit of my business in winter, a season when, anyway, the natives retire inside their huts in a kind of stupor, incapable of exertion.

I was in this region nearly six years, alone among the Indians and naked like them.

From Álvar Núñez Cabeza de Vaca, *Adventures in the Unknown Interior of America*, edited by Cyclone Covey (New York: Macmillan Co., 1961), pp. 66–67.

Álvar Núñez Cabeza de Vaca

Hints of Riches

Among the things the people there gave us was a big copper rattle which they presented Andrés Dorantes. It had a face represented on it and the natives prized it highly. They told Dorantes they had received it from their neighbors. Where did *they* get it? It had been brought from the north, where there was a lot of it, replied the natives, who considered copper very valuable. Wherever it came from, we concluded the place must have a foundry to have cast the copper in hollow form. . . .

They fetched me a man who, they said, had long since been shot in the shoulder through the back and that the arrowhead had lodged above his heart. He said it was very painful and kept him sick. I probed the wound and discovered the arrow had passed through the cartilage. With a flint knife I opened the fellow's chest until I could see that the point was sideways and would be difficult to extract. But I cut on and, at last, inserting my knife-point deep, was able to work the arrowhead out with great effort. It was huge. With a deer bone, I further demonstrated my surgical skill with two stitches while blood drenched me, and stanched the flow with hair from a hide. The villagers asked me for the arrowhead, which I gave them. The whole population came to look at it, and they sent it into the back country so the people there could see it.

They celebrated this operation with their customary dances and festivities. Next day, I cut the stitches and the patient was well. My incision appeared only like a crease in the palm of the hand. He said he felt no pain or sensitivity there at all.

Now this cure so inflated our fame all over the region that we could control whatever the inhabitants cherished.

We showed them the copper rattle we had recently been given, and they told us that many layers of this material were buried in the place whence it came, that this [metal] was highly valued, and that the people who made it lived in fixed dwellings. We conceived the country they spoke of to be on the South Sea, which we had always understood was richer in mineral resources than that of the North. . . .

. . . The people gave us innumerable deerhide and cotton blankets, the latter better than those of New Spain, beads made of coral from the South Sea, fine [and genuine] turquoises from the north—in fact, everything they had, including a special gift to me of five emerald arrowheads such as they use in their singing and dancing. These looked quite valuable. I asked where they came from. They said from lofty mountains to the north, where there were towns of great population and great houses, and that the arrowheads had been purchased with feather brushes and parrot plumes. . . .

From Cabeza de Vaca, *Adventures*, pp. 108, 110, 119.

Álvar Núñez Cabeza de Vaca
Rescued by Christians

We gave many thanks to God our Lord. Having almost despaired of finding Christians again, we could hardly restrain our excitement. Yet we anxiously suspected that these men were explorers who had merely made a flying visit on their voyage of discovery. But having at last some exact information to go on, we quickened our pace and, as we went heard more and more of Christians. We told the natives we were going after those men to order them to stop killing, enslaving, and dispossessing the Indians; which made our friends very glad.

We hastened through a vast territory, which we found vacant, the inhabitants having fled to the mountains in fear of Christians. With heavy hearts we looked out over the lavishly watered, fertile, and beautiful land, now abandoned and burned and the people thin and weak, scattering or hiding in fright. Not having planted, they were reduced to eating roots and bark; and we shared their famine the whole way. Those who did receive us could provide hardly anything. They themselves looked as if they would willingly die. They brought us blankets they had concealed from the other Christians and told us how the latter had come through razing the towns and carrying off half the men and all the women and boys; those who had escaped were wandering about as fugitives. We found the survivors too alarmed to stay anywhere very long, unable or unwilling to till, preferring death to a repetition of their recent horror. While they seemed delighted with our company, we grew apprehensive that the Indians resisting farther on at the frontier would avenge themselves on us.

When we got there, however, they received us with the same awe and respect the others had—even more, which amazed us. Clearly, to bring all these people to Christianity and subjection to Your Imperial Majesty, they must be won by kindness, the only certain way. . . .

When we saw for certain that we were drawing near the Christians, we gave thanks to God our Lord for choosing to bring us out of such a melancholy and wretched captivity. The joy we felt can only be conjectured in terms of the time, the suffering, and the peril we had endured in that land. . . .

The day after that, I overtook four of them on their horses. They were dumbfounded at the sight of me, strangely undressed and in company with Indians. They just stood staring for a long time, not thinking to hail me or come closer to ask questions.

"Take me to your captain," I at last requested; and we

went together half a league to a place [near Ocoroni on the Sinaloa] where we found their captain, Diego de Alcaraz.

When we had talked awhile, he confessed to me that he was completely undone, having been unable to catch any Indians in a long time; he did not know which way to turn; his men were getting too hungry and exhausted. . . .

After this we had a hot argument with them, for they meant to make slaves of the Indians in our train. We got so angry that we went off forgetting the many Turkish-shaped bows, the many pouches, and the five emerald arrowheads, etc., which we thus lost. And to think we had given these Christians a supply of cowhides and other things that our retainers had carried a long distance!

It proved difficult to persuade our escorting Indians to go back to their homes, to feel apprehensive no longer, and to plant their corn. . . .

. . . Alcaraz bade his interpreter tell the Indians that we were members of his race who had been long lost; that his group were the lords of the land who must be obeyed and served, while we were inconsequential. The Indians paid no attention to this. Conferring among themselves, they replied that the Christians lied: We had come from the sunrise, they from the sunset; we healed the sick, they killed the sound; we came naked and barefoot, they clothed, horsed, and lanced; we coveted nothing but gave whatever we were given, while they robbed whomever they found and bestowed nothing on anyone. . . .

To the last I could not convince the Indians that we were of the same people as the Christian slavers. Only with the greatest effort were we able to induce them to go back home. We ordered them to fear no more, re-establish their towns, and farm.

Already the countryside had grown rank from neglect. This is, no doubt, the most prolific land in all these Indies. It produces three crops a year; the trees bear a great variety of fruit; and beautiful rivers and brimming springs abound throughout. There are gold- and silver-bearing ores. The people are well disposed, serving such Christians as are their friends with great good will. . . . This land, in short, lacks nothing to be regarded as blest.

From Cabeza de Vaca, *Adventures*, pp. 122–123, 125–29.

THE WEST AS EL DORADO

Fray Marcos de Niza

The Seven Cities of Cíbola

As it seems to me worth recording here what this Indian, sent to me by Esteban, says about the country, I shall proceed to do so. He says and maintains that, in the first province, there are seven very large cities, all under one ruler, with large houses of stone and lime. The smaller ones are one story high with a terrace above; others are two and three stories high, and the ruler's house is four stories high; these houses are all joined in an orderly manner. He says that the doorways to the best houses have many decorations of turquoises, of which there is a great abundance, and that the people in these cities are very well clothed. He told me many other details, both of these seven cities and of other provinces farther on, each one of which he claims to be much more important than these seven cities. In order to find out from him how he came to know this, we had a good many questions and answers, and I found him quite able to express himself. I rendered thanks to our Lord. . . . Accompanied by them and by my own Indians and interpreters, I proceeded on my journey until coming within view of Cíbola, which is situated in a plain, at the base of a round hill.

This pueblo has a fine appearance, the best I have seen in these regions. The houses are as they had been described to me by the Indians, all of stone, with terraces and flat roofs, as it seemed to me from a hill where I stood to view it. The city is larger than the city of Mexico. At times I was tempted to descend to the pueblo, because I knew I was risking only my life, and this I offered to God the day I set out on this journey. In the end, realizing my danger, I feared that if I died no information would be obtained concerning this land, which in my opinion is the greatest and best of all that have been discovered.

When I told the chieftains who were with me how well impressed I was with Cíbola, they told me that it was the smallest of the seven cities, and that Totonteac is much larger and better than all the seven, that it has so many houses and people that there is no end to it. . . .

On my way back, and although I was not lacking in fear, I determined to approach the valley where the sierras end, which, as I said previously, I had heard about. There I learned that that valley is inhabited for many days' journeys toward the east. I did not dare to enter it without endangering my person and failing to report what I had seen, and it seemed to me that the Spaniards would first have to come and settle and dominate this other land of the seven cities and kingdoms I have mentioned, and that this valley could then be more easily explored. I only saw, from the opening of the valley, seven fair-sized settlements, somewhat distant, and, below, a very verdant valley with very good soil, from which many smokes rose. I was told that there is much gold there and that the natives make it into vessels, and jewels for the ears, and into little blades with which they wipe away their sweat.

From Fray Marcos de Niza, "Report of Fray Marcos de Niza, August 26, 1539," in *Narratives of the Coronado Expedition 1540–1542*, edited by George P. Hammond and Agapito Rey (Albuquerque: University of New Mexico Press, 1940), pp. 66, 78–79, 80.

Pedro de Castañeda

Coronado Enters Cíbola

The next day they entered the settled country in good order, and when they saw the first village, which was Cíbola, such were the curses that some hurled at Friar Marcos that I pray God may protect him from them.

It is a little, unattractive village, looking as if it had been crumpled all up together. There are [haciendas] in New Spain which make a better appearance at a distance. It is a village of about 200 warriors, is three and four stories high, with the houses small and having only a few rooms, and without a courtyard. One yard serves for each section. The people of the whole district had collected here, for there are

seven villages in the province, and some of the others are
even larger and stronger than Cíbola. These folks waited for
the army, drawn up by divisions in front of the village. When
they refused to have peace on the terms the interpreters
extended to them, but appeared defiant, the Santiago was
given, and they were at once put to flight. The Spaniards then
attacked the village, which was taken with not a little difficulty, since they held the narrow and crooked entrance. During the attack they knocked the general [Coronado] down
with a large stone, and would have killed him but for Don
Garcia Lopez de Cardenas and Hernando de Alvarado, who
threw themselves above him and drew him away, receiving
the blows of the stones, which were not few. But the first fury
of the Spaniards could not be resisted, and in less than an
hour they entered the village and captured it. They discovered food there, which was the thing they were most in need
of. After this the whole province was at peace.

From George Parker Winship, "The Coronado Expedition, 1540–1542,"
in *Fourteenth Annual Report of the Bureau of Ethnology*, 1892–93,
Part I (Washington: U.S. Government Printing Office, 1896), p. 483.

Pedro de Castañeda
Rumors of Quivira

The Spaniards enjoyed themselves here for several days and
talked with an Indian slave. . . . This fellow said that there
were large settlements in the farther part of that country
[Quivira]. Hernando de Alvarado took him to guide them to
the cows [buffalo]; but he told them so many and such great
things about the wealth of gold and silver in his country that
they did not care about looking for cows, but returned after
they had seen some few, to report the rich news to the gen-
ral. They called the Indian "Turk," because he looked like
one. . . . He said also that the lord of that country took his
afternoon nap under a great tree on which were hung a great
number of little gold bells, which put him to sleep as they
swung in the air. He said also that everyone had their ordinary dishes made of wrought plate, and the jugs and bowls
were of gold. He called gold acochis. For the present he was

believed, on account of the ease with which he told it and because they showed him metal ornaments and he recognized them and said they were not gold, and he knew gold and silver very well and did not care anything about other metals.

From Winship, "Coronado," pp. 491–492, 493.

Francisco Vázquez Coronado
Report to the King

October 20, 1541

The province of Quivira is 950 leagues from Mexico. Where I reached it, it is in the fortieth degree. The country itself is the best I have ever seen for producing all the products of Spain, for besides the land itself being very fat and black and being very well watered by the rivulets and springs and rivers, I found prunes like those of Spain [*or* I found everything they have in Spain] and nuts and very good sweet grapes and mulberries. I have treated the natives of this province, and all the others whom I found wherever I went, as well as was possible, agreeably to what Your Majesty had commanded, and they have received no harm in any way from me or from those who went in my company. I remained twenty-five days in this province of Quivira, so as to see and explore the country and also to find out whether there was anything beyond which could be of service to Your Majesty, because the guides who had brought me had given me an account of other provinces beyond this. And what I am sure of is that there is not any gold nor any other metal in all that country, and the other things of which they had told me are nothing but little villages, and in many of these they do not plant anything and do not have any houses except of skins and sticks, and they wander around with the cows . . .

I have done all that I possibly could to serve Your Majesty and to discover a country where God Our Lord might be served and the royal patrimony of Your Majesty increased, as your loyal servant and vassal. For since I reached the province of Cíbola, to which the viceroy of New Spain sent me in the name of Your Majesty, seeing that there were none of the things there of which Friar Marcos had told, I have managed to explore this country for 200 leagues and more around Cíbola, and the best place I have found is this river of Tiguex where I am now, and the settlements here. It would not be possible to establish a settlement here, for besides being 400 leagues from the North sea and more than 200 from the South sea, with which it is impossible to have any sort of communication, the country is so cold, as I have written to Your Majesty, that apparently the winter could not possibly be spent here, because there is no wood, nor cloth with which to protect the men, except the skins which the natives wear and some small amount of cotton cloaks.

From Winship, "Coronado," pp. 582–583.

O STRANGE NEW WORLD

Pedro de Castañeda

Frightening Beasts, Remarkable Events

For these things were remarkable and something not seen in other parts. I dare to write of them because I am writing at a time when many men are still living who saw them and who will vouch for my account. Who could believe that 1,000 horses and 500 of our cows and more than 5,000 rams and ewes and more than 1,500 friendly Indians and servants, in traveling over those plains, would leave no more trace where they had passed than if nothing had been there—nothing—so that it was necessary to make piles of bones and cow dung now and then, so that the rear guard could follow the army. The grass never failed to become erect after it had been trodden down, and, although it was short, it was as fresh and straight as before. . . .

Now that I wish to describe the appearance of the [buffalo] bulls, it is to be noticed first that there was not one of the horses that did not take flight when he saw them first, for

they have a narrow, short face, the brow two palms across
from eye to eye, the eyes sticking out at the side, so that,
when they are running, they can see who is following them.
They have very long beards, like goats, and when they are
running they throw their heads back with the beard dragging
on the ground. There is a sort of girdle round the middle of
the body. The hair is very woolly, like a sheep's, very fine,
and in front of the girdle the hair is very long and rough like
a lion's. They have a great hump, larger than a camel's. The
horns are short and thick, so that they are not seen much
above the hair. In May they change the hair in the middle of
the body for down, which makes perfect lions of them. They
rub against the small trees in the little ravines to shed their
hair, and they continue this until only the down is left, as a
snake changes his skin. They have a short tail, with a bunch
of hair at the end. When they run, they carry it erect like a
scorpion. It is worth noticing that the little calves are red and
just like ours, but they change color and appearance with
time and age. . . .

The country they traveled over was so level and smooth
that if one looked at them the sky could be seen between
their legs, so that if some of them were at a distance they
looked like smooth-trunked pines whose tops joined, and if
there was only one bull it looked as if there were four pines.
When one was near them, it was impossible to see the ground
on the other side of them. The reason for all this was that the
country seemed as round as if a man should imagine himself
in a three-pint measure, and could see the sky at the edge of
it, about a crossbow shot from him, and even if a man only
lay down on his back he lost sight of the ground. . . .

Many fellows were lost at this time who went out hunting
and did not get back to the army for two or three days,
wandering about the country as if they were crazy, in one
direction or another, not knowing how to get back where
they started from, although this ravine extended in either
direction so that they could find it. Every night they took account of who was missing, fired guns and blew trumpets and
beat drums and built great fires, but yet some of them went
off so far and wandered about so much that all this did not
give them any help, although it helped others. . . . It is
worth noting that the country there is so level that at midday,
after one has wandered about in one direction and another in
pursuit of game, the only thing to do is to stay near the game

quietly until sunset, so as to see where it goes down, and even then they have to be men who are practiced to it.

From Winship, "Coronado," pp. 541–542, 543.

Garci Rodríguez Ordóñez de Montalvo

Imaginary Island of the West

Know, then, that, on the right hand of the Indies, there is an island called California very close to the side of the Terrestrial Paradise, and it was peopled by black women, without any man among them, for they lived in the fashion of Amazons. They were of strong and hardy bodies, of ardent courage and great force. Their island was the strongest in all the world, with its steep cliffs and rocky shores, their arms were all of gold, and so was the harness of the wild beasts which they tamed and rode. For, in the whole island, there was no metal but gold. They lived in caves wrought out of the rock with much labor. They had many ships with which they sailed out to other countries to obtain booty. . . .

In this island, called California, there were many griffens, on account of the great ruggedness of the country, and its infinite hosts of wild beasts, such as never were seen in any other part of the world. And when these griffens were yet small, the women went out with traps to take them. They covered themselves over with very thick hides, and when they had caught the little griffens, they took them to their caves, and brought them up there. And being themselves quite a match for the griffens, they fed them with the men whom they took prisoners, and with the boys to whom they gave birth, and brought them up with such arts that they got much good from them, and no harm. Every man who landed on the island was immediately devoured by these griffens; and although they had had enough, none the less would they seize them and carry them high up in the air, in their flight, and when they were tired of carrying them, would let them fall anywhere as soon as they died. . . .

. . . [T]here reigned in this island of California a Queen [Calafia], very large in person, the most beautiful of all of them, of blooming years, and in her thoughts desirous of achieving great things, strong of limb and of great courage, more than any of those who had filled her throne before her.

[c. 1510]

From Garci Rodríguez Ordóñdez de Montalvo, *Las Sergas de Esplandián*, translated by Edward Everett Hale, *The Atlantic Monthly*, 82 (March 1864), pp. 266–267.

Father Eusebio Francisco Kino

California Is Not an Island

[B]ecause the many currents from north to south which I experienced in the voyages which I made in the Gulf of California were so continuous and at times so strong that it seemed as if the sea communicated with that of the north, and inclined me to the opinion that California was an island; and as such I sketched it in some of my maps.

But now already, thanks to his Divine Majesty, with various expeditions, and three in particular, of one hundred and seventy, and two hundred leagues, which I have made from here to the north of Nuestra Señora de los Dolores, I have discovered with all minute certainty and evidence, with mariner's compass and astrolabe in my hands, that California is not an island . . .

From Father Eusebio Francisco Kino, "Expedition of Two Hundred Leagues in the Year 1702 . . ." in *Kino's Historical Memoir of Pimería Alta*, edited by Herbert Eugene Bolton (Cleveland: Arthur H. Clark Co., 1919), Vol. 1, p. 334.

Father Eusebio Francisco Kino

These New Heathendoms

With all these expeditions or missions that have been made to a distance of two hundred leagues in these new heathendoms in these twenty-one years, there have been brought to our friendship and to the desire of receiving our holy Catholic faith, between Pimas, Cocomaricopas, Yumas, Quiquimas, etc., more than thirty thousand souls, there being sixteen thousand of Pimas alone. I have solemnized more than four thousand baptisms, and I could have baptized ten or twelve thousand Indians more if the lack of father laborers had not rendered it impossible for us to catechise them and instruct them in advance. But if our Lord sends, by means of his royal Majesty and of the superiors, the necessary fathers for so great and so ripe a harvest of souls, it will not be difficult, God willing, to achieve the holy baptism of all these souls and of very many others, on the very populous Colorado River, as well as in California Alta . . .

If we continue with the promotion and advancement of these new conversions, we shall be able to continue to make correct maps of this North America, the greater part of which has hitherto been unknown, or practically unknown, for some ancients blot the map with so many and such errors and with such unreal grandeurs and feigned riches as a crowned king whom they carry in chairs of gold, with walled cities, and lakes of quick-silver and gold, or amber, and of corals. With reason Father Mariana rebukes them for deceiving us with these riches that do not exist. They do not say a word about the principal riches that exist there, which are the innumerable souls ransomed by the most precious blood of our Redeemer, Jesus Christ . . .

From *Kino's Historical Memoir*, Vol. 2, pp. 252, 264.

LOOKING FAR WEST

Louis-Joseph de la Vérendrye

Route to the Western Sea

Sir:

I take the liberty of giving you an account of the voyage which I have made with one of my brothers and two Frenchmen sent by my father, honored by your orders to proceed to discover the Western Sea by way of the country of the *Mantanes* (Mandans) according to the accounts of the Indians. . . .

On the second day we came upon a village of the tribe of the *Petits Renards* (Little Foxes), who showed great joy upon seeing us. After making them a number of presents I had our guides tell them that I was seeking the *Gens de Chevaux* who, we hoped, would conduct us to the sea. The result of this was that the entire village marched with us, still following the same route. I felt, indeed, at the time that we could hope to find nothing but a known sea. On the second day of the march we encountered a populous village of the same tribe. They showed us great friendliness. I gave them a number of presents, which they looked upon as great novelties, and they seemed to me very grateful for them. They guided us to a village of the *Pioya* which we reached on the fifteenth. We were very well received there. After proffering them some presents I proposed to them that they conduct us to some tribe on the route to the sea. . . .

Up to that time we had been well received in all the villages through which we had passed, but all that was as nothing in comparison with the admirable behavior of the great chief of the Bow tribe, a man who was not at all covetous as the others had been, but always took very great care of all that belonged to us.

I became attached to the chief, who merited all our friendship. In a short time, due to the pains which he took to instruct me, I learned the language sufficiently well to make myself understood and to understand also what he said to me.

I asked him if his tribe knew the white men who lived by the sea and if they could guide us there. He replied: "We know them by what the prisoners of the Snake Indians, whom we are to join shortly, have told us of them. Do not be surprised if you see many villages joined with us. Messages urging them to meet us have been sent out in all directions. Every day you hear the war song chanted; that is not without purpose: we are going to march to the great mountains which are near the sea, to seek the Snakes there. Do not be afraid to come with us, you have nothing to fear, you will be able to see there the ocean for which you are searching."

He continued his speech as follows: "The French who are at the sea coast," he said, "are numerous; they have many slaves, whom they establish upon their lands by tribes; they have separate quarters, they marry among themselves, and they are not oppressed; the result is that they are happy with them (their masters) and they do not seek to run away. They raise a large number of horses and other animals, which they use to work on their lands. They have many leaders for their soldiers, and they have many also for prayer." He pronounced a few words in their language. I recognized that he was speaking Spanish, and what fully assured me of the fact was the account which he gave me of the massacre of the Spaniards who were seeking to discover the Missouri, of which I had heard before. All this dampened my ardor of the search of a known sea; nevertheless I should have liked very much to go there, if it had been feasible. . . .

We continued to march on until January 8th. On the 9th we left the village. I left my brother to guard our baggage, which was in the lodge of the Bow chief. The larger part of the men were on horseback, advancing in good order. At last, on the twelfth day, we reached the mountains. They are for the most part thickly-wooded with all kinds of wood and appear very high.

After approaching the main part of the village of the Snake tribe, the scouts returned to inform us that they (the Snakes) had fled in great haste and had abandoned their huts and a large part of their belongings. This report brought terror to everyone, for it was feared that the enemy, having discovered them, had gone to fall upon their villages and would reach them before they, themselves, could arrive to defend them. The chief of the Bows did what he could to persuade them to the contrary and to prevail upon them to continue. No one would listen to him. "It is very annoying," he told me, "to have brought you to this point and not be able to go further."

I was exceedingly vexed not to be able to ascend the mountains, as I had hoped to do. We determined therefore to return. . . .

Seeing that there was no likelihood of being conducted to the Spanish territory and having no doubt that my father was very uneasy about us, we determined to depart for Fort La Reine, and left the Bow tribe, to the great regret of all.

                                                    [1742–1743]

From "Journal of the Voyage Made by Chevalier de la Vérendrye, with One of his Brothers, in Search of the Western Sea," *Oregon Historical Quarterly* 26 (June 1925), pp. 116, 118, 120–21, 122, 124.

Philip Freneau

The Great Unknown

My friend, the clergyman, informs me, that after passing a
ridge of lofty mountains extending on the western frontiers of
these republics, a new and most enchanting region opens, of
inexpressible beauty and fertility. The lands are *there* of a
quality far superior to those situated in the neighborhood of
the sea coast: the trees of the forest are stately and tall, the
meadows and pastures spacious, supporting vast herds of the
native animals of the country; which own no master, nor expect their sustenance from the hands of men. The climate, he
says, is moderate and agreeable; there the rivers no longer
bend their courses eastward to the Atlantic, but inclining west
and south, and moving with a gentle current through the
channels that Nature has opened, fall at length into that
grand repository of a thousand streams, *Mississippi,* who collecting his waters, derived from a source remote and unknown, rolls onward through the frozen regions of the north,
and stretching his prodigiously extended arms to the east and
west, embraces these savage groves and dreary solitudes, as
yet uninvestigated by the traveller, unsung by the poet, and
unmeasured by the chain of the geometrician; till uniting
with the *Ohio* and turning due south, receiving afterwards the
Missori and a hundred others, this prince of rivers, in comparison of whom the *Nile* is but a small rivulet, and the
Danube a ditch, hurries with his immense flood of waters into
the Mexican sea, laving the shores of many fertile countries
in his passage, inhabited by savage nations to this day almost
unknown and without a name.

From Philip Freneau, "The Philosopher of the Forest," *The Freeman's
Journal: or, The North American Intelligencer* (Philadelphia), 9, January 1782.

Timothy Dwight

Land of Promise

All hail, thou western world! by heaven design'd
Th' example bright, to renovate mankind.
Soon shall thy sons across the mainland roam;
And claim, on far Pacific shores, their home;
Their rule, religion, manners, arts, convey,
And spread their freedom to the Asian sea.
Where erst six thousand suns have roll'd the year
O'er plains of slaughter, and o'er wilds of fear,
Towns, cities, fanes, shall lift their towery pride;
The village bloom, on every streamlet's side;
Proud Commerce' mole the western surges lave;
The long, white, spire lie imag'd on the wave;
O'er morn's pellucid main expand their sails,
And the starr'd ensign court Korean gales.
The nobler thoughts shall savage trains inform;
Then barbarous passions cease the heart to storm:
No more the captive circling flames devour;
Through the war path the Indian creep no more;
No midnight scout the slumbering village fire;
Nor the scalp'd infant stain his gasping sire:
But peace, the truth, illume the twilight mind,
The gospel's sunshine, and the purpose kind.
Where marshes teem'd with death, shall meads unfold;
Untrodden cliffs resign their stores of gold;
The dance refin'd on Albion's margin move,
And her lone bowers rehearse the tale of love.
Where slept perennial night, shall science rise,
And new-born Oxfords cheer the evening skies;
Miltonic strains the Mexic hills prolong,
And Louis murmurs to Sicilian song.

Then to new climes the bliss shall trace its way,
And Tarter desarts hail the rising day;
From the long torpor startled China wake;

Her chains of misery rous'd Peruvia break;
Man link to man; with bosom bosom twine;
And one great bond the house of Adam join:
The sacred promise full completion know,
And peace, and piety, the world o'erflow.

From Timothy Dwight, *Greenfield Hill: A Poem* (New York: Childs and Swaine, 1794), pp. 52–53.

John Boit

Paradise Glimpsed

12. N. Latt. 46°7'; W. Long. 122°47'. This day saw an appearance of a spacious harbour abreast the Ship, haul'd our wind for it, observ'd two sand bars making off, with a passage between them to a fine river. . . . The River extended to the NE. as far as eye cou'd reach, and water fit to drink as far down as the *Bars,* at the entrance. We directed our course up this noble *River* in search of a Village. The beach was lin'd with Natives, who ran along shore following the Ship. Soon after, above 20 Canoes came off, and brought a good lot of Furs, and Salmon, which last they sold two for a board Nail. The furs we likewise bought cheap, for Copper and Cloth. They appear'd to view the Ship with the greatest astonishment and no doubt we was the first civilized people that they ever saw. . . .

. . . Capt. Gray named this river *Columbia's,* and the North entrance Cape Hancock, and the South Point, *Adams.* This River in my opinion, wou'd be a fine place for to set up a *Factory.* The Indians are very numerous, and appear'd very civil (not even offering to steal). During our short stay we collected 150 Otter, 300 Beaver, and twice the Number of other land furs. The river abounds with excellent *Salmon,* and most other River fish, and the Woods with plenty of Moose and Deer, the skins of which was brought us in great plenty, and the Banks produces a ground Nut, which is an excellent substitute for either bread or Potatoes. We found plenty of Oak, Ash, and Walnut trees, and clear ground in plenty, which with little labour might be made fit to raise such seeds as is necessary for the sustenance of inhabitants, and in short a factory set up here, and another at Hancock's River, in the Queen Charlotte Isles, wou'd engross the whole trade of the NW. Coast (with the help [of] a few small coasting vessells).

20. This day left Columbia's River, and stood clear of the bars, and bore off to the Northward. The men, at Columbia's River, are strait lim'd, fine looking fellows, and the Women are very pretty. They are all in a state of Nature, except the females, who wear a leaf Apron—(perhaps *'t was* a fig leaf). But some of our gentlemen, that examin'd them pretty close, and near, both within and without reported, that it was not a leaf, but a nice wove mat in resemblance!! and so we go—thus, thus—and no War!—!

From John Boit, "Log of the Columbia, 1790–1792," *Massachusetts Historical Society Proceedings* 53 (June 1920), pp. 247, 248.

Meriwether Lewis

It Might Be a Dream

June 14, 1805

I therefore determined to ascend the hill behind me which promised a fine prospect of the adjacent country, nor was I disappointed on my arrival at it's summit. from hence I overlooked a most beatifull and extensive plain reaching from the river to the base of the Snowclad mountains to the S. and S. West; I also observed the missoury streching it's meandering course to the South through this plain to a great distance filled to it's even and grassey brim; another large river flowed in on it's Western side about four miles above me and extended itself th[r]ough a level and fertile valley of 3 miles in width a great distance to the N.W. rendered more conspicuous by the timber which garnished it's borders. in these plains and more particularly in the valley just below me immence herds of buffaloe are feeding. the missouri just above this hill makes a bend to the South where it lies a smoth even and unruffled sheet of water of nearly a mile in width bearing on it's watry bosome vast flocks of geese which feed at pleasure in the delightfull pasture on either border. the young geese are now completely feathered except the wings which both in the young and old are yet deficient. after feasting my eyes on this ravishing prospect and resting myself a few minutes I determined to procede as far as the river which I saw discharge itself on the West side of Missouri convinced that it was the river which the Indians call *medecine river* and which they informed us fell into the Missouri just above the falls. I descended the hill and directed my course to the bend of the Missouri near which there was a herd of at least a thousand buffaloe; here I thought it would be well to kill a buffaloe and leave him untill my return from the river and if I then found that I had not time to get back to camp this evening to remain all night here there being a few sticks of drift wood lying along shore which would answer for my fire, and a few s[c]attering cottonwood trees a few hundred yards below which would afford me at least the semblance of a shelter. under this impression I selected a fat buffaloe and shot him very well, through the lungs; while I was gazeing attentively on the poor anamal dischargin blood in streams from his mouth and nostrils, expecting him to fall every instant, and having entirely forgotten to reload my rifle, a large white, or reather brown bear, had perceived and crept on me within 20 steps before I discovered him; in the first moment I drew up my gun to shoot, but at the same instant recolected that she was not loaded and that he was too near for me to hope to perform this opperation before he reached me, as he was then briskly advancing on me; it was an open level plain, not a bush within miles nor a tree within less than three hundred yards of me; the river bank was sloping and not more than three feet above the level of the water; in short there was no place by means of which I could conceal myself from this monster untill I could charge my rifle; in this situation I thought of retreating in a brisk walk as fast as he was advancing untill I could reach a tree about 300 yards below me, but I had no sooner terned myself about but he pitched at me, open mouthed and full speed, I ran about 80 yards and found he gained on me fast, I then run into the water. the idea struk me to get into the water to such debth that I could stand and he would be obliged to swim, and that I could in that situation defend myself with my espontoon; accordingly I ran haistily into the water about waist deep, and faced

about and presented the point of my espontoon, at this instant he arrived at the edge of the water within about 20 feet
of me; the moment I put myself in this attitude of defence he
sudonly wheeled about as if frightened, declined the combat
on such unequal grounds, and retreated with quite as great
precipitation as he had just before pursued me. as soon as I saw
him run of[f] in that manner I returned to the shore and
charged my gun, which I had still retained in my hand
throughout this curious adventure. I saw him run through the
level open plain about three miles, till he disappeared in the
woods on medecine river; during the whole of this distance
he ran at full speed, sometimes appearing to look behind him
as if he expected pursuit. I now began to reflect on this novil
occurrence and indeavoured to account for this sudden retreat of the bear. I at first thought that perhaps he had not
smelt me before he arrived at the waters edge so near me, but
I then reflected that he had pursued me for about 80 or 90
yards before I took [to] the water and on examinination saw
the grownd toarn with his tallons immediately on the
imp[r]ession of my steps; and the cause of his allarm still remains with me misterious and unaccountable. so it was and I
felt myself not a little gratifyed that he had declined the combat. my gun reloaded I felt confidence once more in my
strength; and determined not to be thwarted in my design of
visiting medecine river, but determined never again to suffer
my peice to be longer empty than the time she necessarily required to charge her. I passed through the plain nearly in the
direction which the bear had run to medecine river, found it
a handsome stream, about 200 y^{ds}. wide with a gentle current, apparently deep, it's waters clear, and banks which were
formed principally of dark-brown and blue clay were about
the hight of those of the Missouri or from 3 to 5 feet; yet
they had not the appearance of ever being overflown, a circumstance, which I did not expect so immediately in the
neighbourhood of the mountains, from whence I should have
supposed, that sudden and immence torrants would issue at
certain seasons of the year; but the reverse is absolutely the
case. I am therefore compelled to believe that the snowey
mountains yeald their warters slowly, being partially effected
every day by the influence of the sun only, and never sud-
donly melted down by haisty showers of rain.

having examined Medecine river I now determined to return, having by my estimate about 12 miles to walk. I looked
at my watch and found it was half after six P.M. in returning

through the level bottom of Medecine river and about 200 yards distant from the Missouri, my direction led me directly to an anamal that I at first supposed was a wolf; but on nearer approach or about sixty paces distant I discovered that it was not, it's color was a brownish yellow; it was standing near it's burrow, and when I approached it thus nearly, it couched itself down like a cat looking immediately at me as if it designed to spring on me. I took aim at it and fired, it instantly disappeared in it's burrow; I loaded my gun and ex[a]mined the place which was dusty and saw the track from which I am still further convinced that it was of the tiger kind. whether I struck it or not I could not determine, but I am almost confident that I did; my gun is true and I had a steady rest by means of my espontoon, which I have found very serviceable to me in this way in the open plains. It now seemed to me that all the beasts of the neighbourhood had made a league to destroy me, or that some fortune was disposed to amuse herself at my expence, for I had not proceded more than three hundred yards from the burrow of this tyger cat, before three bull buffaloe, which wer feeding with a large herd about half a mile from me on my left, seperated from the herd and ran full speed towards me, I thought at least to give them some amusement and altered my direction to meet them; when they arrived within a hundred yards they mad[e] a halt, took a good view of me and retreated with precipitation. I then continued my rout homewards passed the buffaloe which I had killed, but did not think it prudent to remain all night at this place which really from the succession of curious adventures wore the impression on my mind of inchantment; at sometimes for a moment I thought it might be a dream, but the prickley pears which pierced my feet very severely once in a while, particularly after it grew dark, convinced me that I was really awake, and that it was necessary to make the best of my way to camp. it was sometime after dark before I returned to the party; I found them extremely uneasy for my safety; they had formed a thousand conjectures, all of which equally forboding my death, which they had so far settled among them, that they had already agreed on the rout which each should take in the morning to surch for me. I felt myself much fortiegued, but eat a hearty supper and took a good night's rest.

From Meriwether Lewis, *Original Journals of the Lewis and Clark Expedition: 1804–1806,* edited by Reuben G. Thwaites (New York: Dodd, Mead & Co., 1904), Vol. 2, pp. 155–159.

Edgar Allan Poe

The Romantic West

In regard to the question of the *first* passage across the Rocky Mountains, it will be seen, from what we have already said, that the credit of the enterprise should never have been given to Lewis and Clark, since Mackenzie succeeded in it, in the year 1793; and that in point of fact, Mr. [Julius] Rodman was the first who overcame those gigantic barriers; crossing them as he did in 1792. . . . He was possessed with a burning love of Nature; and worshipped her, perhaps, more in her dreary and savage aspects, than in her manifestations of placidity and joy. He stalked through that immense and often terrible wilderness with an evident rapture at his heart which we envy him as we read. . . .

The sun shone clearly, but with no great heat. The ice had disappeared from the river, and the current, which was pretty full, conceded all those marshy, and ragged alluvia which disfigure the borders of the Missouri at low water. It had now the most majestic appearance washing up among the willows and cotton-wood on one side, and rushing, with a bold volume, by the sharp cliffs on the other. As I looked up the stream (which here stretched away to the westward, until the waters apparently met the sky in the great distance) and reflected on the immensity of territory through which those waters had probably passed, a territory as yet altogether unknown to white people, and perhaps abounding in the magnificent works of God, I felt an excitement of soul such as I had never before experienced, and secretly resolved that it should be no slight obstacle which should prevent my pushing up this noble river farther than any previous adventurer had done. At that moment I seemed possessed of an energy more than human; and my animal spirits rose to so high a degree that I could with difficulty content myself in the narrow limits of the boat. I longed to be . . . on the bank, that I might give full vent to the feelings which inspired me, by leaping and running in the prairie.

From Edgar Allan Poe, *The Journal of Julius Rodman, Being an Account of the First Passage Across the Rocky Mountains of North America Achieved by Civilized Man*, in *The Complete Works of Edgar Allan Poe*, edited by James A. Harrison (New York: Thomas Y. Crowell & Co., 1902), Vol. 4, p., 148.

Zebulon Montgomery Pike

The Great American Desert

Numerous have been the hypotheses formed by various naturalists to account for the vast tract of untimbered country which lies between the waters of the Missouri, Mississippi, and the Western Ocean, from the mouth of the latter river to 48° north latitude. Although not flattering myself to be able to elucidate that which numbers of highly scientific characters have acknowledged to be beyond their depth of research, still I would not think I had done my country justice did I not give birth to what few lights my examination of those internal deserts had enabled me to acquire. In that vast country of which I speak, we find the soil generally dry and sandy, with gravel, and discover that the moment we approach a stream the land becomes more humid, with small timber. I therefore conclude that this country never was timbered; as, from the earliest age the aridity of the soil, having so few water-courses running through it, and they being principally dry in summer, has never afforded moisture sufficient to support the growth of timber. In all timbered land the annual discharge of the leaves, with the continual decay of old trees and branches, creates a manure and moisture, which is preserved from the heat of the sun not being permitted to direct his rays perpendicularly, but only to shed them obliquely through the foliage. But here a barren soil, parched and dried up for eight months in the year, presents neither moisture nor nutrition sufficient to nourish the timber. These vast plains of the western hemisphere may become in time as celebrated as the sandy deserts of Africa; for I saw in my route, in various places, tracts of many leagues where the wind had thrown up the sand in all the fanciful form of the ocean's rolling wave, and on which not a speck of vegetable matter existed.

But from these immense prairies may arise one great advantage to the United States, viz: The restriction of our population to some certain limits, and thereby a continuation of the Union. Our citizens being so prone to rambling and extending themselves on the frontiers will, through necessity, be constrained to limit their extent on the west to the borders of the Missouri and Mississippi, while they leave the prairies incapable of cultivation to the wandering and uncivilized aborigines of the country.

From Zebulon Montgomery Pike, *The Expeditions of Zebulon Montgomery Pike*, edited by Elliott Coues (New York: Francis P. Harper, 1895), Vol. 2, pp. 524–525.

William Cullen Bryant
The Gardens of the Desert

These are the gardens of the Desert, these
The unshorn fields, boundless and beautiful,
For which the speech of England has no name—
The Prairies. I behold them for the first,
And my heart swells, while the dilated sight
Takes in the encircling vastness. Lo! they stretch
In airy undulations, far away,
As if the Ocean, in his gentlest swell,
Stood still, with all his rounded billows fixed,
And motionless forever. Motionless?—
No—they are all unchained again. The clouds
Sweep over with their shadows, and, beneath,
The surface rolls and fluctuates to the eye;
Dark hollows seem to glide along and chase
The sunny ridges. Breezes of the South!
Who toss the golden and the flame-like flowers,
And pass the prairie-hawk that, poised on high,
Flaps his broad wings, yet moves not—ye have played
Among the palms of Mexico and vines
Of Texas, and have crisped the limpid brooks
That from the fountains of Sonora glide
Into the calm Pacific—have ye fanned
A nobler or lovelier scene than this?
Man hath no part in all this glorious work:
The hand that built the firmament hath heaved
And smoothed these verdant swells, and sown their slopes
With herbage, planted them with island-groves,
And hedged them round with forests. Fitting floor

For this magnificent temple of the sky—
With flowers whose glory and whose multitude
Rival the constellations! The great heavens
Seem to stoop down upon the scene in love,—
A nearer vault, and of a tenderer blue,
Than that which bends above our Eastern hills. . . .

From William Cullen Bryant, "The Prairies," in *Poetical Works of William Cullen Bryant* (D. Appleton & Co., 1878), pp. 184–185.

Zenas Leonard

The *End* of the *Far West*

November 1833

This night we encamped on the bank of the river in a very beautiful situation. Soon after the men went to rest and the camp had become quieted, we were startled by a loud distant noise similar to that of thunder. Whilst lying close to the ground this noise could be distinctly heard for a considerable length of time without intermission. When it was at first observed some of our men were much alarmed, as they readily supposed it was occasioned by an earthquake, and they began to fear that we would all be swallowed up in the bowels of the earth; and others judged it to be the noise of a neighboring cataract. Capt. Walker, however, suggested a more plausible cause, which allayed the fears of the most timid. He supposed that the noise origined by the Pacific rolling and dashing her boisterous waves against the rocky shore. Had any of us ever before been at the coast, we would have readily accounted for the mysterious noise.

The idea of being within hearing of the *end* of the *Far West* inspired the heart of every member of our company with a patriotic feeling for his country's honor, and all were eager to loose no time until they should behold what they had heard. We felt as if all our previous hardships and privations would be adequately compensated, if we would be spared to return in safety to the homes of our kindred and have it to say that we had stood upon the extreme end of the great west. . . .

Most of this vast waste of territory belongs to the Republic of the United States. What a theme to contemplate its settlement and civilization. Will the jurisdiction of the federal government ever succeed in civilizing the thousands of savages now roaming over these plains, and her hardy freeborn population here plant their homes, build their towns and cities, and say here shall the arts and sciences of civilization take root and flourish? yes, here, even in this remote part of the great west before many years, will these hills and valleys be greeted with the enlivening sound, of the workman's hammer, and the merry whistle of the plough-boy. But this is left undone by government, and will only be seen when too late to apply the remedy. The Spaniards are making inroads on the South—the Russians are encroaching with impunity along the seashore to the North, and further North-east the British are pushing their stations into the very heart of our territory, which, even at this day, more resemble military forts to resist invasion than trading stations. Our government should be vigilant. She should assert her claim by taking possession of the whole territory, as soon as possible—for we have good reason to suppose that the territory *west* of the mountain will some day be equally as important to a nation as that on the *east*.

From Zenas Leonard, *Narrative of the Adventures of Zenas Leonard . . . Written By Himself* (Clearfield, Pa.: D. W. Moore, 1839), pp. 47, 49–50.

FRÉMONT MAPS THE WEST

John C. Frémont

The Great Plains

June 22, 1842

At the Big Trees, where we had intended to noon, no water was to be found. The bed of the little creek was perfectly dry, and, on the adjacent sandy bottom, *cacti*, for the first time, made their appearance. We made here a short delay in search of water; and, after a hard day's march of twenty-eight miles, encamped, at 5 o'clock, on the Little Blue, where our arrival made a scene of the Arabian desert. As fast as they arrived, men and horses rushed into the stream, where they bathed and drank together in common enjoyment. We were now in the range of the Pawnees, who were accustomed to infest this part of the country, stealing horses from companies on their way to the mountains, and, when in sufficient force, openly attacking and plundering them, and subjecting them to various kinds of insult. For the first time, therefore, guard was mounted to-night. Our route the next morning lay up the valley, which, bordered by hills with graceful slopes, looked uncommonly green and beautiful. The stream was about fifty feet wide, and three or four feet deep, fringed by cotton wood and willow, with frequent groves of oak tenanted by flocks of turkeys. Game here, too, made its appearance in greater plenty. Elk were frequently seen on the hills, and now and then an antelope bounded across our path, or a deer broke from the groves. The road in the afternoon was over the upper prairies, several miles from the river, and we encamped at sunset on one of its small tributaries, where an abundance of prêle [*equisetum*] afforded fine forage to our tired animals. We had travelled thirty-one miles. A heavy bank of black clouds in the west came on us in a storm between nine and ten, preceded by a violent wind. The rain fell in such torrents that it was difficult to breathe facing the wind, the thunder rolled incessantly, and the whole sky was tremulous with lightning; now and then illuminated by a blinding flash, succeeded by pitchy darkness. Carson had the watch from ten to midnight, and to him had been assigned our young *compagnons de voyage,* Messrs. Brant and R. Benton. This was their first night on guard, and such an introduction did not augur very auspiciously of the pleasures of the expedition. Many things conspired to render their situation uncomfortable; stories of desperate and bloody Indian fights were rife in the camp; our position was badly chosen, surrounded on all sides by timbered hollows, and occupying an area of several hundred feet, so that necessarily the guards were far apart; and now and then I could hear Randolph, as if relieved by the sound of a voice in the darkness, calling out to the sergeant of the guard, to direct his attention to some imaginary alarm; but they stood it out, and took their turn regularly afterward.

The next morning we had a specimen of the false alarms to which all parties in these wild regions are subject. Proceeding up the valley, objects were seen on the opposite hills, which disappeared before a glass could be brought to bear upon them. A man, who was a short distance in the rear, came spurring up in great haste, shouting Indians! Indians! He had been near enough to see and count them, according to his report, and had made out twenty-seven. I immediately halted; arms were examined and put in order; the usual preparations made; and Kit Carson, springing upon one of the hunting horses, crossed the river, and galloped off into the opposite prairies, to obtain some certain intelligence of their movements.

Mounted on a fine horse, without a saddle, and scouring bareheaded over the prairies, Kit was one of the finest pictures of a horseman I have ever seen. A short time enabled him to discover that the Indian war party of twenty-seven consisted of six elk, who had been grazing curiously at our caravan as it passed by and were now scampering off at full speed. This was our first alarm, and its excitement broke agreeably on the monotony of the day.

From John C. Frémont, *Report of the Exploring Expedition to the Rocky Mountains in the Year 1842, and to Oregon and California in the Years 1843–'44* (Washington: Gales and Seaton, 1845), pp. 14–15.

Charles Preuss

Miserable Prairie Life

June 6, 1842

Broke camp and moved fifteen miles up the Kansas river. Annoyed by that childish Frémont. During the night a lot of rain, which made me get up; everything wet. Thought much about the fine Coast Survey.

What a disorder in this outfit; dirty cooking. To be sure, how can a foolish lieutenant manage such a thing.

This is my first day of horseback riding. Fortunately I got a gentle horse. Yet the unaccustomed effort, little though it was, made me quite stiff.

June 12

A lot of rain at night; slept in a poor tent.

Eternal prairie and grass, with occasional groups of trees. Frémont prefers this to every other landscape. To me it is as if someone would prefer a book with blank pages to a good story. The ocean has, after all, its storms and icebergs, the beautiful sunrise and sunset. But the prairie? To the deuce with such a life; I wish I were in Washington with my old girl.

Chased a wolf; the men tried to shoot him but missed.

June 19

No Sunday for us. I don't even have a clean shirt to wear. To the deuce with washing.

Have trapped a large turtle, which is being prepared for soup tonight. If our cook, the rascal, will only know how to fix it.

Our big chronometer has gone to sleep. That is what always happens when an egg wants to be wiser than the hen. So far I can't say that I have formed a very high opinion of Frémont's astronomical manipulations. We have also started to botanize.

I wish I had a drink.

95

June 25

Had a remarkably bad night. First came a thunderstorm with torrential rain, which drenched us thoroughly in our miserable tents. Then it became so warm that the mosquitoes were as if possessed by the devil, and I actually could not sleep a minute.

The others lay safely under their nets; mine had been forgotten because of Frémont's negligence.

This morning toward ten o'clock, after we had been on the march for about three hours, that silly Brant came galloping up and claimed he had seen Indians on the other side of the river. We halted, and our two sharpshooters set out to reconnoiter while the others made ready their rifles and pistols for an emergency. After half an hour it became clear that Mr. Brant had seen elk instead of Indians. After we had laughed at him, we moved on quietly in the roasting heat of the sun (94° Fahrenheit).

July 9

Last night there was a great deal of discussion with the leader [Bridger] of the company about the Indian danger. He advises very earnestly not to continue from Laramie with such a small crew. He regrets that Frémont is not present for a conference. I wonder what the latter will decide.

Daily, several people, White and Indian, have been killed there. If our party cannot be increased at the Fort, it would be best to turn back and limit ourselves to the survey of the Platte. We are no military expedition to fight the Indians. It would be ridiculous to risk the lives of twenty-five people just to determine a few longitudes and latitudes and to find out the elevation of a mountain range. The men are not at all inclined to continue without reinforcements, and Labbok[?] Brant was at the point of going back with the traders.

In a few days everything will be settled in Laramie. I hope we shall get that far surely.

August 2

Yesterday afternoon and this morning Frémont set up his daguerreotype to photograph the rocks; he spoiled five plates that way. Not a thing was to be seen on them. That's the way it often is with these Americans. They know everything, they can do everything, and when they are put to a test, they fail miserably.

Last night a few horses became restless. When we walked up with a lantern, we were told that Indians are near by.

Frémont wasted the morning with his machine. Now, after we have ridden about ten miles and pitched camp, we see smoke rising in the mountains opposite us, about six miles distant. Here that can mean nothing else but Indians. We shall therefore have to be on guard again. We shall probably not be at ease again until we see the Missouri before our eyes. . . .

Oh, strange and miserable prairie life!

This and later selections from Charles Preuss, *Exploring with Frémont: The Private Diaries of Charles Preuss, Cartographer for John C. Frémont on His First, Second, and Fourth Expeditions to the West*, translated and edited by Erwin G. and Elisabeth K. Gudde (Norman: University of Oklahoma Press, 1958), pp. 3–124 *passim*.

John C. Frémont

The Rocky Mountains

August 15, 1842

At intervals we reached places where a number of springs gushed from the rocks, and about 1,800 feet above the lakes came to the snow line. From this point our progress was uninterrupted climbing. Hitherto I had worn a pair of thick moccasins, with soles of *parflêche*; but here I put on a light thin pair, which I had brought for the purpose, as now the use of our toes became necessary to a further advance. I availed myself of a sort of comb of the mountain, which stood against the wall like a buttress, and which the wind and the solar radiation, joined to the steepness of the smooth rock, had kept almost entirely free from snow. Up this I made my way rapidly. Our cautious method of advancing in the outset had spared my strength; and, with the exception of a slight disposition to headache, I felt no remains of yesterday's illness. In a few minutes we reached a point where the buttress was overhanging, and there was no other way of surmounting the difficulty than by passing around one side of it, which was the face of a vertical precipice of several hundred feet.

Putting hands and feet in the crevices between the blocks, I succeeded in getting over it, and, when I reached the top, found my companions in a small valley below. Descending to them, we continued climbing, and in a short time reached the crest. I sprang upon the summit, and another step would have precipitated me into an immense snow field five hundred feet below. To the edge of this field was a sheer icy precipice; and then, with a gradual fall, the field sloped off for about a mile, until it struck the foot of another lower ridge. I stood on a narrow crest, about three feet in width, with an inclination of about 20° N. 51° E. As soon as I had gratified the first feelings of curiosity, I descended, and each man ascended in his turn; for I would only allow one at a time to mount the unstable and precarious slab, which it seemed a breath would hurl into the abyss below. We mounted the barometer in the snow of the summit, and, fixing a ramrod in a crevice, unfurled the national flag to wave in the breeze where never flag waved before. During our morning's ascent we had met no sign of animal life except the small sparrow-like bird already mentioned. A stillness the most profound and a terrible solitude forced themselves constantly on the mind as the great features of the place. Here on the summit, where the stillness was absolute, unbroken by any sound, and the solitude complete, we thought ourselves beyond the region of animated life; but while we were sitting on the rock a solitary bee (*bromus, the bumble bee*) came winging his flight from the eastern valley, and lit on the knee of one of the men.

It was a strange place, the icy rock and the highest peak of the Rocky Mountains, for a lover of warm sunshine and flowers; and we pleased ourselves with the idea that he was the first of his species to cross the mountain barrier—a solitary pioneer to foretell the advance of civilization. I believe that a moment's thought would have made us let him continue his way unharmed; but we carried out the law of this country, where all animated nature seems at war; and, seizing him immediately, put him in at least a fit place—in the leaves of a large book, among the flowers we had collected on our way. The barometer stood at 18.293, the attached thermometer at 44°; giving for the elevation of this summit 13,570 feet above the Gulf of Mexico, which may be called the highest flight of the bee. It is certainly the highest known flight of that insect.

From Frémont, *Report*, pp. 69–70.

Charles Preuss

No Swiss Alps

August 5, 1842

Frémont is roaming through the mountains collecting rocks and is keeping us waiting for lunch. I am hungry as a wolf. That fellow knows nothing about minerology or botany. Yet he collects every trifle in order to have it interpreted later in Washington and to brag about it in his report. Let him collect as much as he wants—if he would only not make us wait for our meal.

Today he said the air up here is too thin; that is the reason his daguerreotype was a failure. Old boy, you don't understand the thing, that is it.

August 8

As I said, these Rocky Mountains are no Swiss Alps. But it is true that they are magnificent, strangely shaped rocks. In a few days I shall be able to say more about them.

August 17

It was a terrible climb over rocks and through water. The actual height which we had to climb we were forced to repeat at least two or three times because we had to go downhill again and again, from one mountain to the other. The leader, Carson, walked too fast. This caused some exchange of words. Frémont got excited as usual and designated a young chap to take the lead—he could not serve as a guide, of course. Frémont developed a headache, and as a result we stopped soon afterwards, about eleven o'clock. He decided to climb the peak the next morning, with renewed strength and cooler blood. . . .

Someone hit upon the idea of trying to cross the snow that was quite soft, and then everything proceeded without danger. The leader, de Couteau, tried every step, carefully, and each of us followed in his tracks. Thus we continued, carefully and slowly, and soon we reached the summit. The highest rock was so small that only one after the other could stand on it. Pistols were fired, the flag unfurled, and we shouted "hurrah" several times. Then the barometer was set up, and I observed twice. The results were 18.320 and 18.293, thermometer, 45.3° and 44°, which will probably correspond to almost 10,000 feet. As on the entire journey, Frémont allowed me only a few minutes for my work. When the time comes for me to make my map in Washington, he will more than regret this unwise haste. . . .

The next morning, it was the sixteenth of August, we started even before sunrise. We wanted to have breakfast at the place where the other nine men waited with the rest of the mules. Our guide, Basil, lost the way or perhaps thought he could find a better one. For that reason we got into such a confusion of rocks and small lakes that we hardly knew how to get out of it. Twenty times we had to dismount and shove the animals by force over the rocks. We climbed after them and mounted again for a short stretch. It was almost noon when we reached the spot, which was only two miles distant as the crow flies. But instead of finding men, mules, and breakfast, we found only a piece of paper fastened to a post, on which Kit Carson informed us that he and the others had moved to the base camp at the lake. He had assumed that we, too, had gone there by a shorter route. Frémont began to rave again, wanted to dismiss everybody, go home immediately, etc., etc. The nonsense naturally ended again with a headache.

From Preuss, *Exploring with Frémont.*

John C. Frémont
Independence Rock

August 23, 1842

Yesterday evening we reached our encampment at Rock Independence, where I took some astronomical observations. Here, not unmindful of the custom of early travellers and explorers in our country, I engraved on this rock of the Far West a symbol of the Christian faith. Among the thickly inscribed names, I made on the hard granite the impression of a large cross, which I covered with a black preparation of India rubber, well calculated to resist the influence of wind and rain. It stands amidst the names of many who have long since found their way to the grave, and for whom the huge rock is a giant grave stone.

From Frémont, *Report*, pp. 71–72.

Charles Preuss
A Miserable Rock

August 22, 1842

What a miserable rock is this Independence Rock compared to the rocks we saw in the mountains. And what a name! Many a human wretch, too, bears a high-sounding name.

August 31

A few remarks about the Indians. They possess an astonishing degree of equanimity. We met three Cheyennes who had nothing to eat for six days. Even the best observer could not have suspected this when they sat down to our evening meal. They only mentioned it casually to Kit, with whom they were already acquainted. What a fuss we white people make if we have to go hungry for only one day.

September 17

The entire prairie teems with buffalo. Yesterday four cows were killed, and the men prepared for further slaughter. To-day we cross the region where we saw the first buffalo on our march west.

There is so much dew that it appears as if it had rained during the night. It is hot at noon. This afternoon Frémont joined the buffalo hunt once more but again did not bag anything. "I knocked down one, and that fellow will not get much farther," etc. That does not mean anything, my dear lieutenant! You have to bring home the tongue—the tongue!

From Preuss, *Exploring with Frémont.*

John C. Frémont

The Sierra Nevada

February 11, 1844

High wind continued, and our trail this morning was nearly invisible—here and there indicated by a little ridge of snow. Our situation became tiresome and dreary, requiring a strong exercise of patience and resolution.

February 13

The meat train did not arrive this evening, and I gave Godey leave to kill our little dog, (Tlamath,) which he prepared in Indian fashion; scorching off the hair, and washing the skin with soap and snow, and then cutting it up into pieces, which were laid on the snow. Shortly afterwards, the sleigh arrived with a supply of horse meat; and we had tonight an extraordinary dinner—pea soup, mule, and dog.

February 14

With Mr. Preuss, I ascended to-day the highest peak to the right; from which we had a beautiful view of a mountain lake at our feet, about fifteen miles in length, and so entirely surrounded by mountains that we could not discover an outlet. We had taken with us a glass; but, though we enjoyed an extended view, the valley was half hidden in mist, as when we had seen it before. Snow could be distinguished on the higher parts of the coast mountains; eastward, as far as the eye could extend, it ranged over a terrible mass of broken snowy mountains, fading off blue in the distance.

From Frémont, *Report*, p. 234.

Charles Preuss
Completely Snowed In

February 11, 1844

We are now completely snowed in. The snowstorm is on top of us. The wind obliterates all tracks which, with incredible effort, we make for our horses. The horses are about twenty miles behind and are expected to arrive tonight—or rather they are now no longer expected. How could they get through? At the moment no one can tell what will really happen. It is certain that we shall have to eat horse meat. I should not mind if we only had salt. But the lack of salt kills me. I feel terribly weak and have little appetite.

March 4

I dig up a few onions, a hard job because I have only a pocketknife and they are deep between the rocks. At two or three o'clock I search for a spot where I can find fungus or enough wood to have a fire for the night. I have no axe to cut wood, nor would I have enough strength. The weather outlook is awful now . . . Oh, my sweetheart! If you knew how badly off I am at the moment! Just now I have scraped up my evening meal. On the way I came across small puddles, where I caught a few frogs. I pulled off their legs and chewed them.

From Preuss, *Exploring with Frémont.*

John C. Frémont

The San Joaquin Valley

March 27, 1844

Over much of this extent, the vegetation was sparse; the surface showing plainly the action of water, which, in the season of flood, the Joaquin spreads over the valley. About 1 o'clock we came again among innumerable flowers; and a few miles further, fields of the beautiful blue-flowering *lupine*, which seems to love the neighborhood of water, indicated that we were approaching a stream. We here found this beautiful shrub in thickets, some of them being 12 feet in height. Occasionally three or four plants were clustered together, forming a grand bouquet, about 90 feet in circumference, and 10 feet high; the whole summit covered with spikes of flowers, the perfume of which is very sweet and grateful. A lover of natural beauty can imagine with what pleasure we rode among these flowering groves, which filled the air with a light and delicate fragrance. We continued our road for about half a mile, interspersed through an open grove of live oaks, which, in form, were the most symmetrical and beautiful we had yet seen in this country. The ends of their branches rested on the ground, forming somewhat more than a half sphere of very full and regular figure, with leaves apparently smaller than usual.

The Californian poppy, of a rich orange color, was numerous today. Elk and several bands of antelope made their appearance.

Our road was now one continuous enjoyment; and it was pleasant, riding among this assemblage of green pastures with varied flowers and scattered groves, and out of the warm green spring, to look at the rocky and snowy peaks where lately we had suffered so much.

From Frémont, *Report*, p. 249.

Charles Preuss

This Valley Is a Paradise

March 27, 1844

It is true; this valley is a paradise. Grass, flowers, trees, beautiful, clear rivers, thousands of deer, elk, wild horses, wonderful salmon. I shall probably settle on Captain Sutter's property.

There are thousands of different kinds of ducks here; geese stand around as if tame. The Indians make pretty blankets of the feathers. One can kill a fat oxen without asking permission; all one has to do is to give the hide and the tallow to the owner. All soil products thrive. The lazy Spaniards just scratch the surface with a spike instead of plowing the ground, yet everything grows wonderfully. Plenty of grapes and figs.

Sutter is starting a vineyard in the German fashion. The Indians are so tame and docile that Sutter can use them for all kinds of work. The wages for fourteen days of labor on a drainage ditch in the wheat field amount to one shirt. To be sure, they all go naked because it is eternal spring. Why is this country with such advantages so little known in the east? Because the whalers and skippers keep everything secret in order not to spoil their advantageous trade in hides and tallow through competition with more intelligent settlers. Even now they refuse to take along letters from the few settlers who are here.

At a dance with which the Indians entertained us, one had painted his penis with the Prussian national colors. Everybody, at least the males, runs around stark naked.

March 28

The wild mules cause us lots of trouble. Already nine o'clock in the morning. This river is called the Stanislaus, a tributary to the San Joaquin. All rivers are at a high-water mark because of the melting of the snow. How pleasant it is to look from the beautiful spring to the white walls where we suffered so much. One thing is certain: if I can not make a liv-

ing in the United States without much soliciting and long
rigamorole in the future, I will move. After this job is finished, I shall go via Vera Cruz, Mexico, and Acapulco to the
San Francisco Bay district and settle there.

From Preuss, *Exploring with Frémont*.

John C. Frémont
Land of Contrast

April 15, 1844

We continued a short distance down the creek, in which our
guide informed us that the water very soon disappeared, and
turned directly to the southward along the foot of the mountain; the trail on which we rode appearing to describe the
eastern limit of travel, where water and grass terminated.
Crossing a low spur, which bordered the creek, we descended
to a kind of plain among the lower spurs; the desert being in
full view on our left, apparently illimitable. A hot mist lay
over it to-day, through which it had a white and glistening
appearance; here and there a few dry-looking *buttes* and iso-
lated black ridges rose suddenly upon it. "There," said our
guide, stretching out his hand towards it [the Mohave
Desert], "there are the great *llanos*, (plains;) *no hay agua;
no hay zacate—nada;* there is neither water nor grass—nothing; every animal that goes out upon them, dies." It was
indeed dismal to look upon, and hard to conceive so great a
change in so short a distance. One might travel the world
over, without finding a valley more fresh and verdant—more
floral and sylvan—more alive with birds and animals—more
bounteously watered—than we had left in the San Joaquin:
here, within a few miles ride, a vast desert plain spread before us, from which the boldest traveller turned away in
despair.

Directly in front of us, at some distance to the southward,
and running out in an easterly direction from the mountains,
stretched a sierra, having at the eastern end (perhaps 50
miles distant) some snowy peaks, on which, by the information of our guide, snow rested all the year.

Our cavalcade made a strange and grotesque appearance; and it was impossible to avoid reflecting upon our position and composition in this remote solitude. Within two degrees of the Pacific ocean; already far south of the latitude of Monterey; and still forced on south by a desert on one hand, and a mountain range on the other; guided by a civilized Indian, attended by two wild ones from the Sierra; a Chinook from the Columbia; and our own mixture of American, French, German—all armed; four or five languages heard at once; above a hundred horses and mules, half wild; American, Spanish, and Indian dresses and equipments intermingled—such was our composition. Our march was a sort of procession. Scouts ahead, and on the flanks; a front and rear division; the pack animals, baggage, and horned cattle, in the centre; and the whole stretching a quarter of a mile along our dreary path. In this form we journeyed; looking more like we belonged to Asia than to the United States of America.

From Frémont, *Report*, pp. 256–257.

Charles Preuss

Bad, Bad Region

April 14, 1844

Yesterday we reached the little stream we have to ascend to cross the mountains. A few miles farther up we left the sandy plains where these small mountain streams lose themselves. We came into pleasant, grassy hills. There we made a fine camp. The same mountain range which a short time ago caused us such misery we crossed in one day today, through a most beautiful pass covered with trees and flowers. To the right and left the snow-capped mountains stared us in the face but could not frighten us. Hummingbirds and warm spring air made us laugh at the snow. Now, to be sure, all this glory is gone. We are camping on the east side of the mountains, have a desert ahead of us, and must prepare for a miserable journey for the next months. The oaks, which we still see here, look absolutely black and wintry, while those which we left yesterday stood in full green splendor. Such a difference is caused by a range of mountains. The *Pisang* [Yucca], a tree I knew before only from paintings, cuts a sorry figure.

April 18

Yesterday we followed a stream until late at night in order to find grass. Found nothing. My Polly ran against a cactus, jumped high in the air, and threw me off. My hips were blue this morning. I lost this diary and other things; luckily, I recovered everything this morning. Bad, bad region! Sand and Yucca trees and cactus.

What are hopes? What are plans?

From Preuss, *Exploring with Frémont*.

WESTERN DREAMS

Josiah Gregg

Land of the Free

I have striven in vain to reconcile myself to the even tenor of civilized life in the United States; and have sought in its amusements and its society a substitute for those high excitements which have attached me so strongly to Prairie life. Yet I am almost ashamed to confess that scarcely a day passes without my experiencing a pang of regret that I am not now roving at large upon those western plains. Nor do I find my taste peculiar; for I have hardly known a man who has ever become familiar with the kind of life which I have led for so many years, that has not relinquished it with regret.

There is more than one way of explaining this apparent incongruity. In the first place the wild, unsettled and independent life of the Prairie trader makes perfect freedom from nearly every kind of social dependence an absolute necessity

of his being. He is in daily, nay, hourly exposure of his life
and property, and in the habit of relying upon his own arm
and his own gun both for protection and support. Is he
wronged? No court or jury is called to adjudicate upon his
disputes or his abuses, save his own conscience; and no powers are invoked to redress them save those with which the
God of Nature had endowed him. He knows no government—no laws, save those of his own creation and adoption.
He lives in no society which he must look up to or propitiate.
The exchange of this untrammeled condition—this sovereign
independence, for a life in civilization, where both his physical and moral freedom are invaded at every turn by the complicated machinery of social institutions, is certainly likely to
commend itself to but few,—not even to all those who have
been educated to find their enjoyments in the arts and elegan-
cies peculiar to civilized society;—as is evinced by the frequent instances of men of letters, of refinement and of
wealth, voluntarily abandoning society for a life upon the
Prairies, or in the still more savage mountain wilds.

From Josiah Gregg, *Commerce of the Prairies* (New York: H.G. Langley, 1844), Vol. 2, pp. 156–157.

William Perkins

Land of Regeneration

Having arranged our traps, I strolled up towards the hills,
and had not proceeded far when I heard my name called out
in tones of surprise. I turned towards a person standing at the
entrance of a large blue tent surrounded with boxes, bales
and barrels.

This was evidently the person who had hailed, and now
strode rapidly towards me, and grasping me heartily by the
hand, dragged me towards his tent. I strove in vain to recognise my new friend. I saw before me a tall, loose-made, bony
individual, with an emaciated, yellow complexion, and hair
and beard in which white was certainly the predominating
colour. He appeared to be a man of about fifty-five years of
age.

"Let's have a drink, first of all," said my new friend. He opened a bottle of liquor and, pouring out its contents into two tin cups, he gave me one.

"Success, old fellow!" said he.

"The same to you, my boy," said I.

I was completely puzzled. I could [not] remember having seen the man in my life, and he was evidently enjoying my bewilderment.

"And so you do not remember me, P———," said he at last. "Well it is no wonder; I do not recognise myself, when I happen to look into the glass, which is seldom enough, now that I have eschewed that cursed operation of shaving. I am what was once H. C———."

I was thunderstruck. It was not six months since I had seen Mr. C———, a dandy of the first water in one of the Atlantic cities, with rosy complexion, brown waving hair, and with an imposing *embonpoint*, that really made him a handsome fellow of some twenty eight or thirty years of age.

"And is the climate of California so deadly?" I asked.

"No, my dear fellow," returned he; "but I will let you into my secret, that is a secret no longer. For twenty years I have lived the life of a martyr in order to wear the appearance of youth. I kept up the deceit until I arrived at Panamá where a severe sickness prostrated me for two weeks. Since then I have thrown off all disguise, and really feel younger at this moment than I did twenty years ago. Thanks to California, I have broken my chains. I am fifty two this year and I don't care who knows it!"

"And those magnificent rounded legs, and gentlemanlike signs of good feeding about the region of the waist; and the broad well-filled chest?" I enquired.

"Padding, my son, padding. I have made the fortune of half a dozen tailors. I was made up artificially, from the foot to the head."

"And the brown glossy hair, the full rosy cheeks?"

"Hair dye, paint and a gold apparatus inside the cheeks to fill them out," he answered. "Oh, my friend, what tortures I have suffered! What a fool have I been! And how happy am I now!"

I congratulated the pseudo-beau heartily, and after another tin cup of wine, we parted.

I met Mr. C———several times during my sojourn in

California and must say that he appeared to be growing younger every day.

From William Perkins, *Three Years in California, William Perkins' Journal of Life at Sonora, 1849–1852* (Berkeley and Los Angeles: University of California Press, 1964), pp. 88–90.

Senator George McDuffie

The West as Waste

What is the character of the country? Why, as I understand it, that about seven hundred miles this side of the Rocky Mountains is uninhabitable, where rain scarcely ever falls—a barren sandy soil. On the other side—we have it from a very intelligent gentleman, sent to explore that country by the State Department, that there are three successive ridges of mountains extending towards the Pacific, and running nearly parallel; which mountains are totally impassable, except in certain parts, where there were gaps or depressions, to be reached only by going some hundreds of miles out of the direct course. Well, now, what are we going to do in such a case as this? . . . Who are to go there, along the line of military posts, and take possession of the only part of the territory fit to occupy—that part lying upon the sea-coast, a strip less than one hundred miles in width; for as I have already stated, the rest of the territory consists of mountains almost inaccessible, and low lands which are covered with stone and volcanic remains, where rain never falls, except during the spring; and even on the coast no rain falls from April to October, and for the remainder of the year there is nothing but rain. Why, sir, sir, of what use will this be for agricultural purposes? I would not, for that purpose, give a pinch of snuff for the whole territory. I wish to God we did not own it. I wish it was an impassable barrier to secure us against the intrusion of others. This is the character of the country. Who are we to send there?

From Speech of Senator George McDuffie, January 25, 1843, in *Abridgement of the Debates of Congress from 1789 to 1856*, edited by Thomas Hart Benton (New York: D. Appleton & Co., 1860), Vol. 14, p. 676.

William Gilpin

Manifest Destiny

There has been a radical misapprehension in the popular mind as to the true character of the *"Great Plains of America,"* as complete as that which pervaded Europe respecting the Atlantic Ocean during the whole historic period prior to COLUMBUS. These PLAINS are not *deserts*, but the opposite, and are the cardinal basis of the future empire of commerce and industry now erecting itself upon the North American Continent.

They are calcareous, and form the PASTORAL GARDEN of the world. . . .

It is not for me, in this season of gathering splendor, to speak *tamely* upon a subject of such intense and engrossing novelty and interest. I may properly here quote the concluding sentences of a report which I was required to make on the 2d of March, 1846, *to the United States Senate,* at that time brimful of illustrious statesmen. What I said then and there, in the first dawning twilight of our glory, I will now repeat:

"The calm, wise man sets himself to study aright and understand clearly the deep designs of Providence—to scan the great volume of nature—to fathom, if possible, the will of the Creator, and to receive with respect what may be revealed to him.

"Two centuries have rolled over our race upon this continent. From nothing we have become 20,000,000. From nothing we are grown to be in agriculture, in commerce, in civilization, and in natural strength, the first among nations existing or in history. So much is our *destiny*—so far, up to this time—*transacted*, accomplished certain, and not to be disputed. From this threshold we read the future.

"The *untransacted* destiny of the American people is to subdue the continent—to rush over this vast field to the Pacific Ocean—to animate the many hundred millions of its people, and to cheer them upward—to set the principle of self-government at work—to agitate these herculean masses—to establish a new order in human affairs—to set free the en-

slaved—to regenerate superannuated nations—to change darkness into light—to stir up the sleep of a hundred centuries—
to teach old nations a new civilization—to confirm the destiny of the human race—to carry the career of mankind to
its culminating point—to cause stagnant people to be re-
born—to perfect science—to emblazon history with the conquest of peace—to shed a new and resplendent glory upon
mankind—to unite the world in one social family—to dis-
solve the spell of tyranny and exalt charity—to absolve the
curse that weighs down humanity, and to shed blessings round
the world!

"*Divine task! immortal mission!* Let us tread fast and joy-
fully the open trail before us! Let every American heart open
wide for patriotism to glow undimmed, and confide with religious faith in the sublime and prodigious destiny of his well-
loved country."

From William Gilpin, *Mission of the North American People, Geographical, Social, and Political*, rev. ed. (Philadelphia: J. B. Lippincott
& Co., 1874), pp. 71, 130.

The West as Eden

Oh, give me a home where the buffalo roam,
Where the deer and the antelope play,
Where seldom is heard a discouraging word
And the skies are not cloudy all day.

Where the air is so pure, the zephyrs so free,
The breezes so balmy and light,
That I would not exchange my home on the range
For all the cities so bright.

The red man was pressed from this part of the West,
He's likely no more to return
To the banks of Red River where seldom if ever
Their flickering campfires burn.

How often at night the heavens are bright
With the light of the glittering stars,

Have I stood here amazed and asked as I gazed
If their glory exceeds that of ours.

Oh, I love these wild flowers in this dear land of ours;
The curlew I love to hear scream;
And I love the white rocks and the antelope flocks
That graze on the mountain-tops green.

Oh, give me a land where the bright diamond sand
Flows leisurely down the stream;
Where the graceful white swan goes gliding along
Like a maid in a heavenly dream.

Then I would not exchange my home on the range,
Where the deer and the antelope play;
Where seldom is heard a discouraging word
And the skies are not cloudy all day.

"A Home on The Range" in John A. Lomax, *Cowboy Songs and Other Frontier Ballads* (New York: Sturgis & Walton Co., 1910), pp. 39–40.

Thomas Hart Benton

Passage to India

The road will be made, and soon and by individual enterprize. The age is progressive, and ultilitarian. It abounds with
talent, seeking employment, and with capital, seeking investment. The temptation is irresistible. To reach the golden California—to put the populations of the Atlantic, the Pacific,
and the Mississippi Valley, into direct communication—to
connect Europe and Asia through our America—and to own
a road of our own to the East Indies: such is the grandeur of
the enterprize! and the time has arrived to begin it. The
country is open to settlement, and inviting it, and receiving it.
The world is in motion, following the track of the sun to its
dip in the western ocean. Westward the torrents of emigration
direct their course; and soon the country between Missouri
and California is to show the most rapid expansion of the hu-

man race that the ages of man have ever beheld. It will all be
settled up, and that with magical rapidity; settlements will
promote the road; the road will aggrandize the settlements.
Soon it will be a line of towns, cities, villages and farms; and
rich will be the man that may own some quarter section on
its track, or some squares in the cities which are to grow up
upon it. . . .

. . . Besides the advantages to our Union in opening direct
communication with that Golden California which completes
our extended dominion towards the setting sun, and a road to
which would be the realization of the Roman idea of annex-
ation, *that no conquest was annexed until reached and pervaded by a road:* besides the obvious advantages, social,
political, commercial, of this communication, another tran-
scendental object presents itself! That oriental commerce
which nations have sought for, and fought for, from the time
of the Phoenicians to the discovery of the Cape of Good
Hope—which was carried on over lines so extended—by conveyances so slow and limited—amidst populations so various
and barbarous, and which considered the merchant their law-
ful prey—and up and down rapid rivers, and across strange
seas, and through wide and frightful deserts:—and which,
under all these perils, burthens, and discouragements, converted Asiatic and African cities into seats of wealth and empire—centres of the arts and sciences—while western Europe
was yet barbarian:—and some branches of which afterwards
lit up Venice, and Genoa, and Florence, and made commercial cities the match for empires, and the wives and daughters
of their citizens, (in their luxurious oriental attire,) the admiration and the envy of queens and princesses. All this commerce, and in a deeper and broader stream than the
"merchant princes" ever saw, is now within your reach! at-
tainable by a road all the way on your soil, and under your
own laws: to be flown over by a vehicle as much superior in
speed and capacity to the steamboat as the boat is to the ship,
and the ship to the camel, and the camel to the Arab's back.
Thanks to the progress of the mechanic arts! which are going
on continually, converting into facilities what stood as obsta-
cles in the way of national communications. . . .

. . . Any other nation, upon half a pretext, would go to
war for such a road, and tax unborn generations for its completion. We may have it without war, without tax, without
treaty with any nation: and when we make it, all nations
must travel it—with our permission—and behave well to re-

ceive permission; or fall behind and lose the trade by following the old track: giving us a bond in the use of our road for their peaceable behaviour. Twenty-five centuries have fought for the commercial road to India: we have it as a peaceable possession: shall we use it? or wear out our lives in strife and bitterness, wrangling over a miserable topic of domestic contention, while a glorious prize lies neglected before us? Vasco de Gama, (in the discovery of the Cape of Good Hope, and the opening of a new route to India, independent of Mussulman power,) eclipsed in his day, the glory of Columbus, balked in the discovery of his well divined route by the intervention of a new world: let us vindicate the glory of Columbus by realizing his divine idea of arriving in the east by going to the west. Take the work into your own powerful and auspicious keeping. Adopt the road.

From Thomas Hart Benton, *Discourse of Mr. Benton, of Missouri, before the Boston Mercantile Library Association, on the Physical Geography of the Country between the States of Missouri and California . . . December 20, 1854* (Washington: J. T. and Lem Towers, 1854), pp. 20–21, 22, 23.

WESTWARD MOVEMENT: METAPHOR AND FACT

Henry David Thoreau

A Country of the Mind

Eastward I go only by force; but westward I go free. Thither no business leads me. It is hard for me to believe that I shall find fair landscapes or sufficient wildness and freedom behind the eastern horizon. I am not excited by the prospect of a walk thither; but I believe that the forest which I see in the western horizon stretches uninterruptedly toward the setting sun, and there are no towns nor cities in it of enough consequence to disturb me. Let me live where I will, on this side is the city, on that the wilderness, and ever I am leaving the city more and more, and withdrawing into the wilderness. I should not lay so much stress on this fact, if I did not believe that something like this is the prevailing tendency of my countrymen. I must walk toward Oregon, and not toward Europe. And that way the nation is moving, and I may say that mankind progresses from east to west. . . .

Every sunset which I witness inspires me with the desire to go to a West as distant and as fair as that into which the sun goes down. He appears to migrate westward daily, and tempt us to follow him. He is the Great Western Pioneer whom the nations follow. We dream all night of those mountain-ridges in the horizon, though they may be of vapor only, which were last gilded by his rays. The island of Atlantis, and the islands and gardens of the Hesperides, a sort of terrestrial paradise, appear to have been the Great West of the ancients, enveloped in mystery and poetry. Who has not seen in imagination, when looking into the sunset sky, the gardens of the Hesperides, and the foundation of all those fables? . . .

To Americans I hardly need to say,—
"Westward the star of empire takes its way."
As a true patriot, I should be ashamed to think that Adam in paradise was more favorably situated on the whole than the backwoodsman in this country. . . .

The West of which I speak is but another name for the Wild; and what I have been preparing to say is, that in Wildness is the preservation of the World.

From Henry David Thoreau, "Walking," in *The Writings of Henry David Thoreau* (Boston and New York: Houghton Mifflin Co., 1893), Vol. 9, pp. 266–267.

Henry David Thoreau

A Country for the Mindless

The whole enterprise of this nation which is not an upward, but a westward one, toward Oregon, California, Japan &c, is totally devoid of interest to me, whether performed on foot or by a Pacific railroad. It is not illustrated by a thought it is not warmed by a sentiment, there is nothing in it which one should lay down his life for, nor even his gloves, hardly which one should take up a newspaper for. It is perfectly heathenish—a filibustiering *toward* heaven by the great western route. No, they may go their way to their manifest destiny which I trust is not mine. May my 76 dollars whenever I get them help to carry me in the other direction. I see them on their winding way, but no music 'is' wafted from their host, only the rattling of change in their pockets. I would rather be a captive knight, and let them all pass by, than be free only to go whither they are bound. What end do they propose to themselves beyond Japan? What aims more lofty have they than the prairie dogs?

From Henry David Thoreau, *The Correspondence of Henry David Thoreau,* edited by Walter Harding and Carl Bode (Washington Square: New York University Press, 1958), p. 296.

A COUNTRY OF EXTREMES

Walt Whitman
New Senses, New Joys

We follow the stream of amber and bronze brawling along its bed, with its frequent cascades and snow-white foam. Through the cañon we fly—mountains not only each side, but seemingly till we get near, right in front of us—every rood a new view flashing, and each flash defying description—on the almost perpendicular sides, clinging pines, cedars, spruces, crimson sumach bushes, spots of wild grass—but dominating all, those towering rocks, rocks, rocks, bathed in delicate vari-colors, with the clear sky of autumn overhead. New senses, new joys, seem develop'd. Talk as you like, a typical Rocky Mountain cañon, or a limitless sea-like stretch of the great Kansas or

Colorado plains, under favoring circumstances, tallies, perhaps expresses, certainly awakes, those grandest and subtlest element-emotions in the human soul, that all the marble temples and sculptures from Phidias to Thorwaldsen—all paintings, poems, reminiscences, or even music, probably never can.

From Walt Whitman, *Specimen Days & Collect* (Philadelphia: David McKay, 1882), pp. 143–144.

Meriwether Lewis
Waterfalls

About ten O'Clock this morning while the men were engaged with the meat I took my Gun and espontoon and thought I would walk a few miles and see where the rappids termineated above, and return to dinner. accordingly I set out and proceeded up the river about S.W. after passing one continued rappid and three small cascades of about for or five feet each at the distance of about five miles I arrived at a fall of about 19 feet; the river is here about 400 y^{ds}. wide. this pitch which I called the crooked falls occupys about threefourths of the width of the river, commencing on the South side, extends obliquly upwards about 150 y^{ds}. then forming an accute angle extends downwards nearly to the commencement of four small Islands lying near the N. shore; among these Islands and between them and the lower extremity of the perpendicular pitch being a distance of 100 yards or upwards, the water glides down the side of a sloping rock with a volocity almost equal to that of it's perpendicular decent. just above this rappid the river makes a suddon bend to the right or Northwardly. I should have returned from hence but hearing a tremendious roaring above me I continued my rout across the point of a hill a few hundred yards further and was again presented by one of the most beatifull objects in nature, a cascade of about fifty feet perpendicular streching at rightangles across the river from side to side to the distance of at least a quartcr of a mile. here the river pitches over a shelving rock, with an edge as regular and as streight as if formed by art, without a nich or brake in it; the water decends in one even and uninterupted sheet to the bottom wher dashing against the rocky bottom [it] rises into foaming billows of great hight and rappidly glides away, hising flashing and sparkling as it departs. the sprey rises from one extremity to the other of 50ᶠ. I now thought that if a skillfull painter had been asked to make a beautifull cascade that he would most probably have p[r]esented the precise immage of this one; nor could I for some time determine on which of those two great cataracts to bestoe the palm, on this or that which I had discovered yesterday; at length I determined between these two great rivals for glory that this was *pleasingly beautifull*, while the other was *sublimely grand*.

From *Journals of Lewis and Clark*, edited by Thwaites, Vol. 2, pp. 153–154.

Father Pierre-Jean De Smet
Colter's Hell

Near the source of the River [Stinking Water, now called Shoshone] which empties into the Big Horn, and the sulphurous waters of which have probably the same medicinal qualities as the celebrated Blue Lick Springs of Kentucky, is a place called Colter's Hell—from a beaver hunter of that name. This locality is often agitated with subterranean fires. The sulphurous gases which escape in great volumes from the burning soil infect the atmosphere for several miles, and render the earth so barren that even the wild wormwood cannot grow on it. The beaver hunters have assured me that the underground noises and explosions are often frightful.

However, I think that the most extraordinary spot in this respect, and perhaps the most marvelous of all the northern half of this continent, is in the very heart of the Rocky Mountains, between the forty-third and forty-fifth degrees of latitude, and the 109th and 111th degrees of longitude; that is, between the sources of the Madison and the Yellowstone. It reaches more than a hundred miles. Bituminous, sulphurous, and boiling springs are very numerous in it. The hot springs contain a large quantity of calcareous matter, and form hills more or less elevated, which resemble in their nature, perhaps, if not in their extent, the famous springs of Pambuk Kalessi, in Asia Minor, so well described by Chandler. The earth is thrown up very high, and the influence of the elements causes it to take the most varied and the most fantastic shapes. Gas, vapor and smoke are continually escaping by a thousand openings from the base to the summit of the volcanic pile; the noise at times resembles the steam let off by a boat. Strong, subterranean explosions occur, like those in "Colter's Hell." The hunters and the Indians speak of it with a superstitious fear, and consider it the abode of evil spirits, that is to say, a kind of hell. Indians seldom approach it without offering some sacrifice, or at least, without presenting the calumet of peace to the turbulent spirits, that they may be propitious. They declare that the subterranean noises proceed from the forging of warlike weapons; each eruption of the earth is, in their eyes, the result of a combat between the infernal spirits, and becomes the monument of a new victory or calamity. Near Gardiner River, a tributary of the Yellowstone, and in the vicinity of the region I have just been describing, there is a mountain of sulphur. I have this report from Captain Bridger, who is familiar with every one of these mounds, having passed thirty years of his life near them.

From Pierre-Jean De Smet, *Life, Letters and Travels of Father Pierre-Jean De Smet, S.J. 1801–1873, among the North American Indians,* edited by Hiram Martin Chittenden and Alfred Talbot Richardson (New York: Francis P. Harper, 1905), Vol. 2, pp. 660–661.

James Fenimore Cooper

The Prairie

The earth was not unlike the Ocean, when its restless waters are heaving heavily after the agitation and fury of the tempest have begun to lessen. There was the same waving and regular surface, the same absence of foreign objects, and the same boundless extent to the view. Indeed so very striking was the resemblance between the water and the land, that, however much the geologist might sneer at so simple a the-

ory, it would have been difficult for a poet not to have felt,
that the formation of the one had been produced by the sub-
siding dominion of the other. Here and there a tall tree rose
out of the bottoms, stretching its naked branches abroad, like
some solitary vessel; and, to strengthen the delusion, far in
the distance appeared two or three rounded thickets, looming
in the misty horizon like islands resting on the waters. It is
unnecessary to warn the practised reader, that the sameness
of the surface, and the low stands of the spectators exagger-
ated the distances; but still, as swell appeared after swell, and
island succeeded island, there was a disheartening assurance
that long, and seemingly interminable, tracts of territory must
be passed, before the wishes of the humblest agriculturist
could be realized.

From James Fenimore Cooper, *The Prairie: A Tale* (Philadelphia:
Carey, Lea & Carey, 1827), Vol. 1, p. 17.

Josiah Gregg

Illusions

We were now approaching the "Round Mound," a beautiful
round-topped cone, rising nearly a thousand feet above the
level of the plain by which it is for the most part surrounded.
We were yet at least three miles from this mound when a
party set out on foot to ascend it, in order to get a view of
the surrounding country. They felt confident it was but a half
mile off—at most, three-quarters; but finding the distance so
much greater than they had anticipated, many began to lag
behind and soon rejoined the wagons. The optical illusions
occasioned by the rarefied and transparent atmosphere of
these elevated plains are often truly remarkable, affording another exemplification of its purity. One would almost fancy
himself looking through a spy-glass, for objects frequently appear at scarce one-fourth of their real distance—frequently
much magnified, and more especially elevated. I have often
seen flocks of antelopes mistaken for droves of elks or wild
horses, and when at a great distance even for horsemen;
whereby frequent alarms are occasioned. I have also known

tufts of grass or weeds, or mere buffalo bones scattered on the prairies, to stretch upward to the height of several feet, so as to present the appearance of so many human beings. Ravens in the same way are not infrequently taken for Indians, as well as for buffalo; and a herd of the latter upon a distant plain often appear so increased in bulk that they would be mistaken by the inexperienced for a grove of trees. This is usually attended with a continual waving and looming, which often so writhe and distort distant objects as to render them too indistinct to be discriminated. The illusion seems to be occasioned by gaseous vapors rising from the ground while the beaming rays of the sun are darting upon it.

But the most curious, and at the same time the most perplexing phenomenon, occasioned by optical deception is the *mirage*, or, as familiarly called upon the Prairies, the "false ponds." Even the experienced traveler is often deceived by these upon the arid plains, where a disappointment is most severely felt. The thirsty wayfarer, after jogging for hours under a burning sky, at length espies a pond—yes, it must be water—it looks too natural for him to be mistaken. He quickens his pace, enjoying in anticipation the pleasure of a refreshing draught. But lo! as he approaches, it recedes or entirely disappears; and when upon its apparent site, he is ready to doubt his own vision—he finds but a parched plain under his feet. It is not until he has been thus a dozen times deceived, that he is willing to relinquish the pursuit: and then, perhaps, when he really does see a pond, he will pass it unexamined, for fear of another disappointment.

From Gregg, *Commerce of the Prairies*, Vol. 1, pp. 97–99.

Mark Twain
Mono Lake

Mono Lake lies in a lifeless, treeless, hideous desert, eight thousand feet above the level of the sea, and is guarded by mountains two thousand feet higher, whose summits are always clothed in clouds. This solemn, silent, sailless sea—this lonely tenant of the loneliest spot on earth—is little graced with the picturesque. It is an unpretending expanse of grayish water, about a hundred miles in circumference, with two islands in its center, mere upheavals of rent and scorched and blistered lava, snowed over with gray banks and drifts of pumice-stone and ashes, the winding sheet of the dead volcano, whose vast center the lake has seized upon and occupied.

The lake is two hundred feet deep, and its sluggish waters are so strong with alkali that if you only dip the most hopelessly soiled garment into them once or twice, and wring it out, it will be found as clean as if it had been through the ablest of washerwomen's hands. While we camped there our laundry work was easy. We tied the week's washing astern of our boat, and sailed a quarter of a mile, and the job was complete, all to the wringing out. If we threw the water on our heads and gave them a rub or so, the white lather would pile up three inches high. This water is not good for bruised places and abrasions of the skin. . . .

A white man cannot drink the water of Mono Lake, for it is nearly pure lye. It is said that the Indians in the vicinity drink it sometimes, though. It is not improbable, for they are among the purest liars I ever saw. [There will be no additional charge for this joke, except to parties requiring an explanation of it. This joke has received high commendation from some of the ablest minds of the age.]

There are no fish in Mono Lake—no frogs, no snakes, no polliwogs—nothing, in fact, that goes to make life desirable. Millions of wild ducks and sea gulls swim about the surface, but no living thing exists *under* the surface, except a white feathery sort of worm, one half an inch long, which looks like a bit of white thread frayed out at the sides. If you dip up a gallon of water, you will get about fifteen thousand of these. They give to the water a sort of grayish-white appearance. . . .

Half a dozen little mountain brooks flow into Mono Lake, but *not a stream of any kind flows out of it*. It neither rises nor falls, apparently, and what it does with its surplus water is a dark and bloody mystery.

There are only two seasons in the region around about Mono Lake—and these are, the breaking up of one Winter and the beginning of the next. More than once (in Esmeralda) I have seen a perfectly blistering morning open up with the thermometer at ninety degrees at eight o'clock, and seen the snow fall fourteen inches deep and that same identical thermometer go down to forty-four degrees under shelter, before nine o'clock at night. Under favorable circumstances it snows at least once in every single month in the year, in the little town of Mono. So uncertain is the climate in summer that a lady who goes out visiting cannot hope to be prepared for all emergencies unless she takes her fan under one arm and her snowshoes under the other. When they have a Fourth of July procession it generally snows on them, and they do say that as a general thing when a man calls for a brandy toddy there, the barkeeper chops it off with a hatchet and wraps it up in a paper, like maple sugar. And it is further reported that the old soakers haven't any teeth—wore them out eating gin cocktails and brandy punches. I do not endorse that statement—I simply give it for what it is worth—and it is worth—well, I should say, millions, to any man who can believe it without straining himself. But I do endorse the snow on the Fourth of July—because I know that to be true.

From Samuel L. Clemens, *Roughing It* (Hartford: American Publishing Co., 1872), pp. 265, 267, 269.

Stephen Crane

Tempests

The sun had been growing prophetically more fierce day by day, and in July there began these winds from the south, mild at first and subtle like the breaths of the panting countries of the tropics. The corn in the fields underwent a preliminary quiver from this breeze burdened with an omen of death. In the following days it became stronger, more threatening. The farmers turned anxious eyes toward their fields where the corn was beginning to rustle with a dry and crackling sound which went up from the prairie like cries.

Then from the southern horizon came the scream of a wind hot as an oven's fury. Its valor was great in the presence of the sun. It came when the burning disc appeared in the east and it weakened when the blood-red, molten mass vanished in the west. From day to day, it raged like a pestilence. The leaves of the corn and of the trees turned yellow and sapless like leather. For a time they stood the blasts in the agony of a futile resistance. The farmers helpless, with no weapon against this terrible and inscrutable wrath of nature, were spectators at the strangling of their hopes, their ambitions, all that they could look to from their labor. It was as if upon the massive altar of the earth, their homes and their families were being offered in sacrifice to the wrath of some blind and pitiless deity.

The country died. In the rage of the wind, the trees struggled, gasped through each curled and scorched leaf, then, as last, ceased to exist, and there remained only the bowed and bare skeletons of trees. The corn shivering as from fever, bent and swayed abjectly for a time, then one by one the yellow and tinder-like stalks, twisted and pulled by the rage of the hot breath, died in the fields and the vast and sometime beautiful green prairies were brown and naked. . . .

Meanwhile, the chill and tempest of the inevitable winter had gathered in the north and swept down upon the devastated country. The prairies turned bleak and desolate.

The wind was a direct counter-part of the summer. It came down like wolves on ice. And then was the time that from this district came that first wail, half impotent rage, half despair. The men went to feed the starving cattle in their tiny allowances in clothes that enabled the wind to turn their bodies red and then blue with cold. The women shivered in the houses where fuel was as scarce as flour, where flour was sometimes as scarce as diamonds. . . .

. . . This town of Eddyville is in the heart of the stricken territory. The thermometer at this time registers eighteen degrees below zero. The temperature of the room which is the writer's bedchamber is precisely one and a half degrees below zero. Over the wide white expanses of the prairie, the icy winds from the north shriek, whirling high sheets of snow and enveloping the house in white clouds of it. The tempest forces fine stinging flakes between the rattling sashes of the window that fronts the storm. The air has remained gloomy the entire day. From other windows can be seen the snowflakes fleeing into the south, traversing as level a line as bullets, speeding like the wind. . . .

A farmer in Lincoln county recently said: "No, I didn't get no aid. I hadter drive twenty-five miles t' git my flour, an' then drive back agin an' I didn't think th' team would stand it, they been poor-fed so long. Besides I'd hadter put up a dollar to keep th' team over night an' I didn't have none. I hain't had no aid!"

"How did you get along?"

"Don't git along, stranger. Who the hell told you I did get along?"

From Stephen Crane, "Nebraska's Bitter Fight for Life," in *The Works of Stephen Crane*, edited by Fredson Bowers (Charlottesville: University Press of Virginia, 1973), Vol. 8, pp. 409–410, 412, 415, 417–418.

Mari Sandoz
Hail

Then suddenly the hail was upon them, a deafening pounding against the shingles and the side of the house, bouncing high from the ground in white sheets. One window after another crashed inward, the force of the wind blowing the blankets and sheets into the room, driving the hail in spurts across the floor, until white streaks reached clear across it. Water ran in streams through the wide cracks between the boards.

The wind turned, and the south windows, unprotected, crashed inward together, the house rocking with the blast. Mary ran to the bedroom, pushed the bed into a far corner, rolled the tick and covers into a pile. Outside the trees about the house were momentarily visible through the gusts of hail, only naked sticks, stripped of all fruit and foliage.

She walked the floor, the hail cracking under her heavy shoes, her knotted fingers twisting her apron, still tucked up.

"Ach, *Gott,* what must we do now? Everything, everything gone."

The next two days the drifts of hail lay thick in the canyons under the summer sun hot on the naked fields and prairie. Even the mockingbird that lived in the brush pile east of the house was gone. The children found him washed against a post, the feathers stripped from his back, dead. Pete Staskiewicz helped them bury the bird, and stole a little of his mother's holy water for the cigar-box coffin.

Jules came in from the garden and sat hunched over on a box before the house. All the trees were stripped, barked on the west and south, gone. Where her garden had been Mary planted radishes and peas and turnips as though it were spring. The corn and wheat were pounded into the ground, the orchard gone, but still they must eat.

From Mari Sandoz, *Old Jules* (Boston: Little, Brown and Co., 1935), p. 251.

Everett Dick

Grasshoppers

Gradually the sun was slightly darkened by a cloud in the northwest which looked like smoke or dust, and it was remarked that it looked as though an April squall might be in the offing. Presently one of the family who had gone to the well for a pitcher of fresh water cried, "Grasshoppers!" The meal so happily begun was never finished. At first there was no thought of the destruction of the crops. All looked upon the insects with astonishment. They came like a driving snow in winter, filling the air, covering the earth, the buildings, the shocks of grain, and everything. According to one observer their alighting on the roofs and sides of the houses sounded like a continuous hail storm. They alighted on trees in such great numbers that their weight broke off large limbs. The chickens and turkeys at first were frightened and ran to hide from them. On recovering from their fright, they tried to eat all the insects. At first when a hopper alighted, a hen rushed forward and gobbled it up and then without moving she ate another and another until her crop was distended to an unusual size and she could hold no more. Then when a hopper flew near her, she would instinctively make a dash for it, then pause and cock her head as if to say, "Can I possibly hold another?" The turkeys and chickens ate themselves sick. One pioneer reported that a herd of forty hogs and a flock of fifty turkeys fattened themselves by eating nothing but grasshoppers and a little prairie hay. The pork and turkey had a peculiar taste of grasshoppers.

At times the insects were four to six inches deep on the ground and continued to alight for hours. Men were obliged to tie strings around their pants legs to keep the pests from crawling up their legs. In the cool of the evening the hoppers gathered so thick on the warm rails of the railroad that the Union Pacific trains were stopped. Section men were called out to shovel the grasshoppers off the track near where Kearney, Nebraska, now stands, so that the trains could get through. The track was so oily and greasy that the wheels spun and would not pull a train.

When people began to see the danger of the destruction of their crops, they brought out bed-clothes and blankets to cover the most valuable garden crops. Yet the insects ate holes in the bedclothes or crawled under the edge and destroyed everything; even hay piled on the plants seldom availed much. Smudges of dry hay and litter were tried. In Dakota old straw was piled around a field and set on fire. Some put a salt solution on the grain, all to no avail. A heavy rain was best; it drowned millions of them. Men with clubs walked down the corn rows knocking the hoppers off, but on looking behind them they saw the insects were as numerous as ever. The grasshoppers alighted in such numbers on the corn that the stalks bent toward the ground. The potato vines were mashed flat. The sound of their feeding was like a herd of cattle eating in a corn field.

From Everett Dick, *The Sod-House Frontier 1854–1890* (New York: D. Appleton-Century Co., 1937), pp. 203–205.

John C. Van Tramp

Mojave Desert

On the "jornada" of which I am about to speak, which is sometimes called the "Jornada del Muerto" (the journey of death), the distance from one water-hole to another can not be less than eighty miles; and on account of the animals it is highly important that it should be traveled at once; to accomplish this we started about three o'clock in the afternoon and reached the other side of the jornada late in the morning of the following day, the greater part of the distance being gone over by moonlight. I shall never forget the impression which that night's journey left upon my mind. Sometimes the trail led us over large basins of deep sand, where the trampling of the mules' feet gave forth no sound; this added to the almost terrible silence, which ever reigns in the solitudes of the desert, rendered our transit more like the passage of some airy spectacle, where the actors were shadows instead of men. Nor is this comparison a constrained one, for our way-worn voyagers, with their tangled locks and unshorn beards (rendered white as snow by the fine sand with which the air in these regions is often filled), had a weird and ghostlike look, which the gloomy scene around, with its frowning rocks and moonlit sands, tended to enhance and heighten.

There were other matters, too, to render the view impressive: scattered along our route we found numerous skeletons of horses, who at some former period had dropped down and died by the wayside.

From John C. Van Tramp, *Prairie and Rocky Mountain Adventures, or, Life in the West* (Columbus, O.: H. Miller, 1860), p. 183.

Clarence King

Yosemite

Late in the afternoon of October 5, 1864, a party of us reached the edge of Yosemite, and, looking down into the valley, saw that the summer haze had been banished from the regions by autumnal frosts and wind. We looked in the gulf through air as clear as a vacuum, discerning small objects upon valley-floor and cliff-front.

That splendid afternoon shadow which divides the face of El Capitan was projected far up and across the valley, cutting it in halves,—one a mosaic of russets and yellows with dark pine and glimpse of white river; the other, a cobalt-blue zone, in which the familiar groves and meadows were suffused with shadow-tones. It is hard to conceive a more pointed contrast than this same view in October and June. Then, through a slumberous yet transparent atmosphere, you look down upon emerald freshness of green, upon arrowy rush of swollen river, and here and there, along pearly cliffs, as from the clouds, tumbles white silver dust of cataracts. The voice of full soft winds swells up over rustling leaves, and, pulsating, throbs like the beating of far-off surf. All stern sublimity, all geological terribleness, are veiled away behind magic curtains of cloud-shadow and broken light. Misty brightness, glow of cliff and sparkle of foam, wealth of beautiful details, the charm of pearl and emerald, cool gulfs of violet shade stretching back in deep recesses of the walls,—these are the features which lie under the June sky.

Now all that has gone. The shattered fronts of walls stand out sharp and terrible, sweeping down in broken crag and cliff to a valley whereon the shadow of autumnal death has left its solemnity. There is no longer an air of beauty. In this cold, naked strength, one has crowded on him the geological record of mountain work, of granite plateau suddenly rent asunder, of the slow, imperfect manner in which Nature has vainly striven to smooth her rough work and bury the ruins with thousands of years' accumulation of soil and debris. . . .

It was impossible for me, as I sat perched upon this jutting rock mass, in full view of all the cañons which had led into this wonderful converging system of ice-rivers, not to imagine a picture of the glacier period. Bare or snow-laden cliffs overhung the gulf; streams of ice, here smooth and compacted into a white plain, there riven into innumerable crevasses, or tossed into forms like the waves of a tempest-lashed sea, crawled through all the gorges. Torrents of water and avalanches of rock and snow spouted at intervals all along the cliff walls. Not a tree nor a vestige of life was in sight, except far away upon ridges below, or out upon the dimly expanding plain. Granite and ice and snow, silence broken only by the howling tempest and the crash of falling ice or splintered rock, and a sky deep freighted with cloud and storm,—these were the elements of a period which lasted immeasurably long, and only in comparatively the most recent geological times have given way to the present marvellously changed condition. Nature in her present aspects, as well as in the records of her past, here constantly offers the most vivid and terrible contrasts. Can anything be more wonderfully opposite than that period of leaden sky, gray granite, and desolate stretches of white, and the present, when of the old order we have only left the solid framework of granite and the indelible inscriptions of glacier work? To-day their burnished pathways are legibly traced with the history of the past. Every ice-stream is represented by a feeble river, every great glacier cascade by a torrent of white foam dashing itself down rugged walls, or spouting from the brinks of upright cliffs.

The very avalanche tracks are darkened by clustered woods, and over the level pathway of the great Yosemite glacier itself is spread a park of green, a mosaic of forest, a thread of river.

From Clarence King, *Mountaineering in the Sierra Nevada* (Boston: James R. Osgood & Co., 1872), pp. 133–134, 152–153.

John Muir
Winds

I heard trees falling for hours at the rate of one every two or three minutes; some uprooted, partly on account of the loose, water-soaked condition of the ground; others broken straight across, where some weakness caused by fire had determined the spot. The gestures of the various trees made a delightful study. Young Sugar Pines, light and feathery as squirrel-tails, were bowing almost to the ground; while the grand old patriarchs, whose massive boles had been tried in a hundred storms, waved solemnly above them, their long, arching branches streaming fluently on the gale, and every needle thrilling and ringing and shedding off keen lances of light like a diamond. The Douglas Spruces, with long sprays drawn out in level tresses, and needles massed in a gray, shimmering glow, presented a most striking appearance as they stood in bold relief along the hilltops. The madroños in the dells, with their red bark and large glossy leaves tilted every way, reflected the sunshine in throbbing spangles like those one so often sees on the rippled surface of a glacier lake. But the Silver Pines were now the most impressively beautiful of all. Colossal spires 200 feet in height waved like supple goldenrods chanting and bowing low as if in worship, while the whole mass of their long, tremulous foliage was kindled into one continuous blaze of white sun-fire. The force of the gale was such that the most steadfast monarch of them all rocked down to its roots with a motion plainly perceptible when one leaned against it. Nature was holding high festival, and every fiber of the most rigid giants thrilled with glad excitement. . . .

Toward midday, after a long, tingling scramble through copses of hazel and ceanothus, I gained the summit of the highest ridge in the neighborhood; and then it occurred to me that it would be a fine thing to climb one of the trees to obtain a wider outlook and get my ear close to the Aeolian music of its top most needles. But under the circumstances the choice of a tree was a serious matter. One whose instep was not very strong seemed in danger of being blown down, or of being struck by others in case they should fall; another was branchless to a considerable height above the ground, and at the same time too large to be grasped with arms and legs in climbing; while others were not favorably situated for clear views. After cautiously casting about, I made choice of the tallest of a group of Douglas Spruces that were growing close together like a tuft of grass, no one of which seemed likely to fall unless all the rest fell with it. Though comparatively young, they were about 100 feet high, and their lithe, brushy tops were rocking and swirling in wild ecstasy. Being accustomed to climb trees in making botanical studies, I experienced no difficulty in reaching the top of this one, and never before did I enjoy so noble an exhilaration of motion. The slender tops fairly flapped and swished in the passionate torrent, bending and swirling backward and forward, round and round, tracing indescribable combinations of vertical and horizontal curves, while I clung with muscles firm braced, like a bobolink on a reed.

From John Muir, *The Mountains of California* (New York: Century Co., 1894), pp. 249–250, 251–252.

John Wesley Powell

The Grand Canyon

Stand at some point on the brink of the Grand Canyon where you can overlook the river, and the details of the structure, the vast labyrinth of gorges of which it is composed, are scarcely noticed; the elements are lost in the grand effect, and a broad, deep, flaring gorge of many colors is seen. But stand down among these gorges and the landscape seems to be composed of huge vertical elements of wonderful form. Above, it is an open, sunny gorge; below, it is deep and gloomy. Above, it is a chasm; below, it is a stairway from gloom to heaven.

The traveler in the region of mountains sees vast masses piled up in gentle declivities to the clouds. To see mountains in this way is to appreciate the masses of which they are composed. But the climber among the glaciers sees the elements of which this mass is composed,—that it is made of cliffs and towers and pinnacles, with intervening gorges, and the smooth billows of granite seen from afar are transformed into cliffs and caves and towers and minarets. These two aspects of mountain scenery have been seized by painters, and in their art two classes of mountains represented: mountains with towering forms that seem ready to topple in the first storm, and mountains in masses that seem to frown defiance at the tempests. Both classes have told the truth. The two aspects are sometimes caught by our painters severally; sometimes they are combined. Church paints a mountain like a kingdom of glory. Bierstadt paints a mountain cliff where an eagle is lost from sight ere he reaches the summit. Thomas Moran marries these great characteristics, and in his infinite masses cliffs of immeasurable height are seen.

Thus the elements of the façade of the Grand Canyon change vertically and horizontally. The details of structure can be seen only at close view, but grand effects of structure can be witnessed in great panoramic scenes. Seen in detail, forges and precipices appear; seen at a distance, in comprehensive views, vast massive structures are presented. The traveler on the brink looks from afar and is overwhelmed with the sublimity of massive forms; the traveler among the gorges stands in the presence of awful mysteries, profound, solemn, and gloomy. . . .

The Grand Canyon of the Colorado is a canyon composed of many canyons. It is a composite of thousands, of tens of thousands, of gorges. In like manner, each wall of the canyon is a composite structure, a wall composed of many walls, but never a repetition. Every one of these almost innumerable gorges is a world of beauty in itself. In the Grand Canyon there are thousands of gorges like that below Niagara Falls, and there are a thousand Yosemites. Yet all these canyons unite to form one grand canyon, the most sublime spectacle on the earth. Pluck up Mt. Washington by the roots to the level of the sea and drop it headfirst into the Grand Canyon, and the dam will not force its waters over the walls. Pluck up the Blue Ridge and hurl it into the Grand Canyon, and it will not fill it.

From John Wesley Powell, *Canyons of the Colorado* (Meadville, Pa.: Flood & Vincent, 1895), pp. 386, 389, 390.

Robert Louis Stevenson
The Big Sky

To one hurrying through by steam there was a certain exhilaration in this spacious vacancy, this greatness of the air, this discovery of the whole arch of heaven, this straight, unbroken, prison-line of the horizon. Yet one could not but reflect upon the weariness of those who passed by there in old days, at the foot's pace of oxen, painfully urging their teams, and with no landmark but that unattainable evening sun for which they steered, and which daily fled them by an equal stride. They had nothing, it would seem, to overtake; nothing by which to reckon their advance; no sight for repose or for encouragement; but stage after stage, only the dead green waste under foot, and the mocking, fugitive horizon. But the eye, as I have been told, found differences even here; and at the worst the emigrant came, by perseverance, to the end of this toil. It is the settlers, after all, at whom we have a right to marvel. Our consciousness, by which we live, is itself but the creature of variety. Upon what food does it subsist in such a land? What livelihood can repay a human creature for a life spent in this huge sameness? He is cut off from books, from news, from company, from all that can relieve existence but the prosecution of his affairs. A sky full of stars is the most varied spectacle that he can hope for. He may walk five miles and see nothing; ten, and it is as though he had not moved; twenty, and still he is in the midst of the same great level, and has approached no nearer to the one object within view, the flat horizon which keeps pace with his advance. We are full at home of the question of agreeable wall-papers, and wise people are of opinion that the temper may be quieted by sedative surroundings. But what is to be said of the Nebraskan settler? His is a wall-paper with a vengeance—one quarter of the universe laid bare in all its gauntness. His eye must embrace at every glance the whole seeming concave of the visible world; it quails before so vast an outlook, it is tortured by distance; yet there is no rest or shelter, till the man runs into his cabin, and can repose his sight upon things near at hand. Hence, I am told, a sickness of the vision peculiar to these empty plains.

From Robert Louis Stevenson, *Across the Plains with Other Memories and Essays* (Leipzig: Bernhard Tauchnitz, 1892), pp. 46–48.

John Noble
Loneliness

Did you ever hear of "loneliness" as a fatal disease? Once, back in the days when Father and I were bringing up long-legged sheep from Mexico, we picked up a man near Las Vegas who had lost his way. He was in a terrible state. It wasn't the result of being lost. He had "loneliness." Born on the plains, you get accustomed to them; but on people not born there the plains sometimes have an appalling effect.

You look on, on, on, out into space, out almost beyond time itself. You see nothing but the rise and swell of land and grass, and then more grass—the monotonous, endless prairie! A stranger traveling on the prairie would get his hopes up, expecting to see something different on making the next rise. To him the disappointment and monotony were terrible. "He's got loneliness," we would say of such a man.

From John Noble, in M.K. Wisehart, " 'Wichita Bill,' Cowboy Artist, Rode Into the Halls of Fame," *The American Magazine*, 104 (August 1927), p. 68.

THE CLOSING OF THE WEST

Frederick Jackson Turner

The Significance of the Frontier in American History

Up to our own day American history has been in a large degree the history of the colonization of the Great West. The existence of an area of free land, its continuous recession, and the advance of American settlement westward, explain American development. . . .

. . . The frontier is the line of most rapid and effective Americanization. The wilderness masters the colonist. It finds him a European in dress, industries, tools, modes of travel, and thought. It takes him from the railroad car and puts him in the birch canoe. It strips off the garments of civilization and arrays him in the hunting shirt and the moccasin. It puts him in the log cabin of the Cherokee and Iroquois and runs an Indian palisade around him. Before long he has gone to planting Indian corn and plowing with a sharp stick; he shouts the war cry and takes the scalp in orthodox Indian fashion. In short, at the frontier the environment is at first too strong for the man. He must accept the conditions which it furnishes, or perish, and so he fits himself into the Indian clearings and follows the Indian trails. Little by little he transforms the wilderness, but the outcome is not the old Europe, not simply the development of Germanic germs, any more than the first phenomenon was a case of reversion to the Germanic mark. The fact is, that here is a new product that is American. At first, the frontier was the Atlantic coast. It was the frontier of Europe in a very real sense. Moving westward, the frontier became more and more American. As successive terminal moraines result from successive glaciations, so each frontier leaves its traces behind it, and when it becomes a settled area the region still partakes of the frontier

137

characteristics. Thus the advance of the frontier has meant a steady movement away from the influence of Europe, a growth of independence on American lines. And to study this advance, the men who grew up under these conditions, and the political, economic, and social results of it, is to study the really American part of our history. . . .

From the conditions of frontier life came intellectual traits of profound importance. The works of travelers along each frontier from colonial days onward describe certain common traits, and these traits have, while softening down, still persisted as survivals in the place of their origin, even when a higher social organization succeeded. The result is that to the frontier the American intellect owes its striking characteristics. That coarseness and strength combined with acuteness and inquisitiveness; that practical, inventive turn of mind, quick to find expedients; that masterful grasp of material things, lacking in the artistic but powerful to effect great ends; that restless, nervous energy; that dominant individualism, working for good and for evil, and withal that buoyancy and exuberance which comes with freedom—these are traits of the frontier, or traits called out elsewhere because of the existence of the frontier. Since the days when the fleet of Columbus sailed into the waters of the New World, America has been another name for opportunity, and the people of the United States have taken their tone from the incessant expansion which has not only been open but has even been forced upon them. He would be a rash prophet who should assert that the expansive character of American life has now entirely ceased. Movement has been its dominant fact, and, unless this training has no effect upon a people, the American energy will continually demand a wider field for its exercise. But never again will such gifts of free land offer themselves. For a moment, at the frontier, the bonds of custom are broken and unrestraint is triumphant. There is not *tabula rasa*. The stubborn American environment is there with its imperious summons to accept its conditions; the inherited ways of doing things are also there; and yet, in spite of environment, and in spite of custom, each frontier did indeed furnish a new field of opportunity, a gate of escape from the bondage of the past; and freshness, and confidence, and scorn of older society, impatience of its restraints and its ideas, and indifference to its lessons, have accompanied the frontier. What the Mediterranean Sea was to the Greeks, breaking the bond of custom, offering new experiences, calling out new institutions and activities, that, and more, the ever retreating frontier has been to the United States directly, and to the nations of Europe more remotely. And now, four centuries from the discovery of America, at the end of a hundred years of life under the Constitution, the frontier has gone, and with its going has closed the first period of American history.

From Frederick Jackson Turner, "The Significance of the Frontier in American History," in *Annual Report of the American Historical Association for the Year 1893* (Washington: U.S. Government Printing Office, 1894), pp. 199, 201, 226–227.

Walt Whitman

Facing West from California's Shores

Facing west from California's shores,
Inquiring, tireless, seeking what is yet unfound,
I, a child, very old, over waves, towards the house of maternity, the land of migrations, look afar,
Look off the shores of my Western sea, the circle almost circled;
For starting westward from Hindustan, from the vales of Kashmere,
From Asia, from the north, from the God, the sage, and the hero,
From the south, from the flowery peninsulas and the spice islands,
Long having wander'd since, round the earth having wander'd,
Now I face home again, very pleas'd and joyous,
(But where is what I started for so long ago?
And why is it yet unfound?)

From Walt Whitman, *Leaves of Grass* (Philadelphia: David McKay, 1891–1892), p. 95.

III

The West as Frontier: The Mountain Men

I must tell you, that there is something in the proximity of the woods, which is very singular. It is with men as it is with the plants and animals that grow and live in the forests; they are entirely different from those that live in the plains.

—J. Hector St. John Crèvecoeur

Introduction to Part III

The mountain men were among our first Westerners. Unlike earlier frontiersmen, they left their homes a thousand miles behind them, and like the Indians, they became full-time, nomadic residents of the Far West. They trapped its rivers, named its mountains, explored its canyons, crossed its deserts, traced its routes to the Pacific, and shaped a way of life to fit its wilderness. Without the explorations of the mountain men, the rapidity of the West's settlement is inconceivable, and yet the original intention of these men was not to blaze trails. They came to the Rocky Mountains on business. In 1822, several of them responded to advertisements in St. Louis newspapers to join an enterprise that eventually revitalized the 200-year-old fur trade of the New World. Others came later. Jim Bridger and James Clyman were originally from Virginia, Joe Walker from Tennessee, Kit Carson from Kentucky, Osborne Russell from Maine, and Jedediah Smith from New York. Many were boys, mostly farm boys, and they were greenhorns; but the mountains changed them. Out of this confrontation with the land, the animals, and the Indians of the West, there emerged a type of man that was distinctly American. Traditions from England and Europe that helped form societies in the East provided few models for these men in the Rockies. Shaped by the wilderness, the mountain man became a special product of the American West.

Washington Irving, most noted for such American classics as "Rip Van Winkle" and "The Legend of Sleepy Hollow," has left two gracefully written and recently undervalued contemporary accounts of the fur trade. Except for his treatment of mountain man Joe Walker, Irving's history of the oldest and most important trade of North America is basically reliable. Irving describes how the mountain men differed from the *voyageurs* and earlier traders, how "free trapping" radically changed the fur business, and how the "rendezvous" and other aspects of the trade shaped the rhythms of trappers' lives. To Irving, the mountain men led a "wild, Robin Hood kind of life," and for correction of this romantic image we must turn to firsthand accounts by the mountain men themselves. Hardship, frustration, and daily grind dominate the journals of James Ohio Pattie, Osborne Russell, Zenas Leonard, and James Clyman. With the exception of Pattie, these men doggedly avoid exaggeration in their views of the trapper's routine and method. In their descriptions of danger and adventure, such as Clyman's account of Jed Smith's battle with a grizzly, their tight-lipped narratives bear silent witness to the values they lived by. The most vivid portraits of mountain men, where we hear the patois they used, are found in Western classics by Lewis Garrard, who traveled the Taos Trail, and George F. Ruxton, a British author who interviewed more mountain men than any other writer of the time. Both Garrard and Ruxton, like Francis Parkman, saw the mountain men in 1846 and 1847, after their heyday and at a time when the mountaineers self-consciously told stories and acted roles that intensified expected images of themselves. It was through such self-promotion, for instance, that the son of a Virginia slave became the legendary figure of *The Life and Adventures of James P. Beckwourth, Mountaineer, Scout, and Pioneer, and Chief of the Crow Nation Indians.*

Intense disgust as well as romantic sentiment marked the reactions of those who observed the mountain men in their own day. In a novel based on his travels in the 1830s, Sir William Drummond Stewart, a Scottish sportsman, stressed the freedom and heroism of "that glorious race, the Free Trappers." In contrast, most Protestant missionaries and their wives, with the exception of the eccentric Reverend Samuel Parker, saw the mountain men only as degenerate savages. According to Myra Eells, who was among the first white women to cross the Rockies in 1838, a group of dancing mountain men "looked like the emissaries of the Devil worshipping their own master." George Ruxton summed up criticism of the mountain men when he wrote, "They may have good qualities, but they are those of the animal; and people fond of giving them hard names call them revengeful, bloodthirsty, drunken (when the wherewithal is to be had), gamblers, regardless of the laws of *meum* and *tuum*—in fact, 'White Indians.' "

Ruxton's closing description probably would have delighted

most mountain men, for while missionaries and pioneers commonly defined themselves by rejecting Indians, the mountain men defined themselves by becoming like Indians. "You cannot pay a free trapper a greater compliment," Irving wrote, "than to persuade him you have mistaken him for an Indian brave." They adopted Indian clothing, habits, and customs, and mastered Indian crafts and skills. When mountain men became "squaw men" by buying Indian wives, they were following local custom. Often, too, they assumed Indian beliefs and values. It is significant that when the hero of Lewis Garrard's most famous tall tale in *Wah-to-yah* finds himself in danger, he does not appeal to a Christian God. Instead, he "makes medicine" and directs an offering to the earth and to the sky, "like Injun." In their actual dealings with Indians, the mountain men were neither friendly nor hostile with consistency. As among the Indians themselves, some tribes were their allies, while others, like the Blackfeet, were their enemies. The West of the mountain man was a time when reckless killing and cruelty were common, just as it was a time when a particular American ideal was dimly visible. Descriptions of the rendezvous show that the mountain men lived in a society where Shoshonis, French, Crows, Scots, Nez Perces, Blacks, Kanakas, Irish, Flatheads, Mexicans, and others could mix together in trade, play, and marriage. It was a passing moment in Western history.

By the 1840s both the depletion of beaver and the switch in fashion from beaver to silk hats brought to a close the West of the mountain men. Some, like Bridger, Carson, Walker, and Fitzpatrick, later served as army scouts or guides for official "explorations" through regions that they had come to know with the intimacy of Indians. Others settled down, or tried unsuccessfully to settle down.

Today, debate continues whether the mountain men really were independent, self-sufficient heroes, or daring retrogrades, or merely aspiring capitalists. What emerges from most of the evidence, including a recent computer study, is that they were a complex group of men who evade generalization. Perhaps the richest source of insight about them is provided not by computer facts, but by the stories they have left behind— their tall tales. Indian in form, these stories are expressions of character and records of the mountain man's sense of himself. If nothing else, they were told by men whose imaginations were as expansive as the land they called home. It is easy to understand why Moses "Black" Harris balked at a lady's description of him as merely a great traveler. We hear him answer in a particularly Western voice—a blend of comic self-derision and fierce self-respect—as he proudly tells the lady who he really is. "Travler, marm," says Black Harris, "this niggur's no travler; I ar' a trapper, marm, a mountain-man, wagh!"

ST. LOUIS WANT ADS: 1822–1823

Missouri Gazette
To Enterprising Young Men

THE SUBSCRIBER WISHES TO ENGAGE ONE HUNDRED MEN, TO ASCEND THE RIVER MISSOURI TO ITS SOURCE, THERE TO BE EMPLOYED FOR ONE, TWO OR THREE YEARS. ——FOR PARTICULARS ENQUIRE OF MAJOR ANDREW HENRY, NEAR THE LEAD MINES, IN THE COUNTY OF WASHINGTON, (WHO WILL ASCEND WITH, AND COMMAND THE PARTY) OR TO THE SUBSCRIBER AT ST. LOUIS.

WM. H. ASHLEY

St. Louis Enquirer
For the Rocky Mountains

THE SUBSCRIBERS WISH TO ENGAGE ONE HUNDRED MEN, TO ASCEND THE MISSOURI TO THE ROCKY MOUNTAINS,

THERE TO BE EMPLOYED AS HUNTERS. AS A COMPENSATION
TO EACH MAN FIT FOR SUCH BUSINESS, $200 PER ANNUM,
WILL BE GIVEN FOR HIS SERVICES, AS AFORESAID.—FOR
PARTICULARS, APPLY TO J. V. GARNIER, OR W. ASHLEY, AT
ST. LOUIS. THE EXPEDITION WILL SET OUT FROM THIS
PLACE, ON OR BEFORE THE FIRST DAY OF MARCH NEXT.
ASHLEY & HENRY

Advertisements in the *Missouri Gazette and Public Advertiser*, February 13, 1822, [p. 3], and *St. Louis Enquirer*, January 18, 1823, [p. 1].

WHITE INDIANS

Washington Irving
The Mountaineers

In the old times of the great Northwest Company, when the trade in furs was pursued chiefly about the lakes and rivers, the expeditions were carried on in batteaux and canoes. The voyageurs or boatmen were the rank and file in the service of the trader, and even the hardy "men of the north," those great rufflers and game birds, were fain to be paddled from point to point of their migrations.

A totally different class has now sprung up:—"the Mountaineers," the traders and trappers that scale the vast mountain chains, and pursue their hazardous vocations amidst their wild recesses. They move from place to place on horseback. The equestrian exercises, therefore, in which they are engaged, the nature of the countries they traverse, vast plains and mountains, pure and exhilarating in atmospheric qualities, seem to make them physically and mentally a more lively and mercurial race than the fur traders and trappers of former days, the self-vaunting "men of the north." A man who bestrides a horse must be essentially different from a man who cowers in a canoe. We find them, accordingly, hardy, lithe, vigorous, and active; extravagant in word, and thought, and deed; heedless of hardship; daring of danger; prodigal of the present, and thoughtless of the future.

A difference is to be perceived even between these mountain hunters and those of the lower regions along the waters of the Missouri. The latter, generally French creoles, live comfortably in cabins and log-huts, well sheltered from the inclemencies of the seasons. They are within reach of frequent supplies from the settlements; their life is comparatively free from danger, and from most of the vicissitudes of the upper wilderness. The consequence is that they are less hardy, self-dependent and game-spirited than the mountaineer. If the latter by chance comes among them on his way to and from the settlements, he is like a game-cock among the common roosters of the poultry yard. Accustomed to live in tents, or to bivouac in the open air, he despises the comforts and is impatient of the confinement of the log-house. If his meal is not ready in his season, he takes his rifle, hies to the forest or prairie, shoots his own game, lights his fire, and cooks his repast. With his horse and his rifle, he is independent of the world, and spurns at all its restraints. The very superintendents at the lower posts will not put him to mess with the common men, the hirelings of the establishment, but treat him as something superior.

There is, perhaps, no class of men on the face of the earth, says Captain Bonneville, who lead a life of more continued exertion, peril, and excitement, and who are more enamoured of their occupations, than the free trappers of the West. No toil, no danger, no privation can turn the trapper from his pursuit. His passionate excitement at times resembles a mania. In vain may the most vigilant and cruel savages beset his path; in vain may rocks and precipices and wintry torrents oppose his progress; let but a single track of a beaver meet his eye, and he forgets all dangers and defies all difficulties. At times, he may be seen with his traps on his shoulder, buffeting his way across rapid streams, amidst floating blocks of ice: at other times, he is to be found with his traps swung on his back clambering the most rugged mountains, scaling or descending the most frightful precipices, searching, by routes inaccessible to the horse, and never before trodden by white man, for springs and lakes unknown to his comrades, and where he may meet with his favorite game. Such is the mountaineer, the hardy trapper of the West; and such, as we have slightly sketched it, is the wild, Robin Hood kind of life, with all its strange and motley populace, now existing in full vigor among the Rocky Mountains. . . .

The mountaineers in their rude hunting dresses, armed with rifles and roughly mounted, and leading their pack-horses down a hill of the forest, looked like banditti returning with plunder. On the top of some of the packs were perched several half-breed children, perfect little imps, with wild black eyes glaring from among elf locks. These, I was told, were children of the trappers; pledges of love from their squaw spouses in the wilderness. . . .

The wandering whites who mingle for any length of time with the savages have invariably a proneness to adopt savage habitudes; but none more so than the free trappers. It is a matter of vanity and ambition with them to discard everything that may bear the stamp of civilized life, and to adopt the manners, habits, dress, gesture, and even walk of the Indian. You cannot pay a free trapper a greater compliment, than to persuade him you have mistaken him for an Indian brave; and, in truth, the counterfeit is complete. His hair, suffered to attain to a great length, is carefully combed out, and either left to fall carelessly over his shoulders, or plaited neatly and tied up in otter skins, or parti-colored ribands. A hunting-shirt of ruffled calico of bright dyes, or of ornamented leather, falls to his knee; below which, curiously fashioned leggins, ornamented with strings, fringes, and a profusion of hawks' bells, reach to a costly pair of moccasons of the finest Indian fabric, richly embroidered with beads. A blanket of scarlet, or some other bright color, hangs from his shoulders, and is girt around his waist with a red sash, in which he bestows his pistols, knife, and the stem of his Indian pipe; preparations either for peace or war. His gun is lavishly decorated with brass tacks and vermilion, and provided with a fringed cover, occasionally of buckskin, ornamented here and there with a feather. . . . Their dark sunburned faces, and long flowing hair, their leggins, flaps, moccasons, and richly-dyed blankets and their painted horses gaudily caparisoned, gave them so much the air and appearance of Indians, that it was difficult to persuade one's self that they were white men, and had been brought up in civilized life.

From Washington Irving, *The Rocky Mountains: Or, Scenes, Incidents, and Adventures in the Far West* (Philadelphia: Carey, Lea, & Blanchard, 1837), Vol. 1, pp. 25–27, 88, 92–93.

James Clyman

Falstaff's Battalion

Haveing been imployed in Public Surveys in the state of Illinois through the winter of 1823 [1822] and the early part of 24 [23] I came to St Louis about the first of February to ricieve pay for past services and rimaining there Some days I heard a report that general William H Ashly was engageing men for a Trip to the mouth of the Yellow Stone river   I made enquiry as to what was the object but found no person who seemed to possess the desired information   finding whare Ashleys dwelling was I called on him the same evening   Several Gentlemen being present he invited me to call again on a certain evening which I did   he then gave me a lengthy account of game found in that Region   Deer, elk Bear and Buffaloe but to crown all immence Quantities of Beaver whose skins ware verry valuable selling from $5 to 8$ per pound at that time in St Louis and the men he wished to engage ware to [be] huters trappers and traders for furs and peltrees   my curiosity now being satisfied St Louis being a fine place for Spending money I did not leave immediately   not having spent all my funds I loitered about without (without) employment.

Haveing fomed a Slight acquaintaince with Mr Ashley we occasionlly passed each other on the street   at length one day Meeting him he told me he had been looking for me a few days back and enquired as to my employment   I informed him that I was entirely unemployed   then that I would assist him ingageing men for his Rocky mountain epedition and he wished me to call at his house in the evening which I accordinly did getting instructions as to whare I would most probably find men willing to engage which [were to be] found in grog Shops and other sinks of degradation   he rented a house & furnished it with provisions Bread from to Bakers—pork plenty, which the men had to cook for themselves

On the 8th [10th] of March 1824 [1823] all things ready we shoved off from the shore fired a swivel which was answered by a Shout form the shore which we returned with a will and porceed up stream under sail

A discription of our crew I cannt give but Fallstafs Battallion was genteel in comparison . . .

From James Clyman, "James Clyman: His Diaries and Reminiscences," edited by Charles L. Camp, *California Historical Society Quarterly* 4 (June 1925), pp. 110–111.

The Reverend Samuel Parker
Wild and Wandering Life

It is worthy of remark, that comparatively few of all those who engage in the fur business about and west of the Rocky Mountains, ever return to their native land, and to their homes and friends. Mr. P. of Fort Walla Walla told me, that to keep their number of trappers and hunters near, but west of the mountains, they were under the necessity of sending out recruits annually, about one third of the whole number. Captain W. has said, that of more than two hundred who had been in his employment in less than three years, only between thirty and forty were known to be alive. From this data it may be seen that the life of hunters in these far western regions averages about three years. And with these known facts, still hundreds and hundreds are willing to engage in the hunter's life, and expose themselves to hardships, famine, dangers, and death. The estimate has been made from sources of correct information, that there are nine thousand white men in the north and in the great west, engaged in the various departments of trading, trapping and hunting, including Americans, Britons, Frenchmen, and Russians. It is more than one hundred and fifty years since white men penetrated far into the forests, in their canoes freighted with goods, coasting the shores of the remote lakes, and following up the still more remote rivers, to traffic with the Indians for their furs, not regarding hunger, toils, and dangers. These enterprises have been extended and pursued with avidity, until every Indian nation and tribe have been visited by the trader. . . .

While we continued in this place, Doct. Whitman was

called to perform some very important surgical operations. He extracted an iron arrow, three inches long, from the back of Capt. Bridger, which was received in a skirmish, three years before, with the Blackfeet Indians. It was a difficult operation, because the arrow was hooked at the point by striking a large bone, and a cartilaginous substance had grown around it. The Doctor pursued the operation with great self-possession and perseverance; and his patient manifested equal firmness. The Indians looked on meanwhile, with countenances indicating wonder, and in their own peculiar manner expressed great astonishment when it was extracted. The Doctor also extracted another arrow from the shoulder of one of the hunters, which had been there two years and a half. His reputation becoming favorably established, calls for medical and surgical aid were almost incessant. . . .

. . . I will relate an occurrence which took place near evening, as a specimen of mountain life. A hunter, who goes technically by the name of the great bully of the mountains, mounted his horse with a loaded rifle, and challenged any Frenchman, American, Spaniard, or Dutchman, to fight him in single combat. Kit Carson, an American, told him if he wished to die, he would accept the challenge. Shunar defied him. C. mounted his horse, and with a loaded pistol, rushed into close contact, and both almost at the same instant fired. C's ball entered S's hand, came out at the wrist, and passed through the arm above the elbow. Shunar's ball passed over the head of Carson; and while he went for another pistol, Shunar begged that his life might be spared. Such scenes, sometimes from passion, and sometimes for amusement, make the pastime of their wild and wandering life. They appear to have sought for a place where, as they would say, human nature is not oppressed by the tyranny of religion, and pleasure is not awed by the frown of virtue. The fruits are visible in all the varied forms to which human nature, without the restraints of civil government, and cultivated and polished society, may be supposed to yield. In the absence of all those motives, which they would feel in moral and religious society, refinement, pride, a sense of the worth of character, and even conscience, give place to unrestrained dissoluteness. Their toils and privations are so great, that they more readily compensate themselves by plunging into such excesses, as in their mistaken judgment of things, seem most adapted to give them pleasure. They disdain the common-place phrases of profanity which prevail among the impious vulgar in civilized countries, and have many set phrases, which they appear to have manufactured among themselves, and which, in their imprecations, they bring into almost every sentence and on all occasions. By varying the tones of their voices they make them expressive of joy, hope, grief, and anger. In their broils among themselves, which do not happen every day, they would not be ungenerous. They would see "fair play," and would "spare the last eye;" and would not tolerate murder, unless drunkenness or great provocation could be pleaded in extenuation.

Their demoralizing influence with the Indians has been lamentable, and they have practiced impositions upon them, in all ways that sinful propensities dictate. It is said they have sold them packs of cards at high prices, calling them the Bible; and have told them, if they should refuse to give white men wives, God would be angry with them and punish them eternally; and on almost any occasion when their wishes have been resisted, they have threatened them with the wrath of God. If these things are true in many instances, yet from personal observation, I should believe, their more common mode of accomplishing their wishes has been by flattery and presents; for the most of them squander away their wages in ornaments for their women and children.

From the Reverend Samuel Parker, *Journal of an Exploring Tour beyond the Rocky Mountains* (Ithaca, N.Y.: Mack, Andrus, & Woodruff, 1838), pp. 188–189, 80, 83–85.

Smith, Jackson & Sublette

Rubbed Out

Amount of Property lost by the firm of Smith, Jackson & Soublette, from depredations of different tribes of Indians from July 1826 to July 1830.

480 head of horses, at the lowest mountain price

$60 per head	$28,000.
Gross amount of Goods lost	10,000.
Traps and Camp Equipage lost	1,000.
Beaver furs taken from us by Indians . . .	4,500.
	$43,500.

Names of Persons Killed belonging to the parties of Wm. H. Ashley and Smith, Jackson & Sublette, &c.

Names of leaders	Names of men killed	Total No.	Places where killed	Year	By whom killed
Major Henry	Mayo, Tyo, Laymay, (one not recollected)	4	Mouth of Smith's river	1823	Blackfeet
same		14	Arickara village	June 1823	Arickaras
	J. Anderson, A. Neil	2	On the way from the Arickaras to the Yellow Stone	1823	Gros Ventres
	Decharle, Trumble, (2 others names not recollected)	4	On the Yellow Stone	1823	Gros Ventres (supposed)
	Stevenson, Kremer	2	Mouth of Cannon ball river	1824	St. Peters Sioux
Clyman	Name not recollected	1	The Seetskeeder, or head of the Colarada	1825	Blackfeet (supposed)
J. S. Smith	David Cunningham, Silas Goble, Francis Deramme, Wm. Campbell, Boatswain Brown, Gregory Ortaga, John B. Ratelle, Pale, Polite Robiseau	10	On the Colerado	Augt 1827	Amuchabas
Samuel Tulock	Pinkney W. Sublette, Batiste, Jeandrois Rariet	3	Port Neuff River	1828	Blackfeet
Robert Campbell	Pierre, an Iroquois Indian	1	Head of the Missouri	1827	Blackfeet
Wm. L. Sublette	J. Cote	1	Godairs river	1828	Blackfeet
	Boileau	1	Little Lake	1828	Blackfeet
J. S. Smith	Bell, Logan, J. Scott & J. O'Hara.*		Snake Country	1827 or 1828	Snakes (supposed)

Men	Company	No.	Location	Date	Tribe
Thos. Virgin Tousaint Marishall, Joseph Lapoint, Jos. Palmer, Marion, Harrison G. Rodgers, Martin McCoy, Peter Rannee, John Gaither, John Hanna, Abraham Laplant, Emanuel Lazarus, Thomas Daw, Charles Swift, & one other		19	On the Umpquah	July 1828	Umpquahs
Ezekiel Abel, Peter Spoon, Adam J. Larimet†		4	Bad pass of Big Horn	1829	Blackfeet (supposed)
A. Chapman, E. More		2	Platte river	1824	Arickaras
Johnson, Godair		2	Bear River	1828	Blackfeet
. . . . . .	Misso fur Co.	7	Yellow Stone	1823	Blackfeet
. . . . . .	French Co.	4	Below the Mandans	1823	Rickaras
. . . . . .	Prevox & La Clere	7	Waters of Uta Lake	1824	Snakes
. . . . . .	Missouri fur Co.	1	Weber's fork	1825	Snakes
. . . . . .	Missouri fur Co.	2	Platte in the Black hills	1828	Crows, (supposed)
. . . . . .	Drips Co.	2	Wind River	1829	Blackfeet (supposed)
. . . . . .	American fur Co.	1	Arickara village	1829	Arickaras
		94			

* The fate of these men is not known, but the conclusion is hardly doubtful. [Footnote in original.]

† Indian report says these (4) men were killed by the Snakes. [Footnote in original.]

This statement will rather fall short than overgo the real amount of our losses from depredations of Indians.

Smith, Jackson & Sublette.

The number of men in our employ for the last four years has varied from   to 120 men.

Smith, Jackson & Sublette.

Deaths of men caused by accidents and other causes not chargeable to Indians.

In 1825   Marshall was lost in the Willow valley near the Salt Lake.

"   "   A woman, a half breed died a natural death on Hams fork.

" 1823   Holly Wheeler died from wounds received from a bear.

" 1822   [1823]. Mike Fink shot Carpenter—Talbot soon after shot Fink, and not long after was himself drowned at the Tetons.

" 1824   Thomas, a half breed, was killed by Williams, on the waters of Bear river, west of the mountains.

" 1828   Bray was killed by a blow from the hand of Mr. Tullock.

Among our parties in the mountains, sickness and natural deaths are almost unknown.

Smith, Jackson & Sublette.

From Papers of the U.S. Superintendency of Indian Affairs, St. Louis, 1807–1855, Manuscript Division, Kansas State Historical Society, Vol. 6, pp. 297, 298, 299–300. Reprinted in Dale L. Morgan, *Jedediah Smith and the Opening of the West* (Indianapolis, Ind.: Bobbs-Merrill Co., 1952), pp. 342–345.

George F. Ruxton

A Trapper's Gear and Method

Trappers are of two kinds, the "hired hand" and the "free trapper": the former hired for the hunt by the fur companies; the latter, supplied with animals and traps by the company, is paid a certain price for his furs and peltries.

There is also the trapper "on his own hook"; but this class

is very small. He has his own animals and traps, hunts where he chooses, and sells his peltries to whom he pleases.

On starting for a hunt, the trapper fits himself out with the necessary equipment, either from the Indian trading-forts, or from some of the petty traders—coureurs des bois—who frequent the western country. This equipment consists usually of two or three horses or mules—one for saddle, the others for packs—and six traps, which are carried in a bag of leather called a *trap-sack*. Ammunition, a few pounds of tobacco, dressed deerskins for moccasons, &c., are carried in a wallet of dressed buffalo-skin, called a possible-sack. His "possibles" and "trap-sack" are generally carried on the saddle-mule when hunting, the others being packed with the furs. The costume of the trapper is a hunting-shirt of dressed buckskin, ornamented with long fringes; pantaloons of the same material, and decorated with porcupine-quills and long fringes down the outside of the leg. A flexible felt hat and moccasons clothe his extremities. Over his left shoulder and under his right arm hang his powder-horn and bullet-pouch, in which he carries his balls, flint, and steel, and odds and ends of all kinds. Round the waist is a belt, in which is stuck a large butcher-knife in a sheath of buffalo-hide, made fast to the belt by a chain or guard of steel, which also supports a little buckskin case containing a whetstone. A tomahawk is also often added; and of course, a long, heavy rifle is part and parcel of his equipment. I had nearly forgotten the pipe-holder, which hangs around his neck, and is generally a gage d'amour, and a triumph of squaw workmanship, in shape of a heart, garnished with beads and porcupine-quills.

Thus provided, and having determined the locality of his trapping-ground, he starts to the mountains, sometimes alone, sometimes with three or four in company, as soon as the breaking up of the ice allows him to commence operations. Arrived on his hunting-grounds, he follows the creeks and streams, keeping a sharp lookout for "sign." If he sees a prostrate cottonwood tree, he examines it to discover if it be the work of beaver—whether "thrown" for the purpose of food, or to dam the stream. The track of the beaver on the mud or sand under the bank is also examined; and if the "sign" be fresh, he sets his trap in the run of the animal, hiding it under water, and attaching it by a stout chain to a picket driven in the bank, or to a brush or tree. A "float-stick" is made fast to the trap by a cord a few feet long, which, if the animal carry away the trap, floats on the water and points out its position. The trap is baited with the "medicine," an oily substance obtained from a gland in the scrotum of the beaver, but distinct from the testes. A stick is dipped into this and planted over the trap; and the beaver, attracted by the smell, and wishing a close inspection, very foolishly puts his leg into the trap, and is a "gone beaver."

When a lodge is discovered, the trap is set at the edge of the dam, at the point where the animal passes from deep to shoal water, and always under water. Early in the morning the hunter mounts his mule and examines the traps. The captured animals are skinned, and the tails, which are a great dainty, carefully packed into camp. The skin is then stretched over a hoop or framework of ossier-twigs and is allowed to dry, the flesh and fatty substance being carefully scraped (grained). When dry, it is folded into a square sheet, the fur turned inward, and the bundle, containing about ten to twenty skins, tightly pressed and corded, is ready for transportation.

During the hunt, regardless of Indian vicinity, the fearless trapper wanders far and near in search of "sign." His nerves must ever be in a state of tension, and his mind ever present at his call. His eagle eye sweeps round the country, and in an instant detects any foreign appearance. A turned leaf, a blade of grass pressed down, the uneasiness of the wild animals, the flight of birds, are all paragraphs to him written in nature's legible hand and plainest language. All the wits of the subtile savage are called into play to gain an advantage over the wily woodsman; but with the natural instinct of primitive man, the white hunter has the advantages of a civilized mind, and, thus provided, seldom fails to outwit, under equal advantages, the cunning savage.

From George F. Ruxton, *Adventures in Mexico and the Rocky Mountains* (New York: Harper & Bros., 1848) pp. 234–235.

James Ohio Pattie
A Trapper's Routine

On the morning of the 26th we concluded, that we must kill a horse, as we had eaten nothing for four day's and a half, except the small portion of a hare caught by my dogs, which fell to the lot of each of a party of seven. Before we obtained this, we had become weak in body and mind, complaining, and desponding of our success in search of beaver. Desirous of returning to some settlement, my father encouraged our party to eat some of the horses, and pursue our journey. We were all reluctant to begin to partake of the hors-flesh; and the actual thing without bread or salt was as bad as the anticipation of it. We were somewhat strengthened, however, and hastened on, while our supply lasted, in the hope of either overtaking those in advance of us, or finding another stream yet undiscovered by trappers.

The latter desire was gratified the first of January, 1825. The stream, we discovered, carried as much water as the Helay, heading north. We called it the river St. Francisco. After travelling up its banks about four miles, we encamped, and set all our traps, and killed a couple of fat turkies. In the morning we examined our traps, and found in them 37 beavers! This success restored our spirits instantaneously. Exhilerating prospects now opened before us, and we pushed on with anticipation. . . .

The right hand fork of this river, and the left of the Helay head in the same mountains, which is covered with snow, and divides its waters from those of Red river. We finished our trapping on this river, on the 14th. We had caught 250 beavers, and had used and preserved most of the meat, we had killed. On the 19th we arrived on the river Helay, encamped, and buried our furs in a secure position, as we intended to return home by this route. . . .

On the 28th we resumed our journey, and pushed down the stream to reach a point on the river, where trapping had not been practised. On the 30th, we reached this point, and found the man, that the Indians had killed. They had cut him in quarters, after the fashion of butchers. His head, with the hat on, was stuck on a stake. It was full of the arrows, which they had probably discharged into it, as they had danced around it. We gathered up the parts of the body, and buried them. . . . March 3d, we trapped down a small stream, that empties into the Helay on the south side, having its head in a south west direction. It being very remarkable for the number of its beavers, we gave it the name of Beaver river. At this place we collected 200 skins; and on the 10th continued to descend the Helay, until the 20th, when we turned back with as much fur, as our beasts could pack. As yet we had experienced no molestation from the Indians, although they were frequently descried skulking after us, and gathering up the pieces of meat, we had thrown away. . . . On the 25th we returned to Beaver river, and dug up the furs that we had buried, or cashed, as the phrase is, and concluded to ascend it, trapping towards its head, whence we proposed to cross over to the Helay above the mountains, where we had suffered so much in crossing. About six miles up the stream, we stopped to set our traps, three being selected to remain behind in the camp to dry the skins, my father to make a pen for the horses, and I to guard them, while they were turned loose to feed in the grass. We had pitched our camp near the bank of the river, in a thick grove of timber, extending about a hundred yards in width. Behind the timber was a narrow plain of about the same width, and still further on was a high hill, to which I repaired, to watch my horses, and descry whatever might pass in the distance. Immediately back of the hill I discovered a small lake, by the noise made by the ducks and geese in it. Looking more attentively, I remarked what gave me much more satisfaction, that is to say, three beaver lodges. I returned, and made my father acquainted with my discovery. The party despatched to set traps had returned. My father informed them of my discovery, and told them to set traps in the little lake. As we passed towards the lake, we observed the horses and mules all crowded together. At first we concluded that they collected together in this way, because they had fed enough. We soon discovered, that it was owing to another cause. I had put down my gun, and stepped into the water, to prepare a bed for my trap, while the others were busy in preparing theirs. Instantly the Indians raised a yell, and the quick report of guns ensued. This noise was almost drowned in the fierce shouts that followed, succeeded by a shower of arrows falling among us like hail. As we ran for the camp leaving all the horses in their power, we saw six Indians stealthily following our trail, as though they were tracking deer. They occasionally stopped, raised themselves, and surveyed every thing around them. We concealed ourselves behind a large cotton-wood tree, and waited until they came within a hundred yards of us. Each of us selected a separate Indian for a mark, and our signal to fire together was to be a whistle. The sign was given, and we fired together. My mark fell dead, and my companions' severely wounded. The other Indians seized their dead and wounded companions, and fled. . . .

We proceeded to bury our furs; and having packed our four horses with provisions and two traps, we commenced our march. Having travelled about ten miles, we encamped in a thicket without kindling a fire, and kept a strict guard all night. Next morning we made an early march, still along the banks of the river. Its banks are still plentifully timbered with cotton-wood and willow. The bottoms on each side afford fine soil for cultivation. . . .

On the 29th, we made our last encampment on this river, intending to return to it no more, except for our furs. We set our two traps for the last time, and caught a beaver in each.—We skinned the animals, and prepared the skins to hold water, through fear, that we might find none on our unknown route through the mountains to the Helay, from which we judged ourselves distant two hundred miles. Our provisions were all spoiled. We had nothing to carry with us to satisfy hunger, but the bodies of the two beavers which we had caught, the night before. We had nothing to sustain us in this disconsolate march, but our trust in providence; for we could not but forsee hunger, fatigue and pain, as the inevitable attendants upon our journey. To increase the depression of our spirits, our moccasins were worn out, our feet sore and tender, and the route full of sharp rocks. . . . We commenced an early march on the 6th, and were obliged to move slowly, as we were bare-footed, and the mountains rough and steep. We found them either wholly barren, or only covered with a stinted growth of pine and cedar, live oak and barbary bushes. On the 8th, our provisions were entirely exhausted, and so having nothing to eat, we felt the less need of water. Our destitute and forlorn condition goaded us on, so that we reached the Helay on the 12th. We immediately began to search for traces of beaver, where to set our traps, but found none. On the morning of the 13th, we killed a raven, which we cooked for seven men. . . .

We arrived at the house of the governor on the 12th. Jacova, his daughter, received us with the utmost affection; and shed tears on observing me so ill; as I was in fact reduced by starvation and fatigue, to skin and bone. Beings in a more wretched plight she could not often have an opportunity to see. My hair hung matted and uncombed. My head was surmounted with an old straw hat. My legs were fitted with leather leggins, and my body arrayed in a leather hunting shirt, and no want of dirt about any part of the whole. . . .

We rested ourselves three days. I had left more decent apparel in the care of Jacova, when we started from the house into the wilderness on our trapping expedition. She had my clothes prepared in perfect order. I once more dressed myself decently, and spared to my companions all my clothes that fitted them. We all had our hair trimmed. All this much improved our appearance. When we started on the 15th, the old gentleman gave each of us a good horse, enabling us to travel at our ease. . . . I took part of my goods, and started back to the mines on the 21st. None of my companions were willing to accompany me on account of the great apprehended danger from the Indians between this place and the mines. In consequence, I hired a man to go with me, and having purchased what horses I wanted, we two travelled on in company. . . .

We left the mines on the 7th, and reached Battle-hill on Beaver river on the 22d. I need not attempt to describe my feelings, for no description could paint them, when I found the furs all gone, and perceived that the Indians had discovered them and taken them away. All that, for which we had hazarded ourselves, and suffered every thing but death, was gone. The whole fruit of our long, toilsome and dangerous expedition was lost, and all my golden hopes of prosperity and comfort vanished like a dream. I tried to convince myself, that repining was of no use, and we started for the river San Francisco on the 29th. Here we found the small quantity buried there, our whole compensation for a year's toil, misery and danger. We met no Indians either going or returning.

From James Ohio Pattie, *The Personal Narrative of James O. Pattie*, edited by Timothy Flint (Cincinnati: John H. Wood, 1831), pp. 55–72 *passim*.

PORTRAIT OF A MOUNTAIN MAN

Jedediah Strong Smith

The Journal of Jedediah Smith

February 20, 1828

My horses freezing, my men discouraged and our utmost exertion necessary to keep them from freezing to death. I then thought of the vanity of riches and of all those objects that lead men in the perilous path of adventure. It seems that in times like those men return to reason and make the true estimate of things. They throw by the gaudy baubles of ambition and embrace the solid comforts of domestic life. But a few days of rest makes the sailor forget the storm and embark again on the perilous Ocean and I suppose that like him I would soon become weary of rest.

February 26, 1828

Two of my trappers, Mareshall and Turner were up 3 or 4 miles from camp and seeing some indians around their traps who would not come to them but attempted to run off they fired at them and Turner killed one and Mareshall wounded another. I was extremely sorry for the occurrence and reprimanded them severely for their impolitic conduct. To prevent the recurrence of such an act the only remedy in my power was to forbid them the privilege of setting traps, for I could not always have the trappers under my eye.

From Jedediah Strong Smith, "The Journal of Jedediah Smith," in *The Travels of Jedediah Smith: A Documentary Outline*, edited by Maurice S. Sullivan (Santa Ana: Fine Arts Press, 1934), pp. 63, 64–65.

James Clyman

A Lesson to Remember

[L]ate in the afternoon while passing through a Brushy bottom
a large Grssely came down the valley we being in single file
men on foot leding pack horses he struck us about the center then turning ran paralel to our line   capt. Smith being in
the advanc he ran to the open ground and as he immerged
from the thicket he and the bear met face to face   Grissly
did not hesitate a moment but sprung on the Capt taking him
by the head first pitc[h]ing sprawling on the earth he gave
him a grab by the middle fortunately cat[c]hing by the ball
pouch and Butcher K[n]ife which he broke but breaking
several of his ribs and cutting his head badly none of us
having any surgical Knowledge what was to be done one Said
come take hold and he wuld say why not you so it went
around I asked the Capt what was best he said one or 2
[go] for water and if you have a needle and thread git it out
and sew up my wounds around my head which was bleeding
freely I got a pair of scissors and cut off his hair and then
began my first Job of d[r]essing wounds upon examination
I [found] the bear had taken nearly all his head in his ca-
pacious mouth close to his left eye on one side and clos to his
right ear on the other and laid the skull bare to near the crown
of the head leaving a white streak whare his teeth
passed one of ears was torn from his head out to the outer
rim after stitching all the other wounds in the best way I
was capabl and according to the captains directions the ear
being the last I told him I could do nothing for his Eare   O
you must try to stich up some way or other said he then I
put in my needle stitching it through and through and over
and over laying the lacerated parts together as nice as I could
with my hands   water was found in about ame mille when we
all moved down and encamped the captain being able to mount
his horse and ride to camp whare we pitched a tent the onley
one we had and made him as comfortable as circumstances

would permit   this gave us a lisson on the character of the
grissly Baare which we did not forget

From "Clyman Diaries," edited by Camp, pp. 122–123.

A Eulogy for The Great American Pathfinder

"Few men have been more fortunate than I have," said Mr.
Smith to the writer, in March, 1831. "I started into the
mountains, with the determination of becoming a first-rate
hunter, of making myself thoroughly acquainted with the
character and habits of the Indians, of tracing out the sources
of the Columbia river, and following it to its mouth; and of
making the whole profitable to me, and I have perfectly
succeeded." Indeed, he did much more than he had planned
out. For nine years and a half he was almost constantly travelling. He became well acquainted with the sources, direction,
and length of most of the tributaries of the Missouri and
Columbia rivers, and of the numerous tribes of Indians that
dwell on their banks. He traversed the Rocky Mountains in
every direction, found out the best hunting grounds and the
best passes through the mountains. The salt lake, salt plains,
and caves of solid salt were familiar to him. He had visited
whole tribes of Indians that had never before seen a white
man or a horse—people more rude and barbarous probably
than any that have ever been described. There is no written
notice of these people anywhere except in the notes of Mr.
Smith. He was a close and accurate observer and a student of
nature. He thought nothing in the true works of God unworthy of his notice, and from constant observation he had
amassed an immense fund of knowledge, exceedingly useful
and interesting in every branch of natural history. More than
this, by his intimate knowledge of the geography of that immense tract of country, he had found that all the maps of it
were full of errors, and worse than useless as guides to travellers. Compare his travels with those of all who had gone before him, of all who have published anything of that country,
and it will appear how much, I had almost said infinitely,
greater, his opportunities have been than all theirs, however
great may have been their pretensions. . . .

. . . The lone wilderness had been his place of meditation, and the mountain top his altar. He made religion an active, practical principle, from the duties of which, nothing could seduce him. He affirmed it to be "the one thing needful," and his greatest happiness; yet was he modest, never obtrusive, charitable, "without guile."

Such is a feeble sketch of J. S. Smith, a man whom none could approach without respect, or know without esteem. And though he fell under the spears of the savages, and his body has glutted the prairie wolf, and none can tell where his bones are bleaching, he must not be forgotten.

From "Captain Jedediah Strong Smith: A Eulogy of That Most Romantic and Pious of Mountainmen," *Illinois Monthly Magazine* (June 1832), reprinted in Edwin L. Sabin, *Kit Carson Days* (Chicago: A.C. McClurg & Co., 1914), pp. 512–513, 517–518.

RENDEZVOUS

Washington Irving

Mountain Business

The American fur companies keep no established posts beyond the mountains. . . . In the months of June and July, when there is an interval between the hunting seasons, a general rendezvous is held, at some designated place in the mountains, where the affairs of the past year are settled by the resident partners, and the plans for the following year arranged.

To this rendezvous repair the various brigades of trappers from their widely separated hunting grounds, bringing in the products of their year's campaign. Hither also repair the Indian tribes accustomed to traffic their peltries with the company. Bands of free trappers resort hither also, to sell the furs they have collected; or to engage their services for the next hunting season.

To this rendezvous the company sends annually a convoy of supplies from its establishment on the Atlantic frontier, under the guidance of some experienced partner or officer. On the arrival of this convoy, the resident partner at the rendezvous depends to set all his next year's machinery in motion.

From Irving, *The Rocky Mountains,* pp. 22–23.

Sir William Drummond Stewart
Days of Jubilee

A small piece of carved bone, often taken from the body of the fox, was held by the gambler, who joining his closed fists together, one above the other, could thus pass it into either, he then separated them and threw his arms wide apart, singing and jerking his body up and down, and again bringing his hands together, and changing or pretending to change the bone, the gamblers choosing only when the hands were held wide apart; if the guess is right, the guesser pulls away his pile with that of the bone holder previously arranged beside it; and if inclined a new bet is made, when the juggler or the bank, as he might be called, has nothing more to bet, he gives up the bone, or if the successful guesser chooses, he may, as is generally the case, take his place. The scene is particularly animating from the exciting song and action, being joined to the deep and desolating passion of play. We looked on a minute, and Kit [Carson] threw down a handsome dagger-knife, a considerable bunch of beads was placed against it, the youth who played had lost the dignity and calm usual to his race, his dark eyes flashed, and his body naked, but for a slight girdle round his waist, was jerked up and down from the hips with frantic eagerness, and his wild song rose high as he eyed the tempting stake. Kit having clapped his hands, and threw out the left, signified that the bone was to be found in that opposite, the Indian opened the other where there was nothing; Kit had won and drew back his knife and beads, making a sign that he did not wish to play, and the game went on. A young squaw of the Utaw tribe, who had lost every thing of her dress to a scanty shirt, stood looking wistfully on, her small hands clasped, and her beautifully formed limbs crossed one over the other, she never took her eyes off the ring, in which her whole desire seemed to be concentrated. My companion threw the beads he had won at her beautiful feet, and with an almost imperceptible look of thanks for the gift, she flung them down again to be risked in the chance of the game. . . .

It was evening, and Indians and whites were flocking back and forth from the excursions of the day, whether those of hunting or pleasure; a war party had returned from the side of the Blackfeet country with scalps, the drum was beating, and the squaws and some of the braves had already begun the dance to its slow and measured music. The Snake camp was full, and the games of the young, as well as the grown up, the shooting with the bow and arrow, as well as throwing an arrow like a javelin, diversified the scene; the bucks paraded in full paint, and the gamblers dotted with their groups the varied scenes. . . .

I had no news to read, and no letters; but the recollections of a former home were not obliterated, nor of country; and I loved to sit in the shade, and let my memory wander over bye-gone years, when tired of a visit to the Snake Camp, or the now frequent jollities of the wild free trappers, who came dropping in from distant and unknown haunts, where they had perilled their lives for the ephemeral joys and riot of the few days of jubilee. The best looking of the young squaws of the neighboring camp, came over in groups to wonder at the riches of the white man, as well as tempt him to dispense them, and many happy matrimonial connections were formed by means of a dower of glittering beads and scarlet cloth.

From Sir William Drummond Stewart, *Edward Warren* (London: G. Walker, 1854), pp. 271, 274–275.

Myra F. Eells
Devil's Den

Thursday, July 5th.—Last night, were troubled exceedingly
by the noise of some drunken men. We were awakened by
the barking of dogs, soon we heard a rush of drunken men
coming directly towards our tent. . . . They then began singing; asked Mr. Eells to sing with them. He told them he did
not know their tunes. They asked if they disturbed him by
keeping him up. He made no reply. They said silence gave
consent and went a little distance to Mr. Curtis, who was
sleeping under a tree. They conversed a while with him and
then made off with themselves giving us no more trouble,
only that we were constantly in fear lest they would return. . . . Capt. Bridger's company comes in about ten
o'clock, with drums and firing—an apology for a scalp dance.
After they had given Capt. Drips company a shout, fifteen or
twenty mountain men and Indians came to our tent with
drumming, firing, and dancing. If I might make the comparison, I should say that they looked like the emissaries of the
Devil worshipping their own master. They had the scalp of a
Blackfoot Indian, which they carried for a color, all rejoicing
in the fate of the Blackfoots in consequence of the small-pox.
The dog being frightened, took the trail across the river and
howled so that we knew him and called him back. . . .

Friday, July 6th.—Last night twelve white men came, dressed
and painted in Indian style, and gave us a dance. No pen can
describe the horrible scene they presented. Could not imagine
that white men, brought up in a civilized land, can appear to
so much imitate the Devil.

From "Journal of Myra F. Eells [1838]," *Transactions of the Oregon
Pioneer Association*, June 18, 1889, pp. 78–79.

ROCKY MOUNTAIN COLLEGE

Osborne Russell

Winter Camp

We encamped near the fort and turned our horses among the springs and timber to hunt their living during the winter, whilst ourselves were snugly arranged in our skin lodge, which was pitched among the large cottonwood trees, and in it provisions to serve us till the month of April. There were four of us in the mess. One was from Missouri, one from Massachusetts, one from Vermont, and myself from Maine. We passed an agreeable winter. We had nothing to do but to eat, attend to the horses and procure firewood. We had some few books to read, such as Byron, Shakespeare and Scott's works, the Bible and Clark's Commentary on it, and other small works on geology, chemistry and philosophy. The winter was very mild and the ground was bare in the valley until the 15th of January, when the snow fell about eight inches deep, but disappeared again in a few days. . . .

. . . The camp keepers' business in winter quarters is to guard the horses, cook and keep fires. We all had snug lodges made of dressed buffalo skins, in the center of which we built a fire and generally comprised about six men to the lodge. The long winter evenings were passed away by collecting in some of the most spacious lodges and entering into debates, arguments or spinning long yarns until midnight, in perfect good humor, and I for one will cheerfully confess that I have derived no little benefit from the frequent arguments and debates held in what we termed "The Rocky Mountain College," and I doubt not but some of my comrades who considered themselves classical scholars have had some little added to their wisdom in the assemblies, however rude they might appear.

From Osborne Russell, *Journal of a Trapper or Nine Years in the Rocky Mountains, 1834–1843* (Boise, Idaho: Syms-York Co., 1921), pp. 109, 55.

Osborne Russell
Mountain Politics

December 25th—It was agreed on by the party to prepare a Christmas dinner, but I shall first endeavor to describe the party and then the dinner. I have already said the man who was the proprietor of the lodge in which I staid was a Frenchman with a Flathead wife and one child. The inmates of the next lodge were a halfbreed Iowa, a Nez Perce wife and two children, his wife's brother and another halfbreed; next lodge was a halfbreed Cree, his wife (a Nez Perce) two children and a Snake Indian. The inmates of the third lodge were a halfbreed Snake, his wife (a Nez Perce) and two children. The remainder were fifteen lodges of Snake Indians. Three of the party spoke English but very broken, therefore that language was made but little use of, as I was familiar with the Canadian French and Indian tongue.

About ten o'clock we sat down to dinner in the lodge where I staid, which was the most spacious, being about thirty-six feet in circumference at the base, with a fire built in the center. Around this sat on clean epishemores all who claimed kin to the white man (or to use their own expression, all who were gens d'esprit), with their legs crossed in true Turkish style, and now for the dinner.

The first dish that came on was a large tin pan eighteen inches in diameter, rounding full of stewed elk meat. The next dish was similar to the first, heaped up with boiled deer meat (or as the whites would call it, venison, a term not used in the mountains). The third and fourth dishes were equal in size to the first, containing a boiled flour pudding, prepared with dried fruit, accompanied by four quarts of sauce made of the juice of sour berries and sugar. Then came the cakes, followed by about six gallons of strong coffee ready sweetened, with tin cups and pans to drink out of, large chips or pieces of bark supplying the places of plates. On being ready, the butcher knives were drawn and the eating commenced at the word given by the landlady. As all dinners are accompanied by conversation, this was not deficient in that respect. The principal topic which was discussed was the political affairs of the Rocky Mountains, the state of governments among the different tribes, the personal characters of the most distinguished warrior chiefs, etc. One remarked that the Snake chief, Pahda-hewakunda, was becoming very unpopular and it was the opinion of the Snakes in general that Moh-woom-hah, his brother, would be at the head of affairs before twelve months, as his village already amounted to more than three hundred lodges, and, moreover, he was supported by the bravest men in the nation, among whom were Ink-a-tosh-a-pop, Fibe-bo-un-to-wat-see and Who-sha-kik, who were the pillars of the nation and at whose names the Blackfeet quaked with fear. In like manner were the characters of the principal chiefs of the Bannock, Nez Perce, Flathead and Crow nations and the policy of their respective nations commented upon by the descendants of Shem and Japhet with as much affected dignity as if they could have read their own names when written, or distinguish the letter B from bull's foot.

Dinner being over, the tobacco pipes were filled and lighted, while the squaws and children cleared away the remains of the feast to one side of the lodge, where they held a sociable tete-a-tete over the fragments. After the pipes were extinguished all agreed to have a frolic shooting at a mark, which occupied the remainder of the day.

From Russell, *Journal of a Trapper*, pp. 114–116.

Capt. J. Lee Humfreville
Jim Bridger and Shakespeare

James Bridger, or, as he was familiarly spoken of in that country, "Old Jim Bridger," was the most efficient guide, mountaineer, plainsman, trapper and Indian fighter that ever

lived in the Far West. He knew more of that country and all
things within its borders than any one who ever lived. He had
been a trapper for various Fur Companies, and had trapped
on his own account for many years, long before the foot of a
white settler entered that territory, having trapped from the
mouth to the source of nearly all its rivers and streams. Although Bridger had little or no education, he could, with a
piece of charcoal or a stick, scratch on the ground or any
smooth surface a map of the whole western country that was
much more correct than those made at that time by skilled
topographical engineers, with all their scientific instruments. I
have seen Bridger look at a printed map, and point out its de-
fects at sight. . . .

I occupied the same quarters with him one whole winter,
where I had ample opportunity to study his character and
learn his peculiar ways and manner of living. He never did
anything until he felt so inclined. For instance, if he grew
sleepy in the afternoon, say by three, four, or five o'clock, he
went to bed, and when he awoke, say in four, five or six
hours afterward, he would rise, make a fire, roast meat, eat
it, and sing "Injun," to use his own term, the rest of the night.
If he had a tin pan, he turned it bottom side up, and with a
stick, beat on the bottom, making a noise like the Indian
tom-tom. He never ate until he was hungry, and, as he lived
largely on meats, he was thin and spare, although strong and
wiry. His manner of living during this winter did not coincide
with my habits or ideas, by any means, so I tried to entertain
him every afternoon and keep him awake until nine or ten
o'clock in the evening. My first effort was in reading to him.
A copy of "Hiawatha," was found among the troops, which I
read to him as long as he permitted it. He would sit bent
over, his long legs crossed, his gaunt hands and arms clasping
his knees, and listen to the reading attentively, until a passage
was reached in which Longfellow portrayed an imaginary Indian, when Bridger, after a period of uneasy wriggling on his
seat, arose very wrathy, and swearing that the whole story
was a lie, that he would listen to no more of it, and that "no
such Injun ever lived." This happened over and over again.
After a while I quieted him, and began reading again, but after a short time he was sure to stop me, swearing that he
would not listen any longer to such infernal lies. However, I
managed to entertain him in this way for two or three weeks,
during which time I secured a reasonable amount of sleep out
of each twenty-four hours.

Bridger became very much interested in this reading, and asked which was the best book that had ever been written. I told him that Shakespeare's was supposed to be the greatest book. Thereupon he made a journey to the main road, and lay in wait for a wagon train, and bought a copy from some emigrants, paying for it with a yoke of cattle, which at that time could have been sold for one hundred and twenty-five dollars. He hired a German boy, from one of the wagon trains, at forty dollars a month, to read to him. The boy was a good reader, and Bridger took great interest in the reading, listening most attentively for hours at a time. Occasionally he got the thread of the story so mixed that he would swear a blue streak, then compel the young man to stop, turn back, and re-read a page or two, until he could get the story straightened out. This continued until he became so hopelessly involved in reading "Richard the Third" that he declared he "wouldn't listen any more to the talk of any man who was mean enough to kill his mother." That ended our reading of Shakespeare, much to my disgust, for I was again doomed to be kept awake at all hours of the night by his aboriginal habits. After that it was amusing to hear Bridger quote Shakespeare. He could give quotation after quotation, and was always ready to do so. Sometimes he seasoned them with a broad oath, so ingeniously inserted as to make it appear to the listener that Shakespeare himself had used the same language.

From J. Lee Humfreville, *Twenty Years Among Our Hostile Indians*, rev. ed. (New York: Hunter and Co., 1903), pp. 462–463, 467–468.

TALL TALES

Capt. J. Lee Humfreville
Indian Fighting

"You must have had some curious adventures with, and hairbreadth escapes from the Indians during your long life among them," observed one of a party of a dozen or more, who had been relentlessly plying [Jim Bridger] with questions.

"Yes, I've had a few," he responded reflectively, "an' I never to my dyin' day shall forget one in particular."

The crowd manifested an eager desire to hear the story. I will not undertake to give his words, but no story was ever more graphically told, and no throng of listeners ever followed a story's detail with more intense interest. He was on horseback and alone. He had been suddenly surprised by a party of six Indians, and putting spurs to his horse sought to escape. The Indians, mounted on fleet ponies, quickly followed in pursuit. His only weapon was a six-shooter. The moment the leading Indian came within shooting distance, he turned in his saddle and gave him a shot. His shot always meant a dead Indian. In this way he picked off five of the Indians, but the last one kept up the pursuit relentlessly and refused to be shaken off.

"We wus nearin' the edge of a deep an' wide gorge," said Bridger. "No horse could leap over that awful chasm, an' a fall to the bottom meant sartin death. I turned my horse suddint an' the Injun was upon me. We both fired to once, an' both horses was killed. We now engaged in a han'-to-han' conflict with butcher knives. He wus a powerful Injun—tallest I ever seen. It wus a long and fierce struggle. One moment I hed the best of it, an' the next the odds wus agin me. Finally—"

Here Bridger paused as if to get breath.

"How did it end?" at length asked one of his breathless listeners, anxiously.

"The Injun killed me," he replied with slow deliberation.

From Humfreville, *Twenty Years Among Our Hostile Indians*, pp. 464–465.

George F. Ruxton

The Petrified Forest

"Well, Mister Harris, I hear you're a great travler."

"Travler, marm," says Black Harris, "this niggur's no travler; I ar' a trapper, marm, a mountain-man, wagh!"

"Well, Mister Harris, trappers are great travlers, and you goes over a sight of ground in your perishinations, I'll be bound to say."

"A sight, marm, this coon's gone over, if that's the way your 'stick floats.' I've trapped beaver on Platte and Arkansa, and away up on Missoura and Yaller Stone; I've trapped on Columbia, on Lewis Fork, and Green River; I've trapped, marm, on Grand River and the Heely (Gila). I've fout the 'Blackfoot' (and d——d bad Injuns they are); I've 'raised the hair' of more *than one* Apach, and made a Rapaho 'come' afore now; I've trapped in heav'n, in airth, and h——, and scalp my old head, marm, but I've seen a putrefied forest."

"La, Mister Harris, a what?"

"A putrefied forest, marm, as sure as my rifle's got hind-sights, and *she* shoots center. I was out on the Black Hills, Bill Sublette knows the time—the year it rained fire—and every body knows when that was. If thar wasn't cold doin's about that time, this child wouldn't say so. The snow was about fifty foot deep, and the bufler lay dead on the ground like bees after a beein'; not whar we was tho', for *thar* was no bufler, and no meat, and me and my band had been livin' on our mocassins (leastwise the parflesh), for six weeks; and poor doin's that feedin' is, marm, as you'll never know. One day we crossed a 'canon' and over a 'divide,' and got into a periara, whar was green grass, and green trees, and green leaves on the trees, and birds singing in the green leaves, and this in Febrary, wagh! Our animals was like to die when they see the green grass, and we all sung out, 'hurraw for summer doin's.'

" 'Hyar goes for meat,' says I, and I jest ups old Ginger at one of them singing birds, and down come the crittur elegant; its darned head spinning away from the body, but never stops singing, and when I takes up the meat, I finds it stone, wagh!

" 'Hyar's damp powder and no fire to dry it,' I says quite skeared.

" 'Fire be dogged,' says old Rube. 'Hyar's a hos as'll make fire come'; and with that he takes axe and lets drive at a cottonwood. Schr-u-k—goes the axe agin the tree, and out comes a bit of the blade as big as my hand. We looks at the animals, and thar they stood shaking over the grass, which I'm dog-gone if it wasn't stone, too. Young Sublette comes up, and he'd been clerking down to the fort on Platte, so he know'd something. He looks and looks, and scrapes the tree with his butcher knife, and snaps the grass like pipe stems, and breaks the leaves a-snappin' like Californy shells.

" 'What's all this, boy?' I asks.

" 'Putrefactions,' says he, looking smart, 'putrefactions, or I'm a niggur.' "

"La, Mister Harris," says the lady; "putrefactions, why, did the leaves, and the trees, and the grass smell badly?"

"Smell badly, marm," says Black Harris, "would a skunk stink if he was froze to stone? No, marm, this child didn't know what putrefactions was, and young Sublette's varsion wouldn't 'shine' nohow, so I chips a piece out of a tree and puts it in my trap-sack, and carries it in safe to Laramie. Well, old Captain [William Drummond] Stewart (a clever man was that, though he was an Englishman), he comes along next spring, and a Dutch doctor chap was along too. I shows him the piece I chipped out of the tree, and he called it a putrefaction too; and so, marm, if that wasn't a putrified peraira, what was it? For this hos doesn't know, and *he* knows 'fat cow' from 'poor bull,' anyhow."

From George F. Ruxton, *Life in the Far West* (New York: Harper & Bros., 1849), pp. 16–18.

Lewis H. Garrard

A Trip to Hell; or, What the Mountain Man Saw during Delirium Tremens

"Thar, in front, was a level kanyon, with walls of black an' brown an' gray stone, an' stumps of burnt pinyon hung down ready to fall onter us; an', as we passed, the rocks and trees shook an' grated an' creaked. . . . Jest then I heerd a laffin'. I looks up, an' two black critters—they was n't human, sure, fur they had tails an' red coats (Injun cloth, like that traded to the Navyhoes), edged with shiny white stuff, an' brass buttons.

"They kem forrad an' made two low bows. I felt fur my scalpknife (fur I thought they was 'proachin' to take me), but I could n't use it—they were so *darned* polite.

"One of the devils said, with a grin an' bow, 'Good mornin', Mr. Hatcher?'

"'H——!' sez I, 'how do you know me? I swar *this* hos never saw you afore.'

"'Oh! we've expected you a long time,' said the other, 'and we are quite happy to see you—we've known you ever since your arrival in the mountains.'

"I was gittin' sorter scared. I wanted a drop of arwerdenty mity bad, but the bottle was gone, an' I looked at them in astonishment, an' said—'the devil!'

"'Hush!' screamed one, 'you must not say that here—keep still, you will see him presently.' . . .

". . . A kind-lookin' smallish old gentleman, with a black coat and briches, an' a bright, cute face, an' gold spectacles, walks up an' pressed my hand softly—

"'How do you do, my dear friend? I have long expected you. You cannot imagine the pleasure it gives me to meet you at home. I have watched your peregrinations in the busy, tiresome world, with much interest. Sit down, sit down; take a chair,' an' he handed me one.

"I squared myself on it, but a ten-pronged buck was n't done sucking, when I last sot on a cheer, an' I squirmed awhile, oneasy as a gut-shot coyote. I jumps up, an' tells the old gentleman them sort of 'state fixins,' did n't suit this beaver, an' he prefers the floor. I sets cross-legged like in camp as easy as eatin' *boudin*. I reached for my pipe—a feller's so used to it—but the devil's in the kanyon had câched *it* too.

"'You wish to smoke, Mr. Hatcher?—we will have cigars. Here!' he called to an imp near him, 'some cigars.'

"They was brought on a waiter, size of my bulletbag. I empties 'em in my hat, for good cigars ain't to be picked up on the peraira every day, but lookin' at the old man, I saw somethin' was wrong. To be polite, I ought to have taken one.

"'I beg pardon,' says I, scratchin' my old scalp, 'this hos did n't think—he's been so long in the mountains, he forgets civilized doins,' an' I shoves the hat to him.

"'Never mind,' says he, wavin' his hand, an' smilin' faintly, 'get others,' speakin' to the boy aside him.

"The old gentleman took one, and touched his finger to the end of my cigar—it smoked as ef fire had been sot to it.

"'Wagh! the devil!' screams I drawin' back.

"'The same!' chimed in he, biting off the little end of his'n, an' bowin' an' spittin' it out—'the same, sir.'

" 'The same! what?'

" 'Why—the Devil.'

" 'H——! this ain't the holler tree for this coon—I'll be makin' 'medicin';' so I offers my cigar to the sky, an' to the earth, like Injun.

" 'You must not do that *here*—out upon such superstition,' says he, sharplike.

" 'Why?'

" 'Do n't ask so many questions—come with me,' risin' to his feet, an' walkin' off slow, a blowin' his cigar smoke, over his shoulder in a long line, an' I gets along side of him, 'I want to show you my establishment—did not expect to find this down here, eh?' . . .

"The place was hot an' smelt bad of brimstone; but the darned screechin' *took* me. I walks up to t'other end of the 'lodge,' an' steal my mule, if thar was n't Jake Beloo, as trapped with me to Brown's Hole! A lot of hellcats was a pullin' at his ears, an' a jumpin' on his shoulders, a swingin' themselves to the ground by his long har. Some was runnin' hot irons in him, but when we came up, they went off in a corner of laffin' and talkin' like wildcats' gibberish on a cold night.

"Poor Jake! he came to the bar, lookin' like a sick buffler in the eye. The bones stuck through the skin, an' his har was matted an' long—all over jest like a blind bull, an' white blisters spotted him, with water runnin' out of 'em. 'Hatch, old feller! *you* here, too? —how are ye?' says he, in a faint-like voice, staggerin' an' catchin' on to the bar fur support—'I'm sorry to see you *here*, what did you'—he raised his eyes to the old man standin' ahind me, who gave him *such* a look; he went howlin' an' foamin' at the mouth to the fur eend of the den, an' fell down, rollin' over the damp stones. The devils, who was chucklin' by a furnis, whar was irons a heatin', approached easy and run one into his back. I jumped at 'em and hollered, 'You owdacious little hellpups, let him alone; ef my sculptaker was hyar, I'd make buzzard feed of your meat, an' *parflêche* of your dogskins,' but they squeaked out to 'go to the devil.' "

" 'Wagh!' says I, 'ef I *ain't* pretty close to his lodge, I'm a niggur!'

"The old gentleman speaks up, 'take care of yourself, Mr. Hatcher,' in a mity soft, kind voice; an' he smiled so calm an' devilish—it nigh on froze me. I thought ef the ground would open with a yairthquake, an' take me in, I'd be much obleeged any how. Think's I—you saint-forsaken, infernal hell-chief, how I'd like to stick my knife in your withered old bread-basket. . . .

" 'It's time to break fur timber, sure,' and I run as ef a wounded buffler was raisin' my shirt with his horns. The place was damp, an' in the narrow rock, lizards an' vipers an' copperheads jumped out at me, an' clum on my legs, but I stompt an' shook 'em off. Owls, too, flopped thar wings in my face, an' hooted at me, an' fire blazed out, an' lit the place up, an' brimstone smoke came nigh on chokin' me. Lookin' back, the whole cavyard of hell was comin', an' devils on devils, nothin' but devils, filled the hole.

"I threw down my hat to run faster, an' then jerked off my old blanket, but still they was gainin'. I made one jump clean out of my moccasins. The big snake in front was closer an' closer, with his head drawed back to strike; then a helldog raked up nearly long side, pantin' an' blowin' with the slobber runnin' outen his mouth, an' a lot of devils hangin' on to him, was cussin' me an' screechin! I strained every jint, but no use, they still gained—not fast—but gainin' they was. I jumped an' swore, an' leaned down, an' flung out my hands, but the dogs was nearer every time, an' the horrid yellin' an' hissin' way back, grew louder an' louder. At last, a prayer mother used to make me say, I had n't thought of fur twenty year or more, came rite afore me clear as a powderhorn. I kept runnin' an' sayin' it, an' the niggurs held back a little. I gained some on them—Wagh! I stopped repeatin', to get breath, an' the foremost dog made such a lunge at me, I forgot it. Turnin' up my eyes, thar was the old gentleman lookin' at me, an' keepin' along-side, without walkin'. His face war n't more than two feet off, an' his eyes was fixed steady an' calm an' devilish. I screamed rite out. I shut my eyes but he was thar too. I howled an' spit an' hit at it, but could n't git the darned face away. A dog ketched hold of my shirt with his fangs, an' two devils, jumpin' on me, caught me by the throat, a tryin' to choke me. While I was pullin' 'em off, I fell down, with about thirty-five of the infernal things, an' the dogs, an' the slimy snakes a top of me, a mashin' an' taren' me. I bit big pieces out of them, an' bit an' bit agin, an' scratched an' gouged. When I was most give out, I heerd the Pawnee skulp yell, an' use my rifle fur a pokin' stick, ef in did n't charge a party of the best boys in the mountains. *They* slayed the devils right an' left, an' sot 'em running' like goats, but this hos was so weak fightin', he fainted away.

When I come to, we was on the Purgatoire, just whar I found the liquor, an' my companyeros was slappin' thar wet hats in my face, to bring me to. Round whar I was layin', the grass was pulled up an' the ground dug with my knife, and the bottle, cached when I traded with the Yutes, was smashed to flinders 'gainst a tree.

" 'Why, what on airth, Hatcher, have ye bin doin' hyar? You was akickin' and taren' up the grass, and yellin' as ef yer 'har' was taken. Why, old hos, this coon do n't *savy* them hifelutin' notions, he does n't!'

" 'The devils from hell was after me,' sez I mity gruff, 'this hos has seen moren ever he wants to agin.'

"They tried to git me outen the notion, but I swar, an' I'll stick to it, this child saw a heap more of the all-fired place than he wants to agin; an' ef it ain't fact, he does n't know 'fat cow' from 'poor bull'—Wagh!"

So ended Hatcher's tale of Wah-to-yah, or what the mountaineer saw when he had the *mania potu*.

From Lewis H. Garrard, *Wah-to-yah and the Taos Trail: or Prairie Travel and Scalp Dances, with a Look at Los Rancheros from Mule-back and the Rocky Mountain Campfire* (Cincinnati: H.W. Derby & Co., 1850), pp. 244–251, 263–265 *passim*.

SHAPING THE LEGEND: KIT CARSON

Kit Carson

Scalping Indians

They informed us that they were a party of Mexicans from New Mexico. They and two men and women were encamped a distance from the main party herding horses . . .

We started for the place where they said they left their animals, found that they had been taken away by the Indians that had followed them.

The Mexican requested Frémont to aid him to retake his animals. He (Frémont) stated to the party that if they wished to volunteer for such a purpose they might do so, that he would furnish animals for them to ride. Godey and myself volunteered with the expectation that some men of our party would join us. They did not. We two and the Mexican took the trail of (the) animals and commenced the pursuit. In twenty miles the Mexican's horse gave out. We sent him back, and continued on. Travelled during the night. It was very dark. Had to dismount to feel for the trail. By sign we became aware that the Indians had passed after sunset. We were much fatigued, required rest, unsaddled, wrapped ourselves in the wet saddle blankets and laid down. Could not make any fire for fear of it being seen. Passed a miserably cold night. In the morning we arose very early, went down in a deep ravine made a small fire to warm ourselves, and, as soon as it was light, we again took the trail.

As the sun was rising (we) saw the Indians two miles ahead of us, encamped having a feast. They had killed five animals. We were compelled to leave our horses, they could not travel. We hid them among the rocks, continued on the trail, crawled in among the horses. A young one got frightened, that frightened the rest. The Indians noticed the commotion among the animals (and) sprung to their arms. We now considered it time to charge on the Indians. They were about thirty in number. We charged. I fired, killed one. Godey fired, missed but reloaded and fired killing another. There was only three shots fired and two were killed. The remainder run. I then took the two rifles and ascended a hill to keep guard while Godey scalped the dead Indians. He scalped the one he shot and was proceeding towards the one I shot. He was not yet dead and was behind some rocks. As Godey approached, he raised (and) let fly an arrow. It passed through Godey's shirt collar. He again fell and Godey finished him.

We gathered the animals (and) drove them to where we had concealed our own, changed horses and drove to camp and safely arrived. Had all the animals, with the exception of those killed (by the Indians) for their feast.

We then marched on to where the Mexicans had left the

two men and women. (The) men we discovered dead,—their bodies horribly mutilated.

From Kit Carson, *Kit Carson's Own Story of His Life*, edited by Blanche C. Grant (Taos, New Mexico, 1926), pp. 61–63.

John C. Frémont

Promoting the Myth

In the afternoon of the next day, a war-whoop was heard, such as Indians make when returning from a victorious enterprise; and soon Carson and Godey appeared, driving before them a band of horses, recognized by Fuentes to be part of those they had lost. Two bloody scalps, dangling from the end of Godey's gun, announced that they had overtaken the Indians as well as the horses. They informed us, that after Fuentes left them, from the failure of his horse, they continued the pursuit alone, and towards nightfall entered the mountains, into which the trail led. After sunset the moon gave light, and they followed the trail by moonshine until late in the night, when it entered a narrow defile, and was difficult to follow. Afraid of losing it in the darkness of the defile, they tied up their horses, struck no fire, and lay down to sleep in silence and in darkness. Here they lay from midnight till morning. At daylight they resumed the pursuit, and about sunrise discovered the horses; and, immediately dismounting and tying up their own, they crept cautiously to a rising ground which intervened, from the crest of which they perceived the encampment of four lodges close by. They proceeded quietly, and had got within thirty or forty yards of their object, when a movement among the horses discovered them to the Indians; giving the war shout, they instantly charged into the camp, regardless of the number which the *four* lodges would imply. The Indians received them with a flight of arrows shot from their long bows, one of which passed through Godey's shirt collar, barely missing the neck; our men fired their rifles upon a steady aim, and rushed in.

Two Indians were stretched on the ground, fatally pierced with bullets; the rest fled, except a lad that was captured. The scalps of the fallen were instantly stripped off; but in the process, one of them, who had two balls through his body, sprung to his feet, the blood streaming from his skinned head, and uttering a hideous howl. An old squaw, possibly his mother, stopped and looked back from the mountain side she was climbing, threatening and lamenting. The frightful spectacle appalled the stout hearts of our men; but they did what humanity required, and quickly terminated the agonies of the gory savage. They were now masters of the camp, which was a pretty little recess in the mountain, with a fine spring, and apparently safe from all invasion. Great preparations had been made to feast a large party, for it was a very proper place for a rendezvous, and for the celebration of such orgies as robbers of the desert would delight in. Several of the best horses had been killed, skinned, and cut up; for the Indians living in mountains, and only coming into the plains to rob and murder, made no other use of horses than to eat them. Large earthen vessels were on the fire, boiling and stewing the horse beef; and several baskets, containing fifty or sixty pairs of moccasins, indicated the presence, or expectation, of a considerable party. They released the boy, who had given strong evidence of the stoicism, or something else, of the savage character, in commencing his breakfast upon a horse's head as soon as he found he was not to be killed, but only tied as a prisoner. Their object accomplished, our men gathered up all the surviving horses, fifteen in number, returned upon their trail, and rejoined us at our camp in the afternoon of the same day. They had rode about one hundred miles in the pursuit and return, and all in thirty hours. The time, place, object, and numbers, considered, this expedition of Carson and Godey may be considered among the boldest and most disinterested which the annals of western adventure, so full of daring deeds, can present. Two men, in a savage desert, pursue day and night an unknown body of Indians into the defiles of an unknown mountain—attack them on sight, without counting numbers—and defeat them in an instant—and for what? To punish the robbers of the desert, and to avenge the wrongs of Mexicans whom they did not know. I repeat: it was Carson and Godey who did this—the former an *American*, born in the Boonslick county of Mis-

souri; the latter a Frenchman, born in St. Louis—and both
trained to western enterprise from early life.

From Frémont, *Report,* pp. 262–263.

Charles Preuss
Deflating the Hero

This afternoon we continue the journey and shall travel all
night until we reach water. Yesterday we stopped here to give
Godey and Kit a chance to pursue the horsethieves. But this
would require a more detailed narration than I could now
give in this heat. I have thrown a blanket over a little wormwood bush in order to have at least my head in the shade.
Two scalps from the hands of Alex Godey. Are these whites
not much worse than the Indians? The most noble Indian
takes from the killed enemy only a piece of the scalp as large
as a dollar, somewhat like the tonsure of a priest. These two
heroes, who shot the Indians creeping up on them from behind, brought along the entire scalp. The Indians are braver
in a similar situation. Before they shoot, they raise a yelling
war whoop. Kit and Alex sneaked, like cats, as close as possible. Kit shot an Indian in the back; the bullet went through
under the chest, and the Indian was able to run two hundred
feet and get behind a rock. In the meantime, Godey had
missed the other Indian, but loaded again and ran after him.
Without knowing it, he passed within a few paces of the
rock, from which the wounded Indian shot an arrow close
past Godey's ears. Turning, he first dispatched this one, and
then he shot the running Indian. Thus he was entitled to both
scalps, for according to Indian custom the scalp belongs to
the one who makes the kill. Godey rode into camp with a
yelling war cry, both scalps on a rod before him. Kit was
somewhat disgruntled because of his bad luck. To me, such
butchery is disgusting, but Frémont is in high spirits. I believe he would exchange all observations for a scalp taken by
his own hand. The woman escaped; a small boy was found

186

nibbling stoically on a horse head. *Pojutoches* is the name of
the poor chap.

From Preuss, *Exploring with Frémont*, pp. 127–128.

Charles Burdett
The Mythic Hero

As, for their intrepid boldness and stern truthfulness, the exploits and deeds of the old Danish sea-kings, have, since the
age of Canute, been justly heralded in song and story; so now
by the world-wide voice of the press, this, their descendent, as
his name proves him, is brought before the world: and as the
stern integrity of the exploits and deeds of the old Danes in
the age of Canute were heralded by song and story; so too, in
this brief and imperfect memoir, are those of one who by
name and birthright claims descent from them. The subject
of the present memoir, Christopher Carson, familiarly known
under the appellation of Kit Carson, is one of the most extraordinary men of the present era. His fame has long been
established throughout this country and Europe, as a most
skillful and intrepid hunter, trapper, guide, and pilot of the
prairies and mountains of the far West, and Indian fighter.
But his celebrity in these characters is far surpassed by that
of his individual personal traits of courage, coolness, fidelity,
kindness, honor, and friendship. The theatre of his exploits is
extended through out the whole western portion of the territory of the United States, from the Mississippi to the Pacific,
and his associates have been some of the most distinguished
men of the present age, to all of whom he has become an object of affectionate regard and marked respect. . . . As an
Indian fighter he was matchless. His rifle, when fired at a red-
skin, never failed him, and the number that fell beneath his
aim, who can tell!

From Charles Burdett, *Life of Kit Carson: The Great Western Hunter
and Guide* (Philadelphia: Porter and Coates, 1869), pp. 13–14, 382.

Kit Carson

The Man Meets the Myth

In October [1849], the train of a Mr. White was attacked by the Jicarilla Apache. He was killed and his wife and child taken prisoner. A command was organized in Taos, Leroux and Fisher as guides. When they reached Rayado, I was employed as one of the guides. We marched to where the depredation had been committed, then took their trail. I was the first man that found the camp where the murder had been committed. Found trunks that were broken open, harness cut, and everything destroyed that the Indians could not carry with them.

We followed them some ten or twelve days. It was the most difficult trail that I ever followed. As they would leave the camps, they (would break up) in numbers (of) from one to two (and travel) in different directions to meet at some appointed place. In nearly every camp we would find some of Mrs. White's clothing, which was the cause of renewed energy to continue the pursuit.

We finally came in view of the Indian Camp. I was in advance, started for their camp, calling to the men to follow. The comdg officer ordered a halt, none then would follow me. I was informed that Leroux, the principal guide, told the officer in command to halt, that the Indians wished to have a parley.

The Indians, seeing that the troops did not intend to charge on them, they commenced packing up in all haste. When the halt was ordered the comdg officer was shot; the ball passing through his coat, gauntlets that were in his pockets, shirts, and to the skin, doing no serious damage, only making him a little sick at the stomach. The gauntlets saved his life leaving to the service of his country, one (man) gallant officer.

As soon as he recovered from the shock given him by the ball, he ordered the men to charge, but the order was too late for the desired effect. There was only one Indian in the camp, he running into the river hard by was shot. In about 200 yards, pursuing the Indians, the body of Mrs. White was found, perfectly warm, had not been killed more than five minutes, shot through the heart with an arrow. She evidently knew that some one was coming to her rescue. She did not see us, but it was apparent that she was endeavoring to make her escape when she received the fatal shot.

I am certain that if the Indians had been charged immediately on our arrival, she would have been saved. The Indians did not know of our approach and perhaps, not paying any particular watch of her, she could (have) run towards us, the Indians fearing to pursue. She could not possibly have lived long for the treatment she had received from the Indians was so brutal and horrible that she could possibly last but a short period. Her life, I think, should never be regretted by her friends. She is surely far more happy in heaven, with her God, than among the friends on this earth.

I do not wish to be understood as attaching any blame to the officer in command or (the) principal guide. They acted as they thought best for the purpose of saving the life of Mrs. White. We merely differed in opinion at the time. But I have no doubt but they now can see that, if my advice had been taken, the life might have been saved, for at least a short period, of the much lamented Mrs. White.

We, however, captured all their baggage and camp equipage. Many running off without any of their clothing, and some animals. We pursued the Indians for about six miles on a level prairie. One Indian was killed and two or three Indian children taken prisoner. I have much regretted the failure of the attempt to save the life of so greatly esteemed and respected a lady.

In camp was found a book, the first of the kind I had ever seen, in which I was made a great hero, slaying Indians by the hundred and I have often thought that as Mrs. White would read the same and knowing that I lived near, she would pray for my appearance and that she might be saved. I did come but had not the power to convince those that were in command over me to pursue my plan for her rescue. They would not listen to me and they failed.

From Carson, *Kit Carson's Own Story*, edited by Grant, pp. 93-96.

LEAVING THE MOUNTAINS

Jim Beckwourth

Ashley's Farewell Address

General Ashley, having disposed of all his goods and completed his final arrangements, departed for St. Louis, taking with him nearly two hundred packs of beaver. Previous to his departure, he summoned all the men into his presence, and addressed them, as nearly as I can recollect, in the following words:

"Mountaineers and friends! When I first came to the mountains, I came a poor man. You, by your indefatigable exertions, toils, and privations, have procured me an independent fortune. With ordinary prudence in the management of what I have accumulated, I shall never want for anything. For this, my friends, I feel myself under great obligation to you. Many of you have served with me personally, and I shall always be proud to testify to the fidelity with which you have stood by me through all danger, and the friendly and brotherly feeling which you have ever, one and all, evinced toward me. For these faithful and devoted services I wish you to accept my thanks; the gratitude that I express to you springs from my heart, and will ever retain a lively hold on my feelings.

"My friends! I am now about to leave you, to take up my abode in St. Louis. Whenever any of you return thither, your first duty must be to call at my house, to talk over the scenes of peril we have encountered, and partake of the best cheer my table can afford you.

"I now wash my hands of the toils of the Rocky Mountains. Farewell, mountaineers and friends! May God bless you all!"

From James P. Beckwourth, *The Life and Adventures of James P. Beckwourth, Mountaineer, Scout, Pioneer, and Chief of the Crow Nation Indians*, Written from his own Dictation by T.D. Bonner (New York: Harper & Bros., 1856), p. 111.

Osborne Russell

A Trapper's Reflections

The ground was frozen hard in the morning and the wind blew cold from the north. . . . Here we had plenty of wood, water, meat and dry grass to sleep on, and taking everything into consideration, we thought ourselves comfortably situated—comfortably, I say, for mountaineers, not for those who never repose on anything but a bed of down or sit or recline on anything harder than silken cushions, for such would spurn the idea of a hunter talking about comfort and happiness. But experience is the best teacher, hunger good sauce, and I really think to be acquainted with misery contributes to the enjoyment of happiness, and to know one's self greatly facilitates the knowledge of mankind. One thing I often console myself with, and that is, the earth will lie as hard upon the monarch as it will upon the hunter, and I have no assurance that it will lie upon me at all. My bones may, in a few years, or perhaps days, be bleaching upon the plains in these regions, like many of my occupation, without a friend to turn even a turf upon them after a hungry wolf has finished his feast. . . .

In the year 1836 large bands of buffalo could be seen in almost every little valley on the small branches of this stream. At this time the only traces of them which could be seen were the scattered bones of those which had been killed. Their deeply indented trails which had been made in former years were overgrown with grass and weeds. The trappers often remarked to each other as they rode over these lonely plains that it was time for the white man to leave the mountains, as beaver and game had nearly disappeared.

From Russell, *Journal of a Trapper*, pp. 77–78, 124.

IV

The West as Promised Land

Come my tan-faced children,
Follow well in order, get your weapons
ready,
Have you your pistols? have you your sharp-
edged axes?
Pioneers! O pioneers!

All the past we leave behind,
We debouch upon a newer mightier world,
varied world,
Fresh and strong the world we seize, world
of labor and the march,
Pioneers! O pioneers!

—Walt Whitman

Introduction to Part IV

The pioneers' West was born in an era of enthusiasms. Steamboats, railroads, canal building were in their infancy as the opening of the trans-Mississippi West commenced, and Americans were ready for the great adventure that an age of progress seemed to herald. Religious enthusiasms too coursed through the country. Millennial religions with their prophecies of destruction and divine wrath provided one outlet for the volatile American imagination of the 1830s and 1840s; but it was an imagination that was just as apt to find expression in the boom in religious and social utopias, heavens on earth with new and visionary rules of sex, diet, economics. (And some religions would combine both doom and boom.) It was an era of political enthusiasms as well. Lansford W. Hastings, the shadowy and ambitious empire builder whose *Emigrants' Guide* would lead one party to disaster, expresses the breathless character of the age. Such expansionist politicking as Hastings' found a slogan and a moral justification in John L. O'Sullivan's phrase "Manifest Destiny," but the impetus had long anticipated the phrase. Revolution in Texas and California, and, finally, the Mexican War of 1847–48, along with the settlement with Britain over possession of Oregon, would make the destiny a fact. Pioneers along the Oregon Trail would stop on the Fourth of July to indulge in a day of elaborate pomp, circumstance, and bombastic oratory—as well as liquid refreshment.

American missionaries did as much as anyone to promote the West as promised land. Arriving in the Oregon country to preach to the Indians with that missionary zeal which was part of the age's enthusiasm, they became the first permanent white settlers. Young Narcissa Whitman and Eliza Hart Spalding, traveling west with their husbands to the Oregon mission field, would have the distinction of being the first white women to cross the Rockies. A devastating epidemic of measles was the last of a series of frictions that turned the Indians against the Whitmans and led to their massacre and the abandonment of the mission at Waiilatpu in 1847, but by then immigration to Oregon had become an established fact. Returning from the East in 1843 after his famous 3,000-mile ride to "save" Oregon for the United States—as well as plead the cause of his own mission—Whitman would join with the first large company of Oregon-bound pioneers, a convoy 1,000 strong.

Who were these pioneers? Anyone looking at their diaries and reminiscences is impressed by how often this trek across a continent was for them a second or third move. They were already children of the frontier, many of them—Missourians, Kentuckians, Illinoisans, pioneers already, or the offspring of pioneers. Some were wealthy by frontier standards—James Reed, of the Donner-Reed party, was one such. Others were of more modest means, but it took some outlay for a family to set off for Oregon or California with the object of settlement. Byron had immortalized the romantic ideal of the American frontiersman in his picture of an aged Daniel Boone surrounded by "A sylvan tribe of children of the chase" whose "free-born forest found and kept them free." Jesse Applegate, one of the leaders of the 1843 Oregon migration, looked back thirty-three years later and saw the pioneer cast in just that light, a proud and freeborn Anglo-Saxon. Francis Parkman, a young Boston Brahman in search of the great adventure among the Indians, would take stock of the pioneers in his classic *The Oregon Trail* and find them a crude and backward lot, although he would have to admit these Missourians could also strike a fine figure. Literate pioneers—and some were downright learned—might have their Byron. For the rest, there were the newspaper and the stump speaker to goad them on. There were substantial reasons for the trek as well. Economic depression, a lack of markets for their produce, and poor transportation at home made the promise of rich, free land—and possibly trade with China—weighty incentives to head west for the farmers of the Mississippi Valley. For some, resistance to slavery and the competition of a slave economy were important inducements, for others the lure of health. The Gold Rush of 1849 and subsequent gold and silver strikes drew others along the trail. The would-be miners were a more heterogeneous lot in manners, morals, and national origin than the farmers, but those who went by land to the "sundown diggings" would also contribute their toil and sometimes their lives to the trail. Whatever the reasons, when all was said and done, it was "Whoo ha! Go it, boys!" And the trek was begun.

Ahead of them lay 2,000 miles of parched and desolate country. They were bound for the rich and timbered lands of the Pacific Coast, but first they would have to cross the Great American Desert that Pike and Long had given a name to. Itineraries such as Frémont's accurate one or Hastings' tragically misinformed one, or the hastily printed Shively guide, whose typographical errors may indicate the rush to capitalize on emigration fever, could not begin to relate the hardships of the trail. Indians were occasionally seen and duly terrified the emigrants. The pressures of emigration did lead to clashes between pioneers and Indians along the western end of the Oregon Trail, but the Indians' usual motives were a little trailside graft or a bit of thievery or simple curiosity. The real dangers were cholera, dysentery, and the ever-looming winter.

There were disasters. The Donner-Reed party of 1846 followed Lansford W. Hastings' pointing finger across an untested trail. Caught in the tortuous canyons of the Wasatch, bogged down in the Utah salt flats, the emigrants would reach the Sierras too late to cross. Twelve-year-old Virginia Reed's letter shows the horrors of starvation and cannibalism of the winter bivouac. But plucky young Virginia is not one to dishearten anyone. Let the emigration come on, but "never take no cutofs and hury along as fast as you can." The later Death Valley party of '49 would make the same mistake as the Donner-Reed party in following an untested trail, and there would be other lost parties as well. But worse tragedy would come with the handcart expeditions of 1856. Mormon leaders had hit on the idea of handcarts as an efficient way to bring the poorest of their horde of European converts to the Utah Zion. The first companies, born up by religious zeal, were amazingly successful. But a desert snowstorm would catch two later parties short of their goal. Weakened with disease and hunger, 225 emigrants would die, while others would lose limbs to frostbite. Mormons were also involved in a disaster of another sort. John D. Lee, who was to be made the sole scapegoat, gives a grim account of the Mountain Meadows Massacre of 1857. Stirred up by the impending invasion of Utah by a federal army, remembering the death of their prophet Joseph Smith at the hands of a "gentile" mob, Mormons of southern Utah, with Indian help, fell upon and almost totally destroyed a band of California-bound emigrants. Of all the disasters of the trail, this remains the most terrible.

For most of the emigrants the trail's most trying test was reserved for its end. If they started the trek with a jaunty adventurousness, its conclusion would find them exhausted by sun and sickness and bad diet and anxiety. Wagons had been abandoned and animals had died and there had been dissension in almost every band. Ahead lay a treacherous raft trip down the Columbia or rugged chains of mountains. J. Goldsborough Bruff, the wise and humane Forty-niner, gives a vivid picture of what the end of the trail meant. If it had tempered some, it had broken others, and certain commentators have seen in the selfishness and brutality the trail could produce the seeds of future Western atrocities such as vigilante justice and the destruction of the peaceful California Indians.

The Mormons were the pioneer anomaly. Unlike the pioneers of Oregon and California, they had been driven west, not lured there. The mobs of Missouri and Illinois had forced them out of their successful communities, and with the murder of Joseph Smith, they turned west. They chose to settle not in the lush lands of the coast, but in the arid interior Great Basin, and there, on the edge of a dead sea, they built their Zion and their bastion. They pioneered dry farming and the extensive system of irrigation that a communal economy and rigid social hierarchy allowed them to undertake. Like the Indians of the West, they were visionaries, and this curious blend of revelation coupled with Yankee shrewdness allowed them to prosper and to become a wonder in the West. It was a must for travelers such as the scandalous scholar-adventurer Sir Richard Burton and young Mark Twain to stop in Salt Lake long enough to pay a call on the "prophet, seer, and revelator" Brigham Young, and to comment on the Peculiar People's peculiar institution of polygamy. They paused to note the curious phonetic alphabet (soon abandoned) by which the mysteries of English spelling were to be made clear to recent immigrants of German or Scandinavian stock, and finally tried to get a glimpse of the ominous Avenging Angels, of whom armchair traveler A. Conan Doyle has left such a fanciful and frightening account.

Have the pioneers left an indelible mark on our national life? Jesse A. Applegate (nephew of Jesse Applegate) in his memories of making do gives us a frontier that seems far from the waste and superabundance of today's America. Erik Erikson, however, sees a continual struggle between the pull of home and the pull of a yonder, a frontier, which he claims marks Americans to this day. Perhaps Joaquin Miller, himself a member of the great trek, comes closest to the truth for all his sentimentality: the legacy of "The Men of Forty-nine" is a memory for our time, and a test.

PROPAGANDA FOR A PROMISED LAND

Lansford W. Hastings

The Emigrants' Guide

I can not but believe, that the time is not distant, when those wild forests, trackless plains, untrodden valleys, and the unbounded ocean, will present one grand scene, of continuous improvements, universal enterprise, and unparalleled commerce: when those vast forests, shall have disappeared, before the hardy pioneer; those extensive plains, shall abound with innumerable herds, of domestic animals; those fertile valleys, shall groan under the immense weight of their abundant products: when those numerous rivers, shall team with countless steam-boats, steam-ships, ships, barques and brigs; when the entire country, will be everywhere intersected, with turnpike roads, rail-roads and canals; and when, all the vastly numerous, and rich resources, of that now, almost unknown region, will be fully and advantageously developed. To complete this picture, we may fancy to ourselves, a Boston, a

New York, a Philadelphia and a Baltimore, growing up in a day, as it were, both in Oregon and California; crowded with a vast population, and affording all the enjoyments and luxuries, of civilized life. And to this we may add, numerous churches, magnificent edifices, spacious colleges, and stupendous monuments and observatories, all of Grecian architecture, rearing their majestic heads, high in the aerial region, amid those towering pyramids of perpetual snow, looking down upon all the busy, bustling scenes, of tumultuous civilization, amid the eternal verdure of perennial spring. And in fine, we are also led to contemplate the time, as fast approaching, when the supreme darkness of ignorance, superstition, and despotism, which now, so entirely pervade many portions of those remote regions, will have fled forever, before the march of civilization, and the blazing light, of civil and religious liberty; when genuine *republicanism*, and unsophisticated *democracy*, shall be reared up, and tower aloft, even upon the now wild shores, of the great Pacific; where they shall forever stand forth, as enduring monuments, to the increasing wisdom of *man*, and the infinite kindness and protection, of an all-wise, and over-ruling *Providence*.

From Lansford W. Hastings, *The Emigrants' Guide to Oregon and California* (Cincinnati: George Conclin, 1845), pp. 151–152.

J. M. Shively

How to Make the Trek

When the emigrants start to the sun-down diggings of Oregon, they should not fancy that they are doing some great thing, and that they need military array, officers, non-commissioned officers, &c: all this is folly. They will quarrel, and try to enforce nonessential duties, till the company will divide and subdivide, the whole way to Oregon. When you start over these wide plains, let no one leave dependent on his best friend for any thing; for if you do, you will certainly have a blow-out before you get far. I would advise all young men who have no families to have nothing to do with the wagons nor stock. . . .

Those who emigrate with families, and consequently, wagons, stock, etc., cannot expect to accomplish the journey in less than four months, under the most favorable circumstances; and, in order that they be prepared in the best possible manner, first buy a light strong wagon, made of the best seasoned materials; for, if the timbers be not well seasoned, your wagon will fall to pieces when you get to the dry, arid plains of the mountains; let the bed of your wagon be made of maple if you can get it, and let the side and end boards be one wide board, without cracks; let them so project the sides and ends of the bottom of the bed as to turn off the water from the bottom. Next, let your wagon sheet be either linen or Osnaburg, well oiled or painted, and fixed to fasten well down the sides; let the bed be straight; procure wooden boxes of half or three-quarter inch pine boards, of the same convenient height, and let them fit tight in the bed of your wagon. In these boxes place your provisions, clothing, ammunition, and whatever articles you choose to take along; close the boxes by hinges or otherwise, and on them is a comfortable place for women and children to ride through the day, secure from dust or rain, and a place to sleep at night for a small family. Take as much tea, coffee, sugar and spices as you please; but above all take plenty of flour and well cured side bacon to last you through if you can. Let each man and lad be provided with five or six hickory shirts, one or two pair of buckskin pantaloons, a buckskin coat or hunting shirt, two very wide brimmed hats, wide enough to keep the mouth from the sun. For the want of such hat thousands suffer nearly all the way to Oregon, with their lips ulcerated, caused by sunburn. Take enough of coarse shoes or boots to last you through—three or four pair a-piece will be sufficient—moccasins will not protect your feet against the large plains of prickly pear along the road. However much help your wives and daughters have been to you at home, they can do but little for you here—hrdeing stock, through either dew, dust, or rain, breaking brush, swimming rivers, attacking grizzly bears or savage Indians, is all out of their line of business. All they can do, is to cook for camps, etceteras, &c.; nor need they have any wearing apparel, other than their ordinary clothing at home. . . .

All equipped, move on in companies of not less than twenty, nor more than fifty wagons together. You will leave this early, and travel in haste until you reach the Platte, for the reason that the district of country along the Kanzas has

many creeks putting into it, which are swollen to very great
depth, by the hardest rains I ever seen. . . . When you arrive
at the crossings of the Kanzas, if it be past fording, there is a
ferry there; or, if you choose, caulk and pitch some of your
wagon beds, made as before described, and you have a ferry
of your own. When you get across, it will be necessary to set
a watch at night—and this watch should be kept up nearly
the whole way—for where there are no Indians, a guard is
necessary to keep the stock out of camp. You will find your
cattle, horses and mules will often take fright at night, and run
into camp with great fury; this is no particular sign of Indians, and is an occurrence you will often witness. Form a
circle or square with your wagons at night, by running the
tongue of each hinder wagon between the hind wheel and bed
of the wagon before, alternately; chain them together, and
you have a secure breast-work against attack by Indians, as
well as a secure place to cook, sleep, &c.

Your road to the Platte passes along the north side of the
Kanzas, some distance from the river, crossing many of its
tributaries; 202 miles from the crossings of Kanzas—wood
and water any where—you will come to the river Platte. There
the whole face of nature begins to change; the earth in many
places is crested with salt—the few springs you meet with are
impregnated with mixed minerals—the pools are many of
them poisonous—and the emigrants should be careful, and
use only the water of the river; for I know of but two good
springs from the head of Blue to the north spring branches of
Sweet Water; one is at Scott's bluff on North Platte—the
other the well known Willow Springs, between the crossings
of North Platte and Sweet Water. You will have several
camps to make along this river, without wood; but there is
plenty of buffalo dung, which is a good substitute for wood.
184 miles will bring you to the forks; you keep up the South
Fork 75 miles to the crossings—(plenty of buffalo and antelope)—if it is past fording, off with some of your best wagon
beds, and in less than two hours you will have a very good
ferry boat. When you are across the river, fill your kegs with
water—for there is none fit to drink 'till you reach the North
fork, a distance of 20 miles, 143 miles up North Platte to
Fort Larima, up a valley similar to the South fork, (thousands of buffalo.) You are now through the Pawnee country,
and must look out for the Sioux; and when you get to
Larima, make as little dela ya s possible, for fear the Indians
molest you.

You are now 640 miles from Independence, and it is discouraging to tell you that you have not yet travelled one-third of the long road to Oregon.

From J. M. Shively, *Route and distances to Oregon and California, with a description of watering places, crossings, dangerous Indians . . . &c. &c . . .* (Washington: W. Greer, 1846), pp. 3-8.

FIRST WHITE WOMEN OVER THE ROCKIES

Eliza Hart Spalding

The Diary of Eliza Hart Spalding

New York, February 1, 1836
This day I have taken final leave of my dear parents' dwelling and all its inmates except dear father, who is to accompany us a few days on our journey. While I witnessed the emotions of grief on the part of my dear friends at parting with us, I was enabled in a great measure to suppress my own feelings, until after I had experienced the painful trail of separation. But I trust that it is the love of Christ which has constrained me to break away from the fond embrace of parents, brothers and sisters, and made me, not only willing, but anxious to spend and be spent in laboring to promote my Master's cause among the benighted Indians, who, though they have some idea of a Great Spirit, know nothing of His requirements, or designs respecting them. O blessed privilege to labor in the vineyard of my Saviour, and point the lost and perishing to Him, for He is the way, the truth, and the life.

From Clifford Merrill Drury, *First White Women over the Rockies* (Glendale, Calif.: Arthur H. Clark Co., 1963), Vol. 1, p. 183.

Narcissa Prentiss Whitman

The Diary of Narcissa Prentiss Whitman

[July] 27th [1836] Had quite a level route today. Came down Bear River and encamped on Tommow's [Thomas] Fork, a small branch. . . . We are still in a dangerous country but our company is large enough for safety. Our cattle endure the journey remarkably well. They are a source of great comfort to us in this land of scarcity, they supply us with sufficient milk for our tea & coffee which is indeed a luxury. We are obliged to shoe some of them on account of sore feet. Have seen no buffalo since we left Rendezvous. Had no game of any kind except a few messes of Antelope which John's Father gave us. We have plenty of dry Buffalo meat which we purchased of the Indians & dry it is for me. I can scarcely eat it, it appears so filthy, but it will keep us alive, and we ought to be thankful for it.

We have had a few meals of fresh fish also, which relished well. Have the prospect of obtaining plenty in one or two weeks more. Found no berries. Neither have I found any of Ma's bread. (Girls do not waste the bread, if you know how well I should relish even the dryest morsal you would save every piece carefully.) Do not think I regret coming. No, far from it. I would not go back for a world. I am contented and happy notwithstanding I sometimes get very hungry and weary.

Have six weeks steady journeying before us. Will the Lord give me patience to endure it. Feel sometime as if it was a long time to be traveling. Long for rest, but must not murmur. . . .

[August] 13th Sat. . . . We have come at least fifteen miles & have had the worst route in all the journey for the cart, we might have had a better one, but for being misled by some of the company who started out before their leaders. It was two o'clock before we came into camp. They are preparing to cross the Snake River.

The river is divided by two islands into three branches & is fordable. The packs are placed upon the top of the highest horses & in this way crossed without wetting. Two of the tallest horses were selected to carry Mrs. S & myself over. Mr McLeod gave me his & rode mine. The last branch we rode as much as a half mile in crossing & against the current too which made it hard for the horses the water being up to their sides. Husband had considerable difficulty in crossing the cart. Both the cart & the mules were capsized in the water and the mules entangled in the harness. They would have drowned, but for a desperate struggle to get them ashore. Then after putting two of the strongest horses before the cart & two men swimming behind to steady it, they succeeded in getting it over. I once thought that crossing streams would be the most dreadful part of the journey. I can now cross the most difficult stream without the least fear. . . .

From Drury, *First White Women over the Rockies*, Vol. 1, pp. 74–75, 85–86.

WHO THEY WERE

Jesse Applegate

A Pioneer's View

But the picture, in its grandeur, its wonderful mingling of colors and distinctness of detail, is forgotten in contemplation of the singular people who give it life and animation. No other race of men with means at their command would undertake so great a journey—none save those could successfully perform it with no previous preparation, relying only on the fertility of their invention to devise the means to overcome each danger and difficulty as it arose. They have undertaken to perform, with slow moving oxen, a journey of two thousand miles. The way lies over trackless wastes, wide and deep rivers, rugged and lofty mountains, and is beset with hostile savages. Yet, whether it were a deep river with no tree upon its banks, a rugged defile where even a loose horse could not pass, a hill too steep for him to climb, or a threatened attack of an enemy, they are always found ready and equal to the occasion, and always conquerors. May we not call them men of destiny? They are people changed in no essential particulars from their ancestors, who have followed closely on the footsteps of the receding savage, from the Atlantic sea-board to the valley of the Mississippi.

From Jesse Applegate, "A Day With the Cow Column," in *Transactions of the Fourth Annual Reunion of the Oregon Pioneer Association for 1876* (Salem, Ore.: 1877). Reprinted in Maude A. Rucker, *The Oregon Trail and Some of Its Blazers* (New York: Walter Neale, 1930), pp. 76–77.

Francis Parkman
A Boston Intellectual's View

We were late in breaking up our camp on the following morning, and scarcely had we ridden a mile when we saw, far in advance of us, drawn against the horizon, a line of objects stretching at regular intervals along the level edge of the prairie. An intervening swell soon hid them from sight, until, ascending it a quarter of an hour after, we saw close before us the emigrant caravan, with its heavy white wagons creeping on in their slow procession, and a large drove of cattle following behind. Half a dozen yellow-visaged Missourians, mounted on horseback, were cursing and shouting among them; their lank angular proportions, enveloped in brown homespun, evidently cut and adjusted by the hands of a domestic female tailor. As we approached, they greeted us with the polished salutation: "How are ye, boys? Are ye for Oregon or California?"

As we pushed rapidly past the wagons, children's faces were thrust out from the white coverings to look at us; while the careworn, thin-featured matron, or the buxom girl, seated in front, suspended the knitting on which most of them were engaged to stare at us with wondering curiosity. By the side of each wagon stalked the proprietor, urging on his patient oxen, who shouldered heavily along, inch by inch, on their interminable journey. It was easy to see that fear and dissension prevailed among them; some of the men—but these, with one exception, were bachelors—looked wistfully upon us as we rode lightly and swiftly past, and then impatiently at their own lumbering wagons and heavy-gaited oxen. Others were unwilling to advance at all, until the party they had left behind should have rejoined them. Many were murmuring against the leader they had chosen, and wished to depose him; and this discontent was fomented by some ambitious spirits, who had hopes of succeeding in his place. The women were divided between regrets for the homes they had left and apprehension of the deserts and the savages before them.

From Francis Parkman, *The California and Oregon Trail* (New York: George P. Putnam, 1849), pp. 72–73.

The Hon. John Minto

A Pioneer Woman

She could read with difficulty, but rarely attempted it in the prime of her life, when her children claimed her attention. Later in life it was a source of great comfort to her, the New Testament being her favorite book.

Of course she was versed and very expert in the domestic labors, which in her early life involved cooking, dairy management, spinning, weaving, and soap boiling, as well as the rougher preparation of flax and hemp for the spinning process. She brought with her across the plains a flax wheel, flax seed, bobbins, weaving sleighs, etc., necessary for the manufacture of clothing. She had another acquirement not usual to womanhood. She could use a rifle with effect. As a frontiersman's daughter, left in early girlhood her father's housekeeper by the death of her mother, she had been taught the use of the rifle, but she never affected it in mannish ways. I have heard her tell of killing a hawk, in defense of her poultry, but never saw her handle the rifle we called her gun, although I did overhear her asking where it and its accompaniments were, one night when the camp was in alarm, expecting a night attack from the Indians.

From a eulogy by the Hon. John Minto of Nancy Irwin Morrison in Bethenia A. Owens-Adair, *Dr. Owens-Adair. Some of Her Life Experiences* (Portland, Oregon: Mann & Beach, Printers, 1906?), pp. 180–181.

ON THE TRAIL

Bernard DeVoto
Alkali Country

They were in the sagebrush and alkali country now. Thornton observed "a remarkable peculiarity in the atmosphere, which made it impossible for me to judge with any tolerable degree of accuracy as to the distance of objects." He meant that sun and thin air made distances deceptive. Thornton speaks of the "white efflorescence of salts" but does not set down how it makes one squint, how it glares like snowfields under the sun, how it glimmers and quivers in the snaky heat waves and fills the plain with lakes that quench no thirst. The sage smelled like turpentine to Thornton; it smells so still but he might have mentioned its rich, aromatic perfume in the dawn wind, the pungency it gives to campfires, and the tang that grilled meat picks up from it. Mirages flickered across the plain in that terrible sun and he noted them with scholarly glosses on the Specter of the Brocken and the distant prospect of Dover Castle. They were another strangeness in a country that grew increasingly to look like Hell. On the horizon they thrust up peaks or pinewoods or blue New England ponds, where there were no mountains and no lakes or forests, either.

For some time now the emigrants had been making their nightly fires out of what Thornton calls the dried excrement of the bison. Children ranged out from the plodding train to collect it in gunnysacks, and it made red coals for cooking in long, shallow pits. Moreover, they were well into the arid country, in a summer drier than usual. The never-ending wind of the plains blew up dust from the wheels in twisting columns that merged and overspread the whole column in a fog and canopy that moved with it. It "filled the lungs, mouth, nose, ears, and hair, and so covered the face that it was sometimes difficult to recognize each other," and "we suffered from this almost insupportable flying sand or dust for weeks if not for months together." Thornton had neglected to supply himself with goggles which "can be purchased in the United States for thirty-seven and a half cents"; near Independence Rock he would have given fifty dollars for a pair. Right. The tortured eyes tortured the brain. The immense sun, the endless wind, and the gritty, smothering, inescapable dust reddened and swelled the eyes, granulated the lids, inflamed the sockets. The excited nerves make shadows horrible—such shadows as there are—and produce illusions of color and shape. The illusions are not less disturbing in that the heat mirage distorts size and pattern so that a healthy eye may see a jack rabbit as a buffalo at a hundred yards or a clump of sage at half a mile as mounted Indians charging down. Trachoma was endemic among the Indians, a number of emigrants went blind, and few came through this country without eye trouble of some sort. The medicine chests held solutions of zinc sulphate, which was proper, but simple boric would have been better for it was alkali that made the dust corrosive. It was also driven into the skin by the daily wind. Most of the movers were burned black now; the rest were burned a less comfortable, fiery red; their cheeks peeled and their lips were deeply cracked by what is, after all, simple lye. . . . When you read of cowboys buying canned tomatoes and laving their cheeks with juice, you observe an elementary reaction in household chemistry.

The hundredth meridian of west longitude, a geographer's symbol of the true beginning of the West (meaning the point beyond which the annual rainfall is less than twenty inches), strikes the Platte near the present town of Cozad, Nebraska, well east of the Forks. The trail up the North Platte moved mainly west or a little north of west to a point opposite the present town of Ogallala, Nebraska, where it took the due northwest bearing it would maintain for hundreds of miles. And between the sites of the present towns of Broadwater and Bridgeport, Nebraska, it struck the Wildcat Range. Here the scattered buttes and bluffs which had been growing common for a considerable distance became a true badlands. The scenery was spectacular but spectacle was only a momentary solace to the emigrants, who had now reached truly tough go-

ing—with cumulative fatigue, anxiety, and mental conflict
piling up. In early June the desert still had the miraculous
brief carpeting of flowers that delights travelers to this day,
but it was late June when the emigrants got there, a wholly
different season, and '46 was now a drouth year. The slow
pitch of the continent which they had been climbing toward
the ridgepole so slowly that they seldom felt the grade here
lost its monotony. The gentle hills that bordered the valley of
the Platte, known as the Coast of Nebraska, suddenly became
eroded monstrosities. Jail Rock, Courthouse Rock, Chimney
Rock, Scott's Bluff, were individual items in creation's slag
heap that had got named, but the whole formation was fantastic. The learned Thornton called it Tadmor of the Desert and
sketched a gift-book description of ruined cities, defeated armies, and ancient peoples put to the sword. (But exactly opposite Chimney Rock one of his hubs locked for want of
grease and he had to interrupt his poetry.) Even such prosy
diarists as Joel Palmer and Overton Johnson were startled
into rhetoric, the realistic Bryant saw Scott's Bluff against the
green and purple murk of an oncoming storm and committed
phrases like "ruins of some vast city erected by a race of
giants, contemporaries of the Megatherii and the Icthyosau-
rii," and Frémont composed a resounding *tutti* passage about
"The City of the Desert." . . .

   The grade was steep now, and once they were in the badlands the trail narrowed and was frequently precipitous.
Crazy gullies and canyons cut every which way, and whoever
gave up in anger and tried to find better going elsewhere only
found worse troubles. The ropes came out and wagons had to
be lowered by manpower down a steep pitch or hauled up over
the vertical side of a gully or between immense boulders—while
those not working sat and swore in level dust and intolerable
sun, far from water. When they moved, the dry axles added a
torturing shriek to the split-reed soprano of the wheels and
the scrape of tires on stone or rubble. Dry air had shrunk the
wheels, too, and without warning tires rolled off or spokes
pulled out and the wagon stalled. The same brittleness might
make a wagon tongue break, which was disastrous unless a
spare pole had been slung beneath the bed, and the violent
stresses sometimes snapped the metal hounds, the side bars
which connected tongue and fore-carriage to reach and hind-
carriage. Sometimes the ropes broke at a cliff or pulled off
the snubbing post, and a wagon crashed. Or crazed oxen capsized one, or defective workmanship or cheap material could

stand no more and the thing went to pieces like the one-hoss shay. Sometimes half a wrecked wagon could be converted by desert blacksmithing into a cart; sometimes a sound wagon had to be so converted because some of the oxen had died. In any event, here was where the "ancient claw-footed tables, well waxed and rubbed" which Parkman saw began to litter the trail, along with "massive bureaus of carved oak." Parkman speculated on these "relics of ancestral prosperity in the colonial time." He saw them as cherished through successive periods of decline (from the grace of the seaboard) as their owners took them across the Alleghenies to Kentucky and on to Illinois or Missouri. . . . Allocate the abandoned household goods as another stress of desert travel, for something of personality and spiritual heritage died when they had to go. Their owners were in the grip of necessity. The desert beat triphammer blows, an overmastering realism, on one's soul, and something permanent came from that forging, the old confirmed forever or the new, frequently the lesser, formed forever.

In sun and dust they went on, the daily distance shortening and no end to the country ahead. They were not yet to South Pass, not yet halfway to the Pacific! Horses and oxen bloated from foul water; many of them died. Their hooves swelled and festered. Even the soundest grew gaunt as the grass diminished: sparse along the upper Platte at any time, it had failed quickly in the drouth summer and many trains had cropped it before our travelers. Men got as gaunt as their stock, in this country, and alkali water was just as bad for them. They saw suddenly that food was limited, and there was an anxious computation of the days ahead, with Hastings' or Frémont's or Parker's mile-by-mile itineraries reckoned over and over. Add to the increasing strain the altitude making the nerves tauter. Though the violent sun was hot and the dust pall breathless, there were suddenly viciously cold days too and all nights were cold. Water froze in the pails—and you remembered how early snow fell in the mountains that were still so far ahead. . . . It was the triphammer, the test itself. You stood it. You went on. Sometimes, in the badlands, you remembered the moist coolness by the elm-bordered pool in the east pasture back home, and how the brook sang falling into it.

From Bernard DeVoto, *The Year of Decision: 1846* (Boston: Little, Brown and Co., 1943), pp. 163–167.

Edmund Ellsworth

A Handcart Company

Soon after, a letter came from Prest. Brigham Young, wishing the hand-cart enterprise to commence this season. My heart was in the enterprise, and I showed the Saints that if it was a hard journey, they were called upon to pass through; and even should they lay down their bodies in the earth before they arrived in Great Salt Lake City, it was better to do so, keeping the commandment of God in gathering, than to wear out their bodies in the old countries; and so the Saints in that country feel now. . . .

I am persuaded that if there had been no wagons for such people, there would have been none sick, or weak, but that their faith would have been strong in the name of the Lord. . . . Consequently I have had to labor with the people incessantly to keep faith in them, to keep them away from the wagons, by showing them that there was honor attached to pulling hand-carts into the valley; by saying, I have walked 1300 miles, old and decrepit as I am, with these crooked legs of mine, and there is honor in that, brethren and sisters, far more than in having to be carried in a wagon to the valleys of the mountains, and thus I believe that I have stimulated those that otherwise would have gone into the wagons. . . .

When we came to the large streams that had to be crossed, such as the Platte, it seemed almost too much for human nature, for men, women, and children to wade through a broad stream nearly two feet deep, and some would tremble at it; but the most, as they were requested, boldly entered and went through freely, not caring for the poor gentile sneaks who were watching them on the banks.

The brethren and sisters felt wonderfully tender of the children, on the commencement of the journey, asking, "What shall we do with them?" and saying that they must get into the wagons. I said let them stick by the hand-carts, and pull-off their heavy shoes so that they can go along light footed, and the journey will be accomplished easily by them; their feet will become tough, and the mothers who will take this course will see the utility of it before the journey is accomplished;

but some were so tender of their children that they nearly killed them by keeping on their heavy stockings and shoes.

Their feet became blistered, and they were soon so crippled as not to be able to walk, only with great pain, and when they could not use their shoes any longer they had to take them off, and their little feet were tender and sore, and altogether unfit to tread on the pebbles and prickly pears scattered on the roads in the latter portion of our journey. If they had been permitted to go barefooted at first, their feet would have been hardened and inured to the journey, and been better prepared for the rough roads in the mountains. . . .

And night after night, day after day, week after week, men, women, and children have come into camp and said that they called upon the Lord, when they felt that they would be obliged to leave their hand-carts behind, and strength seemed to come upon them immediately, and they were enabled to pull their carts up to the camp ground. The Lord has been with us and preserved and blessed us and our teams, and joyful does this company come into these valleys of the mountains; . . .

From Edmund Ellsworth, "Account of His Mission," *The Deseret News* (Salt Lake City), October 8, 1856.

John A. Stone

Crossing the Plains

Air—Caroline of Edinburgh

Come all you Californians, I pray ope wide your ears,
If you are going across the Plains, with snotty mules or steers;
Remember beans before you start, likewise dried beef and ham.
Beware of ven'son, d——n the stuff, it's ofentimes a ram.

You must buy two revolvers, a bowie-knife and belt,

Says you, "Old feller, now stand off, or I will have your
    pelt;"
The greenhorn looks around about, but not a soul can see,
Says he, "There's not a man in town, but what's afraid of
    me."

You shouldn't shave, but cultivate your down, and let it
    grow,
So when you do return, 'twill be as soft and white as snow;
Your lovely Jane will be surprised, your ma'll begin to cook;
The greenhorn to his mother'll say, "How savage I must
    look!"

"How do you like it overland?" his mother she will say,
"All right, excepting cooking, then the devil is to pay;
For some won't cook, and others can't, and then it's curse
    and damn,
The coffee-pot's begun to leak, so has the frying-pan."

It's always jaw about the teams, and how we ought to do,
All hands get mad, and each one says, "I own as much as
    you."
One of them says, "I'll buy or sell, I'm d——d if I care
    which;"
Another says, "Let's buy him out, the lousy son of a b——.'"

You calculate on sixty days to take you over the Plains,
But there you lack for bread and meat, for coffee and for
    brains;
Your sixty days are a hundred or more, your grub you've got
    to divide,
Your steers and mules are alkalied, so foot it—you cannot
    ride.

You have to stand a watch at night, to keep the Indians off,
About sundown some heads will ache, and some begin to
    cough;
To be deprived of health we know is always very hard,
Though every night some one is sick, to get rid of standing
    guard.

Your canteens, they should be well filled, with poison alkali,
So when you get tired of traveling, you can cramp all up and
    die;

The best thing in the world to keep your bowels loose and
free,
Is fight and quarrel among yourselves, and seldom if ever
agree.

There's not a log to make a seat, along the river Platte,
So when you eat, you've got to stand, or sit down square and
flat;
It's fun to cook with buffalo wood, take some that's newly
born,
If I knew once what I know now, I'd a gone around the
Horn!

The desert's nearly death on corns, while walking in the sand,
And drive a jackass by the tail, it's d——n this overland;
I'd rather ride a raft at sea, and then at once be lost,
Says Bill, "Let's leave this poor old mule, we can't get him
across."

The ladies have the hardest time, that emigrate by land,
For when they cook with buffalo wood, they often burn a
hand;
And then they jaw their husbands round, get mad and spill
the tea,
Wish to the Lord they'd be taken down with a turn of the
di-a-ree.

When you arrive at Placerville, or Sacramento City,
You've nothing in the world to eat, no money—what a pity!
Your striped pants are all worn out, which causes people to
laugh
When they see you gaping round the town like a great big
brindle calf.

You're lazy, poor, and all broke down, such hardships you
endure;
The post-office at Sacramento all such men will cure;
You'll find a line from ma' and pa', and one from lovely Sal,
If that don't physic you every mail, you never will get well.

From [John A Stone], *Put's Original California Songster*, 4th ed. (1855;
San Francisco: D.E. Appleton & Co., 1868), pp. 13–15.

DISASTERS

Virginia Reed

The Donner-Reed Tragedy

[I]t was a rain[in]g then in the Vallies and snowing on the mon-
tains   so we went on that way 3 or 4 days till we come to the
big mountain or the Callifornia Mountain   the snow then was
about 3 feet deep   thare was some wagons thare   thay said
thay had atempted to croos and could not. well we thought
we would try it   so we started and thay started again with
those wagons   the snow was then up to the mules side   the
farther we went up the deeper the snow got   so the wagons
could not go   so thay pack thare oxens and started with us
carring a child a piece and driving the oxens in snow up to
thare wast . . . well the Weman were all so tirder caring there
Children that thay could not go over that night   so we made a
fire and got something to eat & ma spred down a bufalo robe
& we all laid down on it & spred somthing over us & ma sit up
by the fire & it snowed one foot on top of the bed   so we got
up in the morning & the snow was so deep we could not go
over & we had to go back to the cabin & build more cabins &
stay thar all winter without Pa   we had not the first thing to
eat   Ma maid arrangements for some cattel giving 2 for 1 in
callifornia   we seldom thot of bread for we had not any since
I [remember] & the cattel was so poor they could not git up
when thay laid down   we stoped thare the 4th of November &
staid till March and what we had to eat i cant hardley tell
you & we had that man & Indians to feed to   well thay started
over a foot and had to come back   so thay made snowshoes
and started again & it come on a storm & thay had to come
back   it would snow 10 days before it would stop   thay wated
till it stoped & started again   I was a going with them & I took
sick & could not go.   thare was 15 started & thare was 7 got
throw   5 weman & 2 men   it come a storme and thay lost the

road & got out of provisions & the ones that got throwe had
to eat them that Died . . . o Mary I would cry and wish I
had what you all wasted Eliza had to go to Mr. Graves cabin
& we staid at Mr Breen thay had meat all the time. & we had
to kill littel cash the dog & eat him we ate his entrails and
feet & hide & evry thing about him o my Dear Cousin you
dont now what trubel is yet. Many a time we had on the last
thing a cooking and did not now wher the next would come
from but there was awl weis some way provided there was 15
in the cabon we was in and half of us had to lay a bed all the
time thare was 10 starved to death then we was hadly abel
to walk . . .

  . . . O Mary I have not rote you half of the truble we
have had but I have rote you anuf to let you now that you
dont now what truble is but thank god we have all got throw
and the onely family that did not eat human flesh we have
left everything but i dont cair for that we have got throw
with our lives but Dont let this letter dish[e]a[r]ten anybody
never take no cutofs and hury along as fast as you can.

From Virginia Reed's letter to her cousin, appendix to George R.
Stewart, *Ordeal by Hunger*, 2nd ed. (Boston: Houghton Mifflin Co.,
1960), pp. 357–360.

John Chislett

A Handcart Disaster

Being surrounded by snow a foot deep, out of provisions,
many of our people sick, and our cattle dying, it was decided
that we should remain in our present camp until the supply-
train reached us. It was also resolved in council that Captain
Willie with one man should go in search of the supply-train
and apprise its leader of our condition, and hasten him to our
help. When this was done we settled down and made our
camp as comfortable as we could. As Captain Willie and his
companion left for the West, many a heart was lifted in
prayer for their success and speedy return. They were absent
three days—three days which I shall never forget. The scanty
allowance of hard bread and poor beef, distributed as de-

scribed, was mostly consumed the first day by the hungry, ravenous, famished souls.

We killed more cattle and issued the meat; but, eating it without bread, did not satisfy hunger, and to those who were suffering from dysentery it did more harm than good. This terrible disease increased rapidly amongst us during these three days, and several died from exhaustion. Before we renewed our journey the camp became so offensive and filthy that words would fail to describe its condition, and even common decency forbids the attempt. Suffice it to say that all the disgusting scenes which the reader might imagine would certainly not equal the terrible reality. It was enough to make the heavens weep. The recollection of it unmans me even now—those three days! During that time I visited the sick, the widows whose husbands died in serving them, and the aged who could not help themselves, to know for myself where to dispense the few articles that had been placed in my charge for distribution. Such craving hunger I never saw before, and may God in his mercy spare me the sight again.

As I was seen giving these things to the most needy, crowds of famished men and women surrounded me and begged for bread! Men whom I had known all the way from Liverpool, who had been true as steel in every stage of our journey, who in their homes in England and Scotland had never known want; men who by honest labour had sustained themselves and their families, and saved enough to cross the Atlantic and traverse the United States, whose hearts were cast in too great a mould to descend to a mean act or brook dishonour; such men as these came to me and begged bread. I felt humbled to the dust for my race and nation, and I hardly know which feeling was strongest at that time, pity for our condition, or malediction on the fates that so humbled the proud Anglo-Saxon nature.

Song of the Handcart Expedition

> Brigham said that they was martyrs,
> My father and my mother;
> For they died a shovin' 'andcarts,
> A-pullin' me an' brother.
>
> Yes, they died a shovin' 'and carts,
> An' they died most awful slow;
> Oh they died travellin' to Zion,
> An' was buried in the snow.

John Chislett's narrative from T. B. H. Stenhouse, *The Rocky Mountain Saints* (New York: D. Appleton and Co., 1873), pp. 323–324. Handcart Song from Claton S. Rice, *Songs of "The Mormon Way"* (Billings, Mont.: Billings Book Binding and Printing Co., 1930), p. 25.

John D. Lee

By Their Own Kind: The Mountain Meadows Massacre

It was then noon, or a little after.

I found that the emigrants were strongly fortified; their wagons were chained to each other in a circle. In the center was a rifle-pit, large enough to contain the entire company. This had served to shield them from the constant fire of their enemy, which had been poured into them from both sides of the valley, from a rocky range that served as a breastwork for their assailants. The valley at this point was not more than five hundred yards wide, and the emigrants had their camp near the center of the valley. On the east and west there was a low range of rugged, rocky mountains, affording a splendid place for the protection of the Indians and Mormons, and leaving them in comparative safety while they fired upon the emigrants. The valley at this place runs nearly due north and south.

When I entered the corral, I found the emigrants engaged in burying two men of note among them, who had died but a short time before from the effect of wounds received by them from the Indians at the time of the first attack on Tuesday morning. They wrapped the bodies up in buffalo robes, and buried them in a grave inside the corral. I was then told by some of the men that seven men were killed and seventeen others were wounded at the first attack made by the Indians, and that three of the wounded men had since died, making ten of their number killed during the siege.

As I entered the fortifications, men, women and children gathered around me in wild consternation. Some felt that the time of their happy deliverance had come, while others, though in deep distress, and all in tears, looked upon me with doubt, distrust and terror. My feelings at this time may be imagined (but I doubt the power of man being equal to even imagine how wretched I felt.) . . . I delivered my message and told the people that they must put their arms in the wagon, so as not to arouse the animosity of the Indians. I ordered the children and wounded, some clothing and the arms, to be put into the wagons. Their guns were mostly Kentucky rifles of the muzzle-loading style. Their ammunition was about all gone—I do not think there were twenty loads left in their whole camp. If the emigrants had had a good supply of ammunition they never would have surrendered, and I do not think we could have captured them without great loss, for they were brave men and very resolute and determined.

Just as the wagons were loaded, Dan. McFarland came riding into the corral and said that Major Higbee had ordered great haste to be made, for he was afraid that the Indians would return and renew the attack before he could get the emigrants to a place of safety.

I hurried up the people and started the wagons off towards Cedar City. As we went out of the corral I ordered the wagons to turn to the left, so as to leave the troops to the right of us. Dan. McFarland rode before the women and led them right up to the troops, where they still stood in open order as I left them. The women and larger children were walking ahead, as directed, and the men following them. The foremost man was about fifty yards behind the hindmost woman.

The women and children were hurried right on by the

troops. When the men came up they cheered the soldiers as if they believed that they were acting honestly. Higbee then gave the orders for his men to form in single file and take their places as ordered before, that is, at the right of the emigrants.

I saw this much, but about this time our wagons passed out of sight of the troops, over the hill. I had disobeyed orders in part by turning off as I did, for I was anxious to be out of sight of the bloody deed that I knew was to follow. I knew that I had much to do yet that was of a cruel and unnatural character. It was my duty, with the two drivers, to kill the sick and wounded who were in the wagons, and to do so when we heard the guns of the troops fire. I was walking between the wagons; the horses were going in a fast walk, and we were fully half a mile from Major Higbee and his men, when we heard the firing. As we heard the guns, I ordered a halt and we proceeded to do our part. . . .

McMurdy and Knight stopped their teams at once, for they were ordered by Higbee, the same as I was, to help kill all the sick and wounded who were in the wagons, and to do it as soon as they heard the guns of the troops. McMurdy was in front; his wagon was mostly loaded with the arms and small children. McMurdy and Knight got out of their wagons; each one had a rifle. McMurdy went up to Knight's wagon, where the sick and wounded were, and raising his rifle to his shoulder, said: *"O Lord, my God, receive their spirits, it is for thy Kingdom that I do this."* He then shot a man who was lying with his head on another man's breast; the ball killed both men.

I also went up to the wagon, intending to do my part of the killing. I drew my pistol and cocked it, but somehow it went off prematurely, and I shot McMurdy across the thigh, my pistol ball cutting his buck-skin pants. McMurdy turned to me and said:

"Brother Lee, keep cool, you are excited; you came very near killing me. Keep cool, there is no reason for being excited."

Knight then shot a man with his rifle; he shot the man in the head. Knight also brained a boy that was about fourteen years old. The boy came running up to our wagons, and Knight struck him on the head with the butt end of his gun, and crushed his skull. By this time many Indians reached our wagons, and all of the sick and wounded were killed almost instantly. I saw an Indian from Cedar City, called Joe, run up to the wagon and catch a man by the hair, and raise his head up and look into his face; the man shut his eyes, and Joe shot him in the head. . . .

Just after the wounded were all killed I saw a girl, some ten or eleven years old, running towards us, from the direction where the troops had attacked the main body of emigrants; she was covered with blood. An Indian shot her before she got within sixty yards of us. That was the last person that I saw killed on that occasion. . . .

After all the parties were dead, I ordered Knight to drive out on one side, and throw out the dead bodies. He did so, and threw them out of his wagon at a place about one hundred yards from the road, and then came back to where I was standing. I then ordered Knight and McMurdy to take the children that were saved alive, (sixteen was the number, some say seventeen, I say sixteen,) and drive on to Hamblin's ranch. . . .

After the wagons, with the children, had started for Hamblin's ranch, I turned and walked back to where the brethren were. . . .

While going back to the brethren, I passed the bodies of several women. In one place I saw six or seven bodies near each other; they were stripped perfectly naked, and all of their clothing was torn from their bodies by the Indians.

I walked along the line where the emigrants had been killed, and saw many bodies lying dead and naked on the field, near by where the women lay. I saw ten children; they had been killed close to each other; they were from ten to sixteen years of age. The bodies of the women and children were scattered along the ground for quite a distance before I came to where the men were killed.

I do not know how many were killed, but I thought then that there were some fifteen women, about ten children, and about forty men killed, but the statement of others that I have since talked with about the massacre, makes me think there were fully one hundred and ten killed that day on the Mountain Meadows, and the ten who had died in the corral, and young Aden killed by Stewart at Richards' Spring, would make the total number one hundred and twenty-one.

When I reached the place where the dead men lay, I was told how the orders had been obeyed. Major Higbee said,

"The boys have acted admirably, they took good aim, and all of the d——d Gentiles but two or three fell at the *first fire*."

From John D. Lee, *Mormonism Unveiled; or The Life and Confessions of the Late Mormon Bishop, John D. Lee* (St. Louis and New York: Bryan, Brand & Co., W. H. Stelle & Co., 1877), pp. 239–244 *passim.*

END OF THE TRAIL

Sarah Royce

Out of the Desert

From near midnight, on through the small hours, it appeared necessary to stop more frequently, for both man and beast were sadly weary, and craved frequent nourishment. Soon after midnight we finished the last bit of meat we had; but there was still enough of the biscuit, rice and dried fruit to give us two or three more little baits. The waning moon now gave us a little melancholy light, showing still the bodies of dead cattle, and the forms of forsaken wagons as our grim way-marks. In one or two instances they had been left in the very middle of the road; and we had to turn out into the untracked sand to pass them. Soon we came upon a scene of wreck that surpassed anything preceding it. As we neared it, we wondered at the size of the wagons, which, in the dim light, looked tall as houses, against the sky. Coming to them, we found three or four of them to be of the make that the early Mississippi Valley emigrants used to call "Prairie Schooners": having deep beds, with projecting backs and high tops. One of them was specially immense, and, useless as we felt it to be to spend time in examining these warning relics of those who had gone before us, curiosity led us to lift the front curtain, which hung down, and by the light of our candle that we had again lit, look in. There from the strong,

high bows, hung several sides of well cured bacon, much better in quality than that we had finished, at our last resting
place. So we had but a short interval in which to say we were
destitute of meat, for, though, warned by all we saw not to
add a useless pound to our load, we thought it wise to take a
little, to eke out our scanty supply of food. And, as to the
young men, who had so rarely, since they joined us, had a bit
of meat they could call their own, they were very glad to
bear the burden of a few pounds of bacon slung over their
shoulders.

After this little episode, the only cheering incident for
many hours, we turned to look at what lay round these monster wagons. It would be impossible to describe the motley
collection of things of various sorts, strewed all about. The
greater part of the materials, however, were pasteboard
boxes, some complete, but most of them broken, and pieces
of wrapping paper still creased, partially in the form of packages. But the most prominent objects were two or three, perhaps more, very beautifully finished trunks of various sizes,
some of them standing open, their pretty trays lying on the
ground, and all rifled of their contents; save that occasionally
a few pamphlets, or, here and there, a book remained in the
corners. We concluded that this must have been a company
of merchants hauling a load of goods to California, that some
of their animals had given out, and, fearing the rest would
they had packed such things as they could, and had fled for
their lives toward the river. There was only one thing,
(besides the few pounds of bacon) that, in all these varied
heaps of things, many of which, in civilized scenes, would
have been valuable, I thought worth picking up. That was a
little book, bound in cloth and illustrated with a number of
small engravings. Its title was "Little Ella." I thought it would
please Mary, so I put it in my pocket. It was an easily carried
souvenir of the desert; and more than one pair of young eyes
learned to read its pages in after years.

Morning was now approaching, and we hoped, when full
daylight came, to see some signs of the river. But, for two or
three weary hours after sunrise nothing of the kind appeared.
The last of the water had been given to the cattle before daylight. When the sun was up we gave them the remainder of
their hay, took a little breakfast and pressed forward. For a
long time not a word was spoken save occasionally to the
cattle. I had again, unconsciously, got in advance; my eyes
scanning the horizon to catch the first glimpse of any change;

though I had no definite idea in my mind what first to expect. But now there was surely something. Was it a cloud? It was very low at first and I feared it might evaporate as the sun warmed it. But it became rather more distinct and a little higher. I paused, and stood till the team came up. Then walking beside it I asked my husband what he thought that low dark line could be. "I think," he said, "it must be the timber on Carson River." Again we were silent and for a while I watched anxiously the heads of the two leading cattle. They were rather unusually fine animals, often showing considerable intelligence, and so faithful had they been, through so many trying scenes, I could not help feeling a sort of attachment to them; and I pitied them, as I observed how low their heads drooped as they pressed their shoulders so resolutely and yet so wearily against the bows. Another glance at the horizon. Surely there was now visible a little unevenness in the top of that dark line, as though it might indeed be trees. "How far off do you think that is now?" I said. "About five or six miles I guess," was the reply. At that moment the white-faced leader raised his head, stretched forward his nose and uttered a low "Moo-o-oo." I was startled fearing it was the sign for him to fall, exhausted. "What is the matter with him?" I said. "I think he smells the water" was the answer. "How can he at such a distance?" As I spoke, the other leader raised his head, stretched out his nose, and uttered the same sound. The hinder cattle seemed to catch the idea, whatever it was; they all somewhat increased their pace, and from that time, showed renewed animation.

But we had yet many weary steps to take, and noon had passed before we stood in the shade of those longed-for trees, beside the Carson River. As soon as the yokes were removed the oxen walked into the stream, and stood a few moments, apparently enjoying its coolness, then drank as they chose, came out, and soon found feed that satisfied them for the present, though at this point it was not abundant. The remainder of that day was spent in much needed rest. The next day we did not travel many miles, for our team showed decided signs of weakness, and the sand became deeper as we advanced, binding the wheels so as to make hauling very hard. We had conquered the desert.

From Sarah Royce, *A Frontier Lady*, edited by Ralph Henry Gabriel (New Haven: Yale University Press, 1932), pp. 53–57.

J. Goldsborough Bruff

Over the Sierra Nevada

                                    Oct. 3rd, 1849
We moved up very early to ascend the Pass.—up a steep,
hard, sandy, and winding road.—The first ascent, of about ¼
m. was gentle enough, and brought us to a sort of valley,
with a spring and rill in it, and some bunch grass.—Here was
a grave, thus enscribed:—

> "Jno. A. Dawson,
> St. Louis, Mo.
> Died Oct. 1st 1849,
> from eating a poisonous
> root at the spring."

The spring just below—In this 1st valley, or platform, above
the base, saw numerous ox-camps, breaking up & moving forward.—Some had a team of 10 yoke of oxen.
   Mein course to the top, N.W. In the 2d valley, or rise,
more ox trains moving ahead.—Reached the foot of the big
hill,—a long and smooth sand drag, pretty steep ascent.—10
dead oxen marked the trail. Across the road, about midway
up this hill, lay an ox on his knees,—dying, and covered with
old gum coat, by his compassionate owner; but it was un-
availing,—the dust was suffocating, and the animals and
wheels went over him, in the haste and trouble of the steep
ascent. The first wagon of my train, which reach'd the top of
the Pass, displayed the Stars and stripes, to encourage those
in the rear. Found many ox-wagons on the flat top of the
Pass. Temp. on top the Pass, at 8 A.M. 44°. . . .
   While on top of the Pass, looking down the En side, at the
bustle, and directing the ascent, I was amused.—
   I thought the infirm ox in the road below, occupied rather
an unenviable position.—In the centre of a very broad,
sandy, and dusty road, men urging their heavy ox-trains up
the steep hill, with lashes, imprecations, & shouts, some riding
up on horses & mules, and clouds of blinding dust & sand flying. There rode up, an old man, on a jaded horse; a matress

covered the horse, the sick man astride and laying over on his breast, with a coverlid thrown over him, and a corner trailing in the dust, he looked pale and haggard; had his arms around the neck of the old horse. He was afflicted with the flux and scurvy. Another unfortunate followed him, on a mule, enveloped in a blue blanket, and barely able to retain his seat; he had the fever and ague. Some small boys, not over 10 years of age, were leading jaded animals up. Women were seen, with the trains, occupied at chocking the wheels, while the oxen were allowed to blow, on the ascent. A man had a baby in his arms, and in midst of the thick dust, was urging up his team. Some wagons had as many as 12 yoke of oxen in them. One wagon, with women and children in it, when near the summit, became uncoupled, and down hill it ran,—*stern-foremost*, with great rapidity.—The women and children screamed, men shouted, and with all the rest of the fuss, there was a great clamor. A dead ox, a short distance in front of a heavy team, and men by them, brought up the backing out vehicle, most luckily without damage to any one.

Oct. 25, 1849

It is a queer sight now, to observe the straggling emigrants coming up and going in. Wagons of every kind, oxen, horses, mules, bulls, cows, and people,—men, women, & children, all packed. A few weeks travel has wrought a great change in their circumstances.—Many of them I recognized as old acquaintances as far back as Pittsburgh, and all along our western waters, and over the long travel. Large companies, fine animals, a great amount of provisions & stores, and smiling faces; were now a scattered, broken, selfish stragglers, dusty in faces and dress, and many of them, thin with hunger, as well as anxiety.

Oct. 26, 1849

One of the travellers informed me, that about 30 miles back, he saw an old man, on the road-side, nearly dead with the scurvy, his *friends* had ejected him from their wagon, and abandoned him to his fate. A Dutchman here, was discarding some tools, which he could carry no further: and was busy breaking saws, &c. over a stump. Willis asked him why he done so, he replied; "Dey cosht me plendy of money, in St. Louis, and nopoty shall have de goot of dem, py Got!"

From J. Goldsborough Bruff, *Gold Rush, The Journals, Drawings and Other Papers of J. Goldsborough Bruff*, edited by G. W. Read and R. Gaines (New York: Columbia University Press, 1944), pp. 202–203; 240–242.

Jesse A. Applegate

Making Do in the Wilderness

In the course of three or four years after we began life in the wilderness of Salt Creek, we had pastures fenced, grain fields and gardens, small apple and peach orchards grown from the seed, comfortable log cabins, barns and other outhouses, and quite a number of cattle, horses, hogs and chickens. We had grain growing and in store and vegetables in abundance. But many things we had always considered necessities were not to be had in the wilderness where we lived. Coffee, tea and sugar were among these. Having an abundance of good milk, a family could do without tea or coffee, and even an old coffee drinker could be consoled by a beverage made of roasted peas crushed in a buckskin bag. Habitual tea drinkers soon became reconciled to what was generally known as "mountain tea," a drink of a spicy odor made from the leaves of a vine found growing in the woods. Many people came to prefer this tea to any tea of commerce. But there was no substitute for sugar. Father and mother had been in the sugar camps in Kentucky and Tennessee and knew how sugar was made from the sap of maple trees. Our spring was surrounded by a grove of maple trees and though the sap was not as sweet as the sap of the sugar maple, they believed sugar could be made from it. The experiment was tried and proved a success and we had plenty of sugar, syrup and candy.

The problem of clothing had become a very serious one. Tents and wagon covers that had seen service from the Mississippi to the Columbia would shed rain when made into coats. Lined with the remnants of some old woolen garment, and with a broad collar and cuffs faced with fur of beaver or otter, these garments would pass without criticism even though their ancestry might be known to everyone by indelible marks that had been on the tent or wagon cover. It would be a mistake to suppose that this was regarded as humiliating or a real hardship. Necessity demanded very plain attire among the first settlers and custom sanctioned it. Buttons for these coats were made of pewter cast in moulds cut in blocks of soapstone. Old spoons, plates and other pieces of worn-out table ware that had seen service around many a camp fire on the plains and in the mountains were used for this purpose. Garments were sometimes made of the wool-like hair of the wolf. At the time we lived in Missouri there were in almost every family a spinning wheel and loom and the women folks spun yarn of wool and cotton out of which they knit socks, stockings and other garments, and wove cloth for family use. They were therefore skilled manufacturers on a small scale in this line, but for some years after settling in Oregon there was neither cotton nor wool to be had, and the hair of the wolf was resorted to as a substitute for wool. It was a poor substitute, for the yarn spun of it was coarse and not strong. Another drawback was that wolves could not be fleeced so long as they were alive, and a man could not kill a sufficient number of the kind that were common, the prairie wolf or coyote, in a month, to make a sweater. The yarn spun from the fleece of one pelt would hardly make a pair of slippers for a child. . . . The skin of the deer, when tanned by the Indians, was soft and pliable and was used by the pioneers. Coats and trousers of buckskin were worn, but I confess to a prejudice against buckskin. I have seen poems printed on this material, notably "The Days of 49," and I have heard men talk of having written on it to hold against parties notoriously slow to meet their obligations, for a note written on buckskin will not wear out. In a climate where it never rains a buckskin suit might be comfortable, but in the climate where we lived, such garments often proved wretchedly disagreeable. . . .

From Jesse A. Applegate, *Recollections of My Boyhood* (Roseburg, Ore.: Press of the Review Publishing Co., 1914). Reprinted in Rucker, *The Oregon Trail and Some of its Blazers*, pp. 192–194.

A MORMON ZION

Wilford Woodruff

Brigham Young's Vision

On the 24th [of July, 1847] I drove my carriage, with
President Young lying on a bed in it, into the open valley,
the rest of the company following. When we came out of the
cañon into full view of the valley, I turned the side of my
carriage around, open to the west, and President Young arose
from his bed and took a survey of the country. While gazing
on the scene before us, he was enwrapped in vision for
several minutes. He had seen the valley before in vision, and
upon this occasion he saw the future glory of Zion and of Is-
rael, as they would be, planted in the valleys of these mountains. When the vision had passed, he said: "It is enough.
This is the right place. Drive on." So I drove to the encampment already formed by those who had come along in advance of us.

From a speech by Wilford Woodruff in *The Utah Pioneers. Celebra-
tion of the Entrance of the Pioneers into Great Salt Lake Valley.
Thirty-Third Anniversary, July 24, 1880* (Salt Lake City: Deseret News
Printing and Publishing Establishment, 1880), p. 23.

Harriet Young

A Pioneer Woman's View

I shall skip to July 24 on account of my health. the fatigue of
traveling togather with my labor prevented my keeping a
daily journal this day we arrived in the valley of the great

White Views of the Indian. ". . . a race of men equal in form and grace (if not superior) to the finest beau ideal ever dreamed of by the Greeks." ("Hunters of San Francisco Bay" by Ludovik Choris) COURTESY OF THE CALIFORNIA HISTORICAL SOCIETY

A Delegation of Pima Chiefs. "We can not hold our own with the white men as we are. We only ask an even chance to live as other men live. We ask to be recognized as men." COURTESY OF THE CALIFORNIA HISTORICAL SOCIETY

White Views of the Indian. "But the Indians are children. . . . Any band of schoolboys, from ten to fifteen years of age, are quite as capable of ruling their appetites, devising and upholding public policy, constituting and conducting a state or community, as an average Indian tribe." (From *The Wasp*, 1885) COURTESY OF THE BANCROFT LIBRARY

Albert Bierstadt, Sunrise in Yosemite. "As I reflected on the immensity of territory . . . as yet altogether unknown to white people, and perhaps abounding in the magnificent works of God, I felt an excitement of soul such as I had never before experienced." (Edgar Allan Poe, *The Journal of Julius Rodman*) COURTESY OF KENNEDY GALLERIES

Timothy O'Sullivan, Desert Sandhills near Sink of Carson, Nevada. "I would not . . . give a pinch of snuff for the whole territory. I wish to God we did not own it." (Senator George McDuffie, 1843) COURTESY OF THE LIBRARY OF CONGRESS

Europeans' First View of the American Bison. "They have very long beards, like goats, and when they are running, they throw their heads back with the beard dragging on the ground." (Pedro de Castañeda, 1540) COURTESY OF HUNTINGTON LIBRARY

Treed by a Bear. "It now seemed to me that all the beasts of the neighbourhood had made a league to distroy me . . . the succession of curious adventures wore the impression on my mind of inchantment . . . I thought it might be a dream." (Meriwether Lewis, 1805). Drawing from Sgt. Patrick Gass's *Journals of the Lewis and Clark Expedition.* COURTESY OF THE NEW YORK PUBLIC LIBRARY

Alfred Jacob Miller, Trappers. "You cannot pay a free trapper a greater compliment, than to persuade him you have mistaken him for an Indian brave." (Washington Irving, 1837) COURTESY OF WALTERS ART GALLERY

Alfred Jacob Miller, Trapper's Bride. ". . . many happy matrimonial connections were formed by means of a dower of glittering beads and scarlet cloth." (Sir William Drummond Stewart, 1854) COURTESY OF WALTERS ART GALLERY

"The Rocky Mountains," by Currier and Ives. "The way lies over trackless wastes, wide and deep rivers, rugged and lofty mountains, and is beset with hostile savages. Yet . . . they are always found ready and equal to the occasion, and always conquerors." COURTESY OF THE BANCROFT LIBRARY

"Your steers and mules are alkalied, so foot it—you cannot ride." (Drawing by J. Goldsborough Bruff) COURTESY OF THE BANCROFT LIBRARY

The mules got through, but the owner ain't— by a long ways.

The Desert

Polygamous Mormon Elders. The Federal Government's view.
COURTESY OF THE UTAH STATE HISTORICAL SOCIETY

Mormon Polygamy. A genteel view. (*Harper's Weekly*, 1857)
COURTESY OF THE UTAH STATE HISTORICAL SOCIETY

Billy the Kid. "There's many a man with a face fine and fair/ Who starts out in life with a chance to be square,/ But just like poor Billy he wanders astray/ And loses his life in the very same way." (*The Ballad of Billy the Kid*) COURTESY OF ARIZONA PIONEERS' HISTORICAL SOCIETY

XIT Cowboys. Cowboy "appearance is striking . . . and picturesque too, with their jingling spurs, the big revolvers stuck in their belts, and bright silk handkerchiefs knotted loosely round their necks over the open collars of flannel shirts." (Theodore Roosevelt, 1888)

Buck Taylor, the First King of the Cowboys. "But no dinginess of travel or shabbiness of attire could tarnish the splendor that radiated from his youth and strength." (Owen Wister, *The Virginian*)

"Then ho! Boys, ho! Who to California go,/ For the mountains cold are covered with gold,/ Along the banks of the Sacramento./ Ho! Ho! Away we go digging up gold in Francisco." (*The Californian*) COURTESY OF BANCROFT LIBRARY

Railroad Poster.
COURTESY OF THE HUNTINGTON LIBRARY

FREE LANDS

— AND —

LOW PRICE

RAILROAD LANDS!

MORE THAN

40,000,000 ACRES

OF EACH,

Open for immediate settlement, along the line of the

NORTHERN PACIFIC R. R.

IN

MINNESOTA, *NORTH DAKOTA,* MONTANA, IDAHO, *WASHINGTON* AND *OREGON*

FARMS AND HOMES FOR ALL

The Great Northwest is being rapidly settled by intelligent and enterprising communities, yet there is ample room for hundreds of thousands of families to build prosperous homes in this region by developing its rich natural resources into profitable industries.

**An Exceptionally Healthful Climate,
Large Areas of Fertile Agricultural Lands
and Extensive Grazing Ranges,
Vast Forests of Fine Timber and
Rich Mining Districts**

INVITE OCCUPANCY AND DEVELOPMENT.

SUPERB TRAIN SERVICE!

"HO! FOR THE WEST! . . . the population now pouring into this region consists of shrewd and well-informed farmers who *know* what is good. . . ." (From a railroad broadside) Photographs by Solomon D. Butcher.

In Nebraska, it was the ranchers who put up the fences and the homesteaders who cut them. Photograph by Solomon D. Butcher.
COURTESY OF THE NEBRASKA STATE HISTORICAL SOCIETY

"We are the whirlwinds that winnow the West—/ We scatter the wicked like straw!/ We are the nemeses, never at rest—/ We are Justice, and Right, and the Law!" (Margaret Ashmun, *The Vigilantes*) COURTESY OF THE CALIFORNIA HISTORICAL SOCIETY

Buffalo Bill's Wild West. COURTESY OF THE LIBRARY OF CONGRESS

Buffalo Bill in Oakland. COURTESY OF THE OAKLAND TRIBUNE

New Pioneers for a Second Frontier. "He compared temporal wealth to stock in the great bank of God, which paid such rich dividends of grace daily, hourly. . . ." COURTESY OF THE BANCROFT LIBRARY

Railroad Poster.

The Triumph of the Machine. "Gentlemen: After using one of your Southwick Horse Power Hay Presses for four years, during which time I baled as high as forty tons in one day, and averaged 32 tons per day, I sold the press for $225.00, and last year I bought one of your 18 x 22 Sandwich Belt Presses. . . . This is a money-making outfit and I cheerfully recommend it to any one who wants to bale hay for a profit. Yours truly, Prosper Bergon." COURTESY OF FRANK BERGON

The Last Trek. "Cars pulled up beside the road, engine heads off, tires mended. Cars limping along 66 like wounded things, panting and struggling." Photograph by Dorothea Lange. COURTESY OF THE LIBRARY OF CONGRESS

Come to where
the flavor is.

Marlboro

You get a lot to like
with a Marlboro.

Salt Lake my feelings were such as I cannot describe every thing looked gloomy and I felt heart sick.

From the "Diary of Lorenzo Dow Young" (in part kept by Harriet Young), edited by Levi Edgar Young and Robert J. Dwyer, *The Utah Historical Quarterly* 14 (January, April, July, October, 1946), p. 163.

Thomas Bullock
Building the Kingdom

After crossing a small creek twenty-one times in about five miles, and between mountains near a mile high, on making a sudden bend in the road, you come in full view of the great Salt Lake, and a valley about thirty miles by twenty; although there is very little timber to be seen, you will be sure to say, "Thank God I am at home at last." On this spot that I am now talking to you about, the pioneers arrived on Thursday, the 23d July last, at five p.m.; the next morning removed to the spot where the city will be built; at noon consecrated and dedicated the place to the Lord; the same afternoon four ploughs were tearing up the ground; next day the brethren had planted five acres with potatoes, and irrigated all the land at night. Sunday was a day of rest—a day of rejoicing before the Lord; His spirit was poured out, and peace dwelt in the "valley of the mountains." The first Sabbath in the valley where a city is to be built unto the Lord, by a holy people, will long be remembered by that little band of pioneers who cried "Hosanna to the Lamb of God."

During the short space between 23d July and 26th August, we ploughed and planted about eighty-four acres with corn, potatoes, beans, buck wheat, turnips, and a variety of garden sauce. We irrigated all the land; surveyed and laid out a city, with streets running east and west, north and south, in blocks of ten acres, divided into eight lots of one and a quarter acre each; the streets will be eight rods wide, having two side walks of twenty feet each, to be ornamented with shade trees; all the houses are to be built twenty feet in the rear of their fence, with flower gardens in the front; one block is reserved for a temple, and three for public grounds, promenades—

having fountains of the purest water running through each square, and ornamented with every thing delightful. One thing wonderful for all you Englishmen to know, is, you have no land to buy nor sell; no lawyers wanting to make out titles, conveyances, stamps, or parchment. We have found a place where the land is acknowledged to belong unto the Lord, and the Saints being his people, are entitled to as much as they can plant, take care of, and will sustain their families with food.

From a letter from Thomas Bullock in *The Latter-Day Saints' Millennial Star*, No. 8, Vol. 10 (Liverpool: Edited and Published by Orson Pratt, April 15, 1848), pp. 117–118.

Sir Richard Burton

A British Adventurer on Mormon Marriage

It will, I suppose, be necessary to supply a popular view of the "peculiar institution," at once the bane and blessing of Mormonism—plurality. I approach the subject with a feeling of despair, so conflicting are opinions concerning it, and so difficult is it to naturalise in Europe the customs of Asia, Africa, and America, or to reconcile the habits of the 19th century A.D. with those of 1900 B.C. A return to the patriarchal ages, we have seen, has its disadvantages. . . .

The "chaste and plural marriage" being once legalised, finds a multitude of supporters. The anti-Mormons declare that it is at once fornication and adultery—a sin which absorbs all others. The Mormons point triumphantly to the austere morals of their community, their superior freedom from maladive influences, and the absence of that uncleanness and licentiousness which distinguish the cities of the civilised world. They boast that if it be an evil they have at least chosen the lesser evil, that they practise openly as a virtue what others do secretly as a sin—how full is society of these latent Mormons!—that their plurality has abolished the necessity of concubinage, cryptogamy, contubernium, celibacy, *mariages du treizième arrondissement*, with their terrible consequences, infanticide, and so forth; that they have removed their ways from those "whose end is bitter as wormwood, and sharp as a two-edged sword." Like its sister institution Slavery, the birth and growth of a similar age, Polygamy acquires *vim* by abuse and detraction; the more turpitude is heaped upon it, the brighter and more glorious it appears to its votaries. . . .

. . . At Gt. S. L. City there is a gloom, like that which the late Professor H. H. Wilson described as being cast by the invading Moslem over the innocent gaiety of the primitive Hindu. The choice egotism of the heart called Love, that is to say, the propensity elevated by sentiment, and not undirected by reason, subsides into a calm and unimpassioned domestic attachment: romance and reverence are transferred, with the true Mormon concentration, from Love and Liberty to Religion and the Church. The consent of the first wife to a rival is seldom refused, and a *ménage à trois*, in the Mormon sense of the phrase, is fatal to the development of that tender tie which must be confined to two. In its stead there is household comfort, affection, circumspect friendship, and domestic discipline. Womanhood is not petted and spoiled as in the Eastern States; the inevitable cyclical revolution, indeed, has rather placed her below par, where, however, I believe her to be happier than when set upon an uncomfortable and unnatural eminence. . . .

For the attachment of the women of the Saints to the doctrine of plurality there are many reasons. The Mormon prophets have expended all their arts upon this end, well knowing that without the hearty co-operation of mothers and wives, sisters and daughters, no institution can live long. They have bribed them with promises of Paradise—they have subjugated them with threats of annihilation. With them once a Mormon always a Mormon. . . . The Mormon household has been described by its enemies as a hell of envy, hatred, and malice—a den of murder and suicide. The same has been said of the Moslem harem. Both, I believe, suffer from the assertions of prejudice or ignorance. The temper of the new is so far superior to that of the old country, that, incredible as the statement may appear, rival wives do dwell together in amity; and to quote the proverb "the more the merrier." . . .

From Richard F. Burton, *The City of the Saints* (London: Green and Roberts, 1861), pp. 517, 519–520, 523–524 *passim.*

C

Mark Twain

On Polygamy and Brigham Young

Our stay in Salt Lake City amounted to only two days, and
therefore we had no time to make the customary inquisition
into the workings of polygamy and get up the usual statistics
and deductions preparatory to calling the attention of the nation at large once more to the matter. I had the will to do it.
With the gushing self-sufficiency of youth I was feverish to
plunge in headlong and achieve a great reform here—until I
saw the Mormon women. Then I was touched. My heart was
wiser than my head. It warmed toward these poor, ungainly,
and pathetically "homely" creatures, and as I turned to hide
the generous moisture in my eyes, I said, "No—the man that
marries one of them has done an act of Christian charity
which entitles him to the kindly applause of mankind, not
their harsh censure—and the man that marries sixty of them
has done a deed of open-handed generosity so sublime that
the nations should stand uncovered in his presence and worship in silence.

The second day, we made the acquaintance of Mr. Street
(since deceased) and put on white shirts and went and paid a
state visit to the king. He seemed a quiet, kindly, easy-man-
nered, dignified, self-possessed old gentleman of fifty-five or
sixty, and had a gentle craft in his eye that probably belonged there. He was very simply dressed and was just taking
off a straw hat as we entered. He talked about Utah, and the
Indians, and Nevada, and general American matters and
questions, with our secretary and certain government officials
who came with us. But he never paid any attention to me,
notwithstanding I made several attempts to "draw him out"
on federal politics and his high handed attitude toward
Congress. I thought some of the things I said were rather fine.
But he merely looked around at me, at distant intervals,
something as I have seen a benignant old cat look around to
see which kitten was meddling with her tail. By and by I sub-
sided into an indignant silence, and so sat until the end, hot

and flushed, and execrating him in my heart for an ignorant savage. But he was calm. His conversation with those gentlemen flowed on as sweetly and peacefully and musically as any summer brook. When the audience was ended and we were retiring from the presence, he put his hand on my head, beamed down on me in an admiring way and said to my brother:

"Ah—your child, I presume? Boy, or girl?"

From Clemens, *Roughing It*, pp. 117-118, 112-113.

Sir Arthur Conan Doyle

Paradise as a Police State

To express an unorthodox opinion was a dangerous matter in those days in the Land of the Saints.

Yes, a dangerous matter—so dangerous that even the most saintly dared only whisper their religious opinions with bated breath, lest something which fell from their lips might be misconstrued, and bring down a swift retribution upon them. The victims of persecution had now turned persecutors on their own account, and persecutors of the most terrible description. Not the Inquisition of Seville, nor the German Vehmgericht, nor the Secret Societies of Italy, were ever able to put a more formidable machinery in motion than that which cast a cloud over the State of Utah.

Its invisibility, and the mystery which was attached to it, made this organization doubly terrible. It appeared to be omniscient and omnipotent, and yet was neither seen nor heard. The man who held out against the Church vanished away, and none knew whither he had gone or what had befallen him. His wife and his children awaited him at home, but no father ever returned to tell them how he had fared at the hands of his secret judges. A rash word or a hasty act was followed by annihilation, and yet none knew what the nature might be of this terrible power which was suspended over them. No wonder that men went about in fear and trembling, and that even in the heart of the wilderness they dared not whisper the doubts which oppressed them.

At first this vague and terrible power was exercised only upon the recalcitrants who, having embraced the Mormon faith, wished afterwards to pervert or to abandon it. Soon however, it took a wider range. The supply of adult women was running short, and polygamy without a female population on which to draw was a barren doctrine indeed. Strange rumours began to be bandied about—rumours of murdered immigrants and rifled camps in regions where Indians had never been seen. Fresh women appeared in the harems of the Elders—women who pined and wept, and bore upon their faces the traces of unextinguishable horror. Belated wanderers upon the mountains spoke of gangs of armed men masked, stealthy, and noiseless, who flitted by them in the darkness. These tales and rumours took substance and shape and were corroborated and re-corroborated, until they resolved themselves into a definite name. To this day, in the lonely ranches of the West, the name of the Danite Band, or the Avenging Angels, is a sinister and an ill-omened one.

Fuller knowledge of the organization which produced such terrible results served to increase rather than to lessen the horror which it inspired in the minds of men. None knew who belonged to this ruthless society. The names of the participators in the deeds of blood and violence done under the name of religion were kept profoundly secret. The very friend to whom you communicated your misgivings as to the Prophet and his mission might be one of those who would come forth at night with fire and sword to exact a terrible reparation. Hence every man feared his neighbour, and none spoke of the things which were nearest his heart.

From Arthur Conan Doyle, *A Study in Scarlet* (1887; London: Ward, Lock, Bowdon, and Co., 1892), pp. 149–151.

LOOKING BACK

Erik H. Erikson

The Frontier and the American Identity

The frontier, of course, remained the decisive influence which served to establish in the American identity the extreme polarization which characterizes it. The original polarity was the cultivation of the sedentary and migratory poles. For the same families, the same mothers, were forced to prepare men and women who would take root in the community life and the gradual class stratification of the new villages and towns and at the same time to prepare these children for the possible physical hardships of homesteading on the frontiers. Towns, too, developed their sedentary existence and oriented their inward life to work bench and writing desk, fireplace and altar, while through them, on the roads and rails, strangers passed bragging of God knows what greener pastures. You had either to follow—or to stay behind and brag louder. The point is that the call of the frontier, the temptation to move on, forced those who stayed to become defensively sedentary, and defensively proud. In a world which developed the slogan, "If you can see your neighbor's chimney, it is time to move on," mothers had to raise sons and daughters who would be determined to ignore the call of the frontier—but who would go with equal determination once they were forced or chose to go. When they became too old, however, there was no choosing, and they remained to support the most sectarian, the most standardized adhesiveness. I think that it was the fear of becoming too old to choose which gave old age and death a bad name in this country. (Only recently have old couples found a solution, the national trailer system, which permits them to settle down to perpetual traveling and to die on wheels.)

236

From Erik H. Erikson, *Childhood and Society,* 2nd ed. (New York: W. W. Norton & Co., 1963), pp. 293–294.

Joaquin Miller

The Men of Forty-nine

> Yea, I remember! The still tears
> that o'er uncoffin'd faces fell!
> The final, silent, sad farewell!
> God! these are with me all the years!
> They shall be with me ever. I
> Shall not forget. I hold a trust.
> They are part of my existence. When
> Swift down the shining iron track
> You sweep, and fields of corn flash back,
> And herds of lowing steers move by,
> And men laugh loud, in mute mistrust,
> I turn to other days, to men
> Who made a pathway with their dust.

Naples, 1874

From Joaquin Miller, *The Complete Poetical Works of Joaquin Miller* (San Francisco: The Whitaker & Ray Co., 1897), pp. 185–186.

V

The Wild West

*... there was a message returned to us by
our frontier that the outlaw is worth more
than the sheriff.*

—Norman Mailer

*Then enter, boys; cheerly, boys, enter and
 rest;
You know how we live, boys, and die in the
 west;
 Oho, boys!—oho, boys!—oho!*

—George Pope Morris

The Wild West

Introduction to Part V

Here is the West as chaos, the missing half of the East's soul: the lawless country of gunfighters, rustlers, claim jumpers, con men, treasure seekers, outlaws, and gamblers—or so it appears through the veil of legend. Gold, cattle, and silver spawned boomtowns in harsh regions ignored by the first pioneers. Restless and reckless energy left over from the Civil War seemed to find a place in new societies that were removed from the laws and institutions of the East. The Wild West reached its height in the 1870s and quickly merged into the last phase of Western settlement. By the early 1890s, a well-known newspaper correspondent, Richard Harding Davis, could mock it as the "Mild West," and only a few more years passed before this most recent of Western eras and regions became affectionately remembered as the "Old West." Romance and nostalgia have come to blur our perception of its fleeting workaday world. At the center of its economy and ethics and ceremonies were the worlds of the prospector and the cowboy, as grueling and brief as any in Western history.

The rush for gold in the 1850s gave reality to the sixteenth-century fantasy of the West as El Dorado. Soon almost half of the world's yearly gold supply was coming out of California. Among the most vivid accounts of life in the early mining camps are the letters that Louise Amelia Knapp Smith Clappe published in *The Pioneer* under the pseudonym "Dame Shirley." While she wrote of those who had reached the mines along the North Fork of the Feather River, Dr. Jacob D.B. Stillman, the founder of the first hospital in Sacramento, observed those who were broken before reaching the mines. "I can think of but very few men," he wrote, "whom I would advise to come to California." An unusual addition to the Gold Rush literature is the recently published journal of William Perkins, who settled as a merchant in Sonora where the southern mines attracted Chileans, Sonorans, Peruvians, Californios, French, Basques, and other "foreigners," and where a significant number of the population were women. Drawn to the Latins he met, Perkins eventually moved to South America, where he married and spent the rest of his life in Argentina. Other gold and silver strikes were made along Cherry Creek in Colorado Territory, the Gila River in Arizona Territory, and the northern territories of Montana, Idaho, and Washington. Soon miners were scurrying all over the West. The richest strike was the $400 million Nevada Comstock Lode, where Mark Twain discovered that the way to real riches in the West might be through speculation but not through hard work. The individual prospector working with a pick or sluice box was soon replaced by the engineers and laborers of corporate ventures as stope and hard-rock mining became fullblown industries.

Nearly as brief as the era of the prospector was the heyday of the cowboy. It began with the Long Trail drives after the Civil War and ended with the Big Die-up of 1886–1887 when overstocked grazing land and blizzards combined with plummeting prices, barbed wire, and new strains of stock to toll the end of the open range. The first cowboy memoirs were by Charlie Siringo, and the best were transposed into a novel by Andy Adams, who reacted to the mythical creature being created in the Roosevelt-Wister-Remington tradition. Despite Owen Wister's claim that cowboys were "Saxon boys of picked courage," their mode of life and lingo were adapted from the *vaqueros*; and Mexican cowboys, along with ex-slaves like James Cape, formed a good number of those hired boys who drove cattle from Texas up the Chisholm Trail to Kansas railheads or up the Goodnight-Loving Trail to the cattle country of Wyoming and Montana.

A phenomenon of this era was the boomtown. The gradual transition from agricultural communities to urban settlements was skipped, and towns were wrenched into existence. Abilene was the first Kansas cowtown to spring up when J. G. McCoy picked it in 1867 as the place where a cattle trail from Texas should meet a railroad line to the East. Abilene was followed by Ellsworth, Wichita, Dodge City, and other shipping points that now evoke rowdy images of the Wild West shared with mining boomtowns such as Deadwood and Hangtown and Tombstone. Beginning in the 1850s, Western vigilantes rose up in communities where law was absent or considered ineffective. Vigilantism, as a tradition, has no apparent European or English models; its roots are strictly American, but its most famous defender and popularizer was Professor Thomas J. Dimsdale, an Oxford-educated Englishman, who became the first editor of the Montana *Post* and the first appointed superintendent of public instruction in the new territory. Other forms of group violence that are connected to the cattle culture, such as the Lincoln County and Johnson County wars, have become staples of the horse opera. Less publicized is how often miners' greed, translated into patriotism, fostered violence against "those who aren't like us." In 1874, Lieutenant Colonel George Custer's reported discovery of gold in the Black Hills of Dakota brought swarms of miners into land reserved for the Sioux and led to the eventual clash between troopers and Crazy Horse. In California, violence against "greasers" was the main offshoot of the Foreign Miners' Tax; and the massacre of Chinese in the Colorado coal mines of Rock Springs in 1885 set off a rash of anti-Chinese incidents throughout the West.

Although Western history is riddled with violence, Howard Mumford Jones and others point out that there is little evidence that violent crime in Western cowtowns was greater than in Eastern cities, or that there were more lynchings, gun duels, and other acts of bloodletting in the West than in the South during the years after the Civil War. Stephen Crane warned readers that "travellers tumbling over each other in their haste to trumpet the radical differences between Eastern and Western life have created a generally wrong opinion. . . . It is this fact which has kept the sweeping march of the West from being chronicled in any particularly true manner." The West had become an escape valve for fantasies of chaos, a complete reversal of the myths and ethos most Americans said they were living by. The Gold Rush knocked the dour work ethic into a cocked hat when it seemed that a man just by *luck* could become a millionaire overnight, and whether he was a criminal or a saint made no difference. Response in the East to mining camps was generally condescending (or frightened) until Bret Harte portrayed them as lovable places where "the greatest scamp had a Raphael face." While Californians gave "The Luck of Roaring Camp" a chilly reception, Easterners sent Harte letters of approval, and *The Atlantic* offered enormous amounts of money for similar stories. The chaotic West had become acceptable as a national morality play. Dime novels and Buffalo Bill's "Wild West" fostered scenes of the West as a bloody arena where forces of good and evil waged battle day and night. The West still was not being taken on its own terms. As Thomas Dimsdale and Dame Shirley tell us, moral distinctions between right and wrong in the West could not be defined easily in terms of the popular image of the sheriff versus the outlaw. The leader of a Montana gang of road agents was Sheriff Plummer, and members of the Committee of Vigilance in Indian Bar were themselves ringleaders of the riotous "Moguls." Ben Thompson and John Wesley Hardin, perhaps the West's most murderous gunslingers, both had brief careers as appointed lawmen.

What kept the worlds of the miner and the cowboy from anarchic disorder was a set of unwritten rules that had little to do with normal legal processes. The cowboy on a trail drive was subservient to the group and the herd. Stern trail bosses and stiff punishments for breaking the code insured that the drive was a cooperative effort. Miners quickly established rules for making and protecting a claim and for the fair use of running water. Accounts of self-ruled mining camps underscore the degree to which unwritten agreements were honored. Yet the figure who is least representative of this picture of the actual Wild West has become its most representative character: the solitary gunslinger. Usually, he was neither cowboy nor miner, and he shared little sense of the fair play or honesty that Owen Wister attributed to his mythical gunfighting cowboy; "the actual prototype of the gun for hire," Bernard DeVoto wrote, "was a repulsive psychopath like anyone who carried a submachine gun for Al Capone." A marginal figure of the West with an inflated reputation, the gunslinger assumed his mythical role as the tough, free individualist at a time when all America, including the West, was watching mining industries, logging companies, farming factories, engineering firms, and speculating corporations rolling across the mild, wild West.

THE CODE OF THE WEST

Ramon F. Adams

Cowboy Wisdom

The bigger the mouth the better it looks when shut
A little hoss is soon curried
A pat on the back don't cure saddle galls
There ain't much paw and beller to a cowboy
A full house divided don't win no pots
A wink's as good as a nod to a blind mule
Brains in the head saves blisters on the feet
Only a fool argues with a skunk, a mule, or a cook
You never know the luck of a lousy calf
Man's the only animal that can be skinned more'n once
The man that always straddles the fence usually has a sore
    crotch
Polishin' your pants on saddle leather don't make you a rider
It's the man that's the cowhand, not the outfit he wears
Success is the size of the hole a man leaves after he dies
The wilder the colt, the better the hoss
Kickin' never gets you nowhere, 'less'n you're a mule
A loose hoss is always lookin' for new pastures
A cow outfit's never better than its hosses
You can judge a man by the hoss he rides
Another man's life don't make no soft pillow at night
A change of pasture sometimes makes the calf fatter
Any hoss's tail kin ketch cockleburs
Montana for bronc riders and hoss thieves, Texas for ropers
    and rustlers
If the saddle creaks, it's not paid for

245

There ain't no hoss that can't be rode,
  There ain't no man that can't be throwed
Tossin' your rope before buildin' a loop don't ketch the calf
It's sometimes safer to pull your freight than pull your gun
Faint heart never filled a flush
Nobody ever drowned himself in sweat
Never call a man a liar because he knows more'n you do

From Ramon F. Adams, *Western Words: A Dictionary of the American West* (Norman: University of Oklahoma Press, 1968), pp. vii–355 *passim.*

Owen Wister

When You Call Me That, *Smile!*

I left that company growing confidential over their leering stories, and I sought the saloon. It was very quiet and orderly. Beer in quart bottles at a dollar I had never met before, but saving its price, I found no complaint to make of it. Through folding doors I passed from the bar proper with its bottles and elk head back to the hall with its various tables. I saw a man sliding cards from a case, and across the table from him another man laying counters down. Near by was a second dealer pulling cards from the bottom of a pack, and opposite him a solemn old rustic piling and changing coins upon the cards which lay already exposed.

But now I heard a voice that drew my eyes to the far corner of the room.

"Why didn't you stay in Arizona?"

Harmless looking words as I write them down here. Yet at the sound of them I noticed the eyes of the others directed to that corner. What answer was given to them I did not hear, nor did I see who spoke. Then came another remark.

"Well, Arizona's no place for amatures."

This time the two card dealers that I stood near began to give a part of their attention to the group that sat in the corner. There was in me a desire to leave this room. So far my hours at Medicine Bow had seemed to glide beneath a sunshine of merriment, of easy-going jocularity. This was suddenly gone, like the wind changing to north in the middle of a warm day. But I stayed, being ashamed to go.

Five or six players sat over in the corner at a round table where counters were piled. Their eyes were close upon their cards, and one seemed to be dealing a card at a time to each, with pauses and betting between. Steve was there and the Virginian; the others were new faces.

"No place for amatures," repeated the voice; and now I saw that it was the dealer's. There was in his countenance the same ugliness that his words conveyed.

"Who's that talkin'?" said one of the men near me, in a low voice.

"Trampas."

"What's he?"

"Cow-puncher, bronco-buster, tin-horn, most anything."

"Who's he talkin' at?"

"Think it's the black-headed guy he's talking at."

"That ain't supposed to be safe, is it?"

"Guess we're all goin' to find out in a few minutes."

"Been trouble between 'em?"

"They've not met before. Trampas don't enjoy losin' to a stranger."

"Fello's from Arizona, yu' say?"

"No. Virginia. He's recently back from havin' a look at Arizona. Went down there last year for a change. Works for the Sunk Creek outfit." And then the dealer lowered his voice still further and said something in the other man's ear, causing him to grin. After which both of them looked at me.

There had been silence over in the corner; but now the man Trampas spoke again.

"*And* ten," said he, sliding out some chips from before him. Very strange it was to hear him, how he contrived to make those words a personal taunt. The Virginian was looking at his cards. He might have been deaf.

"*And* twenty," said the next player, easily.

The next threw his cards down.

It was now the Virginian's turn to bet, or leave the game, and he did not speak at once.

Therefore Trampas spoke. "Your bet, you son-of-a————."

The Virginian's pistol came out, and his hand lay on the table, holding it unaimed. And with a voice as gentle as ever, the voice that sounded almost like a caress, but drawling a very little more than usual, so that there was almost a space between each word, he issued his orders to the man Trampas:—

"When you call me that, *smile!*" And he looked at Trampas across the table. . . .

"I am goin' my own course," he broke in. "Can't yu' see how it must be about a man? It's not for their benefit, friends or enemies, that I have got this thing to do. If any man happened to say I was a thief and I heard about it, would I let him go on spreadin' such a thing of me? Don't I owe my own honesty something better than that? Would I sit down in a corner rubbin' my honesty and whisperin' to it, 'There! there! I know you ain't a thief'? No, seh; not a little bit! What men say about my nature is not just merely an outside thing. For the fact that I let 'em keep on sayin' it is a proof I don't value my nature enough to shield it from their slander and give them their punishment. And that's being a poor sort of a jay."

She had grown very white.

"Can't yu' see how it must be about a man?" he repeated.

"I cannot," she answered, in a voice that scarcely seemed her own. "If I ought to, I cannot. To shed blood in cold blood. When I heard about that last fall,—about the killing of those cattle thieves,—I kept saying to myself: 'He had to do it. It was a public duty. And lying sleepless I got used to Wyoming being different from Vermont. But this—" she gave a shudder—"when I think of to-morrow, of you and me, and of—If you do this, there can be no to-morrow for you and me."

At these words he also turned white.

"Do you mean—" he asked, and could go no farther. Nor could she answer him, but turned her head away.

"This would be the end?" he asked.

Her head faintly moved to signify yes.

He stood still, his hand shaking a little. "Will you look at me and say that?" he murmured at length. She did not move. "Can you do it?" he said.

His sweetness made her turn, but could not pierce her frozen resolve. She gazed at him across the great distance of her despair.

"Then it is really so?" he said.

Her lips tried to form words, but failed.

He looked out of the window, and saw nothing but

shadow. The blue of the mountains was now become a deep purple. Suddenly his hand closed hard.

"Good-bye, then," he said.

The Virginian, for precaution, did not walk out of the front door of the hotel. He went through back ways, and paused once. Against his breast he felt the wedding ring where he had it suspended by a chain from his neck. His hand went up to it, and he drew it out and looked at it. He took it off the chain, and his arm went back to hurl it from him as far as he could. But he stopped and kissed it with one sob, and thrust it in his pocket. Then he walked out into the open, watching. He saw men here and there, and they let him pass as before, without speaking. He saw his three friends, and they said no word to him. But they turned and followed in his rear at a little distance, because it was known that Shorty had been found shot from behind. The Virginian gained a position soon where no one could come at him except from in front; and the sight of the mountains was almost more than he could endure, because it was there that he had been going to-morrow.

"It is quite awhile after sunset," he heard himself say.

A wind seemed to blow his sleeve off his arm, and he replied to it, and saw Trampas pitch forward. He saw Trampas raise his arm from the ground and fall again, and lie there this time, still. A little smoke was rising from the pistol on the ground, and he looked at his own, and saw the smoke flowing upward out of it.

"I expect that's all," he said aloud.

But as he came nearer Trampas, he covered him with his weapon. He stopped a moment, seeing the hand on the ground move. Two fingers twitched, and then ceased; for it was all. The Virginian stood looking down at Trampas.

"Both of mine hit," he said, once more aloud. "His must have gone mighty close to my arm. I told her it would not be me."

From Owen Wister, *The Virginian: A Horseman of the Plains* (New York: Macmillan Co., 1902), pp. 26–29, 474–476, 480–481.

Robert Laxalt

A Basque Learns the Code

My father's head was bent a little, and with one leathered hand he began rubbing a knot in the old wood of the table. "It happened when I was new in America and they sent me into the deserts to herd sheep. You would have to see that country to believe it, but it was so big that even from the top of the highest hill I couldn't see a town or a house, except one little cabin and a corral that were hidden in this gully far below where I had the sheep."

He shook his head and sighed. "Oh, how cruel a country that was. It wasn't like the Pyrenees, where the feed was rich and even when I was twelve years old I could herd the sheep without much trouble. There, for as far as you could see, there was sagebrush and rocks, and the only trees were runted little junipers. Herding in that country was something I never dreamed could be. There was so little feed that the sheep would wake up before daylight and never stop until it was dark, and it was all even a young man could do to keep up with them. If I didn't have the dog, I couldn't have done it. And what dogs they had there then. They were so tough you wouldn't believe it, with strong legs and feet like leather, even though sometimes after a couple of days on the hillsides where it was rocky I would have to wrap my dog's feet in burlap to keep them from bleeding. Those slopes with the rocks were something, even for a man. A pair of boots wouldn't last you two weeks, they would be so torn up.

"The life and the country made my heart sick, and many was the night I cried myself to sleep for ever having come to America. I would get up in the morning when it was still dark, as soon as I heard the sheep moving, and make my coffee, and I would hate for the day to come so that I would have to look at that terrible land."

He straightened in his chair. "Well, anyway, about the cabin," he said. "When they first took me to that range, I used to see a few men walking around down where the cabin was. There were steers and sometimes horses in the corral. Then, after a few days, the men would move the stock out

250

and go north toward the Oregon and Idaho borders, and be gone for a few weeks.

"I asked the camptender once if he knew who they were, and he told me it was an outlaw bunch who rustled cattle and horses, and the leader's name was George Davis, and not to ever get in an argument with them, because they were dangerous men. He said they would probably come up to the camp once in a while and ask for some meat for a change of diet, and to give it to them."

The innkeeper had filled up the wineglasses, and my father took a long swallow. "Well, one day," he went on, "a couple of them came up to my camp at lunch-time, and one of them I could tell was their leader, George Davis, because he had the limp the camptender had told me about. I couldn't talk hardly any English then, but they could talk a few words of Spanish, so I could understand they wanted some mutton. I picked out a nice yearling and showed it to them, and they were pretty pleased. I cut his throat and hung him up on the juniper to bleed, and while we were waiting we ate the mutton stew I already had on the fire.

"George Davis, the leader, was pretty hard looking, but he seemed to be a nice man. He didn't have a big hat like most of the buckaroos those days, but a regular-sized one with the crown up and rounded, like when you first buy it in the store. But the rest of him, except for a long, black silk scarf he had wrapped around his neck a few times, seemed like it was all leather. He had a leather vest and leather arm cuffs, and leather chaps with wings on them, and beaten-up old spurs. He had a big belt with cartridges in it, and a gun that long. His boots weren't the regular cowboy kind, but were laced boots with high heels, maybe because they were easier on his bad leg, I guess."

My father paused and was silent for a while, and when he went on his voice had a softer note in it. "I didn't notice the other outlaw much at the beginning. He never said anything at all for a long time. He was a young man in his twenties, I guess, but not very far along. He was more of a dandy than Davis was, with a clean shirt and a big black hat that was beginning to look sort of beat up, and he had goat-hair chaps that must have been something to see once. At first, he looked to be pretty mean, so I didn't have much to do with him. But when I was butchering the yearling, he helped out like he knew something about sheep, and I found out that he used to herd, and that he wasn't very mean after all.

"Anyway," my father said, "when they left, Davis told me to come down to the cabin sometime, and I said I would if the sheep were pretty near at noonday, when they stopped to rest. So after a few days, I began to go down once in a while, when I would get a little lonesome, to eat with them and watch them shoot. They used to love to shoot, and you wouldn't believe the things they could do with a pistol. But good God, the money they must have spent on cartridges. I bet what they would shoot up on a day like that would be more than a man would make on wages in a week. And I used to think, no wonder men like that were good with a gun.

"*Bainan*," and my father nodded his head gravely, "the shooting was what led to my trouble. One day, when I was in the yard watching them shooting at cans to see who could keep one in the air the longest, George Davis and another outlaw, who was one of the roughest-looking men I ever saw, had an argument. They were both awful good with a gun, and they didn't seem to be able to beat each other that day, although George Davis was almost always the best. So they bet quite a bit of money, and they put a gold piece up on the corral fence and backed away, and when I saw it I just didn't believe how any man could hit it."

A grimness came then to my father's face, and the innkeeper, sensing it, leaned a little forward. By this time, the innkeeper's son had finished in the kitchen, and he came to stand with the girl and listen. My father did not seem to be aware that he had an audience.

"Well," he said, "the rough-looking outlaw didn't hit it. He missed with all three shots, even though one time the gold piece looked like it waved a little. He was mad and swearing like the devil, stamping on the ground like he was trying to find something to take it out on. I was standing off from the cowboys a little bit, holding my dog, because he always got scared and would whimper when there was shooting, and the rough-looking one shouted at me, and I remember it exactly, 'Shut that dog up!'

"Right away," my father said, "I bent down and grabbed the dog by the jaws, because I didn't want to cause any trouble, though I didn't see how a little thing like that could bother anybody's shooting. George Davis didn't seem to think so either because he told me to let the dog go. So I did, and he raised up that long pistol of his and brought it down and knocked that gold piece spinning with the first shot, mind you."

My father stuck his jaw out and jerked his head up and down. "Well, that did it. The rough-looking outlaw blew right up, stamping on the ground and shouting like hell. He turned around and looked at me, and for a second I didn't know what to think. He shouted, 'I told you to keep that dog shut!' and he shot him, right at my feet."

My father let his breath expel slowly, as if he had had it locked in his lungs. "Well, you know," he said, "I went down on my knees to look at the dog, and when I saw his blood pouring out on the ground, the first thing I knew I was crying. I was pretty much of a boy then," he said in apology, "and I guess those things happen when you're young."

He raised his hands helplessly. "The buckaroos didn't do anything, but sort of walked away or went into the cabin. George Davis looked madder than hell, though, but he didn't do anything either, because I guess he didn't want to have trouble in his bunch. He just walked over and picked up the gold piece and leaned against the fence looking at it. And so I took my dog in my arms and carried him up to the camp and buried him."

The innkeeper must have believed that was the end of it, because he had a mystified expression on his face. My father saw it and raised his hand in a gesture that there was more.

"After I buried the dog," he went on, "I began to get a little desperate. The camptender was coming the next day, but I knew it would take him two more days to get another dog back to me from the ranch. And I knew that trying to herd those sheep without a dog would kill me, and that I would lose half of them. Well, that night I rounded them up all right, and it damn near killed me at that. I was sitting by the fire so tired I could barely get any food in my mouth when I heard horses coming up the hill. The first thing that came to my mind was that the rough-looking outlaw was coming back to finish the job, so I went into my tent and got the rifle and came out again. But when the horses got close, I saw who it was.

"It was the young outlaw who had come up to the camp with George Davis that first time, and he was leading a horse with a saddle on him. I couldn't believe it, so I just stood there and didn't say anything. The young outlaw didn't say anything either, but the meanness went out of his face for a second and he sort of grinned like a boy, and then he reined his horse out of the firelight, and I never saw him again, because the whole bunch of them left in a few days.

"Well," my father said, placing both his hands on the table, "even though I knew that horse would last only a few days before getting sorefooted, when I woke up that next morning and saw him there, I can't tell you how I felt, but it was different. I didn't mind seeing the sun come up, and when it did I even felt pretty good about the deserts. For the first time, I didn't feel like a stranger to the land. When I thought about it, I couldn't figure it out, but I knew it sure as hell had something to do with my dog who was dead, and the young outlaw who brought me a horse."

From Robert Laxalt, *Sweet Promised Land* (New York: Harper & Row, 1957), pp. 108–114.

RUSH FOR GOLD

The Californian

We've formed [our band] and are well manned
To journey afar to the promised land,
Where the golden ore is rich in store
On the banks of the Sacramento shore.

Then ho! Boys, ho! who to California go,
For the mountains cold are covered with gold,
Along the banks of the Sacramento.
Ho! Ho! away we go, digging up gold in Francisco.

Oh, the gold is there, most anywhere,
And they dig it out with an iron bar,
And when it's thick, with a spade and pick,
They've taken out lumps as big as a brick.

Oh, don't you cry or heave a sigh,
We'll come back again by and by,
Don't breathe a fear or shed a tear,

But patiently wait about two year.

We expect our share of the coarsest fare,
And sometimes to sleep in the open air,
Upon the cold ground we shall all sleep sound
Except when the wolves are howling 'round.

As off we roam over the dark sea foam,
We'll never forget our friends at home,
For memories kind will bring to mind
The thoughts of those we leave behind.

In the days of old, the Prophets told
Of the City to come, all framed in gold;
Peradventure they foresaw the day
Now dawning in California.

From O. T. Howe, *Argonauts of '49* (Cambridge: Harvard University Press, 1923), p. 79.

J. D. B. Stillman
Gold Rush Letters

Sacramento, November 19th.—Our home is a wooden one, and keeps off the rain. It is made of miscellaneous pieces of boards from dry goods boxes, and is about six feet wide by twelve feet long. A curtain drawn across the middle divides it into a sleeping-room and office. When I passed through this place, in September, there were not more than half a dozen wooden houses in the city, with a population, chiefly floating, of about five thousand. There are now several hundred buildings, and the place is thronged with miners, who are driven from the mines by want of provisions, which are difficult to transport on account of the state of the roads. The early rains came heavier than expected and caught the miners unprepared; consequently, thousands more will be compelled to leave the mines and crowd the towns located on navigable streams. Building material cannot be obtained fast enough to erect shelter from the storms. Many persons are preparing to

Winter in their tents, by covering them with pitch. The consequence will be, that there must be a great amount of suffering and sickness this Winter.

The number of cattle brought over by the overland men was very large, and the supply of feed for them is so nearly exhausted that they die in immense numbers after they have successfully crossed the deserts and the Sierra. Many lie dead by the roads; and around ponds and sloughs, where they have gone for water, they lie in groups, having been too feeble to extricate their feet from the mire. Now the roads are so muddy that wagons are abandoned where they are mired, by men who have come down from the mines for supplies for their companies, and are unable to return.

There is generally good order, and men bear up with cheerfulness. All who are settled in business are making money; but, alas! for the many unfortunates. You have heard of the *Battle of Life*—it is a reality here; the fallen are trampled into the mud, and are left to the tender mercies of the earth and sky. No longer ago than last night, I saw a man lying on the wet ground, unknown, unconscious, uncared for, and dying. To-day, some one, with more humanity than the rest, will have a hole dug for him; some one else will furnish an old blanket; he will be rolled up and buried, and his friends at home, who may be as anxious about him as mine are about me, will never know his fate. Money, money, is the all-absorbing object. There are men here who would hang their heads at home at the mention of their heartless avarice. What can be expected from strangers, when men's own friends will abandon them because they sicken and become an incumbrance? There is no government, no law. Whatever depravity there is in a man's heart shows itself without fear and without restraint.

I know that many will inquire my opinion of California. I have thus far said but little, even now. It is not an unpleasant country for a residence. With the comforts one could bring with him from the States, few places would be more desirable than a choice location on the banks of the Sacramento. The greatest drawback is the long dry season. The rains have been frequent since the first of the month, and grass is growing finely. The weather is cool, but we have not yet felt the want of fire. For several days it has been very pleasant, and the roads are quite passable. The Spring is said to make a perfect flower garden of the whole country. Yet, there are few who intend to make this country a permanent residence; some are going for their families, and the society will be much improved.

So far as making money here is concerned, it is easily done by those who are calculated for it. Too large expectations and too little knowledge of difficulties to be encountered has caused so much disappointment and misfortune. It requires a great deal of determined perseverance under the most trying circumstances to insure success, and then one must have health. Those not thus qualified have succeeded by good luck, while the persevering and healthy have failed.

One of our passengers—a young man of refinement and of excellent family in New York—asked me, the other day, if we could furnish him with employment in the hospital in any capacity. He had brought out a stock of goods, but, for want of energy, had allowed the season to pass, looking for fortune to come to him, but such things do not happen in this country oftener than elsewhere.

A most melancholy instance of the weakness of some young men, when the restraints and support of friends are removed, occurred last evening. A well dressed young man was seen, very drunk, lying on the ground, and a couple of boys we have with us took him to a shelter and medical aid was rendered him, but he died and was buried. No one knew him. He had an ounce of gold in his pocket, a note book and a Bible. To-day he was recognized by these relics as coming from Binghampton (New York), the pride of the village— noble, generous and gifted. He drank, gambled his money away, and drank deeper to drown his trouble. The friends, who claim his effects as his administrators, showed his Bible here to-night. It is the smallest edition, with gilt edges and tucks. In one place was a beautiful card, on which was written, with a lady's hand, "Remember your friend and—." In another was a card, worked with worsted and mounted with silk ribbon, to be used as a book mark; the motto was, "A sister's prayers go with you." It is a case well calculated to stir one's sympathies. If you have a friend who is anxious to come to California and he be not a man of stern virtue, advise him to stay at home. There will be an immense amount of gold dug next season, without a doubt, and there will be many going home discouraged and destitute. A few will go home with higher virtue and characters, formed in the refiner's fire; but by far the greater number will return with gold, perhaps, but with morals and manners ruined, with feelings and habits that will make them poor members of society. The risk is too great for the reward. I can think of but very few men whom I would advise to come to California.

From J.D.B. Stillman, *Seeking the Golden Fleece: A Record of Pioneer Life in California* (San Francisco: A Roman & Co., 1877), pp. 141–146.

William Perkins
Journal of Life at Sonora, 1849–1852

On the seventh day we reached the first *placers*, called James' Diggings. Here we found about four hundred men at work in the bed of a stream, and all the claims already occupied. We proceeded to Sullivan's Diggings, some four miles further, and there put up our large tent, and I was enabled to enjoy the quiet which was so necessary to my health. My companions set to work at once, but they were not very sanguine, as the place seemed pretty thoroughly worked already. My first and almost only experiment gold digging, was made here. Infirm as I was I got down into a pit, and with a knife picked out several dollar's worth of gold, and had I been able to continue, I might have made from twenty to thirty dollars a day but what was this in a country like California in 1849? . . .

When I arrived, at the commencement of June [July?], 1849, I thought I had never seen a more beautiful, a wilder or more romantic spot. The Camp, as it was then termed, was literally embowered in trees. The habitations were constructed of canvas, cotton cloth, or of upright unhewn sticks with green branches and leaves and vines interwoven, and decorated with gaudy hangings of silks, fancy cottons, flags, brilliant goods of every description; the many-tinted Mexican *Zarape*, the rich *manga*, with its gold embroidery, chinese scarfs and shawls of the most costly quality; gold and silver plated saddles, bridles and spurs were strewn about in all directions. The scene irrisistibly reminded one of the descriptions we have read of the brilliant bazaars of oriental countries. Here were to be seen goods of so costly a nature that they would hardly be out of place in Regents' Street. But what article was too costly for men who could pay for it with handfuls of gold dust, the product of a few hours labor!

Here were to be seen people of every nation in all varieties of costume, and speaking fifty different languages, and yet all mixing together amicably and socially and probably not one in a thousand moralizing on the really extraordinary scene in which he was just as extraordinary an actor. . . .

At the time I speak of, Sonora was probably the only place in California where numbers of the gentler sex were to be found. I have mentioned that the camp was formed by an immigration of families from Sonora, in Mexico; this accounts for the presence of women in the place.

The men had constructed brush houses and, leaving their wives and children in charge, separated in all directions in search of the richest diggings, where they would work all the week, to return to the camp and their families on Saturday, when they generally commenced gambling and drinking, and continued both until Monday, never thinking of sleep.

When Peruvian or Chilian women arrived in San Francisco, they soon found out that Sonora was the only place where their own sex were congregated in any number, and at once found their ways to this vicinity. We have consequently always had an abundance of dark-skinned women amongst us, but white—none; except when some South American without indian blood in her veins, made her appearance. These were generally *china-blancas, mestiza-claras* or *quinteras,* and they formed our aristocratic society. . . .

On Saturdays and Sundays the old camp used to wear, night and day, an almost magic appearance. Besides the numberless lights from the gaily decorated houses, all of them with their fronts entirely open to the streets, the streets themselves were strewn with lighted tapers. Where there was an open space, a Mexican would take off his variegated *zarape,* lay it on the ground, put a lighted wax or sperm candle at each corner, and pour into the centre his pile or stock of silver and gold. The *zarape* would soon be surrounded by his countrymen, who, seated on the ground, would stake and generally loose their hard-earned weekly wages.

It would have been difficult to have taken a horse through the crowded streets. As for wheeled carriages, they were not known as yet.

Tables loaded with *dulces,* sweetmeats of every description, cooling beverages, with snow from the *Sierra Nevada* floating in them, cakes and dried fruits, hot meats, pies, every thing in the greatest abundance. One could hardly believe in his senses, the brilliant scene appeared so unreal and fairy-like. . . .

The winter months set in, and the scene changed as if by enchantment. Most of the Sonoraenses, fearful of the cold in these high latitudes, comparatively speaking, either returned to their country or made their way to diggings farther south, about *Mariposa* and King's River. The Yankees now poured into the town, and God knows they soon destroy every thing in the shape of romance.

The *ramadas* or brush houses, and the gay tents were all pulled down, and ugly *adobe*, or rough-hewn log huts were erected in their stead. The fronts of the habitations, once gay with streaming flags, and decorated branches, were changed to gloomy looking architecture, and the place changed its aspect of an Eastern encampment or bazaar, to that of a dirty American country town. . . .

As a sample of what a breakfast cost, even after my arrival, I copy a bill which I paid one morning, riding from one camp to another.

A small box of Sardines	$5	
Sea biscuit, ad lib	1	
a bottle of English ale	8	
8# barley for horse	12	Total Twenty-six dollars

But with all this, as I have said, people did not seem to grow rich. The fact is that gold became a drug, and the class of people then in California did not value it. In those days almost every miner made what is called a "strike" every week or so, that gave him a small fortune, and he then seemed to be on thorns until it was spent. . . .

Sonora [in 1852] is very dull compared to what it used to be; and yet I suppose we must call it improved with its organized police, its halls of Justice, its lawyer's offices, library and printing office; theatres, hotels, balls, dinners and well dressed people; in fact civilization staring us in the face. We have now no rows, no fights, no murders, no rapes, no robberies to amuse us! Dr. Charneaux yesterday pitched a Frenchman from a window of the first floor of the hotel into the street, and we are so hard up for excitable incidents, that even this little affair afforded some gratification. The duel between Miranda and Carmano was too ridiculous in all its

phases to interest any one. I know not what we are coming
to. What with peaceable citizens, picayunish yankees, Jew
clothing shops and down-East strong-minded women, Sonora
will soon be unbearable, and all the old settlers will have to
move off and seek more congenial shades!

From William Perkins, *Three Years in California, William Perkins'
Journal of Life at Sonora, 1849–1852* (Berkeley and Los Angeles: University of California Press, 1964), pp. 95, 101, 103–104, 104–105, 107–
108, 187, 314.

Ralph Waldo Emerson

A View from the East

I do not think very respectfully of the designs or the doings
of the people who went to California in 1849. It was a rush
and a scramble of needy adventurers, and, in the western country, a general jail delivery of all the rowdies of the rivers. Some
of them went with honest purposes, some with very bad ones,
and all of them with the very commonplace wish to find a
short way to wealth. But nature watches over all, and turns
this malfeasance to good. California gets peopled and subdued, civilized in this immoral way, and on this fiction a real
prosperity is rooted and grown. 'Tis a decoy duck; 'tis tubs
thrown to amuse the whale; but real ducks, and whales that
yield oil, are caught. And out of Sabine rapes, and out of
robbers' forays, real Romes and their heroisms come in
fulness of time.

In America the geography is sublime, but the men are not:
the inventions are excellent, but the inventors one is sometimes ashamed of. The agencies by which events so grand as
the opening of California, of Texas, of Oregon, and the junction of the two oceans, are effected, are paltry,—coarse
selfishness, fraud and conspiracy; and most of the great
results of history are brought about by discreditable means.

From Ralph Waldo Emerson, "Considerations by the Way," in *The
Complete Works of Ralph Waldo Emerson* (Cambridge, Mass.: River-
side Press, 1904), Vol. 6, pp. 255–256.

Bret Harte

The Luck of Roaring Camp

The assemblage numbered about a hundred men. One or two of these were actual fugitives from justice, some were criminal, and all were reckless. Physically, they exhibited no indication of their past lives and character. The greatest scamp had a Raphael face, with a profusion of blonde hair; Oakhurst, a gambler, had the melancholy air and intellectual abstraction of a Hamlet; the coolest and most courageous man was scarcely over five feet in height, with a soft voice and an embarrassed, timid manner. The term "roughs" applied to them was a distinction rather than a definition. Perhaps in the minor details of fingers, toes, ears, etc., the camp may have been deficient, but these slight omissions did not detract from their aggregate force. The strongest man had but three fingers on his right hand; the best shot had but one eye.

Such was the physical aspect of the men that were dispersed around the cabin. The camp lay in a triangular valley between two hills and a river. The only outlet was a steep trail over the summit of a hill that faced the cabin, now illuminated by the rising moon. The suffering woman might have seen it from the rude bunk whereon she lay,—seen it winding like a silver thread until it was lost in the stars above.

A fire of withered pine-boughs added sociability to the gathering. By degrees the natural levity of Roaring Camp returned. Bets were freely offered and taken regarding the result. Three to five that "Sal would get through with it"; even that the child would survive; side bets as to the sex and complexion of the coming stranger. In the midst of an excited discussion an exclamation came from those nearest the door, and the camp stopped to listen. Above the swaying and moaning of the pines, the swift rush of the river, and the crackling of the fire rose a sharp, querulous cry,—a cry unlike anything heard before in the camp. The pines stopped

262

moaning, the river ceased to rush, and the fire to crackle. It seemed as if Nature had stopped to listen too.

The camp rose to its feet as one man! It was proposed to explode a barrel of gunpowder, but, in consideration of the situation of the mother, better counsels prevailed, and only a few revolvers were discharged; for whether owing to the rude surgery of the camp, or some other reason, Cherokee Sal was sinking fast. Within an hour she had climbed, as it were, that rugged road that led to the stars, and so passed out of Roaring Camp, its sin and shame, forever. I do not think that the announcement disturbed them much, except in speculation as to the fate of the child. "Can he live now?" was asked of Stumpy. The answer was doubtful. The only other being of Cherokee Sal's sex and maternal condition in the settlement was an ass. There was some conjecture as to fitness, but the experiment was tried. It was less problematical than the ancient treatment of Romulus and Remus, and apparently as successful. . . .

Strange to say, the child thrived. Perhaps the invigorating climate of the mountain camp was compensation for material deficiencies. Nature took the foundling to her broader breast. In that rare atmosphere of the Sierra foothills,—that air pungent with balsamic odor, that ethereal cordial at once bracing and exhilarating,—he may have found food and nourishment, or a subtle chemistry that transmuted ass's milk to lime and phosphorus. Stump inclined to the belief that it was the latter and good nursing. "Me and that ass," he would say, "has been father and mother to him! Don't you," he would add, apostrophizing the helpless bundle before him, "never go back on us."

By the time he was a month old the necessity of giving him a name became apparent. He had generally been known as "The Kid," "Stumpy's Boy," "The Coyote" (an allusion to his vocal powers), and even by Kentuck's endearing diminutive of "The d——d little cuss." But these were felt to be vague and unsatisfactory, and were at last dismissed under another influence. Gamblers and adventurers are generally superstitious, and Oakhurst one day declared that the baby had brought "the luck" to Roaring Camp. It was certain that of late they had been successful. "Luck" was the name agreed upon, with the prefix of Tommy for greater convenience. No allusion was made to the mother, and the father was unknown. "It's better," said the philosophical Oakhurst, "to take a fresh deal all around. Call him Luck, and start him fair." A

day was accordingly set apart for the christening. What was
meant by this ceremony the reader may imagine who has already gathered some idea of the reckless irreverence of Roaring Camp. The master of ceremonies was one "Boston," a
noted wag, and the occasion seemed to promise the greatest
facetiousness. This ingenious satirist had spent two days in
preparing a burlesque of the Church service, with pointed local allusions. The choir was properly trained, and Sandy Tip-
ton was to stand godfather. But after the procession had
marched to the grove with music and banners, and the child
had been deposited before a mock altar, Stumpy stepped before the expectant crowd. "It ain't my style to spoil fun,
boys," said the little man, stoutly eying the faces around him,
"but it strikes me that this thing ain't exactly on the squar.
It's playing it pretty low down on this yer baby to ring in fun
on him that he ain't goin' to understand. And ef there's goin'
to be any godfathers round, I'd like to see who's got any better rights than me." A silence followed Stumpy's speech. To
the credit of all humorists be it said that the first man to acknowledge its justice was the satirist thus stopped of his fun.
"But," said Stumpy, quickly following up his advantage,
"we're here for a christening, and we'll have it. I proclaim
you Thomas Luck, according to the laws of the United States
and the State of California, so help me God." It was the first
time that the name of the Deity had been otherwise uttered
than profanely in the camp. The form of christening was perhaps even more ludicrous than the satirist had conceived;
but strangely enough, nobody saw it and nobody laughed.
"Tommy" was christened as seriously as he would have been
under a Christian roof, and cried and was comforted in as
orthodox fashion.

From Bret Harte, *The Luck of Roaring Camp and Other Sketches*
(Boston: Fields, Osgood, & Co., 1870), pp. 3–5, 9–12.

Mark Twain

Silver Mining in Nevada

Hurry, was the word! We wasted no time. Our party consisted of four persons—a blacksmith sixty years of age, two
young lawyers, and myself. We bought a wagon and two
miserable old horses. We put eighteen hundred pounds of
provisions and mining tools in the wagon and drove out of
Carson on a chilly December afternoon. The horses were so
weak and old that we soon found that it would be better if
one or two of us got out and walked. It was an improvement.
Next, we found that it would be better if a third man got out.
That was an improvement also. It was at this time that I volunteered to drive, although I had never driven a harnessed
horse before and many a man in such a position would have
felt fairly excused from such a responsibility. But in a little
while it was found that it would be a fine thing if the driver
got out and walked also. It was at this time that I resigned
the position of driver, and never resumed it again. Within the
hour, we found that it would not only be better, but was absolutely necessary, that we four, taking turns, two at a time,
should put our hands against the end of the wagon and push
it through the sand, leaving the feeble horses little to do but
keep out of the way and hold up the tongue. Perhaps it is
well for one to know his fate at first, and get reconciled to it.
We had learned ours in one afternoon. It was plain that we
had to walk through the sand and shove that wagon and
those horses two hundred miles. So we accepted the situation,
and from that time forth we never rode. More than that, we
stood regular and nearly constant watches pushing up behind. . . .

We were fifteen days making the trip—two hundred miles;
thirteen, rather, for we lay by a couple of days, in one place,
to let the horses rest. We could really have accomplished the
journey in ten days if we had towed the horses behind the
wagon, but we did not think of that until it was too late, and
so went on shoving the horses and the wagon too when we
might have saved half the labor. Parties who met us, occa-

casionally, advised us to put the horses in the wagon, but Mr. Ballou, through whose ironclad earnestness no sarcasm could pierce, said that that would not do, because the provisions were exposed and would suffer, the horses being "bituminous from long deprivation." The reader will excuse me from translating. What Mr. Ballou customarily meant, when he used a long word, was a secret between himself and his Maker. . . .

True knowledge of the nature of silver mining came fast enough. We went out "prospecting" with Mr. Ballou. We climbed the mountainsides, and clambered among sagebrush, rocks, and snow till we were ready to drop with exhaustion, but found no silver—nor yet any gold. Day after day we did this. Now and then we came upon holes burrowed a few feet into the declivities and apparently abandoned; and now and then we found one or two listless men still burrowing. But there was no appearance of silver. These holes were the beginnings of tunnels, and the purpose was to drive them hundreds of feet into the mountain, and someday tap the hidden ledge where the silver was. Someday! It seemed far enough away, and very hopeless and dreary. Day after day we toiled and climbed and searched, and we younger partners grew sicker and still sicker of the promiseless toil. At last we halted under a beetling rampart of rock which projected from the earth high upon the mountain. Mr. Ballou broke off some fragments with a hammer, and examined them long and attentively with a small eyeglass; threw them away and broke off more; said this rock was quartz, and quartz was the sort of rock that contained silver. *Contained* it! I had thought that at least it would be caked on the outside of it like a kind of veneering. He still broke off pieces and critically examined them, now and then wetting the piece with his tongue and applying the glass. At last he exclaimed:

"We've got it!"

We were full of anxiety in a moment. The rock was clean and white, where it was broken, and across it ran a ragged thread of blue. He said that that little thread had silver in it, mixed with base metals, such as lead and antimony, and other rubbish, and that there was a speck or two of gold visible. After a great deal of effort we managed to discern some little fine yellow specks, and judged that a couple of tons of them massed together might make a gold dollar, possibly. We were not jubilant, but Mr. Ballou said there were worse ledges in the world than that. He saved what he called the "richest" piece of the rock, in order to determine its value by the process called the "fire assay." Then we named the mine "Monarch of the Mountains" (modesty of nomenclature is not a prominent feature in the mines), and Mr. Ballou wrote out and stuck up the following "notice," preserving a copy to be entered upon the books in the mining recorder's office in the town.

NOTICE

We the undersigned claim three claims, of three hundred feet each (and one for discovery), on this silver-bearing quartz lead or lode, extending north and south from this notice, with all its dips, spurs, and angles, variations and sinuosities, together with fifty feet of ground on either side for working the same.

We put our names to it and tried to feel that our fortunes were made. But when we talked the matter all over with Mr. Ballou, we felt depressed and dubious. He said that this surface quartz was not all there was to our mine; but that the wall or ledge of rock called the "Monarch of the Mountains," extended down hundreds and hundreds of feet into the earth—he illustrated by saying it was like a curbstone, and maintained a nearly uniform thickness—say twenty feet— away down into the bowels of the earth, and was perfectly distinct from the casing rock on each side of it; and that it kept to itself, and maintained its distinctive character always, no matter how deep it extended into the earth or how far it stretched itself through and across the hills and valleys. He said it might be a mile deep and ten miles long, for all we knew; and that wherever we bored into it above ground or below, we could find gold and silver in it, but no gold or silver in the meaner rock it was cased between. And he said that down in the great depths of the ledge was its richness, and the deeper it went the richer it grew. Therefore, instead of working here on the surface, we must either bore down into the rock with a shaft till we came to where it was rich—say a hundred feet or so—or else we must go down into the valley and bore a long tunnel into the mountainside and tap the ledge far under the earth. To do either was plainly the labor of months; for we could blast and bore only a few feet a day—some five or six. But this was not all. He said that after we got the ore out it must be hauled in wagons to a distant silver mill, ground up, and the silver extracted by a tedious and costly process. Our fortune seemed a century away!

But we went to work. We decided to sink a shaft. So, for a week we climbed the mountain, laden with picks, drills, gads, crowbars, shovels, cans of blasting powder and coils of fuse and strove with might and main. At first the rock was broken and loose and we dug it up with picks and threw it out with shovels, and the hole progressed very well. But the rock became more compact, presently, and gads and crowbars came into play. But shortly nothing could make an impression but blasting powder. That was the weariest work! One of us held the iron drill in its place and another would strike with an eight-pound sledge—it was like driving nails on a large scale. In the course of an hour or two the drill would reach a depth of two or three feet, making a hole a couple of inches in diameter. We would put in a charge of powder, insert half a yard of fuse, pour in sand and gravel and ram it down, then light the fuse and run. When the exposion came and the rocks and smoke shot into the air, we would go back and find about a bushel of that hard, rebellious quartz jolted out. Nothing more. One week of this satisfied me. I resigned. Claget and Oliphant followed. Our shaft was only twelve feet deep. We decided that a tunnel was the thing we wanted.

We went down the mountainside and worked a week; at the end of which time we had blasted a tunnel about deep enough to hide a hogshead in and judged that about nine hundred feet more of it would reach the ledge. I resigned again, and the other boys only held out one day longer. We decided that a tunnel was not what we wanted. We wanted a ledge that was already "developed." There were none in the camp.

We dropped the "Monarch" for the time being.

Meantime the camp was filling up with people, and there was a constantly growing excitement about our Humboldt mines. We fell victims to the epidemic and strained every nerve to acquire more "feet." We prospected and took up new claims, put "notices" on them and gave them grand eloquent names. We traded some of our "feet" for "feet" in other people's claims. In a little while we owned largely in the "Gray Eagle," the "Columbiana," the "Branch Mint," the "Maria Jane," the "Universe," the "Root-Hog-or-Die," the "Samson and Delilah," the "Treasure Trove," the "Golconda," the "Sultana," the "Boomerang," the "Great Republic," the "Grand Mogul," and fifty other "mines" that had never been molested by a shovel or scratched with a pick. We had not less than thirty thousand "feet" apiece in the "richest mines on earth" as the frenzied cant phrased it—and were in debt to the butcher. We were stark mad with excitement— drunk with happiness—smothered under mountains of prospective wealth—arrogantly compassionate toward the plodding millions who knew not our marvelous canyon—but our credit was not good at the grocer's.

It was the strangest phase of life one can imagine. It was a beggars' revel. There was nothing doing in the district—no mining—no milling—no productive effort—no income—and not enough money in the entire camp to buy a corner lot in an Eastern village, hardly; and yet a stranger would have supposed he was walking among bloated millionaires. Prospecting parties swarmed out of town with the first flush of dawn, and swarmed in again at nightfall laden with spoil— rocks. Nothing but rocks. Every man's pockets were full of them; the floor of his cabin was littered with them; they were disposed in labeled rows on his shelves. . . .

We never touched our tunnel or our shaft again. Why? Because we judged that we had learned the *real* secret of success in silver mining—which was, *not* to mine the silver ourselves by the sweat of our brows and the labor of our hands, but to *sell* the ledges to the dull slaves of toil and let them do the mining!

From Clemens, *Roughing It,* pp. 198, 199, 209–214, 217.

WORKING COWBOYS

William H. Emory

The Prototype: Vaquero

The captured horses were all wild and but little adapted for immediate service, but there was rare sport in catching them, and we saw for the first time the lazo thrown with inimitable skill. It is a saying in Chihuahua that "a Californian can throw the lazo as well with his foot as a Mexican can with his hand," and the scene before us gave us an idea of its truth. There was a wild stallion of great beauty which defied the fleetest horse and the most expert rider. At length a boy of fourteen, a Californian, whose graceful riding was the constant subject of admiration, piqued by repeated failures, mounted a fresh horse, and, followed by an Indian, launched fiercely at the stallion.

His lariat darted from his hand with the force and precision of a rifle ball, and rested on the neck of the fugitive; the Indian, at the same moment, made a successful throw, but the stallion was too stout for both, and dashed off at full speed, with both ropes flying in the air like wings. The perfect representation of Pegasus, he took a sweep, and followed by his pursuers, came thundering down the dry bed of the river. The lazos were now trailing on the ground, and the gallant young Spaniard, taking advantage of the circumstance, stooped from his flying horse and caught one in his hand. It was the work of a moment to make it fast to the pommel of his saddle, and by a short turn of his own horse, he threw the stallion a complete somerset, and the game was secure.

From William H. Emory, *Notes of a Military Reconnoissance* (Washington: Wendell and Van Ben Thuysen, 1848), p. 97.

Charles A. Siringo

How to Become a Cowboy

To begin rounding-up, we went over to Canyon Paladuro, where Chas. Goodnight had a ranch, and where a great many of the river cattle had drifted during the winter. There was about a hundred men and seven or eight wagons in the outfit that went over. We stopped over Sunday in the little Christian Colony and went to church. The Rev. Cahart preached about the wild and woolly Cow Boy of the west; how the eastern people had him pictured as a kind of animal with horns, etc. While to him, looking down from his dry goods box pulpit into the manly faces of nearly a hundred of them, they looked just like human beings, minus the standing collar. . . .

A cow boys outfit is something like a Boston dudes' rig, it can be bought for a small or large amount of money—according to the purchasers' means and inclinations.

If you wish to put on style and at the same time have a serviceable outfit, you can invest $500.00 very handy; that is by going or sending to Western Texas, or Old Mexico, the only place where such costly outfits are kept.

Your saddle would cost $100.00, although the Mexicans have them as high as $300.00. Another $50.00 for a gold mounted Mexican sombraro (hat). And $100.00 for a silver mounted bridle and spurs to match. Now a $50.00 saddle-blanket to match your saddle, another $25.00 for a quirt and "Re-etta" (raw-hide rope). Your Colt's "45" pearl-handled gold mounted pistol would cost $50.00, a Winchester to match, $75.00 and $25.00 for a pair of Angora goat leggings, making a total of $475.00, leaving $25.00 out of the $500.00 to buy a Spanish buggy with.

Years ago costly outfits were worn by nearly all Cow-men, but at this day and age they are seldom indulged in, for the simple reason that now-a-days it requires more rough and tumble hard work than skill to command good wages on a cattle ranch. Cattle are becoming so tame, from being bred

271

up with short horns, that it requires but very little skill and knowledge to be a cow boy. I believe the day is not far distant when cow boys will be armed with prod-poles—to punch the cattle out their way—instead of fire-arms. Messrs. Colt and Winchester will have to go out of business, or else emigrate to "Arkansaw" and open up prod-pole factories.

Well, now for the cost of a common outfit, with a few words of advice to the young "tenderfoot" who wishes to become a cow-boy.

Mount a railroad train and go to any of the large shipping or "cattle-towns." Then purchase a cheap pony, for about $25.00; saddle for $25.00; leather leggings for $5.00; broad-brimmed white hat, $5.00; saddle blankets, which would do to sleep on also, $5.00. Another $5.00 bill for spurs, bridle, stake-rope etc. And now for the most important ornament, the old reliable Colt's "45" pistol, $12.00. If you are foolish enough to go without the latter, the cooks at the different ranches where you happen to stop will not respect you. Instead of putting the handle to your family name they will call you the sore-footed kid, old man Nibbs, or some such names as those. We know from experience that the pistol carries much weight with it, and therefore especially advise the young "tenderfoot" to buy one, even if he has to ride bare-backed, from not having money enough left to buy a saddle with.

Having your outfit all ready, the next thing to be done is, inquire the distance, north, south and west, to the nearest railroad from the town you are in. And which ever one is furthest, strike right out boldly for it. When you get about *half* way there, stop at the first ranch you come to, even if you have to work for your "chuck." The idea is to get just as far from a railroad as possible.

If you got to work for your "chuck", while doing so, work just as hard, and if anything a little harder than if you were getting wages—and at the same time acquire all the knowledge and information possible, on the art of running cattle. Finally one of the Cow Boys on the ranch will quit, or get killed, and you being on hand, will get his place. Or some of the neighboring ranchmen might run short of hands, and knowing of you being out of employment will send after you.

Your wages will be all the way from $15.00 up to $40.00 per month, according to latitude. The further north or north-

west you are the higher your wages will be—although on the
northern ranges your expenses are more than they would be
further south, on account of requiring warmer clothing and
bedding during the long and severe winters.

After you have mastered the cow business thoroughly—
that is, learned how not to dread getting into mud up to your
ears, jumping your horse into a swollen stream when the
water is freezing, nor running your horse at full speed, trying
to stop a stampeded herd, on a dark night, when your course
has to be guided by the sound of the frightened steer's
hoofs—you command *good* wages, which will be from $25.00
to $60.00 per month, according to latitude as I said before.

If you are economical, you can save money very fast on
the range, for your expenses, after your outfit is purchased,
are very light—in fact almost nothing, if you don't use tobacco, gamble nor drink whiskey, when you strike a town.

There are some cattlemen who will let you invest your
wages in cattle and keep them with theirs, at so much a
head—about the average cost per head, per annum, of run-
ing the whole herd, which is a small fraction over $1.00.

From Charles A. Siringo, *A Texas Cow Boy or, Fifteen Years on the
Hurricane Deck of a Spanish Pony* (New York: Rand, McNally & Co.,
1886), pp. 177–178, 337–340.

Chester A. Arthur

A Message to Congress about "Cowboys"

The Acting Attorney-General also calls attention to the disturbance of the public tranquility during the past year
[1881] in the Territory of Arizona. A band of armed desperadoes known as "Cowboys," probably numbering from
fifty to one hundred men, have been engaged for months in
committing acts of lawlessness and brutality which the local
authorities have been unable to repress. The depredations of
these "Cowboys" have also extended into Mexico, which the
marauders reach from the Arizona frontier. With every dis-

position to meet the exigencies of the case, I am embarrassed by lack of authority to deal with them effectually.

From Chester A. Arthur, "First Annual Message to the Senate and House of Representatives of the United Sates," December 6, 1881, in *A Compilation of the Messages and Papers of the Presidents 1789–1897,* edited by James D. Richardson (Washington: U.S. Government Printing Office, 1898), Vol. 8, pp. 53–54.

Theodore Roosevelt

In Defense of the Cowboy

But everywhere among these plainsmen and mountain-men, and more important than any, are the cowboys—the men who follow the calling that has brought such towns into being. Singly, or in twos or threes, they gallop their wiry little horses down the street, their lithe, supple figures erect or swaying slightly as they sit loosely in the saddle; while their stirrups are so long that their knees are hardly bent, the bridles not taut enough to keep the chains from clanking. They are smaller and less muscular than the wielders of ax and pick; but they are as heady and self-reliant as any man who ever breathed—with bronzed, set faces, and keen eyes that look all the world straight in the face without flinching as they flash out from under the broad-brimmed hats. Peril and hardship, and years of long toil broken by weeks of brutal dissipation, draw haggard lines across their eager faces, but never dim their reckless eyes nor break their bearing of defiant self-confidence. They do not walk well, partly because they so rarely do any work out of the saddle, partly because their *chaparajos* or leather overalls hamper them when on the ground; but their appearance is striking for all that, and picturesque too, with their jingling spurs, the big revolvers stuck in their belts, and bright silk handkerchiefs knotted loosely round their necks over the open collars of the flannel shirts. When drunk on the villainous whiskey of the frontier towns, they cut mad antics, riding their horses into the saloons, firing their pistols right and left, from boisterous light-heartedness rather than from any viciousness, and indulging too often in deadly shooting affrays, brought on either by the accidental contact of the moment or on account of some long-standing grudge, or perhaps because of bad blood between two ranches or localities; but except while on such sprees they are quiet, rather self-contained men, perfectly frank and simple and on their own ground treat a stranger with the most whole-souled hospitality, doing all in their power for him and scorning to take any reward in return. Although prompt to resent an injury, they are not at all apt to be rude to outsiders, treating them with what can almost be called a grave courtesy. They are much better fellows and pleasanter companions than small farmers or agricultural laborers; nor are the mechanics and workmen of a great city to be mentioned in the same breath. . . .

Some of the cowboys are Mexicans, who generally do the actual work well enough, but are not trustworthy; moreover, they are always regarded with extreme disfavor by the Texans in an outfit, among whom the intolerant caste spirit is very strong. Southern-born whites will never work under them, and look down upon all colored or half-caste races. One spring I had with my wagon a Pueblo Indian, an excellent rider and roper, but a drunken, worthless, lazy devil; and in the summer of 1886 there were with us a Sioux half-breed, a quiet, hard-working, faithful fellow, and a mulatto, who was one of the best cow-hands in the whole round-up. . . .

There is no eight-hour law in cowboy land; during round-up time we often count ourselves lucky if we get off with much less than sixteen hours; but the work is done in the saddle, and the men are spurred on all the time by the desire to outdo one another in feats of daring and skillful horsemanship. There is very little quarreling or fighting; and though the fun often takes the form of rather rough horse-play, yet the practice of carrying dangerous weapons makes cowboys show far more rough courtesy to each other and far less rudeness to strangers than is the case among, for instance, Eastern miners. Or even lumbermen. When a quarrel may very probably result fatally, a man thinks twice before going into it: warlike people or classes always treat one another with a certain amount of consideration and politeness. The moral tone of a cow-camp, indeed is rather high than otherwise. Meanness, cowardice, and dishonesty are not tolerated. There is a high regard for truthfulness and keeping one's word, intense contempt for any kind of hypocrisy, and a hearty dislike for a man who shirks his work. Many of the men gamble and drink, but many do neither; and the conversation is not worse than in most bodies composed wholly of male human beings. A cowboy will not submit tamely to an insult, and is ever ready to avenge his own wrongs; nor has he an overwrought fear of shedding blood. He possesses, in fact, few of the emasculated, milk-and-water moralities admired by the pseudo-philanthropists; but he does possess, to a very high degree, the stern, manly qualities that are invaluable to a nation. . . .

Cowboys lose much of their money to gamblers; it is with them hard come and light go, for they exchange the wages of six months' grinding toil and lonely peril for three days' whooping carousal, spending their money on poisonous whisky or losing it over greasy cards in the vile dance-houses. As already explained, they are in the main good men; and the disturbance they cause in a town is done from sheer rough light-heartedness. They shoot off boot-heels or tall hats occasionally, or make some obnoxious butt "dance" by shooting round his feet; but they rarely meddle in this way with men who have not themselves played the fool. A fight in the streets is almost always a deal between two men who bear each other malice; it is only in a general melee in a saloon that outsiders often get hurt, and then it is their own fault, for they have no business to be there. One evening at Medora a cowboy spurred his horse up the steps of a rickety "hotel" piazza into the bar-room, where he began firing at the clock, the decanters, etc., the bartender meanwhile taking one shot at him, which missed. When he had emptied his revolver he threw down a roll of bank-notes on the counter, to pay for the damage he had done, and galloped his horse out through the door, disappearing in the darkness with loud yells to a rattling accompaniment of pistol shots firing out of pure desire to enter into the spirit of the occasion,—for it was the night of the Fourth of July, and all the country round about had come into town for a spree.

All this is mere horse-play; it is the cowboy's method of "painting the town red," as an interlude in his harsh, monotonous life.

One curious shooting scrape that took place in Medora was worthy of being chronicled by Bret Harte. It occurred in the summer of 1884, I believe, but it may have been the year following. I did not see the actual occurrence, but I saw both men immediately afterwards; and I heard the shooting, which took place in a saloon on the bank, while I was swimming my horse across the river, holding my rifle up so as not to wet it. I will not give their full names, as I am not certain what has become of them; though I was told that one had since been either put in jail or hung. I forget which. One of them was a saloon-keeper, familiarly called Welshy. The other man, Hay, had been bickering with him for some time. One day Hay, who had been defeated in a wrestling match by one of my own boys, and was out of temper, entered the other's saloon, and became very abusive. The quarrel grew more and more violent, and suddenly Welshy whipped out his revolver and blazed away at Hay. The latter staggered slightly, shook himself, stretched out his hand, and *gave back to his would-be slayer the ball*, saying, "Here, man, here's the bullet." It had glanced along his breast-bone, gone into the body, and come out at the point of the shoulder, when, being spent, it dropped down the sleeve into his hand. Next day the local paper, which rejoiced in the title of "The Bad Lands Cowboy," chronicled the event in the usual vague way as an "unfortunate occurrence" between "two of our most esteemed fellow-citizens." The editor was a good fellow, a college graduate, and a first-class base-ball player, who always stood stoutly up against any corrupt dealing; but, like all other editors in small Western towns, he was intimate with both combatants in almost every fight.

From Theodore Roosevelt, *Ranch Life and the Hunting-Trail* (New York: Century Co., 1888), pp. 9–10, 11, 54–56, 90–92, 95–96.

Andy Adams

On the Trail

Holding the herd this third night required all hands. Only a few men at a time were allowed to go into camp and eat, for the herd refused even to lie down. What few cattle attempted to rest were prevented by the more restless ones. By spells they would mill, until riders were sent through the herd at a break-neck pace to break up the groups. During these milling efforts of the herd, we drifted over a mile from camp; but by the light of moon and stars and the number of riders, scattering was prevented. As the horses were loose for the night, we could not start them on the trail until daybreak gave us a change of mounts, so we lost the early start of the morning before.

Good cloudy weather would have saved us, but in its stead was a sultry morning without a breath of air, which bespoke another day of sizzling heat. We had not been on the trail over two hours before the heat became almost unbearable to man and beast. Had it not been for the condition of the herd, all might yet have gone well; but over three days had now elapsed without water for the cattle, and they became feverish and ungovernable. The lead cattle turned back several times, wandering aimlessly in any direction, and it was with considerable difficulty that the herd could be held on the trail. The rear overtook the lead, and the cattle gradually lost all semblance of a trail herd. Our horses were fresh, however, and after about two hours' work, we once more got the herd strung out in trailing fashion; but before a mile had been covered, the leaders again turned, and the cattle congregated into a mass of unmanageable animals, milling and lowing in their fever and thirst. The milling only intensified their sufferings from the heat, and the outfit split and quartered them again and again, in the hope that this unfortunate out-break might be checked. No sooner was the milling stopped than they would surge hither and yon, sometimes half a mile, as ungovernable as the waves of an ocean. After wasting several hours in this manner, they finally turned back over the trail, and the utmost efforts of every man in the outfit failed to check them. We threw our ropes in their faces, and when this failed, we resorted to shooting; but in defiance of the fusillade and the smoke they walked sullenly through the line of horsemen across their front. Six-shooters were discharged so close to the leaders' faces as to singe their hair, yet, under a noonday sun, they disregarded this and every other device to turn them, and passed wholly out of our control. In a number of instances wild steers deliberately walked against our horses, and then for the first time a fact dawned on us that chilled the marrow in our bones,—*the herd was going blind.*

The bones of men and animals that lie bleaching along the trail abundantly testify that this was not the first instance in which the plain had baffled the determination of man. It was now evident that nothing short of water would stop the herd, and we rode aside and let them pass. As the outfit turned back to the wagon, our foreman seemed dazed by the sudden and unexpected turn of affairs, but rallied and met the emergency.

"There's but one thing left to do," said he, as he rode along, "and that is to hurry the outfit back to Indian Lakes. The herd will travel day and night, and instinct can be depended on to carry them to the only water they know. It's too late to be of any use now, but it's plain why those last two herds turned off at the lakes; some one had gone back and warned them of the very thing we've met. We must beat them to the lakes, for water is the only thing that will check them now. It's a good thing that they are strong, and five or six days without water will hardly kill any. It was no vague statement of the man who said if he owned hell and Texas, he'd rent Texas and live in hell, for if this isn't Billy hell, I'd like to know what you call it."

We spent an hour watering the horses from the wells of our camp of the night before, and about two o'clock started back over the trail for Indian Lakes. We overtook the abandoned herd during the afternoon. They were strung out nearly five miles in length, and were walking about a three-mile gait. Four men were given two extra horses apiece and left to throw in the stragglers in the rear, with instructions to follow them well into the night, and again in the morning as long as their canteens lasted. The remainder of the outfit pushed on without a halt, except to change mounts, and reached the lakes shortly after midnight. There we secured the first good sleep of any consequence for three days.

It was fortunate for us that there were no range cattle at these lakes, and we had only to cover a front of about six miles to catch the drifting herd. It was nearly noon the next day before the cattle began to arrive at the water holes in squads of from twenty to fifty. Pitiful objects as they were, it was a novelty to see them reach the water and slack their thirst. Wading out into the lakes until their sides were half covered, they would stand and low in a soft moaning voice, often for half an hour before attempting to drink. Contrary to our expectation, they drank very little at first, but stood in the water for hours. After coming out, they would lie down and rest for hours longer, and then drink again before attempting to graze, their thirst overpowering hunger. That they were blind there was no question, but with the causes that produced it once removed, it was probable their eyesight would gradually return. . . .

We had undergone an experience which my bunkie, The Rebel, termed "an interesting incident in his checkered career," but which not even he would have cared to repeat. That night while on night herd together—the cattle resting in all contentment—we rode one round together, and as he rolled a cigarette he gave me an old war story:—

"They used to tell the story in the army, that during one of the winter retreats, a cavalryman, riding along in the wake of the column at night, saw a hat apparently floating in the mud and water. In the hope that it might be a better hat than the one he was wearing, he dismounted to get it. Feeling his way carefully through the ooze until he reached the hat, he was surprised to find a man underneath and wearing it. 'Hello, comrade,' he sang out, 'can I lend you a hand?'

" 'No, no,' replied the fellow, 'I'm all right; I've got a good mule yet under me.' "

From Andy Adams, *The Log of a Cowboy: A Narrative of the Old Trail Days* (Boston: Houghton Mifflin Co., 1903), pp. 62–65, 68–69.

James Cape

From Black Slave to Texas Cowboy

I'se born in yonder Southeast Texas and I don't know what month or de year for sure, but 'twas more dan a hundred years ago. My mammy and pappy was born in Africa, dats what dey's told me. Dey was owned by Marster Bob Houston and him had de ranch down dere, where dey have cattle and hosses.

When I'se old 'nough to set on de hoss, dey larned me to ride, tendin' hosses. 'Cause I'se good hoss rider, dey uses me all de time gwine after hosses. I goes with dem to Mexico. We crosses de river lots of times. I 'members once when we was a drivin' about two hundred hosses northwards. Dey was a bad hailstorm comes into de face of de herd and dat herd turns and starts de other way. Dere was five of us riders and we had to keep dem hosses from scatterment. I was de leader and do you know what happens to dis nigger if my hoss stumbles? Right dere's where I'd still be! Marster give me a new saddle for savin' de hosses. . . .

I'se free after de War and goes back to Texas, to Gonzales County, and gets a job doin' cowboy work for Marster Ross herdin' cattle. And right dere's where I'se lucky for not gettin' in jail or hanged. It was dis way: I'se in town and dat man, Ross, says to me, "I understand you's a good cowhand," and he hires me and takes me way out. No house for miles before we comes to de ranch with cattle and I goes to work. After I'se workin' awhile, I wonders how come dey brings in such fine steers so often and I says to myself, "Marster Ross must have heaps of money for to buy all dem steers." Dey pays no attention to de raisin' of cattle, just brings 'em in and drives dem 'way.

One time Marster Ross and six mens was gone a week and when dey comes back, one of 'em was missin'. Dey had no steers dat time and dey talks about getting frusterated and how one man gets shot. I says to myself, "What for was dey chased and shot at?" Den I 'members Martser Bob Houston done told me about rustlers and how dey's hanged when dey's caught, and I know den dat's how come all dem fine steers is drove in and out all de time. But how to get away, dere's de puzzlement. I not know which way to go and dere's no houses anywhere near. I keeps gettin' scareter, and every time somebody comes, I thinks its de law. But Marster Ross drives de cattle north and I says to him, "I'se good hand at de drive. Kin I go with you next time you goes North?" And not long after dat we starts and we gets to Kansas City. After Marster Ross gets shut of de critters, he says, "We'll rest for couple days, den starts back." I says to me, "Not dis nigger."

I sneaks away and was settin' on a bench when along comes a white man and he's tall, had dark hair, and was fine lookin'. He says to me, "Is you a cowhand?" So I tells him I is, and he says he wants a hand on his farm in Missouri and he says, "Come with me." He tells me his name was James and takes me to his farm where I tends cattle and hosses for three years and he pays me well. He gives me more'n I earns. After three years I leaves, but not 'cause I learned he was outlaw, 'cause I learned dat long time afterwards. I'se lonesome for Texas and dat's how I comes to Fort Worth and here's where I'se stayed ever since.

I'se married about forty years ago to a woman dat had eight chillens. We separated 'cause dem chillens cause arguments. I can fight one, but not de army.

From Interview with James Cape, Age 100, in Norman R. Yetman, *Life Under the "Peculiar Institution": Selections from the Slave Narrative Collection* (New York: Holt, Rinehart and Winston, 1970), pp. 50–52.

The Old Chisholm Trail

Come along, boys, and listen to my tale,
I'll tell you of my troubles on the old Chisholm trail.

    Coma ti yi youpy, youpy ya, youpy ya,
    Coma ti yi youpy, youpy ya.

I started up the trail October twenty-third,
I started up the trail with the 2-U herd.

Oh, a ten dollar hoss and a forty-dollar saddle,—
And I'm goin' to punchin' Texas cattle.

My hoss throwed me off at the creek called Mud,
My hoss throwed me off round the 2-U herd.

Last time I saw him he was going cross the level
A-kicking up his heels and a-running like the devil.

It's cloudy in the West, a-looking like rain,
And my damned old slicker's in the wagon again.

Crippled my hoss, I don't know how,
Ropin' at the horns of a 2-U cow.

We hit Caldwell and we hit her on the fly,
We bedded down the cattle on the hill close by.

No chaps, no slicker, and it's pouring down rain,
And I swear, by god, I'll never night-herd again.

Last night I was on guard and the leader broke the ranks,
I hit my horse down the shoulders and I spurred him in the
   flanks.

The wind commenced to blow, and the rain began to fall,
Hit looked, by grab, like we was goin' to loss 'em all.

I popped my foot in the stirrup and gave a little yell,
The trail cattle broke and the leaders went to hell.

Foot in the stirrup and hand on the horn,
Best damned cowboy ever was born.

We rounded 'em up and put 'em on the cars,
And that was the last of the old Two Bars.

Oh it's bacon and beans most every day,—
I'd as soon be a-eatin' prairie hay.

I went to the wagon to get my roll,
To come back to Texas, dad-burn my soul.

I went to the boss to draw my roll,
He had it figgered out I was nine dollars in the hole.

I'll sell my outfit just as soon as I can,
I won't punch cattle for no damned man.

From Lomax, *Cowboy Songs*, pp. 58–61.

INVENTING THE COWBOY

Frederic Remington
The Genesis of a Hero

September 1894

My dear Wister . . .
Great and rising demand for—a cowboy article.—"The Evolution & the Survival of the Cowboy" by O. Wister with 25 illustrations by the eminent artist, Fredrico Remintonio.—just out.

October 1894

Say Wister—Go ahead please—make me an article on the evolution of the puncher—"the passing" as it were—I want to make some pictures of the ponies going over the hell roaring mal-pai after a steer on the jump. I send you a great story by [Montague] Stevens of the S.U. ranche—"front name Dick."

I will give some notes.—
Title "The Mountain Cow-boy—a new type"—
——this idea can be worked in
The early days 1865 to 1878 he was pure Texan &c—cattle boom he was rich—got $75 a month—wore fine clothes—adventurous young men from all parts went into it—just as they would be Kuban Cassacks if they got $100 a month. Cheyenne saddles—fine chaps—$15 hats fringed gloves—$25 boots &c. With the crash of the boom—Yankee ingenuity killed the cattle business as much as anything.—the Chicago packers—the terrible storms, the draught &c.—then the survival of the *Stevens cowboys*—run down a hill like as fast as a steer—over the mal-pai—through juniper.—they fall and are hurt—they run into bear . . .
Jokes—

"I understand you went up a tree with the bear just behind you"—"The bear was not ahead of me" Speaking of good horse "A meal a day is enough for a man who gets to ride that horse".

Well go ahead—will you do it.—get a lot of ponies "just a smokin" in it. Chaps are caught by two buckles. Otherwise they fly loose—

October 1894

Don't know how [the cowboy] was affected by the Mex. war.—he did not exist as an American type—[illegible] was later a combination of the Kentucky or Tennessee man with the Spanish.

In Civil War he sold cattle to Confederate Armies—but was a soldier in Confed army

but as a pure thing he grew up to take the cattle through the Indian country from Texas to meet the R.R.—at Abilene—or before that even he drove to Westport Landing—These were his palmy days—when he literly fought his right of way—he then drove to the north and stocked the ranges—then the thing colapsed and he turned "rustler"—and is now extinct except in the far away places of the Rocky Mountains.—Armor killed him.—Don't mistake the nice young men who amble around wire fences for the "old rider of the Plains."—

And incidentally speak of that puncher who turned horse & cattle thief after the boom slumped and who was incidentally hung and who still lives and occasionally in the most delicate way goes out into the waste land and ship theirs to Kansas City—after driving a great many miles to avoid livestock inspectors. &c &c

February 20, 1895

When will you have in the rest of your cow-boy article? Don't forget to tell about the survival of the fittest 'way down in the back reaches of New Mexico and Arizona.

February 1895

you want to credit the Mexican with the inventing of the whole business—he was the majority of the 'boys who first ran the steers to Abilene Kansas.—

March 9, 1895
Go ahead with your d—— Epic poem . . .
When oh when is the cow-boy to come

From Ben Merchant Vorpahl, *My Dear Wister: The Frederic Reming-ton–Owen Wister Letters* (Palo Alto: American West Publishing Co., 1972), pp. 64, 47, 53, 54–55, 68, 70, 73.

Owen Wister

The Evolution of the Cow-Puncher

The cow-puncher's play-ground in those first glorious days of his prosperity included battle and murder and sudden death as every-day matters. From 1865 to 1878 in Texas he fought his way with knife and gun, and any hour of the twenty-four might see him flattened behind the rocks among the whiz of bullets and the flight of arrows, or dragged bloody and folded together from some adobe hovel. Seventy-five dollars a month and absolute health and strength were his wages; and when the news of all this excellence drifted from Texas eastward, they came in shoals—Saxon boys of picked courage (none but plucky ones could survive) from South and North, from town and country. . . .

With a speech and dress of his own, then, the cow-puncher drove his herds to Abilene or Westport Landing in the Texas times, and the easy abundant dollars came, and left him for spurs and bridles of barbaric decoration. Let it be remembered that the Mexican was the original cowboy, and that the American improved on him. Those were the days in which he was long in advance of settlers, and when he literally fought his right of way. Along the waste hundreds of miles that he had to journey, three sorts of inveterate enemies infested the road—the thief (the cattle-thief, I mean), who was as daring as himself; the supplanted Mexican, who hated the new en-croaching Northern race; and the Indian, whose hand was against all races but his own immediate tribe, and who flayed the feet of his captives, and made them walk so through the mountain passes to the fires in which he slowly burned them. Among these perils the cow-puncher took wild pleasure in existing. No soldier of fortune ever adventured with bolder carelessness, no fiercer blood ever stained a border. If his raids, his triumphs, and his reverses have inspired no minstrel to sing of him who rode by the Pecos River and the Hills of San Andreas, it is not so much the Rob Roy as the Walter Scott who is lacking. And the Flora McIvor! Alas! the stability of the clan, the blessing of the home background, was not there. These wild men sprang from the loins of no similar father, and begot no sons to continue their hardihood. War they made in plenty, but not love; for the woman they saw was not the woman a man can take into his heart. That their fighting Saxon ancestors awoke in them for a moment and made them figures for poetry and romance is due to the strange accidents of a young country, where, while cities flourish by the coast and in the direct paths of trade, the herd-trading interior remains mediæval in its simplicity and violence. . . .

And what has become of them? Where is this latest outcropping of the Saxon gone? Except where he lingers in the mountains of New Mexico he has been dispersed, as the elk, as the buffalo, as all wild animals must inevitably be dispersed. Three things swept him away—the exhausting of the virgin pastures, the coming of the wire fence, and Mr. Armour of Chicago, who set the price of beef to suit himself. But all this may be summed up in the word Progress. When the bankrupt cow-puncher felt Progress dispersing him, he seized whatever plank floated nearest him in the wreck. He went to town for a job; he got a position on the railroad; he set up a saloon; he married, and fenced in a little farm; and he turned "rustler," and stole the cattle from the men for whom he had once worked. In these capacities will you find him to-day. The ex-cowboy who set himself to some new way of wage-earning is all over the West, and his old courage and frankness still stick to him, but his peculiar independence is of necessity dimmed. The only man who has retained that wholly is the outlaw, the horse and cattle thief, on whose grim face hostility to Progress forever sits.

From Owen Wister, "The Evolution of the Cow-Puncher," *Harper's New Monthly Magazine*, 91 (September 1895), pp. 608, 610, 614–615. Reprinted in Vorpahl, *My Dear Wister*.

Owen Wister

The Finished Product: The Virginian

Through the window-glass of our Pullman the thud of their mischievous hoofs reached us, and the strong, humorous curses of the cow-boys. Then for the first time I noticed a man who sat on the high gate of the corral, looking on. For he now climbed down with the undulations of a tiger, smooth and easy, as if his muscles flowed beneath his skin. The others had all visibly whirled the rope, some of them even shoulder high. I did not see his arm lift or move. He appeared to hold the rope down low, by his leg. But like a sudden snake I saw the noose go out its length and fall true: and the thing was done. As the captured pony walked in with a sweet, church-door expression, our train moved slowly on to the station, and a passenger remarked, "That man knows his business." . . .

. . . His broad, soft hat was pushed back; a loose-knotted, dull-scarlet handkerchief sagged from his throat, and one casual thumb was hooked in the cartridge-belt that slanted across his hips. He had plainly come many miles from somewhere across the vast horizon, as the dust upon him showed. His boots were white with it. His overalls were gray with it. The weather-beaten bloom of his face shone through it duskily, as the ripe peaches look upon their trees in a dry season. But no dinginess of travel or shabbiness of attire could tarnish the splendor that radiated from his youth and strength. The old man upon whose temper his remarks were doing such deadly work was combed and curried to a finish, a bridegroom swept and garnished; but alas for age! Had I been the bride, I should have taken the giant, dust and all. . . .

Farewell in those days was not said in Cattle Land. Acquaintances watched our departure with a nod or with nothing, and the nearest approach to "Good-by" was the proprietor's "So-long." But I caught sight of one farewell given without words.

288

As we drove by the eating-house, the shade of a side window was raised, and the landlady looked her last upon the Virginian. Her lips were faintly parted, and no woman's eyes ever said more plainly, "I am one of your possessions." She had forgotten that it might be seen. Her glance caught mine, and she backed into the dimness of the room. What look she may have received from him, if he gave her any at this too public moment, I could not tell. His eyes seemed to be upon the horses, and he drove with the same mastering ease that had roped the wild pony yesterday. We passed the ramparts of Medicine Bow,—thick heaps and fringes of tin cans, and shelving mounds of bottles cast out of the saloons. The sun struck these at a hundred glittering points. And in a moment we were in the clean plains, with the prairie-dogs and the pale herds of antelope. The great, still air bathed us, pure as water and strong as wine; the sunlight flooded the world; and shining upon the breast of the Virginian's flannel shirt lay a long gold thread of hair! . . .

"There's no tellin' in this country," said the Virginian. "Folks come easy, and they go easy. In settled places, like back in the States, even a poor man mostly has a home. Don't care if it's only a barrel on a lot, the fello' will keep frequentin' that lot, and if yu' want him yu' can find him. But out hyeh in the sage-brush, a man's home is apt to be his saddle blanket. First thing yu' know, he has moved it to Texas."

"You have done some moving yourself," I suggested.

But this word closed his mouth. "I have had a look at the country," he said, and we were silent again. Let me, however, tell you here that he had set out for a "look at the country," at the age of fourteen; and that by his present age of twenty-four he had seen Arkansas, Texas, New Mexico, Arizona, California, Oregon, Idaho, Montana, and Wyoming. Everywhere he had taken care of himself, and survived; nor had his strong heart yet waked up to any hunger for a home. Let me also tell you that he was one of thousands drifting and living thus, but (as you shall learn) one in a thousand.

From Wister, *The Virginian*, pp. 2, 4, 49, 51–52.

FRONTIER JUSTICE

Dodge City *Times*

A Day in Court

"The Marshal will preserve strict order," said the Judge. "Any person caught throwing turnips, cigar stumps, beets, or old quids of tobacco at this Court, will be immediately arranged before this bar of Justice." Then Joe [Policeman J. W. Mason] looked savagely at the mob in attendance, hitched his ivory handle a little to the left and adjusted his moustache. "Trot out the wicked and unfortunate, and let the cotillion commence," said his Honor.

City vs. James Martin.—But just then a complaint not on file had to be attended to, and Reverent John Walsh, of Las Animas, took the Throne of Justice, while the Judge stepped over to Hoover's [George M. Hoover, purveyor of wines, liquors and cigars!]. "You are here for horse stealing," says Walsh. "I can clean out the d——d court," says Martin. Then the City Attorney [E. F. Colborn] was banged into a pigeon hole in the desk, the table upset, the windows kicked out and the railing broke down. When order was restored Joe's thumb was "some chawed," Assistant Marshal Masterson's nose sliced a trifle, and the rantankerous originator of all this, James Martin, Esq., was bleeding from a half dozen cuts on the head, inflicted by Masterson's revolver. Then Walsh was deposed and Judge [D. M.] Frost took his seat, chewing burnt coffee, as his habit, for his complexion. The evidence was brief and pointed. "Again," said the Judge, as he rested his alabaster brow on his left paw, "do you appear within this sacred realm of which I, and only I, am high muck-i-muck. You have disturbed the quiet of our lovely village. Why, instead of letting the demon of passion fever your brain into this fray, did you not shake hands and call it all a mistake. Then the lion and the lamb would have lain

290

down together and white-robed peace would have fanned you with her silvery wings and elevated your thoughts to the good and pure by her smiles of approbation; but no, you went to chawing and clawing and pulling hair. It is $10.00 and costs, Mr. Martin."

"Make way for the witnesses," says Joe, as he winks at the two c——s that comes to the front, and plants one on each side of Mr. [W. N.] Morphy, who appears for defendant— "A thorn between two roses." It was the City vs. Monroe Henderson, all being "n——s" except the City Attorney and Mr. Morphy. The prosecuting witness, Miss Carrie, looked "The last rose of summer all faded and gone" to ——. Her best heart's blood (pumped from her nose) was freely bespattering the light folds which but feebly hid her palpitating bosom. Her starboard eye was closed, and a lump like a burnt bisquit ornamented her forehead. The evidence showed that the idol of her affections, a certain moke named Baris, had first busted her eye, loosened her ribs and kicked the stuffing generally out of Miss Carrie. That Carrie then got on the war path, procured a hollow ground razor, flung tin cans at defendant, and used such naughty, naughty language as made the Judge breathe a silent prayer, and caused Walsh to take the open air in horror. But the fact still remained that defendant had "pasted" her one on the nose. The City Attorney dwelt upon the heinousness of a strong giant man smiting a frail woman. Mr. Morphy, for defendant, told two or three good stories, bragged on the Court, winked at the witnesses and thought he had a good case, but the marble jaws of justice snapped with adamantine firmness, and it was $5.00 and costs. Appeal taken.

It was Carrie's turn next to taste the bitter draughts chewed on our Police Court. She plead "Guilty, your Honor, just to carrying that razor in my hand. 'Deed, 'deed, your Honor, I never had it under my clothes at all." Carrie received an eighteen dollar moral lecture and a fine of $5.00 and costs, and court stood adjourned.

From the Dodge City *Times*, August 11, 1877. Reprinted in Nyle H. Miller and Joseph W. Snell, *Great Gunfighters of the Kansas Cowtowns, 1867–1886* (Lincoln: University of Nebraska Press, 1967), pp. 171–172.

Thomas J. Dimsdale

Swift and Terrible Retribution

Finally, swift and terrible retribution is the only preventive of crime, while society is organizing in the far West. The long delay of justice, the wearisome proceedings, the remembrance of old friendships, etc., create a sympathy for the offender, so strong as to cause a hatred of the avenging law, instead of inspiring a horror of the crime. There is something in the excitement of continued stampedes that makes men of quick temperaments uncontrollably impulsive. In the moment of passion, they would slay all round them; but let the blood cool, and they would share their last dollar with the men whose life they sought a day or two before.

Habits of thought rule communities more than laws, and the settled opinion of a numerous class is, that calling a man a liar, a thief, or a son of a b——h, is provocation sufficient to justify instant slaying. Juries do not ordinarily bother themselves about the lengthy instruction they hear read by the court. They simply consider whether the deed is a crime against the Mountain Code; and if not, "not guilty" is the verdict, at once returned. Thieving, or any action which a miner calls *mean*, will surely be visited with condign punishment, at the hands of a Territorial jury. In such cases mercy there is none; but, in affairs of single combats, assaults, shootings, stabbings, and highway robberies, the civil law, with its positively awful expense and delay, is worse than useless.

One other main point requires to be noticed. Any person of experience will remember that the universal story of criminals, who have expiated their crimes on the scaffold, or who are pining away in the hardships of involuntary servitude—tells of habitual Sabbath breaking. This sin is so general in newly discovered diggings in the mountains that a remonstrance usually produces no more than a few jocular oaths and a laugh. Religion is said to be "played out," and a professing Christian must keep straight, indeed, or he will be suspected of being a hypocritical member of a tribe to whom it would be very disagreeable to talk about hemp.

Under these circumstances, it becomes an absolute necessity that good, law-loving, and order-sustaining men should unite for mutual protection and for the salvation of the community. Being united, they must act in harmony, repress disorder, punish crime, and prevent outrage, or their organization would be a failure from the start, and society would collapse in the throes of anarchy. None but extreme penalties inflicted with promptitude are of any avail to quell the spirit of the desperadoes with whom they have to contend; considerable numbers are required to cope successfully with the gangs of murderers, desperadoes, and robbers who infest mining countries, and who, though faithful to no other bond, yet all league willingly against the law. Secret they must be, in council and membership, or they will remain nearly useless for the detection of crime, in a country where equal facilities for the transmission of intelligence are at the command of the criminal and the judiciary; and an organization on this footing is a VIGILANCE COMMITTEE. . . .

The administration of the lex talionis by self-constituted authority is, undoubtedly, in civilized and settled communities, an outrage on mankind. It is there wholly unnecessary; but the sight of a few of the mangled corpses of beloved friends and valued citizens, the whistle of the desperado's bullet, and the plunder of the fruits of the patient toil of years spent in weary exile from home, in places where civil law is as powerless as a palsied arm from sheer lack of ability to enforce its decrees, alter the basis of the reasoning, and reverse the conclusion. In the case of the Vigilantes of Montana, it must be also remembered that the Sheriff himself was the leader of the Road Agents, and his deputies were the prominent members of the band.

From Thomas J. Dimsdale, *The Vigilantes of Montana* (Virginia City, Mont.: D.W. Tiltom & Co., 1866), pp. 12–13, 14.

Louise Amelia Knapp Smith Clappe
("Dame Shirley")

Their Majesties, the Mob

At one o'clock, so rapidly was the trial conducted, the judge charged the jury and gently insinuated that they could do no less than to bring in with their verdict of guilty, a sentence of *death!* Perhaps you know that when a trial is conducted without the majesty of the law, the jury are compelled to decide, not only upon the guilt of the prisoner, but the mode of his punishment also. After a few minutes' absence, the twelve men who had consented to burden their souls with a responsibility so fearful, returned, and the foreman handed to the judge a paper, from which he read the will of the *people*, as follows: "That William Brown, convicted of stealing, etc., should, in one hour from that time, be hung by the neck until he was dead."

By the persuasions of some men more mildly disposed, they granted him a respite of *three* hours, to prepare for his sudden entrance into eternity. He employed the time in writing in his native language (he is a Swede) to some friends in Stockholm; God help them when that fatal post shall arrive; for no doubt *he*, also, although a criminal, was fondly garnered in many a loving heart.

He had exhibited during the trial, the utmost recklessness and *nonchalance*, had drank many times in the course of the day, and when the rope was placed about his neck, was evidently much intoxicated. All at once, however, he seemed startled into a consciousness of the awful reality of his position, and requested a few moments for prayer.

The execution was conducted by the jury, and was performed by throwing the cord, one end of which was attached to the neck of the prisoner, across the limb of a tree standing outside of the Rich Bar grave-yard; when all, who felt disposed to engage in so revolting a task, lifted the poor wretch from the ground, in the most awkward manner possible. The whole affair, indeed, was a piece of cruel butchery, although *that* was not intentional, but arose from the ignorance of those who made the preparations. In truth, life was only

crushed out of him, by hauling the writhing body up and
down several times in succession, by the rope which was
wound round a large bough of his green-leafed gallows. Almost everybody was surprised at the severity of the sentence;
and many, with their hands on the cord, did not believe even
then, that it would be carried into effect, but thought that at
the last moment, the Jury would release the prisoner and substitute a milder punishment.

It is said that the crowd generally, seemed to feel the
solemnity of the occasion; but many of the drunkards, who
form a large part of the community on these Bars, laughed
and shouted, as if it were a spectacle got up for their particular amusement. A disgusting specimen of intoxicated humanity, struck with one of those luminous ideas peculiar to his
class, staggered up to the victim, who was praying at the moment, and crowding a dirty rag into his almost unconscious
hand, in a voice broken by a drunken hiccough, tearfully im-
plored him to take his "handercher," and if he were *innocent*,
(the man had not denied his guilt since first accused), to
drop it as soon as he was drawn up into the air, but if *guilty*,
not to let it fall on any account.

The body of the criminal was allowed to hang for some
hours after the execution. It had commenced storming in the
earlier part of the evening; and when those, whose business it
was to inter the remains, arrived at the spot, they found them
enwrapped in a soft, white shroud of feathery snow-flakes, as
if pitying Nature had tried to hide from the offended face of
heaven, the cruel deed which her mountain children had
committed. . . .

The state of society here has never been so bad as since the
appointment of a Committee of Vigilance. The rowdies have
formed themselves into a company called the "Moguls," and
they parade the streets all night, howling, shouting, breaking
into houses, taking wearied miners out of their beds and
throwing them into the river, and in short, "murdering sleep,"
in the most remorseless manner. Nearly every night they
build bonfires fearfully near some rag shanty, thus endangering the lives, (or I should rather say the property—for as it is
impossible to sleep, lives are emphatically safe) of the whole
community. They retire about five o'clock in the morning;
previously to this blessed event posting notices to that effect,
and that they will throw any one who may disturb them into
the river. I am nearly worn out for want of rest, for truly
they "make night hideous" with their fearful uproar. Mr.

O——, who still lies dangerously ill from the wound received, on what we call the "fatal Sunday," complains bitterly of the disturbance; and when poor Pizarro was dying, and one of his friends gently requested that they would be quiet for half an hour and permit the soul of the sufferer to pass in peace, they only laughed and yelled and hooted louder than ever, in the presence of the departing spirit, for the tenement in which he lay, being composed of green boughs only, could of course shut out no sounds. Without doubt if the "Moguls" had been sober, they would never have been guilty of such horrible barbarity as to compel the thoughts of a dying man to mingle with curses and blasphemies; but alas! they were intoxicated, and may God forgive them, unhappy ones, for they knew not what they did. The poor, exhausted miners, for even well people cannot sleep in such a pandemonium, grumble and complain, but they—although far outnumbering the rioters—are too timid to resist. All say "It is shameful; something ought to be done; something *must* be done," etc. and in the mean time the rioters triumph. You will wonder that the Committee of Vigilance does not interfere; it is said that some of that very Committee are the ringleaders among the "Moguls."

From *The Shirley Letters from the California Mines 1851–1852*, edited by Carl T. Wheat (New York: Alfred A. Knopf, 1949), pp. 95–97, 171–172.

Margaret Ashmun

The Vigilantes

We are the whirlwinds that winnow the West—
We scatter the wicked like straw!
We are the Nemeses, never at rest—
We are Justice, and Right, and the Law!

Moon on the snow and a blood-chilling blast,
Sharp-throbbing hoofs like the heart-beat of fear,
A halt, a swift parley, a pause—then at last
A stiff, swinging figure, cut darkly and sheer
Against the blue steel of the sky; ghastly white

Every on-looking face. Men, our duty was clear;
Yet ah! what a soul to send forth to the night!

Ours is a service brute-hateful and grim;
Little we love the wild task that we seek;
Are they dainty to deal with—the fear-rigid limb,
The curse and the struggle, the blasphemous shriek?
Nay, but men must endure while their bodies have breath;
God made us strong to avenge Him the weak—
To dispense His sure wages of sin—which is death.

We stand for our duty: While wrong works its will,
Our search shall be stern and our course shall be wide;
Retribution shall prove that the just liveth still,
And its horrors and dangers our hearts can abide,
That safety and honor may tread in our path;
The vengeance of Heaven shall speed at our side,
As we follow unwearied our mission of wrath.

We are the whirlwinds that winnow the West—
We scatter the wicked like straw!
We are the Nemeses, never at rest—
We are Justice, and Right, and the Law!

From Margaret Ashmun, in *The Pacific Monthly*, 18 (August 1907),
p. 208.

WESTERN CULTURE

Anthony Trollope

Impressions of a World Traveler

What a night we spent in that inn! They who know America
will be aware that in all hotels there is a free admixture of
different classes. The traveller in Europe may sit down to din-

ner with his tailor and shoemaker; but if so, his tailor and shoemaker have dressed themselves as he dresses, and are prepared to carry themselves according to a certain standard, which in exterior does not differ from his own. In the large Eastern cities of the States, such as Boston, New York, and Washington, a similar practice of life is gradually becoming prevalent. There are various hotels for various classes, and the ordinary traveller does not find himself at the same table with a butcher fresh from the shambles. But in the West there are no distinctions whatever. "A man's a man for a' that" in the West, let the "a' that" comprise what it may of coarse attire and unsophisticated manners. . . .

. . . As regards the people of the West, I must say that they were not such as I expected to find them. With the Northerns we are all more or less intimately acquainted. Those Americans whom we meet in our own country, or on the Continent, are generally from the North, or if not so they have that type of American manners which has become familiar to us. They are talkative, intelligent, inclined to be social, though frequently not sympathetically social with ourselves; somewhat *soi-distant*, but almost invariably companionable. As the traveller goes south into Maryland and Washington, the type is not altered to any great extent. The hard intelligence of the Yankee gives place gradually to the softer, and perhaps more polished manner of the Southern. But the change thus experienced is not so great as that between the American of the western and the American of the Atlantic States. In the West I found the men gloomy and silent,—I might almost say sullen. A dozen of them will sit for hours round a stove, speechless. They chew tobacco and ruminate. They are not offended if you speak to them, but they are not pleased. They answer with monosyllables, or, if it be practicable, with a gesture of the head. They care nothing for the graces,—or shall I say, for the decencies of life? They are essentially a dirty people. Dirt, untidiness, and noise, seem in nowise to afflict them. Things are constantly done before your eyes, which should be done behind your back. No doubt we daily come into the closest contact with matters which, if we saw all that appertains to them, would cause us to shake and shudder. In other countries we do not see all this, but in the western States we do. I have eaten in Bedouin tents, and have been ministered to by Turks and Arabs. I have sojourned in the hotels of old Spain and Spanish America. I have lived in Connaught, and have taken up my quarters with monks of different nations. I have, as it were, been educated to dirt, and taken out my degree in outward abominations. But my education had not reached a point which would enable me to live at my ease in the western States. A man or woman who could do that may be said to have graduated in the highest honours, and to have become absolutely invulnerable, either through the sense of touch, or by the eye, or by the nose. . . . No men love money with more eager love than these western men, but they bear the loss of it as an Indian bears his torture at the stake. They are energetic in trade, speculating deeply whenever speculation is possible; but nevertheless they are slow in motion, loving to loaf about. They are slow in speech, preferring to sit in silence, with the tobacco between their teeth. They drink, but are seldom drunk to the eye; they begin it early in the morning, and take it in a solemn, sullen, ugly manner, standing always at a bar; swallowing their spirits, and saying nothing as they swallow it. They drink often, and to great excess; but they carry it off without noise, sitting down and ruminating over it with the everlasting cud within their jaws. I believe that a stranger might go into the West, and passing from hotel to hotel through a dozen of them, might sit for hours at each in the large everlasting public hall, and never have a word addressed to him. . . .

I cannot part with the West without saying in its favour that there is a certain manliness about its men, which gives them a dignity of their own. It's shown in that very indifference of which I have spoken. Whatever turns up the man is still there,—still unsophisticated and still unbroken. It has seemed to me that no race of men requires less outward assistance than these pioneers of civilization. They rarely amuse themselves. Food, newspapers, and brandy-smashes suffice for life; and while these last, whatever may occur, the man is still there in his manhood. The fury of the mob does not shake him, nor the stern countenance of his present martial tyrant. Alas! I cannot stick to my text by calling him a just man. Intelligence, energy, and endurance are his virtues. Dirt, dishonesty, and morning drinks are his vices.

All native American women are intelligent. It seems to be their birthright. In the eastern cities they have, in their upper classes, superadded womanly grace to this intelligence, and consequently they are charming as companions. They are beautiful also, and, as I believe, lack nothing that a lover can desire in his love. But I cannot fancy myself much in love with a western lady, or rather with a lady in the West. They are as sharp as nails, but then they are also as hard. They know, doubtless, all that they ought to know, but then they know so much more than they ought to know. They are tyrants to their parents, and never practise the virtue of obedience till they have half-grown-up daughters of their own. They have faith in the destiny of their country, if in nothing else; but they believe that that destiny is to be worked out by the spirit and talent of the young women. I confess that for me Eve would have had no charms had she not recognized Adam as her lord. I can forgive her in that she tempted him to eat the apple. Had she come from the West country she would have ordered him to make his meal, and then I could not have forgiven her.

From Anthony Trollope, *North America* (New York: Harper & Bros., 1862), pp. 391, 393–394, 395–396.

Oscar Wilde

Art Criticism in the West

From Salt Lake City one travels over the great plains of Colorado, and up the Rocky Mountains, on the top of which is Leadville, the richest city in the world. It has also got the reputation of being the roughest, and every man carries a revolver. I was told that if I went there they would be sure to shoot me or my travelling manager. I wrote and told them that nothing that they could do to my travelling manager would intimidate me. They are miners—men working in metals, so I lectured to them on the Ethics of Art. I read them passages from the autobiography of Benvenuto Cellini and they seemed much delighted. I was reproved by my hearers for not having brought him with me. I explained that he had been dead for some little time which elicited the enquiry: "Who shot him"? They afterwards took me to a dancing saloon where I saw the only rational method of art criticism I have ever come across. Over the piano was printed a notice:

PLEASE DO NOT SHOOT THE
PIANIST
HE IS DOING HIS BEST

The mortality among pianists in that place is marvellous. Then they asked me to supper, and having accepted, I had to descend a mine in a rickety bucket in which it was impossible to be graceful. Having got into the heart of the mountain I had supper, the first course being whiskey, the second whiskey, and the third whiskey.

I went to the Theatre to lecture and I was informed that just before I went there two men had been seized for committing a murder, and in that theatre they had been brought on to the stage at eight o'clock in the evening, and then and there tried and executed before a crowded audience. But I found these miners very charming and not at all rough. . . .

So infinitesimal did I find the knowledge of Art, west of the Rocky Mountains, that an art patron—one who in his day had been a miner—actually sued the railroad company for damages because the plaster cast of Venus of Milo, which he had imported from Paris, had been delivered minus the arms. And, what is more surprising still, he gained his case and the damages.

From *The Prose of Oscar Wilde* (New York: Cosmopolitan Book Corporation, 1916), 702–704.

GUNSLINGERS

Richard Harding Davis

Ben Thompson Dies with His Boots On

The most notable Englishman who ever came to Texas was Ben Thompson; but he arrived there at so early an age, and became so thoroughly Western in his mode of life, that Texans claim him as their own. I imagine, however, he always retained some of the traditions of his birthplace, as there is a story of his standing with his hat off to talk to an English nobleman, when Thompson at the time was the most feared and best known man in all Texas. The stories of his recklessness and ignorance of fear, and utter disregard of the value of others' lives as well as his own, are innumerable. A few of them are interesting and worth keeping, as they show the typical bad man of the highest degree in his different humors, and also as I have not dared to say half as much about bad men as I should have liked to do. Thompson killed eighteen men in different parts of Texas, and was for this made marshal of Austin, on the principle that if he must kill somebody, it was better to give him authority to kill other desperadoes than reputable citizens. As marshal it was his pleasure to pull up his buggy across the railroad track just as the daily express train was about to start, and covering the engineer with his revolver, bid him hold the train until he was ready to move on. He would then call some trembling acquaintance from the crowd on the platform and talk with him leisurely, until he thought he had successfully awed the engineer and established his authority. Then he would pick up his reins and drive on, saying to the engineer, "You needn't think, sir, any corporation can hurry me." The position of the unfortunate man to whom he talked must have been most trying, with a locomotive on one side and a revolver on the other.

One day a cowboy who was a well-known bully and a would-be desperado, shot several bullet-holes through the high hat of an Eastern traveller who was standing at the bar of an Austin hotel. Thompson heard of this, and, purchasing a high hat, entered the bar-room.

"I hear," he said, facing the cowboy, "that you are shooting plug-hats here to-day; perhaps you would like to take a shot at mine." He then raised his revolver and shot away the cowboy's ear. "I meant," he said, "to hit your ear; did I do it?" The bully showed proof that he had. "Well, then," said the marshal, "get out of here;" and catching the man by his cartridge-belt, he threw him out into the street, and so put an end to his reputation as a desperate character forever.

Thompson was naturally unpopular with a certain class in the community. Two barkeepers who had a personal grudge against him, with no doubt excellent reason, lay in ambush for him behind the bars of the saloon, which stretched along either wall. Thompson entered the room from the street in ignorance of any plot against him until the two men halted him with shot-guns. They had him so surely at their pleasure that he made no effort to reach his revolver, but stood looking from one to the other, and smiling grimly. But his reputation was so great, and their fear of him so actual, that both men missed him, although not twenty feet away, and with shot-guns in their hands. Then Thompson took out his pistol deliberately and killed them.

A few years ago he became involved in San Antonio with "Jack" Harris, the keeper of a gambling-house and variety theatre. Harris lay in wait for Thompson behind the swinging doors of his saloon, but Thompson, as he crossed the Military Plaza, was warned of Harris's hiding-place, and shot him through the door. He was tried for the murder, and acquitted on the ground of self-defence; and in his return to Austin was met at the station by a brass band and all the fire companies. Perhaps inspired by this, he returned to San Antonio, and going to Harris's theatre, then in the hands of his partner, Joe Foster, called from the gallery for Foster to come up and speak to him. Thompson had with him a desperado named King Fisher, and against him every man of his class in San Antonio, for Harris had been very popular. Foster sent his assistant, a very young man named Bill Sims, to ask Thompson to leave the place, as he did not want trouble.

"I have come to have a reconciliation," said Thompson. "I

want to shake hands with my old friend, Joe Foster. Tell him I won't leave till I see him, and I won't make a row."

Sims returned with Foster, and Thompson held out his hand.

"Joe," he said, "I have come all the way from Austin to shake hands with you. Let's make up, and call it off."

"I can't shake hands with you, Ben," Foster said. "You killed my partner, and you know well enough I am not the sort to forget it. Now go, won't you, and don't make trouble."

Thompson said he would leave in a minute, but they must drink together first. There was a bar in the gallery, which was by this time packed with men who had learned of Thompson's presence in the theatre, but Fisher and Thompson stood quite alone beside the bar. The marshal of Austin looked up and saw Foster's glass untouched before him, and said,

"Aren't you drinking with me, Joe?"

Foster shook his head.

"Well, then," cried Thompson, "the man who won't drink with me, nor shake hands with me, fights me."

He reached back for his pistol, and some one—a jury of twelve intelligent citizens decided it was not young Bill Sims—shot him three times in the forehead. They say you could have covered the three bullet-holes with a half-dollar. But so great was the desperate courage of this ruffian that even as he fell he fired, holding his revolver at his hip, and killing Foster, and then, as he lay on his back, with every nerve jerking in agony, he emptied his revolver into the floor, ripping great gashes in the boards about him. And so he died, as he would have·elected to die, with his boots on, and with the report of his pistol the last sound to ring in his ears. King Fisher was killed at the same moment; and the *Express* spoke of it the next morning as "A Good Night's Work."

From Richard Harding Davis, *The West from a Car-Window* (New York: Harper & Bros., 1892), pp. 235–238.

John Wesley Hardin

A Gunslinger's Own Story

I was young then and loved every pretty girl I met, and at Kosse I met one and we got along famously together. I made an engagement to call on her that night and did so. I had not been there long when someone made a row at the door of the house. She got scared and told me it was her sweetheart, and about this time the fellow came in and told me he would kill me if I did not give him $100. I told him to go slow, and not to be in such a hurry; that I only had about $50 or $60 in my pocket, but if he would go with me to the stable I would give more as I had the money in my saddle pockets. He said he would go, and I, pretending to be scared, started for the stable. He said: "Give me what you have got first." I told him all right, and in so doing, dropped some of it on the floor. He stooped down to pick it up and as he was straightening up I pulled my pistol and fired. The ball struck him between the eyes and he fell over, a dead robber. I stopped long enough to get back most of my money and resumed my journey to Brenham. I arrived there about the last of January, 1870, and went to Uncle Bob Hardin's, who was then improving his place. He persuaded me to farm with him and his boys, William, Aaron, and Joe. All the money I had I gave to my aunt to keep for me. I thus became a farmer and made a good plough boy and hoer.

. . . I told my relatives I was in trouble and on my way to Mexico. They told me I could go to Kansas with cattle and make some money and at the same time be free from arrest. I therefore concluded to give up my Mexican trip and went to work helping them gather cattle. We gathered mostly for Jake Johnson and Columbus Carol, who were then putting up herds for Kansas.

I thus soon got acquainted with the country on the Sandies, on Elm and Rocky and on the Guadalupe.

I had not been there long before the boys took me to a Mexican camp where they were dealing monte. I soon learned the rudiments of the game and began to bet with the rest. Finally I turned a card down and tapped the game. My card came and I said: "Pay the queen." The dealer refused. I struck him over the head with my pistol as he was drawing a knife, shot another as he also was drawing a knife. Well, this broke up the monte game and the total casualties were a Mexican with his arm broken, another shot through the lungs, and another with a very sore head. We all went back to camp and laughed about the matter, but the game broke up for good and the Mexican camp was abandoned. The best people of the vicinity said I did a good thing. This was in February, 1871.

I had been drinking pretty freely that day and towards night went into a restaurant to get something to eat. A man named Pain was with me, a Texan who had just come up the trail. While we were in the restaurant several drunken men came in and began to curse Texans. I said to the nearest one:

"I'm a Texan."

He began to curse me and threatened to slap me over. To his surprise I pulled my pistol, and he promptly pulled his. At the first fire he jumped behind my friend Pain, who received the ball in his only arm. He fired one shot and ran, but I shot at him as he started, the ball hitting him in the mouth, knocking out several teeth and coming out behind his left ear. I rushed outside, pistol in hand, and jumped over my late antagonist, who was lying in the doorway, I met a policeman on the sidewalk, but I threw my pistol in his face and told him to "hands up." He did it.

I made my way to my horse and went north to Cottonwood, about thirty-five miles, to await results. While I was there a Mexican named Bideno shot and killed Billy Coran, a cowman who had come up the trail with me. He was bossing a herd then, holding it near by Abilene for the market. His murder by this Mexican was a most foul and treacherous one, and although squad after squad tried to arrest this Mexican, they never succeeded in either killing or arresting him.

Many prominent cowmen came to me and urged me to follow the murderer. I consented if they would go to Abilene and get a warrant for him. They did so and I was appointed a deputy sheriff and was given letters of introduction to cattlemen whom I should meet. . . .

We soon got to Bluff, which was a town of about fifty houses. There were some bar rooms and restaurants in a line and we agreed to ride up like cow boys, hitch our horses, and divide into two parties, each going into different places. Anderson and I went into a restaurant, but before we reached it, we had to go into a saloon. I asked if we could get dinner and if a Mexican herder was eating dinner back there. They said there was; so I told my partner to get out his gun and follow me. We stepped into the entrance and I recognized Bideno. With my pistol by my side I said:

"Bideno, I am after you; surrender; I do not wish to hurt you, and you shall not be hurt while you are in my hands."

He was sitting at the table eating and shook his head and frowned. He then dropped his knife and fork and grabbed his pistol. As he did it, I told him to throw up his hands.

When he got his pistol out, I fired at him across the table and he fell over a dead man, the ball hitting him squarely in the center of the forehead.

Hearing the firing, Coran and Rodgers rushed in also. Coran said:

"I just want to shoot my brother's murderer one time. Is he dead?"

I told him he was, but he wanted to shoot him anyway. I would not let him, but he took his hat as a trophy. . . .

Everybody in Abilene wanted to see the man that killed the murderer of Billy Coran, and I received substantial compliments in the shape of $20, $50 and $100 bills, I did not want to take the money at first but I finally concluded there was nothing wrong about it, so took it as a proof of their friendship and gratitude for what I had done. I think I got about $400 in that way. Besides this, some wealthy cowmen made up a purse and gave me $600, so altogether I got about $1,000 for my work. I wish to say, however, that at the time I killed him I never expected to receive a cent, and only expected to have my expenses paid.

"It is now about 8 o'clock p.m. and I am locked into my cell for the night. By special permission from my keeper I now write you [my wife]. I can tell you that I spent this day in almost perfect happiness, as I generally spend the Sabbaths here, something that I once could not enjoy because I did not know the causes or results of that day. I had no idea before how it benefits a man in my condition. Although we are all prisoners here we are on the road to progress. 'J.S.' and I are both members of our societies and we are looked upon as the leaders by our associates, of which we have a goodly number. John is president of the Moral and Christian Society and I am secretary of our Debating Club. I spoke in our debating club this evening on the subject of Woman's Rights. John held that women should have equal rights with men and I held they shouldn't. We had a lively time. I followed him, winding up the debate for the day. John is the champion of woman's rights, but he failed to convince the judges, who after they had listened to my argument, decided in my favor."

From John Wesley Hardin, *The Life of John Wesley Hardin from the Original Manuscript as Written by Himself* (Sequin, Texas: Smith and Moore, 1896), pp. 33–34, 45–46, 48–49, 51, 134.

Billy the Kid

Billy was a bad man
And carried a big gun,
He was always after Greasers
And kept 'em on the run.

He shot one every morning,
For to make his morning meal.
And let a white man sass him,
He was shore to feel his steel.

He kept folks in hot water,
And he stole from many a stage;
And when he was full of liquor
He was always in a rage.

But one day he met a man
Who was a whole lot badder.
And now he's dead,
And we ain't none the sadder.

From J. Lomax, *Cowboy Songs*, p. 344.

Ramon F. Adams

Facts About Billy the Kid

The Kid is supposed to have been born in New York City, November 23, 1859, but no records have ever been found to substantiate this date. It is based solely upon Ash Upson's questionable authority. Billy's father is said to have died when the Kid was three, and it is a fact that his mother married again in Santa Fe, New Mexico, on March 1, 1873, although most writers have her marrying in Colorado. She was married to William H. Antrim in the First Presbyterian Church, Rev. D. F. McFarland performing the ceremony, with her two sons, Joe and Henry McCarty, as witnesses. Henry later assumed the name William H. Bonney.

The Kid's mother died in Silver City, New Mexico, of consumption on the sixteenth of September, 1874. Shortly afterward Billy got into trouble—for the first time—by stealing some clothing from a pair of Chinamen and was placed in jail, from which he soon escaped. He fled to Arizona, where he killed his first man, E. P. Cahill. It was then that he assumed the name William H. (after his stepfather) Bonney, the source of this surname unknown.

After fleeing from Arizona, he went to Mesilla, New Mexico, but was soon accused of horse stealing and fled to Lincoln County, where he joined Jesse Evans. Rustlers were stealing cattle from John Chisum and selling them to Jim Dolan, of the L. G. Murphy firm, for a fraction of their value. Billy went to work for this outfit, but soon had a quarrel with Billy Morton, the foreman.

Shortly afterward he met J. H. Tunstall, an English rancher and merchant associated with Alexander McSween. Although their stations in life were far apart, they became fast friends. By associating himself with the McSween-Tunstall combination, Billy naturally became the enemy of the Murphy-Dolan faction, and the rest of his life was shaped by the enmity between the two.

When his friend Tunstall was murdered by a posse of Dolan's men, including Morton, Baker, Roberts, and about a dozen others, he became very bitter. He was with a posse which hunted these killers down, and Morton and Baker were killed while trying to escape.

Tunstall, with Dick Brewer, John Middleton, Bob Widenmann, and the Kid, had been apprehensive when they left the ranch to drive a band of horses exempt from the attachment orders of Murphy's court. But after driving until five-thirty in the afternoon without trouble, they relaxed their tension. The Kid and Middleton were some hundred or so yards to the rear hunting turkeys and Brewer and Widenmann were off the trail some distance ahead leaving Tunstall all alone. Morton's posse surrounded Tunstall, who offered no resistance and was shot in the back of the head by Tom Hill, his valuable horse also being killed. This was the spark which exploded the Lincoln County War into action.

The Kid and Fred Waite were seized and held under arrest by Sheriff Brady, a Murphy tool, and so could not attend Tunstall's funeral, despite the many accounts to the contrary. Sheriff Brady made no effort to arrest the men who had murdered Tunstall in spite of the fact that Justice Wilson had signed warrants for their arrest.

Following his release, the Kid, with five companions was sent into Lincoln by Dick Brewer to protect the women of the McSween party. As they came into town, they saw Sheriff Brady, George Hindmann, Billy Matthews, Jack Long, and George Peppin coming up the street. The latter was going to the courthouse to post a notice about the opening of court, but the Kid thought they were after him and his friends. Therefore the Kid's party hid behind a plank gate just east of the rear of Tunstall's store, and as Brady and his men walked down the middle of the street, the gang opened fire, killing Brady and wounding Hindmann, who shortly died from his wounds. The others escaped.

Shortly after this incident, the Kid was joined by a newcomer from Uvalde, Texas, a youth named Tom O'Folliard—a name often misspelled in contemporary and later accounts. From this time on, he was the Kid's constant companion.

Another high light of the Kid's life was the killing of Buckshot Roberts at Blazer's Mill. Charlie Bowdre gave Roberts his mortal wound, though the Kid was accused of the deed. Before Roberts died, he in turn killed Dick Brewer the leader of the McSween faction, and from this time the leadership seemed to fall naturally upon the Kid's shoulders.

The feud reached its climax with the battle of the McSween home. There were several days of desultory firing, during which Sheriff Peppin wrote a note to Colonel Dudley, a commander at Fort Stanton, asking for help. Although the McSween forces were scattered, some being at the Ellis House, some at the Montano House and elsewhere, the Murphy faction concentrated their attack on the McSween home, for McSween was the man they most wanted. Tunstall was dead. Chisum had fled. McSween was the only one left with the money to finance the fight.

On the morning of the third day, Colonel Dudley, with a company of soldiers and two cannon, arrived in Lincoln and pitched camp near the McSween home, threatening to blow the house apart if a shot was fired. During the entire conflict he showed decided favoritism toward the Murphy crowd, and when Mrs. McSween went to him repeatedly with pleas to stop the fight, he became progressively insulting. He looked on as Murphy's men set fire to the McSween home, a fire which burned from room to room until only one room was left. It was then that the Kid and his men made a break for freedom. During this break McSween was killed by Beckwith, who, in turn, was killed by the Kid. When that battle was over, five men lay dead—McSween, Bob Beckwith, Harvey Morris, Vincente Romero, and Francisco Zamora. There was no carnival-like celebration afterward, as some writers claim.

The next high light in the Kid's career was the killing of Bernstein, a clerk at the Mescalero reservation, the true account of which is given later in this book. By now Billy was a hunted man, and Pat Garrett was elected sheriff especially to get him. Although he and the Kid had gambled, danced and stolen cattle together, they were now avowed enemies.

Governor Axtell, of New Mexico, who definitely favored the Murphy crowd and the Santa Fe Ring, was removed from office by the federal government, and General Lew Wallace was sent to take his place. Wallace held some secret meetings with the Kid at Squire Wilson's home and promised the Kid "exemption from prosecution" if he would come in and testify against the murderers of Chapman, Mrs. McSween's lawyer, but the Kid was afraid of treachery.

Chisum had failed to pay the men who fought his war, and the Kid began to hate him for this. He did not, as legend has it, kill one of Chisum's men for every five dollars owed him, but he did make an effort to collect the debt in stolen cattle.

The killing of Carlyle at the Greathouse and Kuck's stage station is another milestone in the Kid's life. Many writers assert positively that Carlyle was killed by the Kid, but there is no proof, since many others were shooting from both sides. Pat Garrett and his posse had surrounded an abandoned stone hut at Stinking Springs in which the Kid and his friends were holed up during a severe snowstorm. It was here that Charlie Bowdre was killed. The tempting smell of cooking food prompted the hungry, half-frozen men inside to surrender. The prisoners were taken to the Wilcox ranch, from which they were transported to Las Vegas in a wagon. After being held there in jail for the night, they were put on the train for Santa Fe. It was at this time that a mob gathered and threatened to take Dave Rudabaugh because he had murdered a native jailer there earlier.

From Santa Fe the Kid was taken to Mesilla to be tried for the killing of Buckshot Roberts, but Judge Leonard had this indictment squashed. Then the Kid was tried for the killing of Sheriff Brady, found guilty, and sentenced to hang. The old legend of the Kid's impudent reply to the Judge's sentence is strictly a myth and is entirely out of character.

The Kid was taken 150 miles to Lincoln, guarded by Bob Olinger, Kinney, an outlaw, and Matthews, the Kid's bitter enemy. He was placed in irons and held upstairs in the old Murphy store, now serving as a courthouse and jail.

Many varying tales have been told about how the Kid got a gun when he made his escape from his Lincoln jail. As near as we can get the truth through the thorough research of such historians as Maurice Garland Fulton and others, it seems that Sam Corbett had hidden a revolver, wrapped in newspaper, in the jail's outdoor privy. He then slipped the Kid a note about the gun, which he secured when Bell, one of his guards, escorted him to the outhouse. On coming out, he covered Bell, disarmed him, and marched him back upstairs. Upon reaching a hall not far from the top landing, Bell made a break for the stairs, but was shot by the Kid when he was halfway down. It is said that the Kid's shot missed Bell but hit the left-hand wall and ricocheted into Bell's right side, and he tumbled down the stairs a dead man.

Hobbling back inside the room (he was still in irons), the Kid grabbed a double-barreled shotgun belonging to Olinger, his other guard, who was absent, and hurried to a window. He saw Olinger returning to investigate the shot. When he got beneath the window, the Kid said, "Hello, Bob," and as Olinger looked up, he filled him with buckshot.

Godfrey Gauss, the jail cook, was next commanded to throw up a file, but the best he could do was a prospector's pick, with which Billy pried loose the rivets on one leg iron. Then securing a horse, he made his escape without any interference from the onlookers across the street.

Some weeks later Garrett, with his deputies Poe and McKinney, came into Fort Sumner searching for the Kid. On the night of July 14, 1881, they went to Pete Maxwell's to seek information. While Poe and McKinney waited outside, Garrett went in to talk with Maxwell, who had gone to bed. While he was there, the Kid came in, seeking a piece of meat for the meal his girl friend was preparing for him. As he approached barefooted, with a butcher knife in his hand and a gun in his pants' waist, he spied the deputies and inquired who they were. Going inside, he asked Maxwell about them. Seeing a figure sitting near the head of Maxwell's bed in the dim light, he jumped back and again asked who was there. Garrett recognized the voice and shot twice, the first shot killing the Kid, the second missing.

This, in brief, is the story of the Kid's life, as nearly accurate as I can reconstruct it from many years of research.

From Ramon F. Adams, *A Fitting Death for Billy the Kid* (Norman: University of Oklahoma Press, 1960), pp. 3–9. Copyright © 1960 by the University of Oklahoma Press.

Billy the Kid

I'll sing you a true song of Billy the Kid,
I'll sing of the desperate deeds that he did,
Way out in New Mexico long, long ago,
When a man's only chance was his own 44.

When Billy the Kid was a very young lad,
In old Silver City he went to the bad;
Way out in the West with a gun in his hand
At the age of twelve years he first killed his man.

Fair Mexican maidens play guitars and sing
A song about Billy, their boy bandit king,
How ere his young manhood had reached its sad end
Had a notch on his pistol for twenty-one men.

'Twas on the same night when poor Billy died
He said to his friends: "I am not satisfied;
There are twenty-one men I have put bullets through
And Sheriff Pat Garrett must make twenty-two."

Now this is how Billy the Kid met his fate;
The bright moon was shining, the hour was late,
Shot down by Pat Garrett, who once was his friend,
The young outlaw's life had now come to its end.

There's many a man with a face fine and fair
Who starts out in life with a chance to be square,
But just like poor Billy he wanders astray
And loses his life in the very same way.

From John A. and Alan Lomax, *American Ballads and Folk Songs*
(New York: The Macmillan Company, 1934), pp. 137–138. Anony-
mous. "Billy the Kid." New words and new music adaptation by John
A. Lomax and Alan Lomax TRO-Copyright 1938 and renewed © 1966
Ludlow Music, Inc. New York, N.Y. Used by permission.

Jorge Luis Borges

The Disinterested Killer, Bill Harrigan

An image of the desert wilds of Arizona, first and foremost,
an image of the desert wilds of Arizona and New Mexico—a
country famous for its silver and gold camps, a country of
breathtaking open spaces, a country of monumental mesas
and soft colors, a country of bleached skeletons picked clean
by buzzards. Over this whole country, another image—that of
Billy the Kid, the hard rider firm on his horse, the young
man with the relentless six-shooters, sending out invisible bullets which (like magic) kill at a distance.

The desert veined with precious metals, arid and blinding-
bright. The near child who on dying at the age of 21 owed to
the justice of grown men 21 deaths—"not counting Mexicans."

Along about 1859, the man who would become known to
terror and glory as Billy the Kid was born in a cellar room of
a New York City tenement. It is said that he was spawned by

a tired-out Irish womb but was brought up among Negroes. In this tumult of lowly smells and woolly heads, he enjoyed a superiority that stemmed from having freckles and a mop of red hair. He took pride in being white; he was also scrawny, wild and coarse. At the age of 12, he fought in the gang of the Swamp Angels, that branch of divinities who operated among the neighborhood sewers. On nights redolent of burnt fog, they would clamber out of that foul-smelling labyrinth, trail some German sailor, do him in with a knock on the head, strip him to his underwear and afterward sneak back to the filth of their starting place. Their leader was a gray-haired Negro, Gas House Jonas, who was also celebrated as a poisoner of horses.

Sometimes, from the upper window of a waterfront dive, a woman would dump a bucket of ashes upon the head of a prospective victim. As he gasped and choked, Swamp Angels would swarm him, rush him into a cellar and plunder him.

Such were the apprentice years of Billy Harrigan, the future Billy the Kid. Nor did he scorn the offerings of Bowery playhouses, enjoying in particular (perhaps without an inkling that they were signs and symbols of his destiny) cowboy melodramas.

If the jammed Bowery theaters (whose top-gallery riffraff shouted "Hoist that rag!" when the curtain failed to rise promptly on schedule) abounded in these blood-and-thunder productions, the simple explanation is that America was then experiencing the lure of the Far West. Beyond the sunset lay the goldfields of Nevada and California. Beyond the sunset were the redwoods, going down before the ax; the buffalo's huge Babylonian face; Brigham Young's beaver hat and plural bed; the red man's ceremonies and his rampages; the clear air of the deserts; endless stretching rangeland; and the earth itself, whose nearness quickens the heart like the nearness of the sea. The West beckoned. A slow, steady rumor populated those years—that of thousands of Americans taking possession of the West. On that march, around 1872, was Bill Harrigan, treacherous as a bull rattler, in flight from a rectangular cell.

History (which like certain film directors, proceeds by a series of abrupt images) now puts forward the image of a danger-filled saloon, located—as if on the high seas—out in the heart of the all-powerful desert. The time, a blustery night of the year 1873; the place, the Staked Plains of New Mexico. All around, the land is almost uncannily flat and

bare, but the sky, with its storm-piled clouds and moon, is
full of fissured cavities and mountains. There are a cow's
skull, the howl and the eyes of coyotes in the shadows, trim
horses and from the saloon an elongated patch of light. Inside, leaning over the bar, a group of strapping but tired men
drink a liquor that warms them for a fight; at the same time,
they make a great show of large silver coins bearing a serpent
and an eagle. A drunk croons to himself, poker-faced.
Among the men are several who speak a language with many
s's, which must be Spanish, for those who speak it are looked
down on. Bill Harrigan, the red-topped tenement rat, stands
among the drinkers. He has downed a couple of *aguardientes*
and thinks of asking for one more, maybe because he hasn't a
cent left. He is somewhat overwhelmed by these men of the
desert. He sees them as imposing, boisterous, happy and hate-
fully wise in the handling of wild cattle and big horses. All at
once there is a dead silence, ignored only by the voice of the
drunk, singing out of tune. Someone has come in—a big,
burly Mexican with the face of an old Indian squaw. He is
endowed with an immense sombrero and with a pair of six-
guns at his side. In awkward English, he wishes a good evening to all the gringo sons of bitches who are drinking.
Nobody takes up the challenge. Bill asks who he is, and they
whisper to him, in fear, that the Dago—that is, the Diego—is
Belisario Villagrán, from Chihuahua. At once, there is a resounding blast. Sheltered by that wall of tall men, Bill has
fired at the intruder. The glass drops from Villagrán's hand;
then the man himself drops. He does not need another bullet.
Without deigning to glance at the showy dead man, Bill picks
up his end of the conversation. "Is that so?" he drawls. "Well,
I'm Billy the Kid, from New York." The drunk goes on singing, unheeded.

One may easily guess the apotheosis. Bill gives out hand-
shakes all around and accepts praises, cheers and whiskeys.
Someone notices that there are no notches on the handle of
his revolver and offers to cut one to stand for Villagrán's
death. Billy the Kid keeps this someone's razor, though he
says that "It's hardly worthwhile noting down Mexicans."
This, perhaps, is not quite enough. That night, Bill lays out
his blanket beside the corpse and—with great show—sleeps
till daybreak.

Out of that lucky blast (at the age of 14), Billy the Kid
the hero was born, and the furtive Bill Harrigan died. The
boy of the sewer and the knock on the head rose to become a

man of the frontier. He made a horseman of himself, learning to ride straight in the saddle—Wyoming- or Texas-style—and not with his body thrown back, the way they rode in Oregon and California. He never completely matched his legend, but he kept getting closer and closer to it. Something of the New York hoodlum lived on in the cowboy; he transferred to Mexicans the hate that had previously been inspired in him by Negroes, but the last words he ever spoke were swearwords in Spanish. He learned the art of the cow-puncher's maverick life. He learned another, more difficult art—how to lead men. Both helped to make him a good cattle rustler. From time to time, Old Mexico's guitars and whorehouses pulled on him.

With the haunting lucidity of insomnia, he organized populous orgies that often lasted four days and four nights. In the end, glutted, he settled accounts with bullets. While his trigger finger was unfailing, he was the most feared man (and perhaps the most anonymous and most lonely) of that whole frontier. Pat Garrett, his friend, the sheriff who later killed him, once told him, "I've had a lot of practice with the rifle shooting buffalo."

"I've had plenty with the six-shooter," Billy replied modestly. "Shooting tin cans and men."

The details can never be recovered, but it is known that he was credited with up to 21 killings—"not counting Mexicans." For seven desperate years, he practiced the extravagance of utter recklessness.

The night of the twenty-fifth of July, 1880, Billy the Kid came galloping on his piebald down the main, or only, street of Fort Sumner. The heat was oppressive and the lamps had not been lighted; Sheriff Garrett, seated on a porch in a rocking chair, drew his revolver and sent a bullet through the Kid's belly. The horse kept on; the rider tumbled into the dust of the road. Garrett got off a second shot. The townspeople (knowing the wounded man was Billy the Kid) locked their window shutters tight. The agony was long and blasphemous. In the morning, the sun by then high overhead, they began drawing near, and they disarmed him. The man was gone. They could see in his face that used-up look of the dead.

He was shaved, sheathed in ready-made clothes and displayed to awe and ridicule in the window of Fort Sumner's biggest store. Men on horseback and in buckboards gathered for miles and miles around. On the third day, they had to use

makeup on him. On the fourth day, he was buried with rejoicing.

From Jorge Luis Borges, *A Universal History of Infamy*, translated
by Norman Thomas di Giovanni (New York: E.P. Dutton & Co.,
1972), pp. 59–66.

Bob Dylan

The Myth Lives On

There's guns across the river aimin' at ya
Lawman on your trail, he'd like to catch ya
Bounty hunters, too, they'd like to get ya
Billy, they don't like you to be so free.

Campin' out all night on the berenda
Dealin' cards 'til dawn in the hacienda
Up to Boot Hill they'd like to send ya
Billy, don't you turn your back on me.

Playin' around with some sweet señorita
Into her dark hallway she will lead ya
In some lonesome shadows she will greet ya
Billy, you're so far away from home.

There's eyes behind the mirrors in empty places
Bullet holes and scars between the spaces
There's always one more notch and ten more paces
Billy, and you're walkin' all alone.

They say that Pat Garrett's got your number
So sleep with one eye open when you slumber
Every little sound just might be thunder
Thunder from the barrel of his gun.

There's always some new stranger sneakin' glances
Some trigger-happy fool willin' to take chances
And some old whore from San Pedro to make advances
Advances on your spirit and your soul.

The businessmen from Taos want you to go down
They've hired Pat Garrett to force a showdown
Billy, don't it make ya feel so lowdown
To be shot down by the man who was your friend.

Hang on to your woman if you got one
Remember in El Paso, once, you shot one
She may have been a whore, but she was a hot one
Billy, you been runnin' for so long.

Guitars will play your grand finale
Down in some Tularosa alley
Maybe in the Rio Pecos valley
Billy, you're so far from home.

From Bob Dylan, "Billy" (New York: Ram's Horn Music, 1976).

THE MILD WEST

Richard Harding Davis

The Trooper

The American private, as he showed himself during the three days in which I was his guest, and afterwards, when Captain Hardie had returned and we went scouting together, proved to be a most intelligent and unpicturesque individual. He was intelligent, because he had, as a rule, followed some other calling before he entered the service, and he was not picturesque, because he looked on "soldiering" merely as a means of livelihood, and had little or no patriotic or sentimental feeling concerning it. This latter was not true of the older men. They had seen real war either during the rebellion or in the Indian campaigns, which are much more desperate affairs than the Eastern mind appreciates, and they were fond

of the service and proud of it. One of the corporals in G
Troop, for instance, had been honorably discharged a year
before with the rank of first sergeant, and had re-enlisted as a
private rather than give up the service, of which he found he
was more fond than he had imagined when he had left it.
And in K Troop was an even more notable instance in a man
who had been retired on three-fourths pay, having served his
thirty years, and who had returned to the troop to act as Captain Hunter's "striker," or man of all work, and who bore the
monotony of the barracks and the hardships of field service
rather than lose the uniform and the feeling of *esprit de
corps* which thirty years' service had made a necessity to him.

But the raw recruit, or the man in his third or fourth year,
as he expressed himself in the different army posts and
among the companies I met on the field, looked upon his
work from a purely business point of view. He had been before enlistment a clerk or a compositor, a cowboy, a day-la-
borer, painter, blacksmith, book-canvasser, almost everything.
In Captain Hardie's troop all of these were represented, and
the average of intelligence was very high. Whether the most
intelligent private is the best soldier is a much-discussed question which is not to be discussed here, but these men were intelligent and were good soldiers, although I am sure they
were too independent in their thoughts, though not in their
actions, to have suited an officer of the English or German
army. That they are more carefully picked men than those
found in the rank and file of the British army can be proved
from the fact that of those who apply for enlistment in the
United States but twenty per cent are chosen, while in Great
Britain they accept eighty and in some years ninety per cent
of the applicants. The small size of our army in comparison,
however, makes this showing less favorable than it at first appears.

In camp, while the captain was away, the privates suggested a lot of college boys more than any other body of individuals. A few had the college boy's delight in shirking their
work, and would rejoice over having had a dirty carbine pass
inspection on account of a shining barrel, as the Sophomore
boasts of having gained a high marking for a translation he
had read from a crib. They had also the college boy's songs,
and his trick of giving nicknames, and his original and sometimes clever slang, and his satisfaction in expressing violent
liking or dislike for those in authority over him—in the one
case tutors and professors, and in the other sergeants and

captains. Their one stupid hitch, in which the officers shared to some extent, was in re-enforcing all they said with profanity; but as soldiers have done this, apparently, since the time of Shakespeare's Seven Ages, it must be considered an inherited characteristic. Their fun around the camp fire at night was rough, but it was sometimes clever, though it was open to the objection that a clever story never failed of three or four repetitions. The greatest successes were those in which the officers, always of some other troop, were the butts. One impudent "cruitie" made himself famous in a night by improvising an interview between himself and a troop commander who had met him that day as he was steering a mule train across the prairie.

" 'How are you?' said he to me. 'You're one of captain Hardie's men, ain't you? I'm Captain ———.'

" 'Glad to know you, captain,' said I. 'I've read about you in the papers.' "

This was considered a magnificent stroke by the men, who thought the captain in question rather too fond of sending in reports concerning himself to headquarters.

" 'Well,' says he, 'when do you think we're going to catch this ——— ——— ——— ——— Garza? As for me,' says he, 'I'm that ——— ——— ——— ——— tired of the whole ——— ——— ——— business that I'm willing to give up my job to any ——— ——— ——— fool that will take it ———'

" 'Well, old man,' says I, 'I'd be glad to relieve you,' says I, 'but I'd a ——— sight rather serve under Captain Hardie than captain such a lot of regular ——— ——— ——— coffee-coolers as you've got under you.' "

The audacity of this entirely fictitious conversation was what recommended it to the men. I only reproduce it here as showing their idea of humor. An even greater success was that of a stolid German, who related a true incident of life at Fort Clarke, where the men were singing one night around the fire, when the colonel passed by, and ordered them into the tents, and to stop that ——— noise.

"And den," continued the soldier, "he come acrost Cabding ———, sitting in frond of his tent, and he says to him quick like that, 'You ged into your tent, *too*.' That's what he said to him, 'You ged into your tent, *too*.' "

It is impossible to imagine the exquisite delight that this simple narrative gave. The idea of a real troop commander having been told to get into his tent just like a common soldier brought the tears to the men's eyes, and the success of his story so turned the German's head that he continued repeating to himself and to any one he met for several days: "That's what he said, 'You ged into your tent, *too*.' That's what he said.". . .

The Eastern mind does not occupy itself much with these guardians of its borders; its idea of the soldier is the comfortable, clubable, likeable fellow they meet in Washington and New York, whose red, white, and blue button is all that marks him from the other clubable, likeable men about him. But they ought to know more and feel more for these equally likeable men of the border posts, whose only knowledge of club life is the annual bill for dues, one of which, with supreme irony, arrived in Captain Hardie's mail at a time when he had only bacon three times a day, and nothing but alkali water to silence the thirst that followed. To a young man it is rather pathetic to see another young man, with a taste and fondness for the pleasant things of this world, pull out his watch and hold it to the camp fire and say, "Just seven o'clock; people in God's country are sitting down to dinner." And then a little later: "And now it's eight o'clock, and they are going to the theatres. What is there at the theatres now?" And when I recalled the plays running in New York when I left it, the officers would select which one they would go to, with much grave deliberation, and then crawl in between two blankets and find the most comfortable angle at which a McClellan saddle will make a pillow.

From Davis, *West from a Car-Window*, pp. 33–39, 40.

Stephen Crane

Galveston, Texas, in 1895

It is the fortune of travellers to take note of differences and publish them to their friends. It is the differences that are supposed to be valuable. The travellers seek them bravely, and cudgel their wits to find means to unearth them. But in this search they are confronted continually by the resemblances and the intrusion of commonplace and most obvious similarity into a field that is being ploughed in the romantic fashion is what causes an occasional resort to the imagination.

The winter found a cowboy in south-western Nebraska who had just ended a journey from Kansas City, and he swore bitterly as he remembered how little boys in Kansas City followed him about in order to contemplate his wide-brimmed hat. His vivid description of this incident would have been instructive to many Eastern readers. The fact that little boys in Kansas City could be profoundly interested in the sight of a wide-hatted cowboy would amaze a certain proportion of the populace. Where then can one expect cowboys if not in Kansas City? As a matter of truth, however, a steam boiler with four legs and a tail, galloping down the main street of the town, could create no more enthusiasm there than a real cow-puncher. For years the farmers have been driving the cattlemen back, back toward the mountains and into Kansas, and Nebraska has come to an almost universal condition of yellow trolly-cars with clanging gongs and whirring wheels, and conductors who don't give a curse for the public. And travellers tumbling over each other in their haste to trumpet the radical differences between Eastern and Western life have created a generally wrong opinion. . . . It is this fact which has kept the sweeping march of the West from being chronicled in any particularly true manner. . . .

If a man comes to Galveston resolved to discover every curious thing possible, and to display every point where Galveston differed from other parts of the universe, he would have the usual difficulty in shutting his eyes to the similarities. Galveston is often original, full of distinctive characters. But it is not like a town in the moon. There are, of course, a thousand details of street color and life which are thoroughly typical of any American city. The square brick business blocks, the mazes of telegraph wires, the trolly-cars clamoring up and down the streets, the passing crowd, the slight fringe of reflective and reposeful men on the curb, all disappoint the traveller, and he goes out in the sand somewhere and digs in order to learn if all Galveston clams are not schooner-rigged.

From Stephen Crane, *The Works of Stephen Crane*, edited by Fredson Bowers (Charlottesville: University Press of Virginia, 1973), Vol. 8, pp. 474–475.

Richard Harding Davis

The West from a Car-Window

The ideas which the stay-at-home Eastern man obtains of the extreme borderland of Texas are gathered from various sources, principally from those who, as will all travellers, make as much of what they have seen as is possible, this much being generally to show the differences which exist between the places they have visited and their own home. Of the similarities they say nothing. Or he has read of the bandits and outlaws of the Garza revolution and he has seen the Wild West show of the Hon. William F. Cody. The latter, no doubt, surprised and delighted him very much. A mild West show, which would be equally accurate, would surprise him even more; at least, if it was organized in the wildest part of Texas between San Antonio and Corpus Christi.

When he leaves this first city and touches at the border of Mexico, at Laredo, and starts forth again across the prairie of cactus and chaparral towards "Corpus," he feels assured that at last he is done with parlor-cars and civilization; that he is about to see the picturesque and lawless side of the Texan existence, and that he has taken his life in his hands. He will be the more readily convinced of this when the young man with the broad shoulders and sun-browned face and wide sombrero in the seat in front raises the car-window, and begins to shoot splinters out of the passing telegraph poles with the melancholy and listless air of one who is performing a casual divertisement. But he will be better informed when the Chicago drummer has risen hurriedly, with a pale face, and has reported what is going on to the conductor, and he hears that dignitary say, complacently: "Sho! that's only 'Will' Scheeley practisin'! He's a dep'ty sheriff."

He will learn in time that the only men on the borders of Texas who are allowed to wear revolvers are sheriffs, State agents in charge of prisoners, and the Texas Rangers, and that whenever he sees a man so armed he may as surely assume that he is one of these as he may know that in New York men in gray uniforms, with leather bags over their shoulders, are letter-carriers. The revolver is the Texan officer's badge of office; it corresponds to the New York policeman's shield; and he toys with it just as the Broadway policeman juggles his club. It is quite as harmless as a toy, and almost as terrible as a weapon.

This will grieve the "tenderfoot" who goes through the West "heeled," and ready to show that though he is from the effete East, he is able to take care of himself.

It was first brought home to me as I was returning from the border, where I had been with the troops who were hunting for Garza, and was waiting at a little station on the prairie to take the train for Corpus Christi. I was then told politely by a gentleman who seemed of authority, that if I did not take off that pistol I would be fined twenty-five dollars, or put in jail for twenty days. I explained to him where I had been, and that my baggage was at "Corpus," and that I had no other place to carry it. At which he apologized, and directed a deputy sheriff, who was also going to Corpus Christie, to see that I was not arrested for carrying a deadly weapon.

This, I think, illustrates a condition of things in darkest Texas which may give a new point of view to the Eastern mind. It is possibly something of a revelation to find that instead of every man protecting himself, and the selection of the fittest depending on who is "quickest on the trigger," he has to have an officer of the law to protect him if he tries to be a law unto himself.

From Davis, *West from a Car-Window*, pp. 6–7.

THE FADING WEST

Leaving Cheyenne

My foot in the stirrup, my pony won't stand;
I'm a-leavin' Cheyenne, I'm off for Montan'.

I'm a-ridin' Old Paint, I'm a-leadin' old Fan
Goodbye, Old Paint, I'm a-leavin' Cheyenne.

Old Paint's a good pony, he paces when he can;
Goodbye, little Annie, I'm off for Cheyenne.

Oh, hitch up your horses and feed 'em some hay,
And seat yourself by me so long as you stay.

My horses ain't hungry, they'll not eat your hay;
My wagon is loaded and rolling away

Goodbye, Old Paint, I'm a-leavin' Cheyenne;
Goodbye, Old Paint, I'm a-leavin' Cheyenne.

From Lomax, *Cowboy Songs*, pp. 329–330.

Zane Grey

Settling Down

Meanwhile sunset had come and the grove of cottonwoods
was a place of color and beauty. A tiny brook tinkled by under a grassy bank; mockingbirds were singing off somewhere
in the distance; a raven croaked overhead. The grass shone
like black-barred gold and there was a redness in the west.
Tranquil, lonely, and sad, the end of day roused feelings in
Laramie that had rendered his breast heavy many a time before.

"Nice place for a little ranch," he said, presently.

"Ain't it, though? I was just thinkin' thet. A bunch of
cattle, some good hosses, plenty of wood, water, an' grass—a
home. . . . Heigho! . . . It's a hell of a life if you don't
weaken."

Laramie had touched on a sensitive chord in his companion's heart. Some how this simple fact seemed to draw them
closer together, in a community of longing, if no more.

"Wal, when yu said home yu said a heap, boy. . . .
Home! Thet means a woman—a wife."

"Sure. But I never got so far in reckonin' as thet," replied
Lonesome, thoughtfully.

"Lonesome, why don't yu marry one of these girls yu
swear bob up heah an' there?"

"My Gawd! What an idear! . . . Thet's one thing thet
never struck me before," ejaculated Mulhall, profoundly
stirred, and his homely young face was good to see on the
moment.

"Wal, since it has struck yu now, how about it?" went on Laramie.

Lonesome threw his rabbit bones away in a violence of contention, with alluring but impossible ideas.

"Marry some girl? On this range—this lone prairee where the wind howls down the wolves? Where there ain't any girls or any cabins for the takin'. When a poor rider can't hold a steady job. . . . When—Aw, hell, Laramie, what's the use talkin'."

"Wal, I wasn't puttin' the difficulties before yu, but just the idee."

"Ahuh. I wisht you hadn't. I've got a weak place in me. Never knowed what it was. But thet's it."

"Like to have a corner to work on—a homestead where every turn of a spade was for yoreself—where every calf an' colt added to yore ranch? Thet how it strikes yu?"

"Sure. I've got pioneer blood. Most of us riders have. But only a few of us beat red liquor, gamblin'-hells, loose wimmin, ropes an' guns."

"Yu said somethin' to think about," mused Laramie.

"Laramie, have you beat them things?"

"I reckon, except mebbe guns—an' I've done tolerable well about them."

"I take it you're ridin' a grub-line, same as I have to now?"

"Shore. But more, Lonesome. I'm ridin' out of this country. Colorado for me, or New Mexico—mebbe even Arizona."

"Laramie, if I ain't too personal—air you on the dodge?"

"Nope. I've a clean slate," retorted Laramie, with the curtness of the Southerner.

"I'm thunderin' glad to hear thet," burst out Lonesome, as if relieved. "I wisht to Gawd I had the nerve to ask you— Aw! never mind. My feelin's run away with me at times."

"Ask me what, Lonesome?" queried Laramie. "I'll lend yu some money, if yu want it."

"Money, hell! You're good to offer, knowin' it'd never be paid back. . . . I meant to let me ride with you out of this flat Kansas prairie—away off some place where you can get on a hill."

"Wal, why not? If yu'll take a chance on me I will on yu."

Lonesome strangled a wild eagerness. The light in his eyes then decided Laramie upon the real deeper possibility of this lad.

"But I'm no good, Laramie, no good atall," he burst out.

"I can ride, I like cattle, I ain't lazy, an' I'm a good camp cook. But thet lets me out."

"How about whiskey?"

"Haven't had a drink for six months an' don't care a damn if I never have another. I'm a pore gambler, too, an' a wuss shot. Reckon I'm some punkins with the girls. But where'd thet ever get a fellow?"

"Lonesome, all yu say 'pears a pretty good reference, if I needed any."

From Zane Grey, *Raiders of Spanish Peaks* (New York: Harper & Bros., 1931), pp. 13–15.

Wallace Stegner
Carrion Spring

The moment she came to the door she could smell it, not really rotten and not coming from any particular direction, but sweetish, faintly sickening, sourceless, filling the whole air the way a river's water can taste of weeds—the carrion smell of a whole country breathing out in the first warmth across hundreds of square miles.

Three days of chinook had uncovered everything that had been under snow since November. The yard lay discolored and ugly, gray ashpile, rusted cans, spilled lignite, bones. The clinkers that had given them winter footing to privy and stable lay in raised gray wavers across the mud; the strung lariats they had used for lifelines in blizzardy weather had dried out and sagged to the ground. Muck was knee deep down in the corrals by the sod-roofed stable, the white-washed logs were yellowed at the corners from dogs lifting their legs against them. Sunken drifts around the hay yard were a reminder of how many times the boys had had to shovel out there to keep the calves from walking into the stacks across the top of them. Across the wan and disheveled yard the willows were bare, and beyond them the floodplain hill was brown. The sky was roiled with gray cloud.

Matted, filthy, lifeless, littered, the place of her winter imprisonment was exposed, ugly enough to put gooseflesh up her backbone, and with the carrion smell over all of it. It was like a bad and disgusting wound, infected wire cut or proud flesh or the gangrene of frostbite, with the bandage off. With her packed trunk and her telescope bag and two loaded grain sacks behind her, she stood in the door waiting for Ray to come with the buckboard, and she was sick to be gone.

Yet when he did come, with the boys all slopping through the mud behind him, and they threw her trunk and telescope and bags into the buckboard and tied the tarp down and there was nothing left to do but go, she faced them with a sudden, desolating desire to cry. She laughed, and caught her lower lip under her teeth and bit down hard on it, and went around to shake one hoof-like hand after the other, staring into each face in turn and seeing in each something that made it all the harder to say something easy: Goodbye. Red-bearded, black-bearded, gray-bristled, clean-shaven (for her?), two of them with puckered sunken scars on the cheekbones, all of them seedy, matted-haired, weathered and cracked as old lumber left out for years, they looked sheepish, or sober, or cheerful, and said things like, "Well, Molly, have you a nice trip, now," or "See you in Malta maybe." They had been her family. She had looked after them, fed them, patched their clothes, unraveled old socks to knit them new ones, cut their hair, lanced their boils, tended their wounds. Now it was like the gathered-in family parting at the graveside after someone's funeral.

She had begun quite openly to cry. She pulled her cheeks down, opened her mouth, dabbed at her eyes with her knuckles, laughed. "Now you all take care," she said. "And come see us, you hear? Jesse? Rusty? Slip? Buck, when you come I'll fix you a better patch on your pants than that one. Goodbye, Panguingue, you were the best man I had on the coal scuttle. Don't you forget me. Little Horn, I'm *sorry* we ran out of pie fixings. When you come to Malta I'll make you a peach pie a yard across."

She could not have helped speaking their names, as if to name them were to insure their permanence. But she knew that though she might see them, or most of them, when Ray brought the drive in to Malta in July, these were friends who would soon be lost for good. They had already got the word: sweep the range and sell everything—steers, bulls, calves, cows—for whatever it would bring. Put a For Sale sign on the ranch, or simply abandon it. The country had rubbed its lesson in. Like half the outfits between the Milk and the CPR, the T-Down was quitting. As for her, she was quitting first.

She saw Ray slumping, glooming down from the buck-board seat with the reins wrapped around one gloved hand. Dude and Dinger were hipshot in the harness. As Rusty and Little Horn gave Molly a hand up to climb the wheel, Dude raised his tail and dropped an oaty bundle of dung on the singletree, but she did not even bother to make a face or say something provoked and joking. She was watching Ray, look-ing right into his gray eyes and his somber dark face and seeing all at once what the winter of disaster had done to him. His cheek, like Ed's and Rusty's, was puckered with frost scars; frost had nibbled at the lobes of his ears; she could see the strain of bone-cracking labor, the bitterness of failure, in the lines from his nose to the corners of his mouth. Making room for her, he did not smile. With her back mo-mentarily to the others, speaking only for him, she said through her tight teeth, "Let's git!"

Promptly—he was always prompt and ready—he plucked whip from whipsocket. The tip snapped on Dinger's haunch, the lurch of the buggy threw her so that she could cling and not have to turn to reveal her face. "Goodbye!" she cried, more into the collar of her mackinaw than to them, throwing the words over her shoulder like a flower or a coin, and tossed her left hand in the air and shook it. The single burst of their voices chopped off into silence. She heard only the grate of the tires in gravel; beside her the wheel poured yel-low drip. She concentrated on it, fighting her lips that wanted to blubber.

"This could be bad for a minute," Ray said. She looked up. Obediently she clamped thumb and finger over her nose. To their right, filling half of Frying Pan Flat, was the bone-yard, two acres of carcasses scattered where the boys had dragged them after skinning them out when they found them dead in the brush. It did not seem that off there they could smell, for the chinook was blowing out in light airs from the west. But when she let go her nose she smelled it rich and rotten, as if it rolled upwind the way water runs upstream in an eddy.

Beside her Ray was silent. The horses were trotting now in the soft sand of the patrol trail. On both sides the willows were gnawed down to stubs, broken and mouthed and gummed off by starving cattle. There was floodwater in the low spots, and the sound of running water under the drifts of every side coulee.

Once Ray said, "Harry Willis says a railroad survey's

coming right up the Whitemud valley this summer. S'pose that'll mean homesteaders in here, maybe a town."

"I s'pose."

"Make it a little easier when you run out of prunes, if there was a store at Whitemud."

"Well," she said, "we won't be here to run out," and then immediately, as she caught a whiff that gagged her, "Pee-you! Hurry up!"

Ray did not touch up the team. "What for?" he said. "To get to the next one quicker?"

She appraised the surliness of his voice, and judged that some of it was general disgust and some of it was aimed at her. But what did he want? Every time she made a suggestion of some outfit around Malta or Chinook where he might get a job he humped his back and looked impenetrable. What *did* he want? To come back here and take another licking? When there wasn't even a cattle outfit left, except maybe the little ones like the Z-X and the Lazy-S? And where one winter could kill you, as it had just killed the T-Down? She felt like yelling at him, "Look at your face. Look at your hands—you can't open them even halfway, for calluses. For what? Maybe three thousand cattle left out of ten thousand, and them skin and bone. Why wouldn't I be glad to get out? Who *cares* if there's a store at Whitemud? You're just like an old bulldog with his teeth clinched in somebody's behind, and it'll take a pry-bar to make you unclinch!" She said nothing; she forced herself to breathe evenly the tainted air.

Floodwater forced them out of the bottoms and up onto the second floodplain. Below them Molly saw the river astonishingly wide, pushing across willow bars and pressing deep into the cutbank bends. She could hear it, when the wheels went quietly—a hushed roar like wind. Cattle were balloonily afloat in the brush where they had died. She saw a brindle longhorn waltz around the deep water of a bend with his legs in the air, and farther on a whiteface that stranded momentarily among flooded rosebushes, and rotated free, and stranded again.

Their bench was cut by a side coulee, and they tipped and rocked down, the rumps of the horses back against the dashboard, Ray's hand on the brake, the shoes screeching mud from the tires. There was brush in the bottom, and stained drifts still unmelted. Their wheels sank in slush, she hung to the seat rail, they righted, the lines cracked across the muscling rumps as the team dug in and lifted them out of the cold, snowbank breath of the draw. Then abruptly, in a hollow on the right, dead eyeballs stared at her from between spraddled legs, horns and tails and legs were tangled in a starved mass of bone and hide not yet, in that cold bottom, puffing with the gases of decay. They must have been three deep—piled on one another, she supposed, while drifting before some one of the winter's blizzards.

A little later, accosted by a stench so overpowering that she breathed it in deeply as if to sample the worst, she looked to the left and saw a longhorn, its belly blown up ready to pop, hanging by neck and horns from a tight clump of alder and black birch where the snow had left him. She saw the wind make catspaws in the heavy winter hair.

"Jesus," Ray said, "when you find 'em in *trees!*"

His boots, worn and whitened by many wettings, were braced against the dash. From the corner of her eye Molly could see his glove, its wrist-lace open. His wrist looked as wide as a double-tree, the sleeve of his Levi jacket was tight with forearm. The very sight of his strength made her hate the tone of defeat and outrage in his voice. Yet she appraised the tone cunningly, for she did not want him somehow butting his bullheaded way back into it. There were better things they could do than break their backs and hearts in a hopeless country a hundred miles from anywhere.

With narrowed eyes, caught in an instant vision, she saw the lilac bushes by the front porch of her father's house, heard the screen door bang behind her brother Charley (screen doors!), saw people passing, women in dresses, maybe all going to a picnic or a ballgame down in the park by the river. She passed the front of McCabe's General Store and through the window saw the counters and shelves: dried apples, dried peaches, prunes, tapioca, Karo syrup, everything they had done without for six weeks; and new white-stitched overalls, yellow horsehide gloves, varnished axe handles, barrels of flour and bags of sugar, shiny boots and workshoes, counters full of calico and flowered voile and crepe de chine and curtain net, whole stacks of flypaper stuck sheet to sheet, jars of peppermints and striped candy and horehound . . . She giggled.

"What?" Ray's neck and shoulders were so stiff with muscle that he all but creaked when he turned his head.

"I was just thinking. Remember the night I used our last sugar to make that batch of divinity, and dragged all the boys in after bedtime to eat it?"

"Kind of saved the day," Ray said. "Took the edge off ever'body."

"Kind of left us starving for sugar, too. I can still see them picking up those little bitty dabs of fluff with their fingers like tongs, and stuffing them in among their whiskers and making faces, *yum yum,* and wondering what on earth had got into me."

"Nothing got into you. You was just fed up. We all was."

"Remember when Slip picked up that pincushion I was tatting a cover for, and I got sort of hysterical and asked him if he knew what it was? Remember what he said? 'It a doll pillar, ain't it, Molly?' I thought I'd die."

She shook her head angrily. Ray was looking sideward at her in alarm. She turned her face away and stared down across the water that spread nearly a half-mile wide in the bottoms. Dirty foam and brush circled in the eddies. She saw a slab cave from an almost drowned cutbank and sink bubbling. From where they drove, between the water and the outer slope that rolled up to the high prairie, the Cypress Hills made a snow-patched, tree-darkened dome across the west. The wind came off them mild as milk. Poisoned! she told herself, and dragged it deep into her lungs.

From Wallace Stegner, *Wolf Willow* (New York: Viking Press, 1962), pp. 222–228.

PROMOTING THE MYTH: BUFFALO BILL

William F. Cody

Buffalo Bill's Own Story

The western end of the Kansas Pacific was at this time in the heart of the buffalo country. Twelve hundred men were employed in the construction of the road. The Indians were very troublesome, and it was difficult to obtain fresh meat for the hands. The company therefore concluded to engage expert hunters to kill buffaloes.

Having heard of my experience and success as a buffalo hunter, Goddard Brothers, who had the contract for feeding the men, made me a good offer to become their hunter. They said they would require about twelve buffaloes a day—twenty-four hams and twelve humps, as only the hump and hindquarters of each animal were utilized. The work was dangerous. Indians were riding all over that section of the country, and my duties would require me to journey from five to ten miles from the railroad every day in order to secure the game, accompanied by only one man with a light wagon to haul the meat back to camp. I demanded a large salary, which they could well afford to pay, as the meat itself would cost them nothing. Under the terms of the contract which I signed with them, I was to receive five hundred dollars a month, agreeing on my part to supply them with all the meat they wanted.

Leaving Rose to complete our grading contract, I at once began my career as a buffalo hunter for the Kansas Pacific. It was not long before I acquired a considerable reputation, and it was at this time that the title "Buffalo Bill" was conferred upon me by the railroad hands. Of this title, which has stuck to me through life, I have never been ashamed.

During my engagement as hunter for the company, which covered a period of eighteen months, I killed 4,280 buffaloes and had many exciting adventures with the Indians, including a number of hairbreadth escapes, some of which are well worth relating. . . .

On our return to camp [after a buffalo-shooting contest with Billy Comstock,] we brought with us the best bits of meat, as well as the biggest and best buffalo heads. The heads I always turned over to the company, which found a very good use for them. They were mounted in the finest possible manner and sent to the principal cities along the road, as well as to the railroad centers of the country. Here they were prominently placed at the leading hotels and in the stations, where they made an excellent advertisement for the road. Today they attract the attention of travelers almost everywhere. Often, while touring the country, I see one of them, and I feel reasonably certain that I brought down the animal it once ornamented. Many a wild and exciting hunt is thus called to my mind.

From William F. Cody, *Buffalo Bill's Life Story: An Autobiography* (New York: Cosmopolitan Book Corporation, 1920), pp. 117-118, 125-126.

Buffalo Bill's Wild West

BUFFALO BILL'S "WILD WEST"
PRAIRIE EXHIBITION, AND ROCKY MOUNTAIN SHOW,
A DRAMATIC-EQUESTRIAN EXPOSITION
OF
LIFE ON THE PLAINS,
WITH ACCOMPANYING MONOLOGUE AND
INCIDENTAL MUSIC
THE WHOLE INVENTED AND ARRANGED BY
W. F. CODY
W. F. CODY AND N. SALSBURY, PROPRIETORS AND MANAGERS
WHO HEREBY CLAIM AS THEIR SPECIAL
PROPERTY THE VARIOUS EF-
FECTS INTRODUCED IN
THE PUBLIC PER-
FORMANCES
OF
BUFFALO BILL'S "WILD WEST"

MONOLOGUE

Ladies and Gentlemen:

I desire to call your attention to an important fact. From time to time it will be my pleasure to announce to you the different features of the programme as they occur. In order that I may do so intelligently, I respectfully request your silence and attention while I am speaking. Our agents will pass among you with the biographical history of the life of Hon. William F. Cody ("Buffalo Bill") and other celebrities who appear before you this afternoon. The Management desires to vouch for the truth and accuracy of all the statements contained in this book, and respectfully submitted to your attention, as helping you to understand and appreciate our entertainment. Before the entertainment begins, however, I wish to impress upon your minds that what you are about to witness is not a performance in the common sense of that term, but an exhibition of skill, on the part of men who have acquired that quality while gaining a livelihood. Many unthinking people suppose that the different features of our exhibition are the result of what is technically called "rehearsals." Such, however, is not the fact, and anyone who witnesses our performance the second time will observe that men and animals alike are the creatures of circumstances, depending for their success upon their own skill, daring and sagacity. In the East, the few who excel are known to all. In the far West, the names we offer to you this afternoon are the synonyms of skill, courage and individual excellence. At the conclusion of the next overture our performance will commence with a grand processional parade of the "Wild West."

Overture, grand processional parade of cowboys, Mexicans, and Indians, with incidental music.

I will introduce the different groups and individual celebrities as they pass before you in review.

Enter a group of Pawnee Indians. Music. Enter Chief. Music. Enter a group of Mexican vaqueros. Music. Enter a group of Wichita Indians. Music. Enter Chief. Music. Enter a group of American Cowboys. Music. Enter King of Cowboys. Music. Enter Cowboy Sheriff of the Platte. Music. Enter a group of Sioux Indians. Music. Enter Chief. Music.

I next have the honor of introducing to your attention a man whose record as a servant of the government, whose skill and daring as a frontiersman, whose place in history as the chief of scouts of the United States Army, under such generals as Sherman, Sheridan, Hancock, Terry, Miles, Hazen, Royal, Merrit, Crook, Carr and others, and whose name as one of the avengers of the lamented Custer, and whose adherence throughout an eventful life to his chosen principle of "true to friend and foe," have made him well and popularly known throughout the world. You all know to whom I allude—the Honorable William F. Cody, "Buffalo Bill."

Enter Cody. Bugle Call. Cody speaks.

Ladies and Gentlemen: Allow me to introduce the equestrian portion of the Wild West Exhibition.

Turns to review.

Wild West, are you ready? Go!

Exeunt omnes.

First on our programme, a — mile race, between a cowboy, a Mexican, and an Indian, starting at ———. You will please notice that these horses carry the heaviest trapping, and that neither of the riders weigh less than 145 pounds.

Next on our programme, the Pony Express. The Pony Express was established long before the Union Pacific railroad was built across the continent, or even before the telegraph poles were set, and when Abraham Lincoln was elected President of the United States, it was important that the election returns from California should be brought across the mountains as quickly as possible. Mr. William Russell, the great government freighter, who at the time was in Washington, first proposed the Pony Express. He was told that it would take too long—17 or 18 days. The result was a wager of $200,000 that the time could be made in less than ten days, and it was, the actual time being nine days, seventeen hours, leaving seven hours to spare, and winning the wager of two hundred thousand dollars. Mr. Billy Johnson will illustrate the mode of riding the Pony Express, mounting, dismounting and changing the mail to fresh horses.

    Music. Enter express rider, changing horses in front of the grandstand, and exit. . . .

Next on our programme, an historical representation between Buffalo Bill and Yellow Hand, fought during the Sitting Bull war, on the 17th of July, 1876, at War Bonnet Creek, Dakota, shortly after the massacre of Custer. The fight was witnessed by General Carr's command and the Sioux army, and resulted in the death of Yellow Hand, and the first scalp taken in revenge of Custer's fate.

    Duel as described above. Cody, supported by cowboys, etc., Yellow Hand by Indians. Music. . . .

Miss Annie Oakley, the celebrated wing and rifle shot. Miss Oakley will give an exhibition of her skill, shooting with a shot gun at Ligowsky patent clay pigeons, holding the gun in various positions.

    Shoots pigeons sprung from trap. . . .

Next on our programme, the cowboy's fun, or the riding of bucking ponies and mules, by Mr. ——, Mr. —— and Mr. ——. There is an impression on the minds of many people that these horses are taught or trained to buck, or that they are compelled to do so by having foreign substances placed under their saddles. This, however, is not the fact. Bucking, the same as balking or running away, is a natural trait of the animal, confirmed by habit.

Riders announced, and mount in succession.

Watch Mr. Taylor pick up his hat.

Taylor rides past at full speed, leans out of his saddle and picks hat from the ground.

Watch Mr. Taylor pick up his handkerchief.

Taylor rides past at full speed, leans out of his saddle and picks up handkerchief.

Hon. William F. Cody, champion all round shot of the world.

Enter Mr. Cody.

Mr. Cody will give an exhibition of his skill, shooting with shot gun, rifle and revolver at clay pigeons and composition balls, shooting first with a shot gun at clay pigeons, pulling the traps himself. (Shoots.) Shooting clay pigeons in the American style of holding the gun, the butt of the gun below his elbow. (Shoots.) Shooting clay pigeons in the English style of holding the gun, the butt of the gun below the arm-pit. Please notice the change of Position. (Shoots.)

Shooting clay pigeons standing with his back to the trap, turning and breaking the pigeon while it is in the air. (Shoots.)

Shooting with his back to the trap, gun over his shoulder, turning and pulling the traps himself. (Shoots.)

Holding the gun with one hand. (Shoots.)

Holding the gun with one hand, pulling the trap with the other. (Shoots.)

Shooting clay pigeons double from two traps sprung at the same time. (Shoots.)

Shooting clay pigeons double pulling the traps himself. (Shoots.)

Shooting twenty clay pigeons inside of one minute and thirty seconds. Any gentleman desiring to hold the time on this feat, will please take it, not from the pulling of the trap, but from the first crack of the gun. (Shoots.)

Mr. Cody will shoot next with a Winchester repeating rifle, at composition balls, thrown from the hand while he rides upon his horse. (Shoots.)

Missing with the first shot, hitting with the second. (Shoots.)

Missing twice, hitting the third time. (Shoots.)

Hitting three balls thrown in the air at the same time. (Shoots.)
Hitting a ball thrown from behind. (Shoots.)
Hitting a ball thrown to either side. (Shoots.)
Hitting a number of balls thrown in the air in rapid succession. (Shoots.)
Hitting a ball thrown in the air while he rides past it at full speed, a shot accomplished by no other marksman. (Shoots.)
Mr. Cody will next attempt the great double shot! Hitting two balls thrown in the air at the same time, as he rides past at full speed. (Shoots.) Hitting composition balls thrown in the air, while marksman and object thrower ride side by side at full speed, thus forming a picture of combined horsemanship and marksmanship never before presented to a public audience. (Shoots.) . . .

———————

A portion of the Pawnee and Wichita tribes will illustrate their native sports and pastimes, giving first the war dance.
    War dance by Indians.
Next the grass dance.
    Grass dance by Indians.
Next, the scalp dance, in which the women of the tribe are allowed to participate.
    Scalp dance by Indians and squaws. . . .

———————

Next on our programme the riding of a wild elk, by Master Voter Hall, a Feejee Indian from Africa.
    Saddled elk ridden as above.

———————

Next on our programme the attack upon a settler's cabin by a band of marauding Indians, and their repulse, by a party of scouts and cowboys, under the command of Buffalo Bill. After our entertainment you are invited to visit the Wild West camp. We thank you for your polite attention, and bid you all good afternoon.
    Battle as above. Review before the grand stand.
    Adieux and dismissal by Mr. Cody.
                    FINIS

From copyright deposit typescript in the Library of Congress, dated June 1, 1885. Entered according to Act of Congress, by W. F. Cody, at Washington, D.C., on the 22nd Day of December, 1883. Reprinted in B.A. Botkin, *A Treasury of American Folklore* (New York: Crown Publishers, 1944), pp. 150–156 *passim*.

William F. Cody

The Wild West in England

Several leading gentlemen of the United States conceived the idea of holding an American Exhibition in the heart of London and to this end a company was organized that pushed the project to a successful issue, aided as they were by several prominent residents of the English capital. . . .

. . . Standing on the deck of a ship, called the "State of Nebraska," whose arrival had evidently been watched for with great curiosity, as the number of yachts, tug boats and other crafts which surrounded us attested, my memory wandered back to the days of my youth, when in search of the necessaries of existence and braving the dangers of the then vast wild plains, a section of which comprised the then unsettled territory of Nebraska. I contrasted that epoch of my life, its lonely duties and its hardships, and all its complex history, as the home and battle-ground of a savage foe, with its present great prosperity and its standing as the empire State of the central West. A certain feeling of pride came over me when I thought of the good ship on whose deck I stood and that her cargo consisted of early pioneers and rude, rough riders from that section, and of the wild horses of the same district, buffalo, deer, elk and antelope—the king game of the prairie,—together with over one hundred representatives of that savage foe that had been compelled to submit to a conquering civilization and were now accompanying me in friendship, loyalty and peace, five thousand miles from their homes, braving the dangers of the to them great unknown sea, now no longer a tradition, but a reality—all of us combined in an exhibition intended to prove to the center of old world civilization that the vast region of the United States, was finally and effectively settled by the English-speaking race. . . .

That the Wild West made a big impression in London could not have been more emphatically proven than it was by the fact that even Queen Victoria became interested and to us came the "command" for a special performance for Her Majesty and suite. . . .

With her Majesty came their Royal Highnesses, the Prince and Princess Henry of Battenberg, the Marquis of Lorne, the

Dowager Duchess of Athole, the Hon. Ethel Cadogan, Sir Henry and Lady Ponsonby, General Lynedoch Gardiner, Colonel Sir Henry Evart, Lord Ronald Gowan, and a collection of brilliantly uniformed military attendants and exquisitely gowned ladies, forming a veritable portiere of living flowers about the temporary throne.

Then another very remarkable incident occurred. Our entire company of performers having been introduced in the usual manner and the American flag sent around the arena at the hands of a graceful and well-mounted horseman, the statement preceded it that this was an "emblem of peace and friendship to all the world." As the standard bearer passed the royal box with "Old Glory" her Majesty arose, bowed deeply and impressively to the banner, and the entire court party came up standing, the noblemen uncovered, the ladies bowed and the soldiers, generals, and all, saluted.

The incident thrilled, unspeakably, every American present, and with the impulse of the West our company gave a shout such as had never before been heard in Britain. Under ordinary circumstances, that yell would have seemed uncouth; but this was a great event, all saw it as such, hence the shout blended harmoniously with the situation.

For the first time in history a British sovereign had saluted the Star-Spangled Banner, and that banner was carried by a delegated and exalted attache of Buffalo Bill's Wild West.

The presence of the Queen gave mighty stimulus to our people and the performance was admirably given. Every member of the company seemed determined to excel. The young women did unusually successful shooting at their targets; my own shooting was the best of its kind that I ever did; the fight of the cowboys and Indians had greater vim, even the bucking bronchos seemed to be under the influence of the contagious enthusiasm and there never had been a more excellent performance in the Wild West Exhibition from beginning to end and in every specialty. Moreover, her Majesty instead of staying only an hour, decided to "sit out" the performance and then she sent the "command" that Buffalo Bill should be presented to her. The compliments, deliberate and unmeasured, that she gave me, that modesty mentioned in the opening of this story forbids me to repeat. . . .

Shortly after this incident of the Queen's visit, came another affair that was to be the third to royalty of the Wild West exhibitions. A royal equerry came to Earl's Court bringing a further "command" from her Majesty. It expressed the

demand that on the 20th of June a special exhibition by the
Wild West should be given in the morning to the kingly and
princely guests of Queen Victoria, on the occasion of her
Jubilee.

Never before, since the world commenced, has such a
gathering honored a public entertainment. Ceasar and his
captive monarchs, the Field of the Cloth of Gold, nothing in
history can compare with that assemblage of the mighty ones
of the earth that honored the Wild West upon this occasion.

From William F. Cody, *Life and Adventures of Buffalo Bill* (Chicago: John R. Stanton & Co., 1917), pp. 314, 321–322, 330, 331–332,
333.

E.E. Cummings

Buffalo Bill's Defunct

Buffalo Bill's
defunct
            who used to
            ride a watersmooth-silver
                            stallion
and break onetwothreefourfive pigeonsjustlikethat
                                        Jesus

he was a handsome man
                    and what i want to know is
how do you like your blueeyed boy
Mister Death

From E. E. Cummings, *Complete Poems 1913–1962* (New York:
Harcourt Brace Jovanovich, 1972), p. 60.

VI

A Second Frontier: Farmers, Miners, Militants

Fly—scatter through the country—go to the Great West. . . . The West is the true destination!

—Horace Greeley

Introduction to Part VI

On May 10, 1869, at Promontory Point, Utah, the rails of the Central Pacific, running from the west, met those of the Union Pacific from the east. At that moment one frontier of the West was closed, while a second frontier was opened. In this second frontier the challenges were not the unknown, the long trail, the Indian, but land and weather and loneliness. The battles to be fought would be by machines against earth and stone, farmers against grasshoppers, hail and drought, laboring men against mine owners and mill bosses and corporations. And in the end the West would be transformed. When the rails touched at Promontory, the old West was ended, although it would take years for it to know it.

The conquest of the farm frontier begins with a myth. By means of this myth the arid plains beyond the 98th meridian, that "Great American Desert" which the pioneers of the 1840s and '50s had labored across on their way to the lush valleys of Oregon and California, were transformed. As early as 1844 the prairie traveler Josiah Gregg had a glimpse of the vision: could not rain somehow be induced to fall on this desert? Would not civilization itself bring the nourishing showers? In 1862 the myth was written into law, and the Homestead Act opened the arid land for the settler. Through propaganda, political pressure, and dubious science, the desert had been changed in the American mind into a hope: it would be the garden of the world.

The pioneers of this farm frontier would partake of another myth of longer standing. Elinore Pruitt Stewart, the energetic Denver widow turned homesteader, and Hamlin Garland's Rob Rodemaker with his 160-acre government claim and his democratic views are echoing a tradition that goes back as far as Jefferson and Crèvecoeur, that of the independent yeoman farmer. The men and women who opened the farm frontier were often pioneers in a second sense as well, for free land and the dream of the garden drew new-comers to the United States such as O. E. Rölvaag's Norwegians, Willa Cather's Bohemians and Scandinavians, the Swiss father of whom Mari Sandoz writes so memorably in *Old Jules*. They would have to struggle with a new language and customs and aching homesickness, as well as with the soil. Pap Singleton's "Exodusters" fleeing the repression of the Reconstruction South show that for at least one group of blacks the West and its land were a promise of independence and prosperity.

Machines made the exploitation of the farm frontier possible. Barbed wire was developed to fence its treeless acres, portable windmills to pump its water. Reapers and steam threshers to harvest the open land made "bonanza" farming an industrial gamble worth taking for those with the lands and the capital to risk.

But the farm frontier and its barbed-wire fences came up against another obstacle: the cattlemen. Teddy Roosevelt, in rationalizing the dispossession of the Indian, had foreseen the eventual disappearance of the cattleman as well, a victim with his grazing herds of the yet more stable civilization of the farmer. Other ranchers were not as willing as Roosevelt to yield. Fence wars and such events as Wyoming's short-lived Johnson County War with its invading cattlemen's "army" of cowpunchers (a war correspondent and a surgeon were included for good measure) would lead to years of bitterness between rancher and farmer.

The farm frontier was pushed forward by fence and wind-mill and harvester, but it was the railroad that got the farmers to their land, just as it was the railroad, with its land sales and publicity, that had as often as not lured the immigrants west in the first place. The railroads gave farmers an international market for their crops, but they also tied the farmer closer than ever to their corporate control. For Frank Norris, the young disciple of Zola, the railroad was an octopus, blindly reaching out to strangle the very farmers it had nurtured.

It was not only the farmers whose West was opened by the railroad. Capitalists and workers, boomers and speculators found their West at the end of the tracks as well. Those hard-headed capitalists to whom Thomas Hart Benton had given a vision of a passage to India and Theodore Judah a practical plan for laying track to it not only built the road, but stayed on to exploit the land through which it ran. And it was a land worth exploiting, rich in timber and coal and copper and oil, and studded with spectacular strikes of silver and gold. The independent operator on his claim, the gold miner working a long tom with a partner, were anachronisms in the New West. It took immense amounts of money to open this industrial West. The new pioneer could dig out a copper mine of incredible engineering complexity in Utah or Arizona or cut down a forest in Oregon with the stroke of a pen in a Wall Street office or a telegram from a Tacoma or San Francisco mansion. Sleepy coast towns and inland settlements awoke to find themselves cities, while new mining towns were born—and often died—overnight. The West was vast and rich and vulnerable. Where once conquistadors had searched fruitlessly for El Dorado, real-estate promotors unrolled plans of imaginary empires. It was boom or bust as stock speculators, oil-well wildcatters, and just plain swindlers strove for the prize.

But the opening of the industrial West brought still another figure on the scene: the worker. To that bubbling stew of races the West had been since fur-trading days were added new races of men to build the railroads and dig the coal and copper and man the mills. Chinese and Irish railroad builders were replaced by Italians, Serbs, Greeks, and Macedonians such as Stoyan Christowe, who would go on to a career as a novelist and Vermont politician. Not only did the New West bring new races—and the usual racism—but it brought that same confrontation between worker and boss that the Industrial Revolution had introduced everywhere. Edward Aveling, with his wife Eleanor (the daughter of no less than Karl Marx), would visit some disgruntled cowboys in a Cincinnati dime museum and wonder at their possibilities as an organized proletariat. It remained for a Westerner, Bill Haywood, himself an ex-cowboy, to attempt to organize them as a union local. But if scattered and wandering cowboys could not be organized, the miners were another matter. The first miners' union in the West was formed in Virginia City in 1863. The free and easy Comstock might tolerate such organizations, but in the lead and silver mines of Idaho and Colorado, in the copper mines of Utah and Montana and Arizona, the gold mines of the Black Hills, and the coal seams that ran throughout the Rocky Mountain states, it was another case. It was an era of industrial violence, and in the West it would reach a state of all-out war between miners on one side and strikebreakers, mine detectives, and state militias on the other. Cripple Creek, Telluride, Coeur d'Alene, Ludlow, and Bisbee are only a few of the grim names.

It was a curious world, this Industrial West. Part frontier, part ostentatiously civilized, with mansions of silver kings overlooking bleak and denuded slopes, a babble of immigrants, Wild West saloons, and telegraph lines running down the canyon for communication with the city men who owned mines they may not have ever seen. The Old West and the New would often meet in the life of the same man. Big Bill Haywood, the one-eyed firebrand of the Western Federation of Miners and, later, of the I.W.W., was born in Salt Lake City in time to hear Brigham Young preach in the Tabernacle. He would die in post-Revolutionary Russia, but not before he had in turn been a miner, a cowboy, and an accused assassin defended by Darrow himself. Up in the Coeur d'Alene, Haywood followed the path of another ex-cowboy—one who had come for a different reason. Charles A. Siringo, whose account of cowboy life is found in Part V, had been working as an undercover detective for the mine owners.

Of the most abused of the Western workers, the bindlestiffs who followed the harvests, the railroad hoboes and the timber beasts of the log camps, the I.W.W.—International Workers of the World—attempted to form the One Big Union that would cut across occupational lines. Their methods—and the response to them—were unashamedly violent. A Swede named Hillstrom gave the Wobblies the best of their songs and he gave them their most famous martyr. Joe Hill, like the West of the period, is impossible to simplify. John Dos Passos gives us a part of the picture—Hill as the debonair martyr-poet of the Left. In Alfred Hayes and Earl Robinson's haunting song Hill has become myth itself. Less admiring investigators have seen Hill as a Wobbly hanger-on with a knack for setting slogans to Salvation Army tunes and a positive genius for self-dramatization. They question the fairness of his trial and sentence but point ominously to his reputation among old Wobblies as a stick-up man.

While the miners and militants of the Second Frontier were fighting their battles, the farmers were fighting—and often losing—their own. Rain did not follow the plow, and as dry cycle succeeded wet, drought parched the farmlands. Irrigation projects were optimistic, but often overextended, as we see in the sad report of Mary Hallock Foote, the genteel writer and illustrator whose letters and journals served as the basis for Wallace Stegner's *Angle of Repose*. The independent yeoman became increasingly scarce in California as land was gathered into immense corporate estates, whose crops were picked by armies of migrants. The farmers of the plains, hemmed in by mortgage and drought, too often found bitterness and defeat instead of the garden. Hamlin Garland would see prairie optimists driven to despair in the bleak and lonely farms and towns which he realistically chronicled. The grievances and special problems—as well as the hopes—of western farmers would find expression in a prairie populism which is still echoed today in our political life—a legacy of the Second Frontier. John Steinbeck's Okies would be later victims of a badly exploited land. Their dustbowl exodus on the roads of 1930s America took them to the only promise they knew: farther west, to the valleys of California.

But if many failed, others did manage to find a foothold in the West. For the people of Saroyan's Fresno, the West has indeed been a land of promise, the garden *has* bloomed.

"[A] thing that is dreamed of in the way I mean, is already an accomplished fact," says Willa Cather's Captain Forrester in *A Lost Lady*. "All our great West has been developed from such dreams; the homesteader's and the prospector's and the contractor's. We dreamed the railroads across the mountains. Just as I dreamed my place on the Sweet Water. All these things will be everyday facts to the coming generation, but to us—" Captain Forrester ends "with a sort of grunt" and in his voice is the "lonely, defiant note that is so often heard in the voices of old Indians." It is a way of saying that the edge of the dream has proved hard, its accomplishment has not been easy. And still the legacy of a West in conflict with itself continues. The immigrant farmers of Saroyan's California, those of Steinbeck's Okies who stayed on the land, find themselves today confronting another force, the farm workers who pick their grapes and lettuce and their struggle for a better life in a land of plenty. They too, like the other strivers of the Second Frontier, are looking, after all, for a West of their own.

THE DREAM OF THE GARDEN

Josiah Gregg
The Dream of the Garden

The high plains seem too dry and lifeless to produce timber; yet might not the vicissitudes of nature operate a change likewise upon the seasons? Why may we not suppose that the genial influences of civilization—that extensive cultivation of the earth—might contribute to the multiplication of showers, as it certainly does of fountains? Or that the shady groves, as they advance upon the prairies, may have some effect upon the seasons? At least, many old settlers maintain that the droughts are becoming less oppressive in the West. . . . Then may we not hope that these sterile regions might yet be thus revived and fertilized, and their surface covered one day by flourishing settlements to the Rocky Mountains?

From Josiah Gregg, *Commerce of the Prairies*, Vol. 2 (New York and London: Henry G. Langley; Wiley and Putnam, 1844), pp. 202–203.

Elinore Pruitt Stewart
Letter from a Woman Homesteader

When I read of the hard times among the Denver poor, I feel like urging them every one to get out and file on land. I am very enthusiastic about women homesteading. It really requires less strength and labor to raise plenty to satisfy a large family than it does to go out to wash, with the added satisfaction of knowing that their job will not be lost to them if they care to keep it. Even if improving the place does go slowly, it is that much done to stay done. Whatever is raised is the homesteader's own, and there is no house-rent to pay. This year Jerrine cut and dropped enough potatoes to raise a ton of fine potatoes. She wanted to try, so we let her, and you will remember that she is but six years old. We had a man to break the ground and cover the potatoes for her and the man irrigated them once. That was all that was done until digging time, when they were ploughed out and Jerrine picked them up. Any woman strong enough to go out by the day could have done every bit of the work and put in two or three times that much, and it would have been so much more pleasant than to work so hard in the city and then be on starvation rations in the winter.

To me, homesteading is the solution of all poverty's problems, but I realize that temperament has much to do with success in any undertaking, and persons afraid of coyotes and work and loneliness had better let ranching alone. At the same time, any woman who can stand her own company, can see the beauty of the sunset, loves growing things, and is willing to put in as much time at careful labor as she does over the washtub, will certainly succeed; will have independence, plenty to eat all the time, and a home of her own in the end. . . .

Here I am boring you to death with things that cannot interest you! You'd think I wanted you to homestead, wouldn't you? But I am only thinking of the troops of tired, worried women, sometimes even cold and hungry, scared to death of losing their places to work, who could have plenty to eat, who could have good fires by gathering wood, and comfortable homes of their own, if they but had the courage and determination to get them.

From Elinore Pruitt Stewart, *Letters of a Woman Homesteader* (Boston: Houghton Mifflin Co., 1914), pp. 214–217.

O. E. Rölvaag

Facing the Great Unknown

After they had milked the cow, eaten their evening porridge, and talked awhile to the oxen, she took the boys and And-Ongen and strolled away from camp. With a common impulse, they went toward the hill; when they had reached the summit, Beret sat down and let her gaze wander aimlessly around. . . . In a certain sense, she had to admit to herself, it was lovely up here. The broad expanse stretching away endlessly in every direction, seemed almost like the ocean—especially now, when darkness was falling. It reminded her strongly of the sea, and yet it was very different. . . . This formless prairie had no heart that beat, no waves that sang, no soul that could be touched . . . or cared. . . .

The infinitude surrounding her on every hand might not have been so oppressive, might even have brought her a measure of peace, if it had not been for the deep silence, which lay heavier here than in a church. Indeed, what was there to break it? She had passed beyond the outposts of civilization; the nearest dwelling places of men were far away. Here no warbling of birds rose on the air, no buzzing of insects sounded; even the wind had died away; the waving blades of grass that trembled to the faintest breath now stood erect and quiet, as if listening, in the great hush of the evening. . . . All along the way, coming out, she had noticed this strange thing: the stillness had grown deeper, the silence more depressing, the farther west they journeyed; it must have been over two weeks now since she had heard a bird sing! Had they travelled into some nameless, abandoned region? Could no living thing exist out here, in the empty, desolate, endless wastes of green and blue? . . . How *could* existence go on, she thought, desperately? If life is to thrive and endure, it must at least have something to hide behind! . . .

From O. E. Rölvaag, *Giants in the Earth*, translated by O. E. Rölvaag and Lincoln Colcord (New York: Harper & Bros., 1927, 1929), pp. 37–38.

O. E. Rölvaag

A First Crop

When Per Hansa left the house next morning to finish the dragging, the air was raw and heavy; a penetrating wind blew over the prairie, as if searching for signs of life to wither and blight; not a trace remained of the mildness and pleasantness of the previous days.

Before he had finished covering the oats, the rain began to fall; along with the rain came huge flakes of snow, floating silently down and turning to slush as they struck the ground. After a while the rain ceased, but the snow only came faster; the flakes were firmer now, and fell in a businesslike manner. Before long a veritable blizzard was raging over the whole prairie—there had hardly been anything worse that winter.

Throughout that day and the following night the storm continued with unabated fury. Early on the next morning, the weather cleared; but now the cold was so intense that it nipped the skin as soon as one stuck one's head out-of-doors. Spring seemed a thousand miles off.

That night Per Hansa did not sleep a wink. How could he sleep, with this tragedy going on? He was nothing but an old sailor; he didn't know the least thing about farming. God Almighty! hadn't he good reason to lie awake? . . . Here he had gone to work and wasted all his precious seed—had simply thrown it away, because he was foolish and hasty! And there wasn't even a chance to extricate himself from the mess he had made! Out in the field, under the snow, lay all that priceless wheat, smothered to death and frozen as hard as flint. . . . He could stand the loss of the oats, perhaps—but, God! the wheat! Twenty-five bushels he had sacrificed, all the work gone to no purpose, and no possible way of getting a fresh supply of seed. . . . As he opened the door that morning, saw two feet of snow covering the ground, and felt the bitter cold stinging his face, he had an irresistible impulse to fling himself down in the snowdrift and cry like a baby! . . .

In the afternoon the sun shone strong and brilliant, but the cold was too intense for it to make any impression on the snow. . . . Per Hansa was still lying in bed; the bright sun-

354 O. E. RÖLVAAG

shine outside, reflecting on the white walls of the room, seemed to sear his eyeballs; he felt that the only thing that would give him relief would be to get up, strike out wildly, and curse everything around him—for he was fighting an unseen enemy. . . . He had come to his great decision; he had done the seeding; he had felt clearly that it was the most momentous day of his life; but no sooner had the last kernel fallen to the ground than the very powers of heaven had stepped down to defeat him! . . . Powers of heaven . . . ? A certain image came before his eyes, and would not go away. One Sunday not very long ago, Store-Hans had sat by the table reading to his mother; Per Hansa remembered it vividly, because the words had sounded so awful to him. At last he had gotten up to look over the boy's shoulder; Store-Hans was reading in a loud voice, throwing great emphasis into the words:

"And the Lord said unto Satan, whence comest thou? Then Satan answered the Lord, and said, From going to and fro in the earth, and from walking up and down in it. . . ."

One day as Per Hansa was pottering about out-of-doors, hardly knowing which way to turn, he caught sight of Tönseten, who had commenced his seeding. Like a condemned man about to be executed Per Hansa walked over. . . . Tönseten is an aboriginal American, he thought, bitterly. I might as well let him polish off the damned fool of a newcomer!

But to-day Tönseten was too busy even to talk. Per Hansa didn't feel inclined to open up the subject of his own troubles; he began on a different tack, to head the other off:

"I must say you certainly sow it even!"

Tönseten spat a prodigious distance. . . . "You think so?" . . . But he didn't stop for a moment; his arms continued to cut wide semicircles in the air; golden grain flew out of his hand and rained down to the ground through the warm sunlight, there to begin the mystic dream of life.

This is beautiful! thought Per Hansa. . . . I couldn't sow it as even as that.

"I was a fool for not waiting to get you to do the seeding for me," he observed.

Tönseten spat another great mouthful before he answered:

"Well, some people are bound to cut off their nose to spite their face. . . . But then—this is a free country, you know!"

. . . He walked on with measured steps, his arm sweeping in long, graceful curves; the kernels flew far and wide, catching the sunlight a moment as they fell.

Per Hansa turned abruptly, and began to walk toward home. When Tönseten noticed this, he stopped his work and called out:

"Did you want anything, Per Hansa?"

"Hell—no!"

"All right. To-day, you see, I'm a busy man!"

Per Hansa started to answer, choked, and continued to walk away. His head was in a whirl as he went on toward his own field, which seemed to be making faces at him as he drew nearer; it was indeed a forbidding countenance that he saw there, lifeless and black and bare. Reaching the field, he fell on his knees, dug into the soil, and picked up the first kernel he came across; he laid it in the palm of his left hand and turned it over and over with the forefinger of his right; the seed was black with clammy dirt, which clung tightly to it. Slowly and carefully he picked off the particles of soil— and there it lay, a pale little thing, greyish-white and dirty, the golden sheen through which he had read the fairy tale, entirely gone, the magic departed, the seed cold and dead. Per Hansa dropped it without a word, and dug in the ground until he had found another kernel. The one he now picked up had the same lifeless color, but it was swollen and seemed about to burst open. . . . "This is the frost!"—he mumbled, hoarsely.—"It's all begun to rot!" . . . He rose to his feet and stood there as if chained to the spot, the very personification of gloom, gazing out over the face of his dead dream. . . . *"Then Satan answered the Lord, and said, From going to and fro in the earth, and from walking up and down in it."* . . . There can't be much doubt that he's found *this* place, all right—the devil salt and pickle his guts! . . .

Over on the piece of field which Per Hansa had broken during the last few days the boys were now busy at work with the dragging. He had set them to the task early that morning, but had not yet made up his mind what to put into the field. Now he walked over to them.

One of the boys was driving; the other sat on the harrow, making grooves with his heels in the loose dirt; on each round of the field they exchanged places. They had quarreled considerably over who could drive the straightest; now they were trying to decide this momentous question by judging the straightness of the grooves made on each round.

The boys stopped as they saw their father approaching.

"Isn't this piece four acres?" Ole demanded, boisterously.

"It should be," their father answered in a tired voice.

"All right," beamed Ole. "If we plant potatoes in the whole piece and get a hundred and fifty bushels to the acre, we'll have six hundred bushels in all!"

"Then we'll sell 'em!" Store-Hans broke in, his eye snapping.

"Shut up, you! This is my idea!" Ole turned again to his father and kept on with his arithmetic: "We can't get less than thirty cents a bushel, can we? I'll be able to help you haul them to town. And that'll be exactly *one hundred and eighty dollars*. Gee! What a lot!" The boy looked proudly at his father, and added with a grown-up air, "We ought to get the potatoes planted at once—that's my opinion!"

But then Store-Hans had a great inspiration, and flashed out:

"When we get as much money as that, just for potatoes, we'll buy a shotgun. Hurrah!"

"Stop your nonsense and get to work!" said Per Hansa, harshly. "You need a pair of pants to cover your bottom, more than you do a gun. . . . Move on, now, I tell you!"

On the way home that morning, Per Hansa realized one thing more clearly than ever before—unless he could find something to occupy his body and mind, and find it right away, he would go all to pieces one of these fine days. . . . Well, why not do as Ole suggested? Here was this piece of new field, and it had to be put to some use. . . . If *that fellow* was loose around these parts, Per Hansa might as well give him a run for his money! . . .

The minute Per Hansa reached home he opened the root cellar and began carrying out potatoes. He took out all that he judged they could possibly spare and began to cut them up into small pieces; he was determined to have enough seed to cover the whole field. . . . Oh yes, no doubt this was insanely foolish, too, but, damn it all, he might as well come to ruination at once and be done with it! . . .

The planting kept the three of them busy for the rest of that week. When Sunday morning came, Per Hansa rose at the usual time, ate his breakfast in silence, and then went back to bed. And-Ongen crawled into bed with him and stirred up a terrible commotion; he must wake now and tell her a story. Getting no answer, she pulled his hair and pinched his cheek and tugged at his nose. The carrying-on of the child made a pleasant diversion for him in his dark mood. Beret sat by the table, reading the Bible. To his great relief, she said little these days. . . . As he lay there brooding he was turning over and over in his mind a new idea—mightn't he make another trip to the Sioux River? Perhaps he could yet scare up a couple of sacks of wheat there. The seeding would be far behind-hand, that's true; but barring any more bad luck, he would at least be able to harvest enough seed grain for another year. . . . But it was so late now—too late, really, to think of such a thing. Perhaps he had better go to Sioux Falls or Worthington and try to get work for the summer. Beret and the boys could easily get along without him. . . . No, he couldn't quite make up his mind as to what would be best. . . . All the while And-Ongen was pommelling him because he wouldn't tell her a story.

Suddenly a violent stamping of feet sounded outside; some one came running up, with another close at his heels.

Ole jerked the door open, took one leap, and landed in the middle of the floor. The boy was wild-eyed with excitement.

"Per Hansa!" he cried, calling his father by name. "The wheat is up!" Then he took another leap and stood leaning over the bed. "The wheat is up, I say! . . . Can't you hear me?" . . .

But now Store-Hans came storming in, all out of breath:

"Father Per Hansa—the wheat is *so high!*"

"You shut up!" raged his brother. "I came first!"

"I guess I can tell it, too!" Store-Hans paid no further attention to his brother; he was standing now by the bed, measuring on his finger. "The wheat is *so high*, the oats about up to *here! . . .* Don't you suppose we can buy a shotgun?"

Per Hansa said never a word; he got up, trembling in every limb, and put the child aside. In a moment he had left the house and rushed up to the field. There he stood spellbound, gazing at the sight spread before him. His whole body shook; tears came to his eyes, so that he found it difficult to see clearly. And well he might be surprised. Over the whole field tiny green shoots were quivering in the warm sunshine.

Store-Hans was standing now by his father's side: he looked at him in consternation.

"Are you sick, father?"

No answer.

"Why, you're crying!"

"You're . . . so—foolish, Store-Hans!" Per Hansa was blowing his nose violently. . . . *"So terribly foolish!"* he added, softly, and straightened himself up with a new energy.

From Rölvaag, *Giants in the Earth,* pp. 300–307.

Pap Singleton
A Black Moses in Kansas

I commenced getting the emigration up in 1875; I think it was in 1875.

Q. Well, tell us about it?

A. I have been fetching out people; I believe I fetched out 7,432 people.

Q. You have brought out 7,432 people from the South to Kansas?

A. Yes, sir; brought and sent.

Q. How did you happen to send them out?

A. The first cause, do you mean, of them going?

Q. Yes; What was the cause of your going out, and in the first place how did you happen to go there, or to send these people there?

A. Well, my people, for the want of land—we needed land for our children—and their disadvantages—that caused my heart to grieve and sorrow; pity for my race, sir, that was coming down, instead of going up—that caused me to go to work for them. I sent out there perhaps in '66—perhaps so; or in '65, any way—my memory don't recollect which; and they brought back tolerable favorable reports; then I jacked up three or four hundred, and went into Southern Kansas, and found it was a good country, and I thought Southern Kansas was congenial to our nature, sir; and I formed a colony there, and bought about a thousand acres of ground—the colony did—my people.

Q. Have they any property now?

A. Yes; I have carried some people in there that when they got there they didn't have fifty cents left, and now they have got in my colony—Singleton colony—a house, nice cabins, their milch cows, and pigs, and sheep, perhaps a span of horses, and trees before their yards, and some three or four or ten acres broken up, and all of them has got little houses that I carried there. They didn't go under no relief assistance; they went on their own resources; and when they went in there first the country was not overrun with them; you see, they could get good wages; the country was not overstocked with people; they went to work, and I never helped as soon as I put them on the land.

These men would tell all their grievances to me in Tennessee—the sorrows of their heart. You know I was an undertaker there in Nashville, and worked in the shop. Well, actually, I would have to go and bury their fathers and mothers. You see we have the same heart and feelings as any other race and nation. (The land is free, and it is nobody's business, if there is land enough, where the people go. *I* put that in my people's heads.) Well, that man would die, and I would bury him; and the next morning maybe a woman would go to that man [meaning the landlord], and she would have six or seven children, and he would say to her, "Well, your husband owed me before he died;" and they would say that to every last one of them, "You owe me." Suppose he would? Then he would say, "You must go to some other place; I cannot take care of you." Now, you see, that is something I would take notice of. That woman had to go out, and these little children was left running through the streets, and the next place you would find them in a disorderly house, and their children in the State's prison.

Well, now, sir, you will find that I have a charter here. You will find that I called on the white people in Tennessee about that time. I called conventions about it, and they sot with me in my conventions, and "Old man," they said, "you are right." The white people said, "You are right; take your people away." And let me tell you, it was the white people—the ex-governor of the State, felt like I did. And they said to me, "You have tooken a great deal on yourself, but if these negroes, instead of deceiving one an other and running for office, would take the same idea that you have in your head, you will be a people."

I then went out to Kansas, and advised them all to go to Kansas; and, sir, they are going to leave the Southern country. The Southern country is out of joint. The blood of a white man runs through my veins. That is congenial, you know, to my nature. That is my choice. Right emphatically, I tell you to-day, I woke up the millions right through me! The great God of glory has worked in me. I have had open air interviews with the living spirit of God for my people; and we are going to leave the South. We are going to leave it if there ain't an alteration and signs of a change. I am going to advise the people who left that country [Kansas] to go back. . . .

Mr. WINDOM. You consider yourself the father of the exodus, then, Mr. Singleton?

The WITNESS. Yes, sir; I am the father of it!

The CHAIRMAN. You are called "Pap Singleton," I believe?

The WITNESS. I am sir; I love everybody!

The CHAIRMAN. They call you "Pap" Singleton, because you are father of the exodus, is that it?

The WITNESS. I reckon they honor me with that name for my old age, sir.

Pap Singleton's Testimony from Senate Report No. 693, part 3, 46th Congress, 2nd Session, "Negro Exodus from Southern States," pp. 379–381, 384.

Song of the Exodusters: Marching to Kansas

We are on our rapid march to Kansas, the land that gives birth to freedom. May God Almighty bless you all.
Farewell, dear friends, farewell.

Many dear mothers are sleeping in the tomb of clay, have spent all their days in slavery in old Tennessee.
Farewell, dear friends, farewell.

It seems to me that the year of jubilee has come; surely this is the time that is spoken of in history.
Farewell, dear friends, farewell.

"We are on our rapid march to Kansas" from Walter L. Fleming, "'Pap' Singleton, the Moses of the Colored Exodus," *The American Journal of Sociology*, Vol. 15, No. 1 (June–July, 1909), p. 67.

Hamlin Garland

Democracy on the Sodhouse Frontier

Seagraves, "holding down a claim" near Rob, had come to see his neighboring "bach" because feeling the need of company; but now that he was near enough to hear him prancing about getting supper, he was content to lie alone on a slope of the green sod.

The silence of the prairie at night was well-nigh terrible. Many a night, as Seagraves lay in his bunk against the side of his cabin, he would strain his ear to hear the slightest sound, and be listening thus sometimes for minutes before the squeak of a mouse or the step of a passing fox came as a relief to the aching sense. In the daytime, however, and especially on a morning, the prairie was another thing. The pigeons, the larks, the cranes, the multitudinous voices of the ground-birds and snipes and insects, made the air pulsate with sound—a chorus that died away into an infinite murmur of music.

"Hello, Seagraves!" yelled Rob from the door. "The biscuit are 'most done."

Seagraves did not speak, only nodded his head, and slowly rose. The faint clouds in the west were getting a superb flame-color above and a misty purple below, and the sun had pierced them with lances of yellow light. As the air grew denser with moisture, the sounds of neighboring life began to reach the ear. Children screamed and laughed, and afar off a woman was singing a lullaby. The rattle of wagons and the voices of men speaking to their teams multiplied. Ducks in a neighboring lowland were quacking sociably. The whole scene took hold upon Seagraves with irresistible power.

"It is American," he exclaimed. "No other land or time can match this mellow air, this wealth of color, much less the strange social conditions of life on this sunlit Dakota prairie."

Rob, though visibly affected by the scene also, couldn't let his biscuit spoil or go without proper attention.

"Say, ain't y' comin' t' grub?" he asked, impatiently.

"In a minute," replied his friend, taking a last wistful look at the scene. "I want one more look at the landscape."

"Landscape be blessed! If you'd been breakin' all day—Come, take that stool an' draw up."

"No; I'll take the candle-box."

"Not much. I know what manners are, if I am a bull-driver."

Seagraves took the three-legged and rather precarious-looking stool and drew up to the table, which was a flat broad box nailed up against the side of the wall, with two strips of board nailed at the outer corners for legs.

"How's that f'r a lay-out?" Rob inquired proudly.

"Well, you *have* spread yourself! Biscuit and canned peaches and sardines and cheese. Why, this is—is—prodigal."

"It ain't nothin' else."

Rob was from one of the finest counties of Wisconsin, over toward Milwaukee. He was of German parentage, a middle-sized, cheery, wide-awake, good-looking young fellow—a typical claim-holder. He was always confident, jovial, and full of plans for the future. He had dug his own well, built his own shanty, washed and mended his own clothing. He could do anything, and do it well. He had a fine field of wheat, and was finishing the ploughing of his entire quarter section.

"This is what I call settin' under a feller's own vine an' fig-tree"—after Seagraves's compliments—"an' I like it. I'm my own boss. No man can say 'come here' 'r 'go there' to me. I get up when I'm a min' to, an' go t' bed when I'm a min' t'."

"Some drawbacks, I s'pose?"

"Yes. Mice, f'r instance, give me a devilish lot o' trouble. They get into my flour-barrel, eat up my cheese, an' fall into my well. But it ain't no use t' swear."

Seagraves quoted an old rhyme:

"The rats and the mice they made such a strife
He had to go to London to buy him a wife,"

"Don't blush. I've probed your secret thought."

"Well, to tell the honest truth," said Rob, a little sheepishly, leaning across the table, "I ain't satisfied with my style o' cookin'. It's good, but a little too plain, y' know. I'd like a change. It ain't much fun to break all day, and then go to work an' cook y'r own supper."

"No, I should say not."

"This fall I'm going back to Wisconsin. Girls are thick as

huckleberries back there, and I'm goin' t' bring one back, now you hear me."

"Good! That's the plan," laughed Seagraves, amused at a certain timid and apprehensive look in his companion's eye. "Just think what a woman would do to put this shanty in shape; and think how nice it would be to take her arm and saunter out after supper, and look at the farm, and plan and lay out gardens and paths, and tend the chickens!"

Rob's manly and self-reliant nature had the settler's typical buoyancy and hopefulness, as well as a certain power of analysis, which enabled him now to say: "The fact is, we fellers holdin' down claims out here ain't fools clear to the *rine*. We know a *couple* o' things. Now I didn't leave Waupac County f'r fun. Did y' ever see Waupac? Well, it's one o' the handsomest counties the sun ever shone on, full o' lakes and rivers and groves of timber. I miss 'em all out here, and I miss the boys an' girls; but they wa'n't no chance there f'r a feller. Land that was good was so blamed high you couldn't touch it with a ten-foot pole from a balloon. Rent was high, if you wanted t' rent, an' so a feller like me had t' get out, an' now I'm out here, I'm goin' t' make the most of it. Another thing," he went on, after a pause—"we fellers workin' out back there got more 'n' more like *hands*, an' less like human beings. Y'know, Waupac is a kind of a summer resort, and the people that use' t' come in summers looked down on us cusses in the fields an' shops. I couldn't stand it. By God!" he said, with a sudden impulse of rage quite unusual, "I'd rather live on an iceberg and claw crabs f'r a livin' than have some feller passin' me on the road an' callin' me 'fellah!' "

Seagraves knew what he meant, but listened in astonishment at his outburst.

"I consider myself a sight better 'n any man who lives on somebody else's hard work. I've never had a cent I didn't earn with them hands." He held them up and broke into a grin. "Beauties, ain't they? But they never wore no gloves that some other poor cuss earned."

Seagraves thought them grand hands, worthy to grasp the hand of any man or woman living.

"Well, so I come West, just like a thousand other fellers, to get a start where the cussed European aristocracy hadn't got a holt on the people. I like it here—course I'd like the lakes an' meadows of Waupac better—but I'm my own boss, as I say, and I'm goin' to *stay* my own boss if I have to live on crackers an' wheat coffee to do it; that's the kind of a hair-pin I am."

In the pause which followed, Seagraves, plunged deep into thought by Rob's words, leaned his head on his hand. This working farmer had voiced the modern idea. It was an absolute overturn of all the ideas of nobility and special privilege born of the feudal past.

"I'd like to use your idea for an editorial, Rob," he said.

"*My* ideas!" exclaimed the astounded host, pausing in the act of filling his pipe. "My ideas! Why, I didn't know I had any."

"Well, you've given me some, anyhow."

Seagraves felt that it was a wild, grand upstirring of the modern democrat against the aristocrat, against the idea of caste and the privilege of living on the labor of others. This atom of humanity (how infinitesimal this drop in the ocean of humanity!) was feeling the nameless longing of expanding personality. He had declared rebellion against laws that were survivals of hate and prejudice. He had exposed also the native spring of the emigrant by uttering the feeling that it is better to be an equal among peasants than a servant before nobles.

"So I have good reasons f'r liking the country," Rob resumed, in a quiet way. "The soil is rich, the climate good so far, an' if I have a couple o' decent crops you'll see a neat *upright* goin' up here, with a porch and a bay-winder."

"And you'll still be livin' here alone, frying leathery slap-jacks an' chopping 'taters and bacon."

"I think I see myself," drawled Rob, "goin' around all summer wearin' the same shirt without washin', an' wipin' on the same towel four straight weeks, an' wearin' holes in my socks, an' eatin' musty ginger-snaps, mouldy bacon, an' canned Boston beans f'r the rest o' my endurin' days! Oh yes; I guess *not!*" He rose. "Well, see y' later. Must go water my bulls."

As he went off down the slope, Seagraves smiled to hear him sing:

"I wish that some kind-hearted girl
    Would pity on me take,
    And extricate me from the mess I'm in.
    The angel—how I'd bless her,

> If this her home she'd make,
> In my little old sod shanty on the plain."

From Hamlin Garland, "Among the Corn-Rows," in *Main-Traveled Roads* (1891; Cambridge and Chicago: Stone and Kimball, 1893), pp. 141–147.

Walter Prescott Webb

A Defense of Cattlemen

It was not until 1916 that Congress recognized in its land legislation that such a class as cattlemen existed in the West. Until that time not a land law made in favor of the cattleman had been passed. The attitude had long been that he was a trespasser on the public domain, an obstacle to settlement, and at best but a crude forerunner of civilization of which the farmer was the advance guard and the hoe the symbol. Major Powell had recommended in his report that the pasturage lands be disposed of in units of 2560 acres. He did this in 1878, but nearly forty years went by before Congress got round to the cattleman. It still could see no reason for such a large unit. The maximum was fixed at 640 acres; the land must be fit only for grazing (improvements were to serve in lieu of cultivation) and must contain no timber, have no minerals, and no irrigation facilities; and the water holes were reserved to the public, as well as land on trails leading to the water holes. The farmer was to raise cattle and drought-resistant forage crops.

Those who have lived in the West know that cattlemen have a hardihood all their own; yet in this law Congress made strong demands even on the toughest of these. They were to set up a "ranch" on 640 acres of land without timber, with little cultivable land, and without water for irrigation. Investigators had found out that a family could support itself on this land under such conditions!

It has been reported that a species of lizard which evolved on the Great Plains lived for thirty years in a western Texas corner stone. No one has asserted that he enjoyed his experience; yet his life must have been a round of pleasure as com-

pared with that of the grazing homesteader in the arid region
had the latter complied with the law. . . .

Again we come back to the central theme of this study;
namely, that our civilization and methods of pioneering were
worked out east of the ninety-eighth meridian and were well
suited to conditions there, but that when these institutions of
the East undertook to cross into the Great Plains they broke
down and had to be modified. The land laws illustrate this in
a most forceful way, except that the modification was not
made until it was almost too late. All legislation was made in
favor of the farmer; none was ever made for the cattleman,
so far as the disposal of the public domain was concerned,
except in Texas. The cattleman had to hold his own (and he
did it pretty well) by evading the law and, as he would say,
"throwing in" with nature. He violated every land law made,
in order that he might survive.

From Walter Prescott Webb, *The Great Plains* (Boston: Ginn and
Co., 1931), pp. 423–424; 428.

Asa Shinn Mercer
Fence War Begins in Wyoming

During the latter period under review material changes had
come about. The luxuriant growth of grass was found only in
small areas; the brush along the streams was largely
destroyed, so that browsing, that in the early days saved the
lives of thousands of cattle, was no longer a resource; the
homeseeker had squatted along the rich valleys, and long
lines of wire fences obstructed the free movement of cattle
before the storm; the railroad lands had been sold and largely
fenced, thus more effectually hemming in the storm-pushed
animals. A striking peculiarity of the range-raised cattle is
that if you destroy the perfect liberty of action they at once
become dependent—lose their will power and rustling qualities. Illustrative of this numerous instances could be cited
where range cattle, drifting before a storm, came upon a
fence that they could not pass through and in utter helpless-

ness walked back and forth along the fence until they fell exhausted, one upon another, and died by the hundred.

With their ranges restricted and fence obstructions on all sides, it became evident to cattle owners that the open range business must soon be reduced to a matter of history, or the settlements in the country be discouraged and the obstructions removed. The paramount question was: "Which of these conditions shall be permitted to materialize?" . . .

The first open and murderous attack made upon the settler by the cattlemen of the then territory, was in the summer of 1889, on the Sweetwater, in Carbon county. James Averill had taken a claim on the rich valley lands and opened a small store, where a postoffice had been established, with Averill as postmaster. Adjoining Averill's claim "Cattle Kate" (Ella Watson) had also taken a claim. These claims were in the center of a large section of country occupied by a cattle ranch, and the presence of the squatters, or settlers there was distasteful to the "Lord of the Manor." Averill sold whisky, but was a quiet, peaceably disposed person, with many friends among the cowboys and the settlers in the outlying districts. He was never accused of cattle stealing. Cattle Kate was a lewd woman and spent part of her time in an annex of Averill's house. She had a small pasture enclosed and gradually accumulated a bunch of young cattle, variously reported at from fifty to eighty head. These she had purchased from the cowboys and ranchmen. The large cattlemen charged that these cattle had been stolen from them by the cowboys and given to Cattle Kate in the way of business exchange; but no civil or criminal action was ever begun in the courts to prove these allegations.

Defying all forms of law, ten cattlemen rode up to Averill's store and with guns pointing at their victims, took Averill and the woman out of the house and hanged them until they were dead. There was known to be one young man present as a witness, and another party was reported to have been near enough to identify the lynchers. The boy was an invalid and was taken in charge by the cattlemen. He lingered some weeks and died—rumor strongly insisting, at the hands of his protectors, by the administration of a slow poison. The second party gave the list of those engaged in the tragedy and they were reported to the Carbon County Grand Jury. Meantime the informant was hunted like a wild beast, and as he failed to appear before the grand jury, and has never been seen or heard from since a few days after the hanging, the supposition is that he sleeps beneath the sod in some lonely mountain gorge where naught but the yelp of the passing wolf disturbs the solemnity of his last resting place. Or, perchance, this same howling beast picked the bones and left them to bleach on the barren hillside.

From Asa Shinn Mercer, *The Banditti of the Plains or the Cattlemen's Invasion of Wyoming in 1892* (Cheyenne: 1894), pp. 9–10, 12–13.

C. C. Coffin
Bonanza Farming Triumphant

Ride over these fertile acres of Dakota, and behold the working of this latest triumph of American genius. You are in a sea of wheat. On the farms managed by Oliver Dalrymple are 13,000 acres in one field. There are other farmers who cultivate from 160 to 6000 acres. The railroad train rolls through an ocean of grain. Pleasant the music of the rippling waves as the west wind sweeps over the expanse. We encounter a squadron of war chariots, not such as once swept over the Delta of the Nile in pursuit of an army of fugitive Israelites, not such as the warriors of Rome were wont to drive, with glittering knives projecting from the axles to mow a swath through the ranks of an enemy, to drench the ground with blood, to cut down the human race, as if men were noxious weeds, but chariots of peace, doing the work of human hands for the sustenance of men. There are twenty-five of them in this one brigade of the grand army of 115, under the marshalship of this Dakota farmer. A superintendent upon a superb horse, like a brigadier directing his forces, rides along the line, accompanied by his staff of two on horseback. They are fully armed and equipped, not with swords, but the implements of peace—wrenches, hammers, chisels. They are surgeons in waiting, with nuts and screws, or whatever may be needed.

This brigade of horse artillery sweeps by in echelon—in close order, reaper following reaper. There is a sound of wheels. The grain disappears an instant, then reappears; iron arms clasp it, hold it a moment in their embrace, wind it with wire, then toss it disdainfully at your feet. You hear in the rattling of the wheels the mechanism saying to itself, "See how easy I can do it!"

An army of "shockers" follow the reapers, setting up the bundles to ripen before threshing. The reaping must ordinarily all be done in fifteen days, else the grain becomes too ripe. The first fields harvested, therefore, are cut before the ripening is complete. Each reaper averages about fifteen acres per day, and is drawn by three horses or mules.

The reaping ended, threshing begins. Again memory goes back to early years, to the pounding out of the grain upon the threshing-floor with the flail—the slow, tedious work of the winter days. Poets no more will rehearse the music of the flail. The picture for February in the old *Farmer's Almanac* is obsolete. September is the month for threshing, the thresher doing its 600 or 700 bushels per day, driven by a steam-engine of sixteen horse-power. Remorseless that sharp-toothed devourer, swallowing its food as fast as two men can cut the wire bands, requiring six teams to supply its demands! And what a cataract of grain pours from its spout, faster than two men can bag it!

The latest triumph of invention in this direction is a straw-burning engine, utilizing the stalks of the grain for fuel.

The cost of raising wheat per bushel is from thirty-five to forty cents; the average yield, from twenty to twenty-five bushels per acre. The nearness of these lands to Lake Superior, and the rates established by the railroad—fifteen cents per bushel from any point between Bismarck and Duluth—give the Dakota farmers a wide margin of profit.

Since the first furrow was turned in the Red River Valley, in 1870, there has been no failure of crops from drought, excessive rains, blight, mildew, rust, or other influence of climatology. The chinch-bug has not made its appearance; the grasshoppers alone have troubled the farmers, but they have disappeared, and the fields are smiling with bounty. With good tilth, the farmer may count upon a net return of from eight to ten dollars per acre per annum. The employment of capital has accomplished a beneficent end, by demonstrating that the region, instead of being incapable of settlement, is one of the fairest sections of the continent. Nor is it a wonder that the land-offices are besieged by emigrants making entries, or that the surveyors find the lands "squatted" upon before they can survey them; that hotels are crowded; that on every hand there is activity.

From C. C. Coffin, "Dakota Wheat Fields," *Harper's New Monthly Magazine,* Vol. 60, No. 358 (March 1880), pp. 533–535.

THE OPENING OF THE INDUSTRIAL WEST

Theodore D. Judah

The Railroad: A Practical Plan

The project for construction of a great Railroad through the United States of America, connecting the Atlantic with the Pacific ocean, has been in agitation for over fifteen years.

It is the most magnificent project ever conceived.

It is an enterprise more important in its bearings and results to the people of the United States, than any other project involving an expenditure of an equal amount of capital.

It connects these two great oceans.

It is an indissoluble bond of union between the populous States of the East, and the undeveloped regions of the fruitful West.

It is a highway which leads to peace and future prosperity. An iron bond for the perpetuation of the Union and independence which we now enjoy.

Many projects for the prosecution of this enterprise have been presented.

Various schemes for the fulfilment of these projects have been devised.

Our wisest statesmen, most experienced politicians, scientific engineers, and shrewdest speculators, have each and all discussed the subject in nearly every point of view, and given the results of their wisdom and experience to the world.

Yet—

Their projects have proved abortive.

Their schemes have failed. . . .

This highway, the greatest and most important of them all, remains unbuilt, it may be said unsurveyed, simply reconnoitered.

Why is this?

Its popularity is universal.

Its importance admitted.

Its practicability believed in.

Its profitableness unquestioned.

1st. It is because these projects have been speculative in their nature; and the people are disposed to look with distrust upon grand speculations.

2dly. There are different routes, advocated by diverse interest, each eager that the road be built to subserve its own particular interest, but unwilling to make common cause upon a common route.

3dly. From the lack of confidence in private capitalists, dissuading them from investing in any project, through which they cannot see their way clear.

This plan assumes to obviate these objections; and,

1st. To build the Pacific Railroad.

2dly. To accomplish the same in ten years.

3dly. To raise the capital therefor. . . .

When a Boston capitalist is invited to invest in a Railroad project, it is not considered sufficient to tell him that somebody has rode over the ground on horseback and pronounced it practicable.

He does not care to be informed that there are 999 different variety and species of plants and herbs, or that grass is abundant at this point, or Buffalo scarce at that; that the latitude or longitude of various points are calculated, to a surprising degree of accuracy, and the temperature of the atmosphere carefully noted for each day in the year.

His inquiries are somewhat more to the point. He wishes to know the length of your road. He says, let me see your map and profile, that I may judge of its alignment and grades.

How many cubic yards of the various kinds of excavation and embankment have you, and upon what sections?

Have you any tunnels, and what are their circumstances?

How much masonry, and where are your stone?

How many bridges, river crossings, culverts, and what kind of foundations?

How about timber and fuel?

Where is the estimate of the cost of your road, and let me
see its details?

What will be its effect upon travel and trade? What its
business revenue?

All this I require to know, in order to judge if my investment is likely to prove a profitable one.

It will be remembered that we start with these grounds assumed, viz: That the Pacific Railroad must be built with private capital.

This can only be had by inspiring the capitalist with confidence.

The only manner in which this can be accomplished, is by
laying before him the results of an actual reliable survey;
such an one as *he* can understand, and upon which he feels
justified in forming his opinions.

From Theodore D. Judah, *A Practical Plan for Building the Pacific
Railroad* (Washington: Henry Polkinhorn, Printer, 1857), pp. 3–6.

Wallace A. Clay

Personal Life of a Chinese Coolie

It was in the summer of 1891 at old Blue Creek Station and I
was just 7 years old. That was the year the Central Pacific
Railroad had an extra gang of about 100 Chinamen housed
in a long string of remodeled box-cars on the back side-track
during a period of "graveling" the roadbed of the main line
from Balfour to Kolmar of the total distance between Cor-
inne and Promontory Summit. . . . I was a lonesome, inquis-
itive kid at that time but ingenious enough to practically
become a Chinaman myself during that summer. You may
wonder that I did it but I got myself renamed "Wah Lee Me
licum Boy" and nearly every Chinaman there knew me by
that name. Under the guise of this "transmutation" I was able
to penetrate parts of their secret private lives and sacred religious beliefs. . . .

There were a number among them I called "my very best
friends." All these Chinamen were "coolies" who had been
shipped to America to work hard for the "Central Pacific" a

railroad section-hands for just a few years out of their lives and they had crossed the Pacific Ocean with the fond hope of saving up a few hundred American Dollars which they could later exchange for a great deal more of Chinese Money so that after a certain few years in America they would return to China as "Money Lords" instead of living out their lives as just plain coolies. Many of them never did return to China for various reasons. Some got killed while others preferred to stay in the United States in special occupations such as cooks, laundrymen or gardeners. Most of them belonged to "Tongs" which were their brand of Secret Societies which were often at odds with different other Tongs so that some Chinamen were killed by other Chinamen instead of the many hazards of railroad construction work. The Tong wars persisted throughout the early part of the Golden Spike Era, the writer having seen a dead Chinaman at Bonneville in 1894 which the section-boss there, Jim Tombs, said was the result of a dispute between two "Chinese Tong Societies." Mostly the section-bosses were burly Irishmen and all section-laborers were Chinese coolies with maybe the "track-walker" being a white man, and this was the rule all the way from Sacramento to Ogden. . . .

I will now describe how my "Chinese friends" lived at old Blue Creek Station in 1891. The antiquated box-car they lived in had been remodeled into a "work-car" in one end of which a series of small bunk-beds had been built as a vertical column of three bunks one above the other on both sides of the car-end from floor to ceiling so that around 18 Chinamen could sleep in the bedroom end of the car, while the other end of the car served as a kitchen and dining-room wherein there was a cast-iron cook-stove with its stovepipe going up through the roof of the car and with all kinds of pots and pans and skillets hanging around on the walls plus cubby-holes for tea-cups and big and little blue china bowls and "chop-sticks" and wooden spoons etc. There was also a wooden table and benches about like we now find in Forest Service camp grounds occupying the middle of the car. Some of the bunks had little windows about 8 inches square cut in the wall of the car so that when the assorted smokes got too dense inside, a non-smoking Chinaman could open his window and get a breath of fresh air. . . .

Each cook would have the use of a very big iron kettle hung over an open fire and into it they would dump a couple of measures of Chinese unhulled brown rice, Chinese noodles, bamboo sprouts and dried seaweed, different Chinese seasonings and American chickens cut up into small pieces including heads, legs and all, plus more water than would seem necessary and even then the kettle would be only half full. When the cook stirred up the fire and the concoction began to boil, then the rice would begin to swell until finally the kettle would be nearly full of steaming, nearly dry brown rice with the cut up chickens all through it.

Each Chinaman would take his big blue bowl and ladle it full of the mixture and deftly entwine his chopsticks between his fingers and string the mixture into his mouth in one continuous operation, while in the meantime he would be drinking his cup of tea and still more tea. I was the curious watching kid, so the cook would ladle up a little blue bowlful for me (little Wah Lee) and hand me a pair of chopsticks and with them I would try to eat like the rest of my buddies but I never could get the "knack" so I ended up eating with my fingers which would make the Chinamen laugh and I would get no tea. If I got a chicken head in my rice I could not eat it due to some kind of American prejudice so in the future the cook would see that I got no chicken-heads.

Nearly all the food a Chinaman ate came from China, with the exception of American chickens, so about once a week a supply car would come in from San Francisco and would be set out on the back sidetrack and all the cooks would come with their long "tote-poles" or totebars which were long sticks about 8 feet long with a notch near each end and a padded shoulder rest near the middle, and they would hang a box of supplies on one end and a bamboo fiber sack of brown rice or raw brown sugar balanced on the other end. They would shoulder the totepole near its middle and trot off to their car with this near 200 pound load of supplies which had come direct from China via ship and C. P. supply-car. . . .

. . . The opium den I will now describe (I have been in others) was under an old tie and dirt shack used as a bunk house. I was guided down a ladder covered by a trap door in the floor of the bunk house since I had some American candy for a dear friend who was down there. The den was dimly lit and had a dirt floor and the air fairly reeked with the sickening sweet smell of opium smoke. I would guess if one was down there long enough a person could go into a happy opium dream without ever drawing an opium pipe. There were the usual tiered bunks around three sides of that underground den. Nearly every bunk held a Chinaman who was "doping up" his opium-pipe or else he had gone to sweet slumber and the pleasant dreams of the opium addict. Several of them I recognized as being among my best friends and the friend I had gone down to talk with was not smoking opium. I could see sleeping Chinamen with big smiles on their faces because they were dreaming the nicest kind of opium dreams. Sometimes that sweet dream would change to a bad dream as the narcotic effect waned and my Chinaman friend would be waking up from a nightmare as was shown by the troubled expression on his face. I was allowed underground there for quite a while that evening which showed that my friends trusted little Wah Lee who had promised not to blab to Papa or Mamma.

From Wallace A. Clay, an unpublished family letter (1969).

Stoyan Christowe
Working on the Great Northern

The track ahead was but a thin stripe upon the earth's white expanse. And upon this band of steel the hundred men, like animated tumbleweeds, bent and twisted, bored and scratched. Upon the white bosom of American earth we engraved a necklace of steel—set in tie plates, clasped with bolts and angle bars, brocaded with spikes. And there it lay secured to the earth, immovable.

Not a tree was upon the plain, not a habitation in sight. Now and then a ground wind prowled over the surface, stirring the powdery snow, gathering drapes of it and twirling them about like the robes of spirits which seemed to weave and dance to the whining of the wind, to the mysterious moaning of the telephone and telegraph wires, and to the orchestra of bars and hammers.

The cold was there—ever present, glued to everything, pressing upon the earth, stinging the steel itself. If we stepped on a rail or a tie plate, the soles of our boots stuck to the steel; we heard the sizzle as though we had stepped on live coals. The cold was real. It needled my face, stung my eyes, penetrated to my feet, swaddled though they were in woolen socks, felt slippers, and arctics. My feet thumped like clumsy, separate bodies, like hedgehogs; my hands pawed the bolts through the fur-lined mittens, fitting the bolts into the round holes of the fishplates. Then I would put my shoulder to the bar and turn the wrench till the bolts were tight, till they squeaked like pups in the cold.

I had always thought that the building of a railway was a complicated business, as mysterious as the building of a steamboat or a locomotive. And I had believed that we would be carrying the steel while others—Americans—would be doing the skillful work. Seeing now a hundred erstwhile plowmen and shepherds tear off the old track and build it anew as fast as they tore it down, the whole thing struck me as too simple to be true. There was the feeling in me that the hundred men, adults though they were, were just children pretending to be building a railway, over which maybe a toy train could pass, but no real one.

There was not an engineer in sight, nor an American, to lend credence to this thing, to impute reality to what was being done. The boss was an Irishman with the fantastic name of Pat—just Pat. Could a man named Pat build a railway? Besides, Pat did nothing anyway. Wrapped in a bearskin cloak which reached to his galoshes, in which his trouser legs were tucked, and upon his head a beehive fur hat, he walked up and down the track, from the claw bars to the spike malls, doing nothing, saying nothing. . . .

Around eleven o'clock, when some sixty or seventy new rails had been strung upon the line, Pat called a stop. A short time before he had talked with some distant place through a portable telephone, which was part of the equipment carried on the pushcar. Afterward Pat kept consulting his watch frequently, and then ordered the claw bars to cease opening more track. The claw-bar men stuck their bars in the snow on the embankment and sat on the track to rest their bodies. Some of them took out handkerchiefs to mop the cold dampness from their foreheads, for despite the cold their hair was moist from the labor and matted down to their skulls. . . .

Pat's thin voice announced the approach of the train. "Here she comes, fellows, everybody up now."

The men stirred, picking up their tools as they stood up. I looked up ahead to the east. And there, where the track vanished, a bundle of black smoke was visible. That and nothing else. But that was the *Fast Mail*. That patch of black smoke upon the steel-gray horizon began to rouse the plain. We could detect a faint sound emitted by the rails.

By and by the bundle of smoke assumed the shape of an inverted cone, with its apex spinning on the edge of the plain. And soon I saw the engine, a black point upon the rim of the horizon. There was now a distinct vibration upon the rails, with the emission of an occasional sound as when you pick at an over-stretched wire. . . .

Pat stood in the middle of the track signaling to the engineer to continue on with caution. Pat did that by describing low arcs with his arm. Two short blows of the whistle acknowledged Pat's signal and he stepped out onto the embankment.

The engine appeared immense. Its cowcatcher was sculptured in ice, but its stack belched smoke, for there was a fire in the heart of the engine which no cold could stifle. And as long as the wheels stayed on the rails, the engine was a mighty power. It moved on, its wheels rolling with earth-shaking ponderosity.

There were only three mail cars attached to the engine, and these were loaded with letters and packages, with bonds, shares, gold certificates, with jewels and gold, and other precious stuffs. They would be delivered to the doors of houses, or into steam-heated offices in cities on the Coast, and some would be put on steamships to go to the Orient.

The pistons shuttled visibly like gigantic arms bending at the elbow to propel the wheels, under whose weight the rails bent into the frozen earth and sprang up in their resilience as soon as released.

The locomotive was still over old track, and the wheels turned slowly, cautiously, feeling their way, as if suspicious of the new track ahead, laid by us. The engine itself sniffed, scented, its many valves spurting out jets of vapor.

The men withdrew farther down toward the ditch, and I too stepped back with them, but my eyes were on the front wheel, watching it come closer and closer to the point of connection. High up in the cab the engineer had slid open a section of the glass that enclosed him, and his goggled eyes held the rail below like a pair of binoculars.

My heart thumped in my breast as the front wheel turned onto the switchpoint. The next instant it was on the new rail, and then upon the joint which I had made secure with the bolts and the fishplates, and on it rolled, over the new track which I had thought was a toy track.

I gave out an involuntary cry and brandished my line wrench like a mace. And then a chorus of a hundred voices waked the plain from its frozen lethargy. There was warmth and cheer in every voice, as if the locomotive were a rescue party from a peopled world come to us forsaken upon the nakedness of a cold and desolate America. The engineer gave out a prolonged, heartening whistle, and the train gathered speed upon the new and firmer track.

I watched the *Fast Mail* disappear into the unknown West, and I felt less alone now, less cold. Some of the awe had gone out of the desolation, and the plain was not so unencompassable.

"All right, men, rip her up now," Pat yelled in his high-pitched voice.

A new energy seized the workers. The claw bars clamped the spikes with the iron fangs of the bars and jerked them out like frozen worms. The tong-men slung in the new thirty-three-foot rails with the lightness of sticks. I unclasped the metal hooks of my sheepskin-lined coat so as to breathe more freely, and I took off my mittens that I might touch the steel with my bare hands. And then I felt as if a candle were suddenly lit inside me, glowing within me and warming my body. In crowded St. Louis I had never felt so close to America as I did now in this pathless plain. I knew that as I touched the steel, linking one rail to another, I was linking myself to the new country and building my own solid road to a new life.

From Stoyan Christowe, *My American Pilgrimage* (Boston: Little, Brown and Co., 1947) pp. 193–196; 198–202 *passim*.

Frank Norris

The Railroad Squeezes the Farmers

As he stood for a moment at the counter in front of the wire partition, waiting for the clerk to make out the order for the freight agent at the depot, Dyke was surprised to see a familiar figure in conference with Ruggles himself, by a desk inside the railing.

The figure was that of a middle-aged man, fat, with a great stomach, which he stroked from time to time. As he turned about, addressing a remark to the clerk, Dyke recognized S. Behrman. The banker, railroad agent, and political manipulator seemed to the ex-engineer's eyes to be more gross than ever. His smooth-shaven jowl stood out big and tremulous on either side of his face; the roll of fat on the nape of his neck, sprinkled with sparse, stiff hairs, bulged out with greater prominence. His great stomach, covered with a light brown linen vest, stamped with innumerable interlocked horseshoes, protruded far in advance, enormous, aggressive. He wore his inevitable round-topped hat of stiff brown straw, varnished so bright that it reflected the light of the office windows like a helmet, and even from where he stood Dyke could hear his loud breathing and the clink of the hollow links of his watch chain upon the vest buttons of imitation pearl, as his stomach rose and fell.

Dyke looked at him with attention. There was the enemy, the representative of the Trust with which Derrick's League was locking horns. The great struggle had begun to invest the combatants with interest. Daily, almost hourly, Dyke was in touch with the ranchers, the wheat-growers. He heard their denunciations, their growls of exasperation and defiance. Here was the other side—this placid, fat man, with a stiff straw hat and linen vest, who never lost his temper, who smiled affably upon his enemies, giving them good advice, commiserating with them in one defeat after another, never ruffled, never excited, sure of his power, conscious that back of him was the Machine, the colossal force, the inexhaustible coffers of a mighty organization, vomiting millions to the League's thousands.

The League was clamorous, ubiquitous, its objects known to every urchin on the streets, but the Trust was silent, its ways inscrutable, the public saw only results. It worked on in the dark, calm, disciplined, irresistible. Abruptly Dyke received the impression of the multitudinous ramifications of the colossus. Under his feet the ground seemed mined; down there below him in the dark the huge tentacles went silently twisting and advancing, spreading out in every direction, sapping the strength of all opposition, quiet, gradual, biding the **time to reach up and out and grip with a sudden unleashing** of gigantic strength.

"I'll be wanting some cars of you people before the summer is out," observed Dyke to the clerk as he folded up and put away the order that the other had handed him. He remembered perfectly well that he had arranged the matter of transporting his crop some months before, but his rôle of proprietor amused him and he liked to busy himself again and again with the details of his undertaking.

"I suppose," he added, "you'll be able to give 'em to me. There'll be a big wheat crop to move this year and I don't want to be caught in any car famine."

"Oh, you'll get your cars," murmured the other.

"I'll be the means of bringing business your way," Dyke went on; "I've done so well with my hops that there are a lot of others going into the business next season. Suppose," he continued, struck with an idea, "suppose we went into some sort of pool, a sort of shippers' organization, could you give us special rates, cheaper rates—say a cent and a half?"

The other looked up.

"A cent and a half! Say *four* cents and a half and maybe I'll talk business with you."

"Four cents and a half," returned Dyke, "I don't see it. Why, the regular rate is only two cents."

"No, it isn't," answered the clerk, looking him gravely in the eye, "it's five cents."

"Well, there's where you are wrong, m'son," Dyke retorted genially. "You look it up. You'll find the freight on hops from Bonneville to 'Frisco is two cents a pound for car load lots. You told me that yourself last fall."

"That was last fall," observed the clerk. There was a silence. Dyke shot a glance of suspicion at the other. Then, reassured, he remarked:

"You look it up. You'll see I'm right."

S. Behrman came forward and shook hands politely with the ex-engineer.

"Anything I can do for you, Mr. Dyke?"

Dyke explained. When he had done speaking, the clerk turned to S. Behrman and observed respectfully:

"Our regular rate on hops is five cents."

"Yes," answered S. Behrman, pausing to reflect; "yes, Mr. Dyke, that's right—five cents."

The clerk brought forward a folder of yellow paper and handed it to Dyke. It was inscribed at the top "Tariff Schedule No. 8," and underneath these words, in brackets, was a smaller inscription, *"Supersedes No. 7 of Aug. 1."*

"See for yourself," said S. Behrman. He indicated an item under the head of "Miscellany."

"The following rates for carriage of hops in car load lots," read Dyke, "take effect June 1, and will remain in force until superseded by a later tariff. Those quoted beyond Stockton are subject to changes in traffic arrangements with carriers by water from that point."

In the list that was printed below, Dyke saw that the rate for hops between Bonneville or Guadalajara and San Francisco was five cents.

For a moment Dyke was confused. Then swiftly the matter became clear in his mind. The Railroad had raised the freight on hops from two cents to five.

All his calculations as to a profit on his little investment he had based on a freight rate of two cents a pound. He was under contract to deliver his crop. He could not draw back. The new rate ate up every cent of his gains. He stood there ruined.

"Why, what do you mean?" he burst out. "You promised me a rate of two cents and I went ahead with my business with that understanding. What do you mean?"

S. Behrman and the clerk watched him from the other side of the counter.

"The rate is five cents," declared the clerk doggedly.

"Well, that ruins me," shouted Dyke. "Do you understand? I won't make fifty cents. *Make!* Why, I will *owe*,—I'll be—be—That ruins me, do you understand?"

The other raised a shoulder.

"We don't force you to ship. You can do as you like. The rate is five cents."

"Well—but—damn you, I'm under contract to deliver. What am I going to do? Why, you told me—you promised me a two-cent rate."

"I don't remember it," said the clerk. "I don't know anything about that. But I know this; I know that hops have gone up. I know the German crop was a failure and that the crop in New York wasn't worth the hauling. Hops have gone up to nearly a dollar. You don't suppose we don't know that, do you, Mr. Dyke?"

"What's the price of hops got to do with you?"

"It's got *this* to do with us," returned the other with a sudden aggressiveness, "that the freight rate has gone up to meet the price. We're not doing business for our health. My orders are to raise your rate to five cents, and I think you are getting off easy."

Dyke stared in blank astonishment. For the moment, the audacity of the affair was what most appealed to him. He forgot its personal application.

"Good Lord," he murmured, "good Lord! What will you people do next? Look here. What's your basis of applying freight rates, anyhow?" he suddenly vociferated with furious sarcasm. "What's your rule? What are you guided by?"

But at the words, S. Behrman, who had kept silent during the heat of the discussion, leaned abruptly forward. For the only time in his knowledge, Dyke saw his face inflamed with anger and with the enmity and contempt of all this farming element with whom he was contending.

"Yes, what's your rule? What's your basis?" demanded Dyke, turning swiftly to him.

S. Behrman emphasised each word of his reply with a tap of one forefinger on the counter before him:

"All—the—traffic—will—bear."

From Frank Norris, *The Octopus* (New York: Doubleday, Page & Co., 1901), pp. 345–350.

Dan De Quille

A Mine in the Comstock Lode

Crossing this thoroughfare of the 1,500-foot level and advancing a few steps further to the eastward, we reach the vast deposit of ore known as the "Big Bonanza." Cross cuts pass through the ore, east and west, and cross-drifts from north to south, cutting it into blocks from fifty to one hundred feet square, as the streets run through and divide a town into blocks. It is indeed a sort of subterranean town, and is more populous than many towns on the surface, as it numbers from 800 to 1,000 souls, and nearly all are voters.

Passing to the south end of the bonanza, to the place where it was first crossed by a drift, we find it to be one hundred and forty-eight feet in width—all a solid mass of ore of the richest description. Here a large stope is opened, and we see the miners at work in the vein, blasting and digging down the ore. They are working upward from the floor of the level, and as they progress they build up square sets of supporting timbers in the cavities or chambers cut out in extracting the ore from the bonanza. Even here, well toward its south end—as far as explored—the ore-body is by no means small, being over nine and one half rods in width! This is not a mixture of ore and worthless rock, but is a solid mass of rich silver-ore which is sent to the mills just as it is dug or blasted down—ore that will pay from $100 to $300 per ton. As thirteen cubic feet make a ton of ore, we have here for every block of ore three feet square from $200 to $600 in pure silver and gold.

We may take our stand here, where the miners are digging out the ore, and for a distance of seventy-five feet on each side of us all is ore, while we may gaze upward to nearly that height to where the twinkling light of candles shows us miners delving up into the same great mass of wealth. On all sides of the pyramidal scaffold of timbers to its very apex, where the candles twinkle like stars in the heavens, we see the miners cutting their way into the precious ore—battering it with sledge-hammers and cutting it to pieces with their picks as though it were but common sandstone. . . .

Two mining superintendents were one day discussing the bonanza, when one of them said to his brother silver-hunter: "Supposing the Almighty to have given you full power and authority to make such a body of ore as you pleased, could you have made a better than this?"

"I don't know that I could," said the other, "but I should have made it still bigger."

"Well," said the first speaker, "you have more cheek than any man I ever saw!"

From Dan De Quille, *History of the Big Bonanza* (Hartford, Conn.; San Francisco: American Publishing Co.; A. L. Bancroft & Co., 1876), pp. 480–481; 485–486.

Woody Guthrie

Boomtown Philosophy in Oklahoma

People had been slinking around corners and ducking behind bushes, whispering and talking, and running like wild to swap and trade for land—because tests had showed that there was a whole big ocean of oil laying under our country. And then, one day, almost out of a clear sky, it broke. A car shot dust in the air along the Ozark Trail. A man piled out and waved his hands up and down Main Street running for the land office. "Oil! She's blowed 'er top! Gusher!" And then, before long—there was a black hot fever hit our town—and it brought with it several whole armies, each running the streets, and each hollering, "Oil! Flipped 'er lid! Gusher!"

They found more oil around town along the river and the creek bottoms, and oil derricks jumped up like new groves of tall timber. Thick and black and flying with steam, in the pastures, and above the trees, and standing in the slushy mud of the boggy rivers, and on the rocky sides of the useless hills, oil derricks, the wood legs and braces gummed and soaked with dusty black blood.

Pretty soon the creeks around Okemah was filled with black scum, and the rivers flowed with it, so that it looked like a stream of rainbow-colored gold drifting hot along the waters. The oily film looked pretty from the river banks and from on the bridges, and I was a right young kid, but I remember how it came in whirls and currents, and swelled up as it slid along down the river. It reflected every color when the sun hit just right on it, and in the hot dry weather that is called Dog Days the fumes rose up and you could smell them for miles and miles in every direction. It was something big and it sort of give you a good feeling. You felt like it was bringing some work, and some trade, and some money to everybody, and that people everywhere, even way back up in the Eastern States was using that oil and that gas.

Oil laid tight and close on the top of the water, and the fish couldn't get the air they needed. They died by the wagon

384

loads along the banks. The weeds turned gray and tan, and never growed there any more. The tender weeds and grass went away and all that you could see for several feet around the edge of the oily water hole was the red dirt. The tough iron weeds and the hard woodbrush stayed longer. They were there for several years, dead, just standing there like they was trying to hold their breath and tough it out till the river would get pure again, and the oil would go, and things could breathe again. But the oil didn't go. It stayed. The grass and the trees and the tanglewood died. The wild grape vine shriveled up and its tree died, and the farmers pulled it down.

The Negro sharecroppers went out with their bread balls and liver for bait. You saw them setting around the banks and on the tangled drifts, in the middle of the day, or along about sundown—great big bunches of Negro farmers trying to get a nibble. They worked hard. But the oil had come, and it looked like the fish had gone. It had been an even swap.

Trains whistled into our town a hundred coaches long. Men drove their heavy wagons by the score down to pull up alongside of the cars, and skidded the big engines, the thick-painted, new and shiny machinery, and some old and rusty machines from other oil fields. They unloaded the railroad cars, and loaded and tugged a blue jillion different kinds of funny-looking gadgets out into the fields. And then it seemed like all on one day, the solid-tired trucks come into the country, making such a roar that it made your back teeth rattle. Everybody was holding down one awful hard job and two or three ordinary ones.

People told jokes:

Birds flew into town by the big long clouds, lasting two or three hours at a time, because it was rumored around up in the sky that you could wallow in the dust of the oiled roads and it would kill all kinds of fleas and body lice.

Dogs cured their mange, or else got it worse. Oil on their hair made them hotter in hot weather and colder in cold weather.

Ants dug their holes deeper, but wouldn't talk any secrets about the oil formation under the ground.

Snakes and lizards complained that wiggling through so many oil pools made the hot sun blister their backs worse. But on the other hand they could slide on their belly through the grass a lot easier. So it come out about even.

Oil was more than gold ever was or ever will be, because you can't make any hair salve or perfume, TNT, or roofing

material or drive a car with just gold. You can't pipe that
gold back East and run them big factories, either.

The religion of the oil field, guys said, was to get all you
can, and spend all you can as quick as you can, and then end
up in the can.

From Woody Guthrie, *Bound for Glory* (New York: E. P. Dutton &
Co., 1943), pp. 113–115.

Willa Cather

Bust in El Dorado, Kansas

At last spring came, that fabled spring, when all the business
men were to return to El Dorado, when the Gump Academy
was to be built, when the waterworks were to be put in, when
the Gumps were to welcome their wives and children. Ches-
terfield, Hezekiah and Aristotle had gone East to see to bringing out their families, and the Colonel was impatiently
awaiting their return, as the real estate business seemed to be
at a standstill and he could get no satisfaction from Apollo
about the condition of affairs. One night there came a telegram from New York, brought posthaste across the country
from the nearest station, announcing that the father of the
Gumps was dying, and summoning the other brothers to his
bedside. There was great excitement in El Dorado at these ti-
dings, and the sympathy of its inhabitants was so genuine
that they scarcely stopped to think what the departure of the
Gumps might mean.

De Witt and Ezekiel left the next day accompanied by
Miss Venus and Miss Almira. Apollo and Isaiah remained to
look after the bank. The Colonel began to feel anxious, realizing that the Gumps had things pretty much in their own
hands and that if the death of their father should make any
material difference in their projects and they should decide to
leave Kansas for good, the town and his interests would be
woefully undone. Still, he said very little, not thinking it a
time to bring up business considerations; for even Apollo
looked worried and harassed and was entirely sober for days
together.

The Gumps left on Monday. On the following Sunday Isaiah delivered a particularly powerful discourse on the mutability of riches. He compared temporal wealth to stock in the great bank of God, which paid such rich dividends of grace daily, hourly. He earnestly exhorted his hearers to choose the good part and lay up for themselves treasures in heaven, where moths cannot corrupt nor thieves break through and steal. Apollo was not at church that morning. The next morning the man who took care of Apollo's blooded horses found that two of them were missing. When he went to report this to Apollo he got no response to his knock, and, not succeeding in finding Isaiah, he went to consult the Colonel. Together they went back to Apollo's room and broke in the door. They found the room in wretched disorder, with clothing strewn about over the furniture; but nothing was missing save Apollo's grip and revolver, the picture of the theatrical looking person that had hung in his sleeping room, and Apollo himself. Then the truth dawned upon the Colonel. The Gumps had gone, taking with them the Gump banking funds, land funds, city improvement funds, academy funds, and all funds, both public and private.

As soon as the news of the hegira of the Gumps got abroad, carriages and horses came from all the towns in the country, bringing to the citizens of El Dorado their attentive creditors. All the townsmen had paid fabulous prices for their land, borrowed money on it, put the money into the Gump bank, and done their business principally on credit obtained on the Gump indorsement. Now that their money was gone, they discovered that the land was worth nothing, was a desert which the fertile imagination of the Gumps had made to blossom as the rose. The loan companies also discovered the worthlessness of the land, and used every possible means to induce the tenants to remain on it; but the entire country was panic-stricken and would hear no argument. Their one desire was to get away from this desolate spot, where they had been duped. The infuriated creditors tore down the houses and carried even the foundation stones away. Scarcely a house in the town had been paid for; the money had been paid to Aristotle Gump, contractor and builder, who had done his business in the East almost entirely on credit. The loan agents and various other creditors literally put the town into wagons and carried it off. Meanwhile, the popular indignation was turned against the Colonel as having been immediately associated with the Gumps and implicated in their dishonesty. In vain did he protest his innocence. When men are hurt they must have something to turn upon, like children who kick the door that pinches their fingers. So the poor old Colonel, who was utterly ruined and one of the heaviest losers, was accused of having untold wealth hidden away somewhere in the bluffs; and all the tempest of wrath and hatred which the Gumps had raised broke over his head. He was glad, indeed, when the town was utterly deserted, and he could live without the continual fear of those reproachful and suspicious glances. Often as he sat watching those barren bluffs, he wondered whether some day the whole grand delusion would not pass away, and this great West, with its cities built on borrowed capital, its business done on credit, its temporary homes, its drifting, restless population, become panic-stricken and disappear, vanish utterly and completely, as a bubble that bursts, as a dream that is done. He hated Western Kansas; and yet in a way he pitied this poor brown country, which seemed as lonely as himself and as unhappy. No one cared for it, for its soil or its rivers. Every one wanted to speculate in it. It seemed as if God himself had only made it for purposes of speculation and was tired of the deal and doing his best to get it off his hands and deed it over to the Other Party.

From Willa Cather, "El Dorado: A Kansas Recessional," *The New England Magazine*, Vol. 24, No. 4 (June 1901), pp. 363–364.

WORKERS ON THE
SECOND FRONTIER

J. G. Brown

A Lumberjack's Life

The worst thing I find that the men in the logging camps
have to contend with is the bad conditions. There is one logging camp on Grays Harbor where they have a bunk house
with room in the bunk house for about 50 persons. Those
men sleep in wooden bunks; those bunks are double tiers running clear around the building. Those bunk houses have only
one window in one end of them. A man would have to light a
lamp to read in the middle of the day. They have a big stove
in the center of that, and the only other comfort is a bench
that runs around on a level with the lower bunk. A man can
sit on those benches, or perhaps have a box or something of
that sort to sit on if they want to sit around the table and
play cards or something of that character. They have stoves,
and in the periods of the year when it is raining the stoves
are hung all about with wet clothing. That is their only
method that these loggers and woodmen have of drying their
clothes. The men naturally in the bunks have to inhale the
steam that comes off of these drying clothes. In the winter-
time or fall of the year the men keep the door open in order
that they can be more comfortable from the heat of the
stoves. When the fire dies out that makes a sudden change in
the temperature. They are victims of colds and other diseases
that come from that—rheumatism and the like of that. They
work these men in the fall and winter all of the daylight
there is. In the summer time they work them about 12 hours
a day. They start out from the bunk house at 6 o'clock, pre-
sumably; frequently it is 20 minutes to 6. They walk anywhere from 20 rods to a mile and a half to their work. They

reach their work and leave at 6 o'clock at night and have to go that distance back home on their own time. They theoretically walk one way on the company's time and the other way on their own time. It frequently happens that what is theoretically 10 hours is stretched into a 12-hour day, sometimes even longer than that. Those long hours of employment, the uncertainty of it, and the bad conditions under which they live are the main complaints that the loggers have. . . . Usually these men are tired out, and have no chance to, or care or desire to improve their conditions. They just come in and sleep. Nearly all of these camps are infested with bedbugs, some of them have fleas, and some of them are lousy. One camp down on Grays Harbor—the men last summer went out and slept out doors out in the woods, rather than tolerate the conditions in the bunk house.

From J. G. Brown, President of the International Union of Timber Workers, testimony in *Final Report and Testimony, U. S. Commission on Industrial Relations*, Vol. 5, 64th Congress, 1st Session, Document No. 415 (Washington: U. S. Government Printing Office, 1916), pp. 4211–4212.

Edward and Eleanor Marx Aveling

Cowboy Proletarians

In the present chapter we desire to show the reader that which the cowboys themselves have made plain to us, that they are distinctly members of the non-possessing and yet producing and distributing class, that they are as much at the mercy of the capitalist as a New or Old England cotton-operative, that their supposed "freedom" is no more of a reality than his. Further, evidence will be given that the cowboys, as a class, are beginning to recognise these facts, are becoming anxious that the general public should know them, and, best of all, are desirous, through the medium of either the Knights of Labour, or some other working-class organisation, to connect themselves with the mass of the labouring class and with the general movement of that class against the tyranny of their employers.

Our first acquaintance with these facts was made at Cincinnati, and in a sufficiently odd way. Some delightful German-American friends, in their anxiety to show us all the sights of the city, had lured us into a dime museum. The chief attraction at this show, pending the arrival of Sir Roger Tichborne, who came the next week, was not seen and did not conquer, was a group of cowboys. They were sitting in twos and threes on various little raised platforms, clad in their picturesque garb, and looking terribly bored. Presently, a spruce gentleman, in ordinary, commonplace garments, began to make stereotyped speeches about them in a voice metallic enough for stereotyping. But, at one platform, he mercifully stopped short, and told us that Mr. John Sullivan, *alias* Broncho John, would take up the parable.

Thereupon, a cowboy of singularly handsome face and figure, with the frankest of blue eyes, rose and spoke a piece. To our great astonishment he plunged at once into a denunciation of capitalists in general and of the ranch-owners in particular. We were struck both by the manner and the matter of this man's talk. It had the first and second and third qualifications for oratorical success—earnestness. Broncho John evidently knew what he was talking about, and felt what he said. The gist of his speech is embodied in the last paragraph but one. To that need only be added John's appeal to the newspapers of the East that they should do what the Western ones were afraid or unwilling to do, and state clearly the case of the cowboys, their complaints, and their demands. . . .

There are some 8,000 to 10,000 cowboys (this is Broncho John's estimate, and is considerably below the actual number), and "no class is harder worked, . . . none so poorly paid for their services." The reason why they are so poorly paid and hard worked is simple enough.—"They have no organisation back of them," while their employers have "one of the strongest and most systematic and, at the same time, despotic unions that was ever formed to awe and dictate to labour." . . . The conditions under which the cowboys work are such that organisation is immensely difficult, in many cases well-nigh impossible. They are dispersed over miles upon miles of huge plains and desolate wastes, a few here and a few there, so that concerted action seems almost out of the question. Yet so many are, it appears, "awakened to the necessity of having a league of their own" that a Cowboy Assembly of the K. of L. or a Cowboy Union is sure to be started in the near future. Meanwhile, the fact that such a league is desired by the cowboys is significant enough, and even more significant is their employers' fear of any such combination. One means by which the bosses hope to ward it off is by issuing orders that the men "must not read books or newspapers." Small wonder the cowboys regard such an "order" as "tyrannical in the extreme." A pathetic example of the belief of the cowboys in a movement of some sort we found in Broncho John's conviction that a return of Blaine (as president) would mean that "all the thieving would go on," while the election of Henry George would "make a change."

As to the actual work and wages of the cowboy. The work is necessarily extremely arduous and dangerous. For some six to eight months in the year—*i.e.*, the working time on the plains—he has not only to be in the saddle from morn to night, but often the whole night through as well. To look after these huge Western herds of cattle, to keep a cool head during stampedes and "milling" is no small matter. . . . Further, there are innumerable dangers from bands of marauders, Indians, and prairie fires to face; and, into the bargain, the herd must not only be delivered safe and all told, but they must have increased in weight since leaving the ranch. "The rule is, the cowboy must fatten the cattle on the trail, *no matter how thin he may grow himself.*"

From Edward and Eleanor Marx Aveling, *The Working-Class Movement in America*, 2nd Ed. (London: Swan Sonnenschein & Co., 1891), pp. 155–161.

Bill Haywood

Big Bill Haywood Goes to the Coeur d'Alene

When the power drills were introduced the work of the miners was changed. The men did not object to the installation of the machines, but many skillful miners were not physically capable of handling one of the big sluggers. No consideration was shown to them; they were put to running cars, shoveling ore, or as roustabouts at fifty cents a day less than the miners had been receiving. This would make a corresponding reduction in their standard of living. Fifteen dollars a month less for all miners, thirty dollars a month less for miners who could not handle the big drills. It could be summed up as less food, less clothes, less house-room, less schooling for the children, less amusements, less everything that made life worth living. The situation was discussed in all its different phases at all the meetings of the union. There was no means of escape from the gigantic force that was relentlessly crushing all of them beneath its cruel heel. The people of these dreadful mining camps were in a fever of revolt. There was no method of appeal; strike was their only weapon.

On April 29, 1899, a big demonstration was held at Wardner. All the members of all the unions in the district were there. The last warning had been sounded. The fuses were lit. Three thousand pounds of dynamite exploded. The Bunker Hill and Sullivan mill was blown up, ripped and smashed, a mass of twisted steel, iron and splintered timbers. The miners had released their pent-up resentment. There may have been some who regretted the destruction of that which workers had built, but the constraint of the entire population was for the time-being relieved. . . .

At Salt Lake City I found the shadow of the Coeur d'Alenes pervading the convention. The delegates could think or talk of little else. Twelve hundred members were in prison, nine of them indicted for murder, women and children were living under the dark menace of martial law. The legislature, the courts and the army were against us. Every man brought the question home to himself. If this dreadful thing happened in Leadville in the Coeur d'Alenes, how long before it happens in Butte, in the Black Hills, in Nevada? What is to stop it happening in the camp where I live? Must wages and hours and the conditions under which we live and work always be subject to the will and whim of the boss?

The only answer I could find in my own mind was to organize, to multiply our strength. As long as we were scattered and disjointed we could be victimized. . . .

In approaching Butte I marveled at the desolation of the country. There was no verdure of any kind; it had all been killed by the fumes and smoke of the piles of burning ore. The noxious gases came from the sulphur that was allowed to burn out of the ore before it was sent to the smelter. It was so poisonous that it not only killed trees, shrubs, grass and flowers, but cats and dogs could not live in the city of Butte, and the housewives complained that the fumes settling on the clothes rotted the fiber.

The city with the copper soul was built around the mines of Butte. The people of this mining camp breathed copper, ate copper, wore copper, and were thoroughly saturated with copper. The smoke, fumes and dust penetrated everywhere and settled on everything. Many of the miners were suffering from rankling copper sores, caused by the poisonous water. The old iron and tin cans were gathered up and dumped into a pool where the water from the mines percolated and precipitated copper on the scrap iron, eating out the iron and converting the cans into copper.

The toll of death in Butte was abnormal. The sick benefits paid to the members of Butte Miners' Union aggregated hundreds of thousands of dollars. The funeral benefits were frightfully large. The city of the dead, mostly young miners, was almost as large as the living population, even in this very young city. Human life was the cheapest by-product of this great copper camp. . . .

We left Butte and caught the Great Northern at Missoula. Burke was to be our first stop. That part of the Rocky Mountains where the Coeur d'Alenes mining district is situated, is scarred and gashed with gulches and deep canyons. The mountain sides are rugged, with cliffs and outcroppings of rock. There are old and rotten stumps of the trees that have been cut for mining timber, railroad ties and firewood. Everywhere bushes and shrubs, wild strawberries and other wild fruit grow in abundance. Where the forests have not been depleted either with the ax or with devastating fires, there are bear, deer, and other game. In the cold, clear streams are mountain trout. The Coeur d'Alenes lake is like a transparent gem in the rough setting of the mountains. It is a delightful place for a summer outing, but a frightful place to live during the long winters, with the continual fear of snowslides, the digging out of the snow-bound houses, the floundering to and from work through snow waist-deep. The railroad runs around the mountains, through tunnels, across deep chasms on skeletons of steel, up and down narrow canyons where there is just room enough for the roadbed. Before the coming of the iron horse, the burro was the only means of transportation, the hunter, the prospector and the Indian were the only inhabitants. . . .

We stopped at Mrs. Fox's boarding house at Burke, which was well known to most of the miners of the West. I have heard many stories of her warm-heartedness. A miner coming to Burke was always welcome to a meal at her place. She caused much amusement among her boarders. One time when new cabbage was just in, the old lady had cooked up a lot. It was just what the miners were longing for and they kept asking for more. Bringing up the last plate full, she said:

"Take that, ye sons of batches, and I'll bring yez a bale of hay in the marnin'."

Burke's one street was so narrow that there was just room enough for the railroad track. When the train was in, a wagon could not pass on either side. The canyon was so deep that the sun had to be nearly at zenith to shine down into the town.

At Mullen we met Paddy Burke and a few other members of the union. Our activities were of necessity under cover, because of the district being under martial law. We avoided the hang-out of the soldiers. Our purpose was to get a word of encouragement to the men in the bull-pen. We wanted them to know that we had come to the Coeur d'Alenes to bring to them the sympathy and the united support of the organization, in the interests of which they were enduring the degradation of imprisonment in the vermin-infested hole. The miners in the bull-pen had gotten some scantlings and long planks, and had lifted the end of the roof and hung out a sign that they had painted on sheets. It read, "The American Bastille." This got under the hide of General Merriam, who seemed to think that his up-to-date bull-pen was not appreciated. . . .

We saw that vile bull-pen from the train windows as we passed. A low, rambling one story building. There was a prison! Hundreds of men, many of whom I had worked with, were confined in it in squalor. They were men of my own kind. They were fighting my fight. If their wages had been cut, my wages would have been cut. They were the men who had made these mining camps. They had dug every pound of ore that ever came out of a mine. They and men like them had made the West. Their very lives, the living of their wives and children, were in jeopardy. Their appeals to the corporations went unheard. A mill had been blown up. If it was for this that they were in the bull-pen I should be there with them. I had not been in person at the demonstration at Wardner; but I was there in desire, in support. So was every miner of the West. We were united with the lead miners of the Coeur d'Alenes in their struggle against oppression.

From William D. Haywood, *Bill Haywood's Book* (New York: International Publishers, 1929), pp. 80–88 *passim*.

Bill Haywood
Big Bill Organizes the Bronc Busters

That fall there was a Mountain and Plains Festival in Denver, of which one of the features was a broncho-busting contest. My brother-in-law, Tom Minor, was one of the riders. I met many of the cowboys and invited them to the headquarters of the Federation, and suggested that their wages and conditions could be improved if they were organized. I said:

"It seems to me you fellows take a lot of chances riding in these contests. For this dangerous work you should get at least fifty dollars a day, and much higher wages than you get now while breaking bronchos on the ranch."

As the result of our meeting the Broncho Busters' and Ranger Riders' Union of the I.W.W. was organized. Harry Brennan, the champion rider, was elected president and Minor, secretary. Wages for riding in contests were fixed at fifty dollars a day, and fifty dollars a month for broncho busting and range riding on the ranch. They asked me to act as secretary until they were better organized or until Minor had a permanent address. The seal of the union was a cowboy on a bucking broncho which was branded on the hip B.B.R.R. I got out letter heads and envelopes with the same design, but with the cowboy throwing a rope around the return address, saying: "If not rounded up in ten days return to————." The union did not grow or even live very long, and I had but little time to devote to it.

From Haywood, *Bill Haywood's Book*, p. 190.

John D. Rockefeller, Jr., and L. M. Bowers
Labor War in Colorado

203 Main Street,
Binghamton, N. Y
September 4, 1913

Dear Mr. Rockefeller:

Reports are about completed for our fiscal year, and we are well pleased with the showing all things considered. Our profits would have exceeded 1912 if wages had not been advanced, costing us about $260,000 over the former year. The net profit, however, comes within $50,000 of 1912, the best year in the history of the company. . . .

There has been a group of labor-union agitators in southern Colorado for more than a month and threatening to call a strike for the purpose of securing a recognition of the Western Federation of Miners, but protests have come from nearly all the State officals from the governor on down, together with the protests from the boards of trade and of commercial bodies, so that the matter has quieted down, though their national officials are still in Colorado.

This has kept us all in a state of unrest, so that my vacation has been a season of worry. A disaster of this sort would put us up against a fight that would be serious indeed.

I expect to leave for Denver the 15th.

Yours, very truly,
L. M. BOWERS

26 Broadway,
New York,
October 6, 1913

Dear Mr. Bowers:

I have your letter of September 29, with reference to the coal strike in southern Colorado. We know how earnestly desirous you have always been to have the men in your employ work under the best possible conditions and receive every consideration and advantage. We also know that you and Mr.

Welborn have spared no pains to provide for the well-being and look out for the interests of the employees of the Colorado Fuel & Iron Co. Your letter simply confirms what we knew to be the case.

You gentlemen can not be more earnest in your desire for the best interests of the employees of your company than we are. We feel that what you have done is right and fair and that the position which you have taken in regard to the unionizing of the mines is in the interest of the employees of the company. Whatever the outcome may be, we will stand by you to the end.

Very truly,
JOHN D. ROCKEFELLER, JR.

October 11, 1913

Dear Mr. Rockefeller:

I am in receipt of your favor of the 6th, and I want to express the appreciation of Mr. Welborn and myself, together with that of several coal operators who have seen your letter, for the stand you have taken in supporting us in fighting this unjust, uncalled-for, and iniquitous strike, called by the officials of what is supposed to be a very important union.

I can say that I have never known such falsehoods and disregard for law and common decency as these men are the perpetrators of in this State. It is now proven beyond any sort of question that Winchester rifles in large numbers and revolvers with large quantities of ammunition are being supplied to the sluggers whom these men have brought in from other States together with the bloodthirsty Greeks who have just returned from the Turkish war. . . .

When this Government places in the Cabinet men like Commissioner of Labor Wilson, who was for many years secretary of the United Mine Workers of America, which has been one of the unions that permitted more disorder and bloodshed than any class of labor organization in this country, we are not skating upon thin ice, but we are on top of a volcano. When such men as these, together with the cheap college professors and still cheaper writers in muckraking magazines, supplemented by a lot of milk-and-water preachers with little or no religion and less common sense, are permitted to assault the business men who have built up the great industries and have done more to make this country what it is than all other agencies combined, it is time that

vigorous measures are taken to put a stop to these vicious
teachings which are being sown broadcast throughout this
country. . . .

You know very well that I am not a pessimist of the dys-
peptic sort, but I believe—that if the business men do not
awaken from their indifference and take aggressive measures
on a large scale to right the wrongs that are being inflicted
upon the business of this country, we will see a revolution,
we will be under military government and our Republic will
end where so many others have ended.

> Yours, very truly,
> L. M. Bowers

> 26 Broadway,
> New York,
> April 14, 1914

Dear Mr. Bowers:

I inclose herewith a letter from the secretary of the industrial department of the Young Men's Christian Association,
with a pamphlet regarding their work.

It may be that it would be worth while to consider the establishment, in connection with the steel mills, if not in the
mining camps, of a Young Men's Christian Association under
the management of the industrial department.

I send the data to you for such consideration as you and
Mr. Welborn may see fit to give it.

> Very truly,
> John D. Rockefeller, Jr.

[Telegram.]

> Denver, Colorado
> April 21, 1914

John D. Rockefeller, Jr.,
26 Broadway, New York:

Following withdrawal of troops by order of governor an
unprovoked attack upon small force of militia yesterday by
200 strikers. Forced fight resulting in probable loss of 10 or
15 strikers. Only one militiaman killed. Ludlow tent colony
of strikers totally destroyed by burning; 200 tents; generally
followed by explosions, showing ammunition and dynamite
stored in them. Expect further fighting to-day. Militia being

reenforced. Suggest your giving this information to friendly
papers.

L. M. BOWERS

[Telegram.]

April 21, 1914

L. M. Bowers,
Boston Building, Denver, Colo:

Telegram received. New York papers have published full
details. To-day's news is appearing on ticker. We profoundly
regret this further outbreak of lawlessness with accompanying
loss of life.

JOHN D. ROCKEFELLER, JR.

From *Final Report of the United States Commission on Industrial
Relations,* Vol. 9, 64th Congress, 1st Session, Senate Document No. 415
(Washington: U. S. Government Printing Office, 1916), pp. 8413,
8419–8420, 8429, 8430.

John Reed

The Ludlow Massacre

It was premeditated and merciless. Militiamen have told me
that their orders were to destroy the tent colony and everything living in it. . . . The three bombs were a signal to the
mine guards and Baldwin-Felts detectives and strikebreakers
in the neighboring mines; and they came swarming down out
of the hills fully armed—400 of them.

. . . Suddenly the terrible storm of lead from the machine
guns ripped their coverings to pieces, and the most awful
panic followed. Some of the women and children streamed
out over the plain, to get away from the tent colony. They
were shot at as they ran. Others with the unarmed men took
refuge in the arroyo to the north. Mrs. Fyler led a group of
women and children, under fire, to the deep well at the railroad pump house, down which they climbed on ladders. Others still crept into the bulletproof cellars they had dug for
themselves under their tents.

The fighting men, appalled at what was happening, started for the tent colony; but they were driven back by a hail of bullets. And now the mine guards began to get into action, shooting explosive bullets, which burst with the report of a six-shooter all through the tents. The machine guns never let up. Tikas had started off with the Greeks; but he ran back in a desperate attempt to save some of those who remained; and stayed in the tent colony all day. He and Mrs. Jolly, the wife of an American striker, and Bernardo, leader of the Italians, and Domeniski, leader of the Slavs, carried water and food and bandages to those imprisoned in the cellars. There was no one shooting from the tent colony. Not a man there had a gun. Tikas thought that the explosive bullets were the sound of shots being fired from the tents, and ran round like a crazy man to tell the fool to stop. It was an hour before he discovered what really made the noise.

Mrs. Jolly put on a white dress; and Tikas and Domeniski made big red crosses and pinned them on her breast and arms. The militia used them as targets. Her dress was riddled in a dozen places, and the heel of her shoe shot off. So fierce was the fire wherever she went that the people had to beg her to keep away from them. Undaunted, she and the three men made sandwiches and drew water to carry to the women and children. . . .

It was growing dark. The militia closed in around the tent colony. At about 7:30, a militiaman with a bucket of kerosene and a broom ran up to the first tent, wet it thoroughly, and touched a match to it. The flame roared up, illuminating the whole countryside. Other soldiers fell upon the other tents; and in a minute the whole northwest corner of the colony was aflame. A freight train came along just then with orders to stop on a siding near the pump house; and the women and children in the well took advantage of the protection of the train to creep out along the right-of-way fence to the protection of the arroyo, screaming and crying. . . .

When the fire started Mrs. Jolly went from tent to tent, pulling the women and children out of the cellars and herding them before her out on the plain. She remembered all of a sudden that Mrs. Petrucci and her three children were in the cellar under her tent, and started back to get them out. "No," said Tikas, "you go ahead with that bunch. I'll go back after the Petruccis." And he started toward the flames.

There the militia captured him. He tried to explain his errand; but they were drunk with blood lust and would not listen to him. Lieutenant Linderfelt broke the stock of his rifle over the Greek's head, laying it open to the bone. Fifty men got a rope and threw it over a telegraph wire to hang him. But Linderfelt cynically handed him over to two militiamen, and told them they were responsible for his life. Five minutes later Louis Tikas fell dead with three bullets in his back; and out of Mrs. Petrucci's cellar were afterward taken the charred bodies of thirteen women and children.

From John Reed, "The Colorado War," *Metropolitan*, Vol. 40, No. 3 (July 1914), pp. 69–70.

Henry George
Hard Times in a Land of Plenty

And over our ill-kept, shadeless, dusty roads, where a house is an unwonted landmark, and which run frequently for miles through the same man's land, plod the tramps, with blankets on back—the laborers of the California farmer—looking for work, in its seasons, or toiling back to the city when the ploughing is ended or the wheat crop is gathered.

From Henry George, "Our Land and Land Policy, National and State" (San Francisco: White & Bower, W. F. Loomis, 1871), p. 25.

Jack London
Hoboes That Pass in the Night

In the early evening I came down to the depot at Ogden. The overland of the Union Pacific was pulling east, and I was bent on making connections. Out in the tangle of tracks ahead of the engine I encountered a figure slouching through the gloom. It was the Swede. We shook hands like long-lost brothers, and discovered that our hands were gloved.

"Where'd ye glahm 'em?" I asked. "Out of an engine-cab," he answered; "and where did you?" "They belonged to a fire-man," said I; "he was careless."

We caught the blind as the overland pulled out, and mighty cold we found it. The way led up a narrow gorge between snow-covered mountains, and we shivered and shook and exchanged confidences about how we had covered the ground between Reno and Ogden. I had closed my eyes for only an hour or so the previous night, and the blind was not comfortable enough to suit me for a snooze. At a stop, I went forward to the engine. We had on a "double-header" (two engines) to take us over the grade.

The pilot of the head engine, because it "punched the wind," I knew would be too cold; so I selected the pilot of the second engine, which was sheltered by the first engine. I stepped on the cowcatcher and found the pilot occupied. In the darkness I felt out the form of a young boy. He was sound asleep. By squeezing, there was room for two on the pilot, and I made the boy budge over and crawled up beside him. It was a "good" night; the "shacks" (brakemen) didn't bother us, and in no time we were asleep. Once in a while hot cinders or heavy jolts aroused me, when I snuggled closer to the boy and dozed off to the coughing of the engines and the screeching of the wheels.

The overland made Evanston, Wyoming, and went no far-ther. A wreck ahead blocked the line. The dead engineer had been brought in, and his body attested the peril of the way. A tramp, also, had been killed, but his body had not been brought in. I talked with the boy. He was thirteen years old. He had run away from his folks in some place in Oregon, and was heading east to his grandmother. He had a tale of cruel treatment in the home he had left that rang true; besides, there was no need for him to lie to me, a nameless hobo on the track.

From Jack London, *The Road* (New York: Macmillan Co., 1907), pp. 131–133.

Around a Western Water Tank

Around a western water tank
A-waitin' for a train,
A thousand miles away from home
A-sleepin' in the rain,
I walked up to the brakeman
And give him a line of talk.
He said, 'if you've got money
I'll see that you don't walk.'

'I haven't got a nickel,
Not a penny can I show.'
'Get off, get off, you railroad bum—'
And he slammed the boxcar door.
He put me off in Texas,
A state I dearly love.
Wide open spaces all round me,
The moon and stars above.

Standing on the platform
Smoking a cheap cigar,
A-listenin' for the next freight train
To catch an empty car.
My pocket-book was empty,
My heart was full of pain,
A thousand miles away from home,
A-bummin' a railroad train.

I next got off in Danville,
Got stuck on a Danville girl.
You can bet your life she was out of sight,
She wore those Danville curls.
She took me in her kitchen,
She treated me nice and kind,
She got me in the notion
Of bummin' all the time.

As I left the kitchen
And went down in the town,
I heard a double-header blow
And she was western bound.
My heart began to flutter
And I began to sing,
'Ten thousand miles away from home
A-bummin' a railroad train.'

I pulled my cap down over my eyes,
And walked on down the tracks,
Then I caught an empty car
And never did look back.

From Alan Lomax, *The Folk Songs of North America in the English Language* (Garden City, N.Y.: Doubleday & Co., 1960), pp. 419–420. "Around a Western Water Tank" collected, adapted, and arranged by John A. Lomax and Alan Lomax TRO= copyright 1934 and renewed © 1962 Ludlow Music, Inc., New York, N. Y. Used by permission.

John Dos Passos

Wobbly Mythology

A young Swede named Hillstrom went to sea, got himself calloused hands on sailingships and tramps, learned English in the fo'c'stle of the steamers that make the run from Stockholm to Hull, dreamed the Swede's dream of the West;

when he got to America they gave him a job polishing cuspidors in a Bowery saloon.

He moved west to Chicago and worked in a machineshop.

He moved west and followed the harvest, hung around employment agencies, paid out many a dollar for a job in a construction camp, walked out many a mile when the grub was too bum, or the boss too tough, or too many bugs in the bunkhouse;

read Marx and the I.W.W. Preamble and dreamed about forming the structure of the new society within the shell of the old.

He was in California for the S.P. strike (*Casey Jones, two locomotives, Casey Jones*), used to play the concertina outside the bunkhouse door, after supper, evenings (*Longhaired preachers come out every night*), had a knack for setting rebel words to tunes (*And the union makes us strong*).

Along the coast in cookshacks flophouses jungles wobblies hoboes bindlestiffs began singing Joe Hill's songs. They sang 'em in the county jails of the State of Washington, Oregon, California, Nevada, Idaho, in the bullpens in Montana and Arizona, sang 'em in Walla Walla, San Quentin, and Leavenworth,
    forming the structure of the new society within the jails of the old.

At Bingham, Utah, Joe Hill organized the workers of the Utah Construction Company in the One Big Union, won a new wagescale, shorter hours, better grub. (The angel Moroni didn't like labororganizers any better than the Southern Pacific did.)
    The angel Moroni moved the hearts of the Mormons to decide it was Joe Hill shot a grocer named Morrison. The Swedish consul and President Wilson tried to get him a new trial, but the angel Moroni moved the hearts of the Supreme Court of the State of Utah to sustain the verdict of guilty. He was in jail a year, went on making up songs. In November 1915 he was stood up against the wall in the jail yard in Salt Lake City.
    "Don't mourn for me organize," was the last word he sent out to the workingstiffs of the I.W.W. Joe Hill stood up against the wall of the jail yard, looked into the muzzles of the guns, and gave the word to fire.
    They put him in a black suit, put a stiff collar around his neck and a bow tie, shipped him to Chicago for a bangup funeral, and photographed his handsome stony mask staring into the future.
    The first of May they scattered his ashes to the wind.

From John Dos Passos, *Nineteen Nineteen* (Boston: Houghton Mifflin Co., 1946), pp. 487–488.

Alfred Hayes and Earl Robinson

Remembering Joe Hill

I dreamed I saw Joe Hill again
Alive as you and me.
Says I "But Joe, you're ten years dead."
"I never died," says he.
"I never died," says he.

"In Salt Lake, Joe, by God," says I,
Him standing by my bed,
"They framed you on a murder charge."
Says Joe, "But I ain't dead."
Says Joe, "But I ain't dead."

"The copper bosses killed you, Joe.
They shot you, Joe," says I.
"Takes more than guns to kill a man,"
Says Joe, "I didn't die."
Says Joe, "I didn't die."

And standing there as big as life,
And smiling with his eyes,
Joe says, "What they forgot to kill
Went on to organize.
Went on to organize."

"Joe Hill ain't dead," he says to me.
"Joe Hill ain't never died.
Where workingmen are out on strike
Joe Hill is at their side.
Joe Hill is at their side."

"From San Diego up to Maine
In every mine and mill
Where workers strike and organize,"
Says he, "you'll find Joe Hill."
Says he, "you'll find Joe Hill."

> I dreamed I saw Joe Hill last night
> Alive as you and me.
> Says I "But Joe, you're ten years dead."
> "I never died," says he.
> "I never died," says he.

From *The Daily Worker* (Sept 4, 1936), p. 5.

BLEAK VISTAS,
RECLAIMED DREAMS

A. M. Simons

Beyond the 98th Meridian

From the 98th meridian West to the Rocky Mountains there is a stretch of country whose history is filled with more tragedy, and whose future is pregnant with greater promise than perhaps any other equal expanse of territory within the confines of the Western Hemisphere. For many years it was marked upon the maps as a great white blank indicating an inhospitable desert. Finally as the territory bordering upon it became more thickly settled and the pressure for land became ever fiercer, the line of settlements encroached more and more upon this stretch of apparently worthless soil. Following the times of occasional rainy seasons, this line of social advance rose and fell with rain and drouth, like a mighty tide beating against the tremendous wall of the Rockies. And every such wave left behind it a mass of human wreckage in the shape of broken fortunes, deserted farms and ruined homes. . . .

From A. M. Simons, *The American Farmer* (Chicago: Charles H. Kerr & Co., 1903), p. 54.

Mari Sandoz

Drought in Nebraska

The early nineties were so dry even the old-timers wondered if it would ever rain again in the Panhandle. They had learned not to expect too much moisture in June or July, but when the young August moon, horned as an antelope, settled into the black wool bed of the horizon, and the hay was down, there should be rain.

All summer the homesteaders cultivated deep, under the spur of hunger, cracking the clodding earth, trying to maintain the mulch Old Jules believed would hold the moisture. But there was none to hold. They watched the skies until their eyes were like old wounds, and still it did not rain. A man on Box Butte Creek fortunate enough to get a shower from a June thunderhead won first prize for winter wheat at the state fair. But on the Flats the wheat never headed; oats sat white and curled as grass, the root soil baked and cracked.

About the time the clouds of blackbirds from the painted wood of the river darkened the fields in search of nubbins, the settlers began to leave. The Iowa colony went first, leaving only Elmer Sturgeon and Johnny Burrows. Several of them had shipped in carloads of goods and stock. They let their claims go to Eastern loan companies for the money they once needed for cattle, horses, implements, seed, wire, lumber. They drove out with nothing except a crowbait team and wagon. Scarcely were they over the horizon before their homes were torn down and hauled away by those who needed the lumber to hang on a little longer. First the stores, then the banks of the Panhandle, went bankrupt. Of the four banks in Rushville only one weathered these years.

"Now is the time to buy land cheap," Jules pointed out, but there was no money—and his father with five thousand dollars out at 2 per cent in the Old Country. Jules did not go to Mirage much any more. To him a hundred sixty acres of wild Susans was not a field of gold but a field going back to sod, a dead venture.

Rain makers arose. In eastern Nebraska a Pawnee Indian

promised a shower for ten dollars, a soaking rain for twenty. Someone gave him a jug of whiskey and the hail pounded the grass into the ground. It was a good story, told not without envy.

At Goodland, Kansas, Melbourne and his assistants produced half an inch of rain within forty-eight hours for a thousand dollars. They were given the same offer at Sidney, south of the Platte. Jules, mounted on a sturdy pinto he got from the Indians for two eagles, rode down with several of the Flatters. From their horses they watched the three men carry a long black box into an old barn, well guarded. Three times a day baskets were taken in full of food and came out empty. Once, the second day, the sky clouded over and awe swept the watching crowd like wind in a young field of wheat. Thunder rumbled, a few heavy drops splattered like shot in the dust, the wind blew, and the sun was out with a double rainbow.

"I'll keep catching skunks for a living," Jules told his neighbors.

Rushville tried powder and the Flats, both the Lutherans and the Catholics, prayer. Some said that the church steeples split the clouds. Jules laughed—only empty houses with the dead smell of religion in them.

When the settlers got clear down in the mouth a walking sky pilot appeared and called a revival at Alkali Lake, on the Flats, not far from Hay Springs.

"Wouldn't you jest know them critters'd have to come to pester us! Ain't we got troubles enough as 't is?" Ma Green told Jules as she stopped her team for a rest at the river. The boys were haying and the freighting had to be done, so she had climbed the heavy wagon.

"Guess I kin handle them eight broncs 's well as anybody!"

She was timing her loading at Hay Springs so she would make Alkali in time for the revival.

Two days later she stopped while her horses blew before they took the long climb out of the river valley. It had been a fine spectacle, with folks thick as flies around a puddle of syrup, and that sky pilot, with his red beard cut like Christ's in the Sunday-school pictures, preaching hell and damnation from the back of a grasshopper buggy, and women crying and men ripping their only shirts. Then they all moved into the lake and the preacher stuck them under like so many old rag dolls until the Flats smelled of stale water and dead salamanders. "It done me more good to see that dirty parson get wet to his middle. I'll bet he ain't ever had a bath all the way up."

Mrs. Schmidt, with eight children at home and a husband laid out behind a saloon somewhere, sang all the way home from the revival. The next week they sent her to the insane asylum and scattered the children. The youngest Frahm girl took pneumonia and died, and a lone Bohemian from the Breaks hung himself. Henriette came away sad. Only Ma Green seemed to have enjoyed it.

Still there was no rain.

While the hard-land settlers talked of artesian well and surface irrigation, those along the Niobrara and Pine Creek got along somehow. The wet years would come, Jules preached, pointing to the rain graphs of the state. Nebraska rainfall came in cycles. There must be wet years just ahead.

Hans looked at him dully. He had taken to drinking lately and the last shreds of the boy his Anna kissed goodbye were going. "It will be dry all the time," he said. He would plant no more.

When the Flats no longer had socials and dances, no longer saw anything amusing in the drouth parodies of church hymns, the Pine Creek settlers and the small cattlemen took them up, singing lustily:—

> I've reached the land of drouth and heat,
> Where nothing grows for man to eat,
> The wind that blows with burning heat,
> O'er all our land is hard to beat.

> O! Nebraska land, sweet Nebraska land!
> As on your burning soil I stand,
> I look away across the plains,
> And wonder why it never rains,
> Till Gabriel calls, with trumpet sound,
> And says the rain has gone around.

From Mari Sandoz, *Old Jules* (Boston: Little, Brown and Co., 1935), pp. 148–150, 152.

Mary Hallock Foote

A Plan That Failed

No one remembers Kuna. It was a place where silence closed about you after the bustle of the train, where a soft, dry wind from great distances hummed through the telegraph wires and a stage road went out of sight in one direction and a new railroad track in another; but that wind had magic in it. It came across immense dry areas without an object to harp upon except the man-made wires. There was not a tree in sight—miles and miles of pallid sagebrush: as moonlight unto sunlight is that desert sage to other greens. It gives a great intensity to the blue of the sky and to the deeper blue of the mountains lifting their snowcapped peaks, the highest light along the far horizon. As to foreground—we were the foreground, bowling along in our light livery rig. We did not go over to Boise by stage, and there were no protests from the family economist this time. . . .

From time to time the front seat looked back to see how the back seat was "making it," and how we liked it on the whole. We liked it very much! Over there, we were told, was the Sawtooth Range where the Boise River heads up in southern Idaho; War Eagle [Mountain] and his brethren of the Owyhees might be fifty miles away—there was no guessing distances in that pure light and featureless perspective. We were driving "straight across the drainage," and the wife of the new irrigation engineer marked the phrase as part of the language she was expected to know. We came out on the last long bench above the valley of the Boise and saw, across a bridge in the distance, the little city which was called the metropolis of the desert plains, the heaven of old teamsters and stage drivers crawling in at nightfall; saw the wild river we had come to tame, slipping from the hold of the farms along its banks that snatched a season's crops from it as it fled. Multiply that inconstant water a hundredfold, store it in those reservoirs the man talked of building up in the crotches of the hills, cover the valley with farms, and even to the mind of the misbeliever, here was a work worth spending a lifetime

412

A Plan That Failed

for, even the one life that is man's in this world. Confucius says: "I can find no flaw in the character of Yu. . . . He lived in a low mean house, but expended all his strength on the ditches and water-channels."

By the first of June [1890] the irrigation boom was well started. New people were coming in, and many of our old friends who had been kind but skeptical were filing now on desert land themselves, copying our confidence. The engineers were not inventing work for themselves, in these days. The Cañon House was open again and every room a Junior's room, windows gloriously unwashed and floors printed all over with boot nails. Above Coston's ranch (the last one on the river "along the way that goest up to Beth-horon") there was a huge contractor's base camp—their lights were like a little city at night. The canal which had been a matter of diagrams and cross sections and dotted lines on paper (when it wasn't a subject for ridicule and pity) was now the great show of the countryside. An unroofed gallery eighty feet across the top, fifty on the bottom, swept in a mathematical curve round the shoulder of the hill; fifteen horsemen might ride down it abreast "nor be pressed." When the sloped walls were finished they kept their alignment, twelve feet high, and where they were not finished an endless procession of scraper teams crawled up and dumped and slid down to load and crawl up again. . . .

The year following our first planting on the Mesa was fated to be one of the dryest on record. The wheat did not sprout, for there were no spring rains. The canal stopped two miles above us and we died—slowly, keeping up the fight to the last. Our orchards were the greatest tragedy; hundreds of little nursery trees struggled along watered by hand from a nose cart making the rounds from tree to tree—but that could not go on. It was the year of our private ruin and nothing was lacking to us in the way of conspicuousness. An old pioneer capitalist of Boise who drove out to look at the grave of our folly remarked to the man in charge of what was left, "I could have told him he'd find it cheaper to buy his wheat than raise it."

Wheat was not the commodity in question, however; it was faith we planted and that did not die—not with him who planted. It took twenty-five years for that crop to show above ground! The Reclamation Bureau under [Theodore] Roosevelt built the New York and Idaho canal following the old line our poor men laid out and left behind them. We did not leave our bones on that battlefield, but we left pretty much everything else we had. My husband left the crown of his years and the greatest of his hopes, the dream that satisfied the blood of farmers and home-makers in him, and the brain of the constructor he was born to use. . . .

But even now, on our continental journeys, when we have reached that country of the high valleys and the old lava flows between the knees of the ranges; when we halt at some lone junction or water tank in the sagebrush and step out to breathe that air again and listen to the "essential silence" after the roar of the train—it is there, that whisper of the desert wind—it all comes back, the shiver of an old longing and doubt and expectancy. . . . We see the long, low house stretched out on the Mesa raised above the valley, we see the ring of mountains lifting and lowering down to the great gate where the sun is setting in a storm of gold. Then purple shadows darken in their cañons; the color mounts to the zenith and the plains are flushed with light. I remember one evening when we sat out there with Mr. Harvey and the glow was in all the faces that stared into the future of that valley. He pointed where a railroad station should be on the lands he had picked for a colony of young Englishmen whom he dreamed of planting there; not wasters, whose people would gladly be rid of them, but nephews of his own and younger sons of those upper-middle-class families which I remember Edith Angus said were the backbone of England. There were long futures in his mind. And many things of the highest importance would have been altered for our children had we anchored them there.

The Congress that winter refused to appropriate for anything that looked as frivolous to them as the Irrigation Survey, so that died too. We shut down the Mesa as tight as we could without throwing it away; we stripped our rooms once more, sold our more rational belongings to Bessie who was furnishing her new house, and stored our fads and collections in her clean and empty attic. An attic that spoke of a house that has no history; it began to accumulate history very fast.

From Mary Hallock Foote, *A Victorian Gentlewoman in the Far West*, edited by Rodman W. Paul (San Marino, Calif.: Huntington Library, 1972), pp. 275–276, 322, 328–330.

Hamlin Garland

A Town of the Plain

A shadeless clump of yellow blocks,
It stands upon the sod, ringed
With level lands and draped in mist,
Wavering in air so dry, it seems
The very clouds might burn.

A mighty wind roars from the south,
Silencing all other tumult. Its wings
Horizon-wide, welters the grass
And tears the dust and stubble;
And yet the mist remains. Beneath
The wind, flat to earth, teams crawl
Like beetles seeking shelter.

In the glimmering offing
Ricks of grain stand like walls
Of scattered Spanish huts, and like
The easy magic of dreams
Lakes of gray-blue water, bloom
On the hot palpitant plain,
So sweet and fair, the heart
Aches with longing deep as grief.

They mock the eyes a moment
And are gone—and under the wind
The teams crawl on blind with dust,
And faint with thirst.

From Hamlin Garland, *Prairie Songs* (Cambridge and Chicago: Stone and Kimball, 1893), p. 97.

William Saroyan

Fresno

A man could walk four or five miles in any direction from
the heart of our city and see our streets dwindle to land and
weeds. In many places the land would be vineyard and orchard land, but in most places it would be desert land the
weeds would be the strong dry weeds of desert. In this land
there would be the living things that had had their being in
the quietness of deserts for centuries. There would be snakes
and horned-toads, prairie-dogs and jack-rabbits. In the sky
over this land would be buzzards and hawks, and the hot sun.
And everywhere in the desert would be the marks of wagons
that had made lonely roads.

Two miles from the heart of our city a man could come to
the desert and feel the loneliness of a desolate area, a place
lost in the earth, far from the solace of human thought.
Standing at the edge of our city, a man could feel that we
had made this place of streets and dwellings in the stillness
and loneliness of the desert, and that we had done a brave
thing. We had come to this dry area that was without history,
and we had paused in it and built our houses and we were
slowly creating the legend of our life. We were digging for
water and we were leading streams through the dry land. We
were planting and ploughing and standing in the midst of the
garden we were making.

Our trees were not yet tall enough to make much shade, and
we had planted a number of kinds of trees we ought not to
have planted because they were of weak stuff and would
never live a century, but we had made a pretty good beginning. Our cemeteries were few and the graves in them were
few. We had buried no great men because we hadn't had
time to produce any great men. We had been too busy trying
to get water into the desert. The shadow of no great mind
was over our city. But we had a playground called Cosmos
Playground. We had public schools named after Emerson and
Hawthorne and Lowell and Longfellow. Two great railways
had their lines running through our city and trains were al-

ways coming to us from the great cities of America and somehow we could not feel that we were wholly lost. We had two newspapers and a Civic Auditorium and a public library one-third full of books. We had the Parlor Lecture Club. We had every sort of church except a Christian Science church. Every house in our city had a Bible in it, and a lot of houses had as many as four Bibles in them. A man could feel our city was beautiful.

Or a man could feel that our city was fake, that our lives were empty, and that we were the contemporaries of jack-rabbits. Or a man could have one viewpoint in the morning and another in the evening. The dome of our court-house was high, but it was ridiculous and had nothing to do with what we were trying to do in the desert. It was an imitation of something out of Rome. We had a mayor but he wasn't a great man and he didn't look like a mayor. He looked like a farmer. He *was* a farmer, but he was elected mayor. We had no great men, but the whole bunch of us put together amount-ed to something that was very nearly great. Our mayor was not above carrying on a conversation with an Armenian farmer from Fowler who could speak very little English. Our mayor was not a proud man and he sometimes got drunk with his friends. He liked to tell folks how to dig for water or how to prune muscat vines in order to get a good crop, and on the whole he was an admirable man. And of course we had to have a mayor, and of course *somebody* had to be mayor.

Our enterprise wasn't on a vast scale. It wasn't even on a medium-sized scale. There was nothing slick about anything we were doing. Our enterprise was neither scientific nor inhu-man, as the enterprise of a growing city ought to be. Nobody knew the meaning of the word efficiency, and the most frightening word ever used by our mayor in public orations was *progress*, but by *progress* he meant, and our people un-derstood him to mean, the paving of the walk in front of the City Hall, and the purchase by our city of a Ford automobile for the mayor. Our biggest merchant was a small man named Kimball, who liked to loaf around in his immense department store with a sharpened pencil on his right ear. He liked to wait on his customers personally, even though he had over two dozen alert clerks working for him. They were alert dur-ing the winter, at any rate, and if they sometimes dozed dur-ing the long summer afternoons, it was because our whole city slept during those afternoons. There was nothing else to do. This sort of thing gave our city an amateur appearance, as if we were only experimenting and weren't quite sure if we had more right to be in the desert than the jack-rabbits and the horned-toads, as if we didn't believe we had started something that was going to be very big, something that would eventually make a tremendous change in the history of the world.

From William Saroyan, "Fresno," in *The Saroyan Special* (New York: Harcourt, Brace & Co., 1948), pp. 58–59.

John Steinbeck

The Last Trek

Highway 66 is the main migrant road. 66—the long concrete path across the country, waving gently up and down on the map, from the Mississippi to Bakersfield—over the red lands and the gray lands, twisting up into the mountains, crossing the Divide and down into the bright and terrible desert, and across the desert to the mountains again, and into the rich California valleys.

66 is the path of a people in flight, refugees from dust and shrinking land, from the thunder of tractors and shrinking ownership, from the desert's slow northward invasion, from the twisting winds that howl up out of Texas, from the floods that bring no richness to the land and steal what little richness is there. From all of these the people are in flight, and they come into 66 from the tributary side roads, from the wagon tracks and the rutted country roads. 66 is the mother road, the road of flight.

Clarksville and Ozark and Van Buren and Fort Smith on 64, and there's an end of Arkansas. And all the roads into Oklahoma City, 66 down from Tulsa, 270 up from McAlester. 81 from Wichita Falls south, from Enid north. Edmond, McLoud, Purcell. 66 out of Oklahoma City; El Reno and Clinton, going west on 66. Hydro, Elk City, and Texola; and there's an end to Oklahoma. 66 across the Panhandle of Texas. Shamrock and McLean, Conway and Amarillo, the yellow. Wildorado and Vega and Boise, and there's an end of

Texas. Tucumcari and Santa Rosa and into the New Mexican mountains to Albuquerque, where the road comes down from Santa Fe. Then down the gorged Rio Grande to Los Lunas and west again on 66 to Gallup, and there's the border of New Mexico.

And now the high mountains. Holbrook and Winslow and Flagstaff in the high mountains of Arizona. Then the great plateau rolling like a ground swell. Ashfork and Kingman and stone mountains again, where water must be hauled and sold. Then out of the broken sun-rotted mountains of Arizona to the Colorado, with green reeds on its banks, and that's the end of Arizona. There's California just over the river, and a pretty town to start it. Needles, on the river. But the river is a stranger in this place. Up from Needles and over a burned range, and there's the desert. And 66 goes on over the terrible desert, where the distance shimmers and the black center mountains hang unbearably in the distance. At last there's Barstow, and more desert until at last the mountains rise up again, the good mountains, and 66 winds through them. Then suddenly a pass, and below the beautiful valley, below orchards and vineyards and little houses, and in the distance a city. And, oh, my God, it's over.

The people in flight streamed out on 66, sometimes a single car, sometimes a little caravan. All day they rolled slowly along the road, and at night they stopped near water. In the day ancient leaky radiators sent up columns of steam, loose connecting rods hammered and pounded. And the men driving the trucks and the overloaded cars listened apprehensively. How far between towns? It is a terror between towns. If something breaks—well, if something breaks we camp right here while Jim walks to town and gets a part and walks back and—how much food we got?

Listen to the motor. Listen to the wheels. Listen with your ears and with your hands on the steering wheel; listen with the palm of your hand on the gear-shift lever; listen with your feet on the floor boards. Listen to the pounding old jalopy with all your senses; for a change of tone, a variation of rhythm may mean—a week here? That rattle—that's tappets. Don't hurt a bit. Tappets can rattle till Jesus comes again without no harm. But that thudding as the car moves along—can't hear that—just kind of feel it. Maybe oil isn't gettin' someplace. Maybe a bearing's startin' to go. Jesus, if it's a bearing, what'll we do? Money's goin' fast.

And why's the son-of-a-bitch heat up so hot today? This

ain't no climb. Le's look. God Almighty, the fan belt's gone
Here, make a belt outa this little piece a rope. Le's see how
long—there. I'll splice the ends. Now take her slow—slow
till we can get to a town. That rope belt won't last long.

'F we can on'y get to California where the oranges grow
before this here ol' jug blows up. 'F we on'y can.

And the tires—two layers of fabric worn through. On'y a
four-ply tire. Might get a hunderd miles more outa her if we
don't hit a rock an' blow her. Which'll we take—a hunderd
maybe, miles, or maybe spoil the tube? Which? A hunderd
miles. Well, that's somepin you got to think about. We got
tube patches. Maybe when she goes she'll only spring a leak
How about makin' a boot? Might get five hunderd more
miles. Le's go on till she blows.

We got to get a tire, but, Jesus, they want a lot for a ol
tire. They look a fella over. They know he got to go on. They
know he can't wait. And the price goes up.

Take it or leave it. I ain't in business for my health. I'm
here a-sellin' tires. I ain't givin' 'em away. I can't help what
happens to you. I got to think what happens to me.

How far's the nex' town?

I seen forty-two cars a you fellas go by yesterday. Where
you all come from? Where all of you goin'?

Well, California's a big State.

It ain't that big. The whole United States ain't that big. I
ain't that big. It ain't big enough. There ain't room enough
for you an' me, for your kind an' my kind, for rich and poor
together all in one country, for thieves and honest men. For
hunger and fat. Whyn't you go back where you come from?

This is a free country. Fella can go where he wants.

That's what *you* think! Ever hear of the border patrol on
the California line? Police from Los Angeles—stopped you
bastards, turned you back. Says, if you can't buy no real es
tate we don't want you. Says, got a driver's license? Le's see
it. Tore it up. Says you can't come in without no driver'
license.

It's a free country.

Well, try to get some freedom to do. Fella says you're jus
as free as you got jack to pay for it.

In California they got high wages. I got a han'bill here tell
about it.

Baloney! I seen folks comin' back. Somebody's kiddin' you
You want that tire or don't ya?

Got to take it, but Jesus, mister, it cuts into our money! We ain't got much left.

Well, I ain't no charity. Take her along.

Got to, I guess. Let's look her over. Open her up, look a' the casing—you son-of-a-bitch, you said the casing was good. She's broke damn near through.

The hell she is. Well—by George! How come I didn' see that?

You did see it, you son-of-a-bitch. You wanta charge us four bucks for a busted casing. I'd like to take a sock at you.

Now keep your shirt on. I didn' see it, I tell you. Here— tell ya what I'll do. I'll give ya this one for three-fifty.

You'll take a flying jump at the moon! We'll try to make the nex' town.

Think we can make it on that tire?

Got to. I'll go on the rim before I'd give that son-of-a-bitch a dime.

What do ya think a guy in business is? Like he says, he ain't in it for his health. That's what business is. What'd you think it was? Fella's got— See that sign 'longside the road there? Service Club. Luncheon Tuesday, Colmado Hotel? Welcome, brother. That's a Service Club. Fella had a story. Went to one of them meetings an' told the story to all them business men. Says, when I was a kid my ol' man give me a haltered heifer an' says take her down an' git her serviced. An' the fella says, I done it, an' ever' time since then when I hear a business man talkin' about service, I wonder who's get-tin' screwed. Fella in business got to lie an' cheat, but he calls it somepin else. That's what's important. You go steal that tire an' you're a thief, but he tried to steal your four dollars for a busted tire. They call that sound business.

Danny in the back seat wants a cup a water.

Have to wait. Got no water here.

Listen—that the rear end?

Can't tell.

Sound telegraphs through the frame.

There goes a gasket. Got to go on. Listen to her whistle. Find a nice place to camp an' I'll jerk the head off. But, God Almighty, the food's gettin' low, the money's gettin' low. When we can't buy no more gas—what then?

Danny in the back seat wants a cup a water. Little fella's thirsty.

Listen to that gasket whistle.

Chee-rist! There she went. Blowed tube an' casing all to

hell. Have to fix her. Save that casing to make boots; cut 'em out an' stick 'em inside a weak place.

Cars pulled up beside the road, engine heads off, tires mended. Cars limping along 66 like wounded things, panting and struggling. Too hot, loose connections, loose bearings, rattling bodies.

Danny wants a cup a water.

People in flight along 66. And the concrete road shone like a mirror under the sun, and in the distance the heat made it seem that there were pools of water in the road.

Danny wants a cup a water.

He'll have to wait, poor little fella. He's hot. Nex' service station. *Service* station, like the fella says.

Two hundred and fifty thousand people over the road. Fifty thousand old cars—wounded, steaming. Wrecks along the road, abandoned. Well, what happened to them? What happened to the folks in that car? Did they walk? Where are they? Where does the courage come from? Where does the terrible faith come from?

And here's a story you can hardly believe, but it's true, and it's funny and it's beautiful. There was a family of twelve and they were forced off the land. They had no car. They built a trailer out of junk and loaded it with their possessions. They pulled it to the side of 66 and waited. And pretty soon a sedan picked them up. Five of them rode in the sedan and seven on the trailer, and a dog on the trailer. They got to California in two jumps. The man who pulled them fed them. And that's true. But how can such courage be, and such faith in their own species? Very few things would teach such faith.

The people in flight from the terror behind—strange things happen to them, some bitterly cruel and some so beautiful that the faith is refired forever.

From John Steinbeck, *The Grapes of Wrath* (New York: Viking Press, 1939), pp. 160–166.

Stan Steiner

The War of the Flowers

It began with the "War of the Flowers," in the town of McFarland.

On the morning of May 3, 1965, at sunrise, a man rises from his knees in the fields of flowers of the Mount Arbor Nurseries, the largest grower of roses in California. He has been grafting young rosebush shoots, and his fingers are bleeding. He yells, "*Huelga!*" Strike! It is the signal. Eighty rose grafters walk out of the fields. The first strike has begun for Cesar Chavez's still unborn National Farm Workers Association, with the "Strike of the Roses."

"Here where the blood is made, here in the heart of the strike," proclaims the newspaper of the farm workers, *El Malcriado*, "here it shall be won in the hearts of our brothers."

Epifanio Camacho is the man who got off his knees. He is an intense man with black eyes and black angers, who sings of his sorrows in a *corrido* he writes for the "Strike of the Roses":

> I am the cry of the poor
> Who work in the fields
> Who water the earth
> With our sweat.
>
> Our huts and hovels
> Are always full of sorrow
> For we live as animals
> In the midst of riches

He has worked on his knees all his life. The farm worker stoops in the fields. But a rose grafter kneels. He crawls from rosebush to rosebush, with his fingers torn by the thorns, as he cuts the shoots into the young plants. It is skilled work, for the plants are delicate and easily damaged. Hundreds of tiny cuts from the thorns turn the fingers of the rose grafter black with scars. The deft fingers have to work quickly, for the pay is by the number of rosebushes. At the time of the rebellion in the rose gardens, the pay was about $7 for one thousand bushes. Many of the flower workers are women and few complain loudly.

> My poor Mexican race
> Evil has been your lot
> So many have wished
> To see you downtrodden
>
> Awaken, oh Mexicans
> Who wouldn't look up
> Who work like slaves
> Who don't want to know.

But now Epifiano Camacho has risen from his knees. He has been talking with three young dreamers in nearby Delano: Cesar Chavez, Gilbert Padilla, and Dolores Huerta. Quietly they organized the strike.

> Long have we suffered
> Being sold like slaves
> Now we can all see
> Our triumph is coming.

It is symbolic to Luiz Valdez, the poet of El Teatro Campesino, that the *huelga* began in the fields of flowers. "We are a people who believe in symbols," he says. "The last divine Aztec emperor Cuauhtémoc was murdered and his descendants were put to work in the fields. We are still there in the fields of America." The renaissance of La Raza had to begin again where it ended.

"History is a flower. If a single seed remains, it will bloom again," says Valdez.

From Stan Steiner, *La Raza: The Mexican Americans* (New York: Harper & Row, Publishers, 1969, 1970), pp. 276–278.

VII

Beyond the West

For our country here at the west of things
Is pregnant of dreams; and west of the west
I have lived; where the last low land
   outflings
Its yellow-white sand to the edge of the bay;
And the west wind over us every day
Blows, and throws with the landward spray
Dreams on our minds, and a dreamy unrest.

                —Robinson Jeffers

Introduction to Part VII

The contemporary West is where you find it. Picked up as a hint here, a flavor there, it is more than an imaginary line that runs down a map—call it the 98th meridian—or the beginning of the rise to the Rockies, or the first cowboy you see loitering on a Nebraska street. It is perhaps a present played out against the myth of the past: an attitude. It is the teasing deadpan talk of the cowboy, where silence is a value understood, and it is a notion of space and spaciousness. It expresses itself as a hint of something lost in the freeways of California slicing through a once paradisic country, and in a sense of something that cannot ever be said to be lost in the arid vastness of Georgia O'Keeffe's desert. The closed and grimly unlovely towns of the plains and valleys and their defiant refusal of the spirit are as Western as the awesome spiritual sustenance of the Cascades. That the ceremonial West still lives, at least in the mind, is found in its astonishing access to parody in both film and fiction. Judith Rascoe's tongue-in-cheek cowboys, with their painful cowboy seriousness, and Simon Ortiz' San Francisco Indians are figures who cut both ways. They express both the death of the West, but also, in their persistent attitudes, its survival. The film West has been shown us so many times, mythologized, debunked, parodied, and resurrected, that it has assumed, detached from time and place, its own reality.

The West is still a place of testing, a place where you measure yourself and your individuality and self-sufficiency against a hard land and—incidentally—against that mythical pioneer who is always looking over your shoulder. Search for the West, if you will. Just when you think you have it, on some downtown street in Denver or Phoenix or Los Angeles, or at the ragged edge of a desert golf course, it vanishes. Were it not for the mountains or a forlorn and out-of-place-looking cactus or two, you could be anywhere.

And yet above all, in myth and in reality, the West remains a place. A landscape to be confronted. It is a sense of life played out against an immensity that can still overwhelm, a message to the East in its questioning of Eastern values of scale, of form, of propriety. It is a land exploited and plundered and a land to be saved. The West, as it continues to exist in the mind and on the map of a shrinking planet, has become everyone's West. It is a challenge to man's sense of his purpose. It is bigger than him still.

LOOKING FOR THE WEST

Jack Kerouac

Wild West Week in Cheyenne

We arrived at Council Bluffs at dawn; I looked out. All winter I'd been reading of the great wagon parties that held council there before hitting the Oregon and Santa Fe trails; and of course now it was only cute suburban cottages of one damn kind and another, all laid out in the dismal gray dawn. Then Omaha, and, by God, the first cowboy I saw, walking along the bleak walls of the wholesale meat warehouses in a ten-gallon hat and Texas boots, looked like any beat character of the brickwall dawns of the East except for the getup. We got off the bus and walked clear up the hill, the long hill formed over the millenniums by the mighty Missouri, alongside of which Omaha is built, and got out to the country and stuck our thumbs out. We got a brief ride from a wealthy rancher in a ten-gallon hat, who said the valley of the Platte was as great as the Nile Valley of Egypt, and as he said so I saw the great trees in the distance that snaked with the riverbed and the great verdant fields around it, and almost agreed with him. Then as we were standing at another crossroads and it was starting to get cloudy another cowboy, this one six feet tall in a modest half-gallon hat, called us over and wanted to know if either one of us could drive. Of course Eddie could drive, and he had a license and I didn't. Cowboy had two cars with him that he was driving back to Montana. His wife was at Grand Island, and he wanted us to drive one of the cars there, where she'd take over. At that point he was going north, and that would be the limit of our ride with him. But it was a good hundred miles into Nebraska, and of course we jumped for it. Eddie drove alone, the cowboy and myself following, and no sooner were we out of town than Eddie started to ball that jack ninety miles an hour out of sheer exuberance. "Damn me, what's that boy doing!" the cowboy shouted, and took off after him. It began to be like a race. For a minute I thought Eddie was trying to get away with the car—and for all I know that's what he meant to do. But the cowboy stuck to him and caught up with him and tooted the horn. Eddie slowed down. The cowboy tooted to stop. "Damn, boy, you're liable to get a flat going that speed. Can't you drive a little slower?"

"Well, I'll be damned, was I really going ninety?" said Eddie. "I didn't realize it on this smooth road."

"Just take it a little easy and we'll all get to Grand Island in one piece."

"Sure thing." And we resumed our journey. Eddie had calmed down and probably even got sleepy. So we drove a hundred miles across Nebraska, following the winding Platte with its verdant fields.

"During the depression," said the cowboy to me, "I used to hop freights at least once a month. In those days you'd see hundreds of men riding a flatcar or in a boxcar, and they weren't just bums, they were all kinds of men out of work and going from one place to another and some of them just wandering. It was like that all over the West. Brakemen never bothered you in those days. I don't know about today. Nebraska I ain't got no use for. Why in the middle nineteen-thirties this place wasn't nothing but a big dustcloud as far as the eye could see. You couldn't breathe. The ground was black. I was here in those days. They can give Nebraska back to the Indians far as I'm concerned. I hate this damn place more than any place in the world. Montana's my home now—Missoula. You come up there sometime and see God's country." Later in the afternoon I slept when he got tired talking—he was an interesting talker.

We stopped along the road for a bite to eat. The cowboy went off to have a spare tire patched, and Eddie and I sat down in a kind of homemade diner. I heard a great laugh, the greatest laugh in the world, and here came this rawhide old-timer Nebraska farmer with a bunch of other boys into the diner; you could hear his raspy cries clear across the plains, across the whole gray world of them that day. Everybody else laughed with him. He didn't have a care in the world and had the hugest regard for everybody. I said to myself, Wham, listen to that man laugh. That's the West, here I am in the West. He came booming into the diner, calling Maw's name, and she made the sweetest cherry pie in Nebraska, and I had some with a mountainous scoop of ice cream on top. "Maw, rustle me up some grub afore I have to start eatin myself raw or some damn silly idee like that." And he threw himself on a stool and went hyaw hyaw hyaw hyaw. "And thow some beans in it." It was the spirit of the West sitting right next to me. I wished I knew his whole raw life and what the hell he'd been doing all these years besides laughing and yelling like that. Whooee, I told my soul, and the cowboy came back and off we went to Grand Island. . . .

As the truck reached the outskirts of Cheyenne, we saw the high red lights of the local radio station, and suddenly we were bucking through a great crowd of people that poured along both sidewalks. "Hell's bells, it's Wild West Week," said Slim. Big crowds of businessmen, fat businessmen in boots and ten-gallon hats, with their hefty wives in cowgirl attire, bustled and whooped on the wooden sidewalks of old Cheyenne; farther down were the long stringy boulevard lights of new downtown Cheyenne, but the celebration was focusing on Oldtown. Blank guns went off. The saloons were crowded to the sidewalk. I was amazed, and at the same time I felt it was ridiculous: in my first shot at the West I was seeing to what absurd devices it had fallen to keep its proud tradition. . . .

I was with Montana Slim and we started hitting the bars. I had about seven dollars, five of which I foolishly squandered that night. First we milled with all the cowboy-dudded tourists and oilmen and ranchers, at bars, in doorways, on the sidewalk; then for a while I shook Slim, who was wandering a little slaphappy in the street from all the whisky and beer; he was that kind of drinker; his eyes got glazed, and in a minute he'd be telling an absolute stranger about things. I went into a chili joint and the waitress was Mexican and beautiful. I ate, and then I wrote her a little love note on the back of the bill. The chili joint was deserted; everybody was somewhere else, drinking. I told her to turn the bill over. She read it and laughed. It was a little poem about how I wanted her to come and see the night with me.

"I'd love to, Chiquito, but I have a date with my boyfriend."

"Can't you shake him?"

"No, no, I don't," she said sadly, and I loved the way she said it.

"Some other time I'll come by here," I said, and she said, "Any time, kid." Still I hung around, just to look at her, and had another cup of coffee. Her boy friend came in sullenly and wanted to know when she was off. She bustled around to close the place quick. I had to get out. I gave her a smile when I left. Things were going on as wild as ever outside, except that the fat burpers were getting drunker and whooping up louder. It was funny. There were Indian chiefs wandering around in big headdresses and really solemn among the flushed drunken faces. I saw Slim tottering along and joined him.

He said, "I just wrote a postcard to my Paw in Montana. You reckon you can find a mailbox and put it in?" It was a strange request; he gave me the postcard and tottered through the swinging doors of a saloon. I took the card, went to the box, and took a quick look at it. "Dear Paw, I'll be home Wednesday. Everything's all right with me and I hope the same is with you. Richard." It gave me a different idea of him; how tenderly polite he was with his father. I went in the bar and joined him. We picked up two girls, a pretty young blonde and a fat brunette. They were dumb and sullen, but we wanted to make them. We took them to a rickety night-club that was already closing, and there I spent all but two dollars on Scotches for them and beer for us. I was getting drunk and didn't care; everything was fine. My whole being and purpose was pointed at the little blond. I wanted to go in there with all my strength. I hugged her and wanted to tell her. The nightclub closed and we all wandered out in the rickety dusty streets. I looked up at the sky; the pure, wonderful stars were still there, burning. The girls wanted to go to the bus station, so we all went, but they apparently wanted to meet some sailor who was there waiting for them, a cousin of the fat girl's and the sailor had friends with him. I said to the blonde, "What's up?" She said she wanted to go home, in Colorado just over the line south of Cheyenne. "I'll take you in a bus," I said.

"No, the bus stops on the highway and I have to walk across that damn prairie all by myself. I spent all afternoon looking at the damn thing and I don't aim to walk over it tonight."

"Ah, listen, we'll take a nice walk in the prairie flowers."

"There ain't no flowers there," she said. "I want to go to New York. I'm sick and tired of this. Ain't no place to go but Cheyenne and ain't nothing in Cheyenne."

"Ain't nothin in New York."

"Hell there ain't," she said with a curl of her lips.

The bus station was crowded to the doors. All kinds of people were waiting for buses or just standing around; there were a lot of Indians, who watched everything with their stony eyes. The girl disengaged herself from my talk and joined the sailor and the others. Slim was dozing on a bench. I sat down. The floors of bus stations are the same all over the country, always covered with butts and spit and they give a feeling of sadness that only bus stations have. For a moment it was no different from being in Newark, except for the great hugeness outside that I loved so much.

From Jack Kerouac, *On the Road* (New York: Viking Press, 1957), pp 19–21, 32–33, 33–35.

Paul Johnson

Moving to New Mexico

The most pervasive fact about the southwest-mountain region is that this is still the West. There's Wilderness, just plain Emptiness, on a scale that's been unimaginable Back East for more than a century. The trips some people are into here are much more rugged-independent-frontiersman than would be possible in New England or California. So are the costumes, the imagery, the styles. In spite of barbed wire and paved roads, it's still feasible to travel long distances on horseback. Folks come out of the hills looking like they've been up there trapping beaver since the spring of 1810. Fur and leather clothing, hand-sewn and home-tanned, is the acme of fashion. So, for men, are a big sheath knife and a gun. For women, high moccasins, heavy ankle-length skirts, everything else that goes with the squaw look.

Some functioning communes still exist, mostly in the Taos valley, but the call of communal open land is muted in these parts, to say the least. Farmers want land *of their own,* possibly with a few close, long-term partners if they can't swing the payments by themselves. A lot of freaks aren't looking for land to settle on at all; their trip is horses, mobility, wilderness survival. A set-up like our own—seven partner/families and the room and resources for, ultimately, a village-scale economy with reciprocal skills and services—is definitely not the usual out here.

"Self-sufficiency" is one (maybe the only) common goal, but everyone seems to have a different model and means of getting there, and everybody that I know is still a long way from making, raising, hunting, or gathering everything they require. Outside of Santa Fe, I haven't encountered a single vegetarian, though there are lots of vehement ex-vegies. Hunting is a big thing and so is raising your own meat: pigs, goats, and poultry. Not beef, which is a cash-crop up here and definitely a rip-off. Kill-what-you-eat, eat-what-you-kill is the ideal, but nobody is terribly purist about this or anything else, and almost everybody who can gets food stamps. . . .

I don't mean to paint too pretty a picture, only to counter the unrelieved grimness that both straight and underground media have been projecting for several years now about New Mexico. It's important that you keep in mind that this is still the wild-and-wooly West. The basic ethic has hardly changed since Territorial days, and folks prefer to settle their disputes in their own fashion, without recourse to Law'n'Order. Our county seat is one paved road, the highway running through it, with four or five stores, the court house, the central school complex, the pool hall, and at least a dozen bars; anyone who's not spoiling for a fight stays out of those bars after dark, especially on week-ends. Spanish-speaking friends of mine in Santa Fe kid me about living in a place where people are always knifing or shooting each other. . . .

. . . Our neighbors are truly impressed with the amount of work they've seen us do towards fixing up our place and healing the land. They know we've come to stay, and if they judge us at all, it's not on what we look like or what we tell them, but what we as individuals have actually accomplished. Help or advice is seldom volunteered, but all you have to do is ask for it to get all you can use, and then some.

The most important gift, from the oldtimers to us newcomers, is an attitude that's much-maligned but absolutely essential to the kind of lives we're trying to put together for ourselves. The phrase is *siempre mañana*: there's always tomorrow. Back there in the cities, in what we called The Movement for a relatively happy while, we lived as though the whole world teetered daily on the crumbling crust of climactic castastrophe—as it certainly did, and undeniably still does, today. But you can't go on that way, not in the country: you've got to live as if there'll always be another spring to plant again, another fall to harvest, better years to follow poor ones. *Siempre mañana*.

From Paul Johnson, "The Country Trip," *Place*, Vol. 1, No. 2 (July 1972), pp. 67, 68, 69.

Simon J. Ortiz

The San Francisco Indians

The Chief and a couple of members of his tribe went to the American Indian Center at Mission and 16th. They had walked all the way from their street. A lock hung on the door of the Center, and they stood by the door wondering whether they should go back, call somebody up, or wait around.

"I wonder where they're all at," one of them said.

"Maybe it's a day off or something," another offered.

The Chief pushed against the door again and searched for a notice or something. He read the Fuck FBIs scribble again and felt sad. "I guess there isn't going to be anybody here," he said and pulled his blanket tighter to ward off the cold. He motioned to the others and they began to leave. "We'll come back later," the Chief said.

At that moment a man walked around the corner and looked up at the plastic sign reading American Indian Center. One of the Chief's companions called, "Hey, Chief Black

Bear." The Chief and the others stopped and watched the man.

The man was around seventy years old. His gray suit was wrinkled and his shoes were scuffed. He looked at the door with the lock and then stepped back into the street. He held a grip bag in his hand.

"Hey, there's an Indian," one of the tribal members said. He smiled happily.

"Yes, there's an Indian," Chief Black Bear said. He straightened up and walked toward the Indian. The Indian man watched them approach.

"Hello," the Chief said. He offered a handshake.

"Hello," the Indian said, shaking hands lightly. He was nervous, and he looked at the pavement and then at the young man with the blanket and beads before him. The others, both young men also, stood to one side. They were not as dressed in Indian attire as their chief was.

The Chief and his companions noticed that the Indian was very tired. They felt his tiredness and his age. The Chief said, "We want to invite you to our home. It is not far from here."

"Yes," the Indian said. "But first, I have to find out where all the Indians go. Is this where all the Indians go?" He indicated the locked-up Center.

"Yes," Chief Black Bear said. "They come here, but not all of them. They're all over the city. Some are up on the street."

"Yes, Indians are everywhere," the Indian said.

"Come with us, and you can come back later when you have eaten and rested."

The Indian thought about this for a while. He didn't know where to go. He had come this far, and he didn't know where to go.

"I came to look for my grandchild. She came to go to school in Oakland, to learn about business work, months ago. She wrote to tell us she was O.K. But we got letters from the school that she was not going any more, and then she stopped writing. I asked the government, but they don't know about her any more. I came to see her, to find her, but I haven't found her. Someone said she came to San Francisco. That's why I came to where the Indians come. Maybe somebody knows her and where she lives."

The Chief and his tribe were saddened by the old man's search. They wanted to comfort him somehow. "There are Indians on our street," the youthful chief said. "Maybe they will know."

The Indian and Chief Black Bear and his tribe walked through gray streets busy with traffic. Some people stared at them, and some didn't. They walked up and down hills. The walking reminded the Indian of the hills and mesas at home. He couldn't see much except buildings and traffic and Chinamen hurrying to some place. Once in a while he could see the ocean to the west. He wanted to ask questions of the young men, but they were intent in their walking and were quiet.

Haight Street was crowded as usual. The Indian saw that some people were just sitting, some were walking around or driving past. He wondered if it was Sunday or a day off. There were a few dressed like the young men he walked with. Chief Black Bear and his companions called greetings to people they met. They walked into a building and up some stairs and entered a room.

"You are welcome here," Chief Black Bear said. He pointed to a small cot. "You can sit down there and sleep there, too." The other two left the room.

The Indian sat down, and he wondered if he would find his grandchild here. There was fast music coming from somewhere behind the walls, and muffled sounds came from the street. The Chief offered him a boloney sandwich and a bottle of wine.

"I'll see if I can find some Indian kids," Chief Black Bear said, and left.

After he had finished eating, the Indian lay down and closed his eyes. He was very tired. He had almost fallen asleep when a girl's voice called, "Chief." He came fully awake to face a girl with blond hair, wearing a colored band around her head.

"Hi," she said. "I'm looking for Chief Black Bear. I heard he brought an Indian back." She was smiling.

"Hello," the Indian said and sat up.

They watched each other. "We have some peyote from Mexico," the girl said. She brought a large coffee can filled with some of the dried buttons. "We have some songs," she said and showed him some records of Indian chants. "This will be the first time, and we wanted someone who knows how to show us." The girl fingered her beads.

The Indian had never seen peyote before, but he had heard songs and prayers for the ceremonials. Maybe it will do O.K., he thought, but he was doubtful. He didn't know the labels on the records, but he thought the chants were not what they would need.

"We want it to be good," the girl said. She felt some of the old man's tiredness too, and his searching and sadness, even without his telling her. She reached out and touched him.

The Chief came back. "There are no Indians around," he said.

The Indian thought, Maybe they have all left for their homes. He looked about the room and wondered if he should leave too. Yes, maybe he should, he thought. But he had come this far, to some place, he was tired, he had seen glimpses of the ocean he had heard about, he had not found his grandchild, and he did not really know where else to look. He had come to look for her because the girl's parents had not. They said, She'll be all right, she's grown up, our people are going some place every day, there are Indians all over the place, she'll be O.K. And that's why he had come.

The People were going all over the world. Indians were everywhere. He had met some at bus stations in Arizona and California. They stood around looking into jukeboxes, magazines in their hands, and getting on and off the buses. And he had met these San Francisco Indians. He looked over at the Chief and the girl who sat on the floor opposite him. They smiled at him.

"I think I'll go now," he said. And he got up to get his bag. "Thank you for your food and wine."

"Wait," Chief Black Bear said. The girl looked worried. And they both looked as if they would grab and hold the Indian. "Won't you stay tonight? We want you to be with us. We have all the things ready," the Chief said.

The Indian looked at the coffee can. "I don't know anything about the peyote stuff. I have heard the songs and prayers, but I think you need more than that. I think I will go," he said.

"But your granddaughter, aren't you going to wait and see if you can find somebody who knows where she is?" Chief Black Bear asked.

"I came to look for my grandchild, but I haven't been able to find her. I am getting to be an old man, and I am tired, and I should be home. My grandchild will be all right, I think. Indians are everywhere."

The Chief and the girl watched helplessly as the Indian left. When he got down to the street, he called a cab from a bar. The cab drove him to the bus station.

As the bus went south toward Palo Alto, the day was getting dark. He thought of a scene a long time back. My prayers were for rain. Pray for rain, my mother said. The *koshare* were going to the east. They were going home. Let us go home, brothers, they sang. I watched them with my prayers.

From Simon J. Ortiz, "The San Francisco Indians," in *The Man to Send Rain Clouds*, edited by Kenneth Rosen (New York: The Viking Press, 1974), pp. 9–13.

Judith Rascoe
A Lot of Cowboys

When it began to snow all the cowboys came into town and rented motel rooms with free TV. One of the cowboys said his favorite program was "Bonanza." "It's pretty authentic."

"Aw, shit, what do you know about authentic?"

"Well, I know. I'm a cowboy, ain't I?"

"Well, so am I, and I think 'Bonanza' is a bunch of bull-pucky. Now if you want authentic stuff you ought to watch 'Gunsmoke.' "

"Well, you old cuss, I will show you what's authentic." So the cowboy hit the other cowboy with his fist.

"No fighting in here, so you cut that out," said the motel manager.

"You're right," the cowboys said. They got some ice and some White Horse and some Coca-Cola. The motel manager said to his wife, "By God, you can't tell them dumb cowhands nothing. They mix good scotch with Coca-Cola."

"I knew I never wanted to marry a cowboy," his wife said. "I knew *all* about them. They weren't the fellows for me." She was keeping her eye on a young couple who weren't married; the girl seemed to have made a wedding ring out of a gold cellophane strip from a cigarette package. Looked mean; good thing the poor fellow hadn't married her yet. That night in the bar the motel manager's wife told him he shouldn't marry her.

"Huh?" he inquired.

A number of cowboys went to see the Ford dealer. He turned on the lights in his office and brought out two fifths of bourbon. The cars stood around the showroom like cows around a campfire, reflecting little gleams from the office and little gleams from the street. You could almost hear them sighing.

"Goddamn, that Maverick is a pretty little car," a cowboy said.

"Yeah, yeah," another cowboy said. "But I tell you, I got my eye on a pickup so pretty you'd like to cry. Dark-green gold-flecked. Air conditioning. And I'd hang toolboxes on the side. And maybe—"

He had their attention.

"—and maybe I do and maybe I don't know a Mexican fellow who wants to make me hand-tooled leather seat covers."

"Aaaaoooooow-*ha*. WooooooooowwEEEEE."

Also little tsk-tsk-tsk noises. Head shakes. Lip bites. Breaths indrawn.

"Pwuh," said the Ford dealer. He was a classicist. He couldn't stand to think of a hand-tooled Mexican leather seat cover. Of course he was a town fellow.

"When I was in the Army," one of the cowboys said illustratively, "I got me a tailor over in Munich, and I went in and I said—well, I drew him what I wanted, and he made me a suit, *bitte schön*! Mama, oh that were a suit! It had six slantpockets in the jacket. Course, uh, course, I don't wear it too often, you understand."

Oh, yes, they understood!

There were those cowboys laughing like they were fit to be tied.

An old woman living above the Western Auto store stuck her head out the window and listened to the cowboys come and go. The snow was falling slowly, and down the street Stan Melchek was sitting in his car waiting for a speeder. A pair of lights appeared in the distance but it was a big tractor-trailer rig, after all, pulling slowly through town, and its tail-lights went past the All Nite Truck Café, and the old woman pulled her head back inside and closed the window.

One cowboy lay on one twin bed and another cowboy lay on the other. One cowboy said, "I like Tammy Wynette. I sure get a kick out of her. My favorite record is 'Stand By Your Man.' My little sister sings it just like her. You close your eyes and you don't know it ain't Tammy Wynette singing. She wants me to get a guitar and learn to play and accompany her."

"I wrote a song once," the other cowboy said. "I showed it

to this fellow works in Denver, and he said maybe I could publish it and maybe I couldn't.

"Oh, there's money there," the first cowboy said.

"Oh, you better believe it."

"What's on now?"

" 'Hawaii Five-O.' "

"Shee-it."

"Well?"

"We sure as hell ain't going to no drive-in tonight."

We had all these cowboys in town because of the snow, and they were mostly drinking whiskey and watching television and talking about cars. It was Saturday night, but you sure couldn't tell it from any other night because of the snow. The Basque Hall advertised a dance, but the group they were going to have didn't have chains or something and anyway called from Salt Lake and said nothing doing, so there wasn't even a dance. Some of the older fellows went to the motel bar and danced, but it was mostly Guy Lombardo, which the bartender's wife favored. Maud, the motel manager's wife, had different ideas; she sat down next to a cowboy she knew and said, "We need to light a fire under some of these old cayuses. Play some of the music the kids like."

"I don't like it," the cowboy said.

"Well, hell, no, *you* don't like it, an old fart like you. Hell, you can't dance that way with one foot in the grave."

"Now, cut it out."

"I'll wash out my mouth, Carl."

"I don't like to hear you talk like that, Maud." His eyes filled with tears. "Honest to Christ, Maud, you was the most beautiful girl I ever saw. You wore your hair the sweetest little way with two little curls in front of your ears, and you wore a green silk dress. You were the sweetest little thing."

"Now, don't start crying here."

"Well, God help me, I can't help it."

"You'll just make me cry too." She had handkerchiefs for both of them. She got another round of drinks. That mean little thing with the cellophane wedding ring was looking, and Maud bet *she'd* never known a real man like Carl. These cowboys were always getting drunk and bawling, and it made her bawl too, to tell the truth.

So, you see, everybody was either in a motel room or in the motel bar, and it was snowing pretty heavily, and then

George Byron Cutler drove into town. He was something of a celebrity because his picture was up in post offices, and he was known as G. Byron Cutler and Byron George Cutler and G. B. Cutler, to give only a few of his aliases. He was wanted mostly for mail fraud, but he had also held up a post office and was armed, and considered himself dangerous. He usually wore khaki shirts and trousers, but he wore good boots. Most criminals have a peculiarity like that. Anyhow, George Bryon Cutler went to the motel and asked for a room, and then stuck his head in the bar and yelled, "Where's the action?"

"Well, now, I thought you was bringing it," somebody yelled back.

"Well, I was, but she didn't have a friend."

"Well, bring her in."

It kind of fell flat. He winked at Maud.

"Is my old man at the desk?" she yelled.

"Yeah, your old man is at the desk," said a voice behind George Byron Cutler. And so Cutler went on to his room, and about an hour later two sheriff's men came by and said they were looking for him.

"Christ almighty! I got to tell Maud," her husband said. "Don't you do nothing 'til I tell Maud. She won't forgive me if we got a bandido in the motel and she's not here."

"You done us a favor," the sheriff's men said, agreeable. They accepted a Coke apiece. They left snow on the Astroturf. "That's Astroturf," Maud's husband said.

"God almighty," the sheriff's men said.

So Maud's husband went in to get Maud, and she said real loud, "You mean we got a criminal in this here motel? Oh, I don't know why this hasn't happened before. We are the only motel for fifty miles. The only motel you'd stop at, that's to say. Of course there's always Mrs. Oldon's place. You boys don't stop there, you hear?" A lot of coarse laughter greeted this remark, because the cowboys knew that Mrs. Oldon had a prostitute come through in the summer. Every summer she had a different prostitute, and these girls were known as Winnemucca Discards. It was a common joke that only sheepherders went to Mrs. Oldon. "I am feeling like a sheepherder tonight," a cowboy would say, and the reply to that was, "I'd get a sheep instead."

"What sort of a criminal is this fellow?" Maud asked.

"He's a mail fraud," her husband said.

"Sounds like a pansy to me," a cowboy said.

"I want to see the police capture him anyways," Maud said. She rose to her feet, showing a lot of bosom to the assembled, and led the way to the motel lobby, and all the cowboys and even the mean girl with the cellophane wedding ring and her "husband" followed. The sheriff's men were feeling the Astroturf.

"Snowing like all hell," one of the sheriff's men said.

"Is this fellow dangerous?" Maud said.

"Well he is armed and considered dangerous," one of the patrolmen said.

"He's in 211," her husband said.

"Then everybody can see," Maud said. They all looked outside and saw the two layers of rooms, and 211 was pretty well located, being close to the big light and close to the middle of the balcony. The sheriff's men told everybody their names and shook some hands and then went out while everybody watched from the lobby. They went up to 211, and you could see them knock at the door. They didn't even have their guns out.

"He can't be very dangerous if they don't even take out their guns," Maud said.

"It's a Supreme Court rule now," somebody said.

"I don't know how they catch anybody."

Then there was an awful sound like a board breaking and nobody knew what it was at first and then one of the sheriff's men started yelling and all the cowboys and everybody else started yelling, "He's been shot! Jesus Christ, he shot him! Oh, get out of the way." The other sheriff's man started running, and then 211 opened the door and George Byron Cutler stood there with a gun in his hand.

He was shouting something but nobody heard it. Finally a cowboy lying on the Astroturf slid open the double glass door and yelled back, "What did you say?"

"I said I just want to get out of here," yelled George Byron Cutler. "I have killed a man, and I have nothing to lose now."

"Did you hear what he said?" Maud asked somebody. "I would never have featured it."

"Where is that other sheriff's man? Did he shoot him too?"

It turned out the other sheriff's man was back in his car calling for help. And all the cowboys in the motel rooms were calling to find out what was going wrong. Maud got on the switchboard and told everybody, "Don't peek out. God almighty, don't peek out. Just keep your door locked and lie low. He has a gun, and he has killed a police officer."

George Byron Cutler walked toward the lobby with his gun shaking. All the cowboys and women were on top of each other on the floor or crawling away, and a lot of people were crying. Maud said to the switchboard, "Dear Lord, he is coming in here. I got to hang up now. Do not come here. You cannot help us."

Then George Byron Cutler tried to open the lobby door, but it was cold and stuck. He began making faces and pounding at it. "Wait wait wait wait." A cowboy got up real slow and opened the door for him.

"Just stay as you are," Cutler said to everybody. "Give me your money."

"I'll give it to you," Maud said. "But I haven't got much cash."

He thought a long time. Then he told everybody to throw down their credit cards. He took the whole pile of credit cards and put them in his shirt and said, "This will take some time to work out, boys."

Later Maud said she'd thought at first he was scared but he surely showed he was a cool customer.

Then he went out again and they heard a car start and make lots of noise and roar away, and then they heard some more shots, and finally somebody went out and found the cowboys from the Ford dealer's place all standing around the street where George Byron Cutler was lying dead, shot by Stan Melchek.

"I thought at first he was a speeder, but when I stopped him he fired his gun at me."

"I guess you didn't tell him his rights," one of the cowboys said.

"Oh, shut your mouth," another cowboy said. "This fellow has been killed."

Nobody could sleep after that. Maud opened the coffee shop and heated up some bear claws. She sat down with Carl and a couple of the younger fellows.

"Stan Melchek is a cowboy," she said. "He is a cowboy by nature. Those fellows shoot first and ask questions later. That's the code of the West. These big-city criminals don't realize they're out in the Wild West. Out on the frontier here."

"They don't realize," Carl said.

In a very sad voice Maud said, "Well, I guess he learned."

"You don't fool around with a cowboy. You don't fool around in this country," Carl said.

"The cowboy is a vanishing race," one of the cowboys said.

"But he's not finished yet," Maud said.

"Not by a long shot," said one of the cowboys.

Judith Rascoe, "A Lot of Cowboys," *The Atlantic*, 226 (November 1970), pp. 56–58.

Henry Kissinger

Cowboy Politics

Q: But, Dr. Kissinger, how do you explain your incredible superstar status, how do you explain the fact that you have become almost more famous and popular than a president? Have you any theories?

A: Yes, but I won't tell you what they are. Because they don't coincide with the common theory. . . . My theory is quite different, but, I repeat, I won't tell you what it is. Why should I, while I'm still in the middle of my job? Instead, you tell me yours. I'm sure you too have some theory on the reasons for my popularity.

Q: I'm not sure, Dr. Kissinger, I'm looking for a theory in this interview. But I haven't found one yet. I expect the root of all lies in success. What I mean is, like a chess player you've made two or three clever moves. China, first of all. People admire a chess player who makes away with his opponent's king.

A: Yes, China was an important element in the mechanics of my success. And yet, that isn't the main point. The main point . . . Well, why not? I'll tell you. What do I care after all? The main point stems from the fact that I've always acted alone. Americans admire that enormously. Americans admire the cowboy leading the caravan alone astride his horse, the cowboy entering a village or city alone on his horse. Without even a pistol, maybe, because he doesn't go in for shooting. He acts, that's all: aiming at the right spot at the right time. A Wild West tale, if you like.

Q: I see. You see yourself as a kind of Henry Fonda, unarmed and ready to fight with his bare fists for honest ideals. Solitary, brave.

A: Not necessarily brave. This cowboy doesn't need courage. It's enough that he be alone, that he show others how he enters the village alone and does everything on his own. This romantic, surprising character suits me, because being alone has always been part of my style, or of my technique if you prefer. Independence too. Yes, that's very important to me and in me. And, finally, conviction. I am always convinced of the necessity of whatever I'm doing.

From "Kissinger: An Interview with Oriana Fallaci," *New Republic*, Vol. 167, No. 23 (Dec. 16, 1972), p. 21.

Bill Moyers

A West to Be Saved

Without any explanation he had slowed down to twenty miles per hour. "Up in that high country is the most fragile soil you can imagine. There's a short growing season up on those slopes, which means you don't have much time to recover if you disturb the vegetation. When the vegetation is injured, the soil isn't going to hold the water. There's one year in a hundred when things are going to be just right and you can begin to recover the conditions that protect the soil and keep it from running off.

"I was up there on horseback once during this study and I heard people coming down the trail. I looked up and it was the worst thing I ever saw. There were about 150 people riding through the high country on horses. That's the most sensitive country we've got. I could feel the soil breaking up and shifting under those horses. I shouted at them: 'What in the hell do you think you're doing?' And they said they were members of the Sierra Club out for a ride. Can you imagine? Up there a group of 30 or 40 horses is okay, but 150! Now I work with the Sierra Club and we do a lot of things together, but you can kill something you love if you're not careful.

"You've heard of crop rotation? We're going to have to manage these lands like that. If we want timber for scenery, we've got to plan for it. It takes longer to grow trees for scenic purposes than for cutting. And we're going to have to tell the lumber industry that we cannot cut these lands over as rapidly as they would like because we have to build access roads at a proper rate, and remove vegetation at a proper rate or we'll upset the hydrological function of the slopes. They'll also have to come up with other ways of getting the timber out once it's cut, than by road. They use balloons up in Washington, I think, and they're going to have to do that here, too. Just lift the logs up and out. Fifty years ago it was the public against the interests. It still is. But we've got to protect these lands against abuse and overuse by the public, too. They're going to ruin it through ignorance. I mentioned crop rotation. There's going to have to be people rotation on our lakes and in these parks. People will scream, but every generation has to give up something for the sake of the next."

If you could get the people who want to do something about conservation and preservation into one big stadium to speak to them, what would you say?

"I'd like to get the whole damn country in there. I'd like to say to the whole damn pot of them: Put your money where your mouth is and get with it."

We pulled off the road just before it crossed the South Fork of the Salmon. We were alone. The only sound came from the cold mountain water washing the rocks and the roots of dark green pines and firs along the banks. When Butterworth spoke, he whispered; it was that kind of place. "It looks clear and beautiful," John Arnold said. "But it's full of sand. The soils that come down don't have much clay so you don't get color in the stream. Used to be holes in there so deep you had to swim across them. Now you can walk across. The sand has filled them up. It just sandblasts everything in there. A river can be dying while you look at it, and you can't even see death coming. The sand is choking it. There are still some salmon spawning in there. Not many, but some. We've got to hurry or there won't be any left. Then the river will look just like it does now, but it won't be the same."

From Bill Moyers, *Listening to America* (New York: Harper's Magazine Press, in association with Harper & Row, 1971), pp. 160–161.

THE WEST ON FILM

William S. Hart

The Search for Authenticity: A Mechanical Horse

While playing in Cleveland, I attended a picture show. I saw a Western picture. It was awful! I talked with the manager of the theater and he told me it was one of the best Westerns he had ever had. None of the impossibilities or libels on the West meant anything to him—it was drawing the crowds. The fact that the sheriff was dressed and characterized as a sort of cross between a Wisconsin wood-chopper and a Gloucester fisherman was unknown to him. I did not seek to enlighten him. I was seeking information. In fact, I was so sure that I had made a big discovery that I was frightened that some one would read my mind and find it out.

Here were reproductions of the Old West being seriously presented to the public—in almost a burlesque manner—and they were successful. It made me tremble to think of it. I was an actor and I knew the West. . . . The opportunity that I had been waiting for years to come was knocking at my door.

Cliff Smith, my director, and I went to look at the location. The first drop before we struck earth was about twelve feet, and the distance to the bottom which must be rolled was easily one hundred and fifty feet. I knew the little horse could do it, but there was that fear that I knew I had of injuring him. I knew I could not do him justice and help him as I should. I weakened. . . .

We had tried several times to have dummy horses made for the little chap, but outside of using them as a staked down wild horse, or a dead horse, we could never use them. Cliff Smith and I had a talk with two expert mechanics at the Lasky Studio. They took the job. They worked five weeks at a cost of about $2000, and made a horse that was as nearly like Fritz as it would be possible for anything to be. Every measurement was perfect. The mane and tail were real horse-hair. We had an artist paint all the markings. Every joint worked on springs. The head swung in the most natural man-ner, and the weight was within a hundred pounds of what Fritz himself would weigh.

At the conclusion of the picture, we got the scene. It was done in the following manner. I brought Fritz at a gallop and threw him. Then the dummy horse was fixed up with the same outfit we used on Fritz and held in an upright position by pi-ano wires so I could mount. Golly! What a job it was! It took about thirty carpenters and helpers to get the mechanical horse to the top of the precipice and get him set up.

"Are you going to go over with that brute?" asked one of the workmen, a well-set-up young chap.

"Yes," I said.

"Then from now on I'm satisfied to work at my trade," he replied.

When the camera started to grind and I swung over my lifeless steed, the wire was cut and down we went.

From William S. Hart, *My Life East and West* (Boston: Houghton Mifflin Co., 1929), pp. 198-199; 321-322.

Sherwood Anderson

Dreaming of Cowboys

Even to-day I cannot go into a movie theatre and see there some such national hero as, say, Bill Hart, without wishing myself such another. In the theatre I sit looking at the people and see how they are all absorbed in the affairs of the man on the stage. Now he springs lightly off a horse and goes toward the door of a lonely cabin. We, in the theatre, know that within the cabin are some ten desperate men all heavily armed with guns and with them, bound to a chair, is a fair woman, another virgin got off the reservation, as it were. Bill stops at the door of the cabin and takes a careful look at his guns, and we, in the audience, know well enough that in a few minutes now he will go inside and just shoot all of those ten fellows in there to death, fairly make sieves of them, and that he will get wounded himself but not seriously—just enough to need the help of the virgin in getting out of the cabin and onto his horse—so he can ride to her father's ranch house and go to bed and get well after a while, in time for the wedding.

All these things we know, but we love our Bill and can hardly wait until the shooting begins. As for myself I never see such a performance but that I later go out of the theatre and, when I get off into a quiet street alone, I become just such another. Looking about to see that I am unobserved, I jerk two imaginary guns out of my hip pockets and draw a quick bead on some near-by tree. "Dog," I cry, "unhand her!" All my early reading of American literature comes into my mind and I try to do a thing that is always being spoken of in the books. I try to make my eyes narrow to pin points. Bill Hart can do it wonderfully in the pictures and why not I? As I sat in the movie house it was evident that Bill Hart was being loved by all the men, women and children sitting about and I also want to be loved—to be a little dreaded and feared, too, perhaps. "Ah! there goes Sherwood Anderson! Treat him with respect. He is a bad man when he is aroused. But treat him kindly and he will be as gentle with you as any cooing dove."

From Sherwood Anderson, *A Story Teller's Story* (New York: Garden City Publishing Co., 1924), pp. 119–120.

Helen Zeese Papanikolas

Dream and Waking: Cowboys

Coming home from school in the late twenties and early thirties, I sometimes saw the strangers on the one street of the town. They were not the immigrant miners and their wives from the thirty or more coal camps in the surrounding draws and arid mountainsides, who surreptitiously came to town on paydays, defying the edict of mine management to trade at mine company stores. These strangers came from the sagebrush plain southward or from the borders of the Ute reservation to the north; they had that certain combination of looks, actions, an indefinable aura that even children recognized as that of "low-class Americans."

The women leaned against store fronts waiting for their men, packages at their feet. They were scrawny, their hair frizzed with permanent waves, their skin taut with myriad wrinkles, their blue eyes squinting, even on gray days, from the wind and sun of their open terrain. In late fall and early spring they shivered in black or gray-striped suit coats worn over J. C. Penney gingham dresses. In summer they wore the faded dresses without the coats. They were always waiting, looking up and down the street, their eyes following each passerby with hard, unwavering stares.

The men were wiry, stunted. Their faces weathered brown from the sun, misshapen. Hand-rolled cigarettes stuck to their bleached lips, and their stockmen's hats—not the Stetsons of the prosperous Greek, French and Mormon sheepmen—were discolored above the band from years of sweat. They wore either overalls too big for their frames or Levis slipped down on their narrow hips. Their half-ton Ford trucks stood at the curb, dusty, bleached by the sun and pitted by rutted roads. In the back were bales of wire fencing, a few lengths of board, sometimes a trussed lamb or calf that brought dry grief, for they were at the mercy of the mean-eyed. At times a child stood pressed to the spackled windshield of the truck, looking out big-eyed at the people passing by. His hair was the color of straw and whacked close to his head.

Sometimes the strangers were inside the Chinese-American

Cafe. They never went into the Grill Cafe, although they sometimes stood at the window and looked at the tank of green water in which trout swam. At the Grill Cafe the manager, Bill White (he had changed his name from Vassilis Ghiourghiotis), presided over leather-upholstered booths and tables set with white cloth napkins; the waitresses wore black with small white aprons and white starched crowns; the counter stools were also upholstered and the wide, long mirror on the wall facing the counter reflected pyramids of glassware and a large glass bowl of fresh fruit. At the Chinese cafe two signs were taped to the window: WHITES ONLY and WHITE HELP ONLY. The booths were plain wood, the tables without cloths, the counter stools also plain, and there was no mirror to reflect anything. When the strangers paid their bill, the Chinese proprietor nodded his head and with wide smiles rang up their money. The strangers looked at him closely, unsmiling, put toothpicks in their mouths, got into their old Ford, drove down the one street and disappeared, the child gazing back for a last look at town.

I always stopped at the Strand Theater where I stood for long minutes in front of the glass-encased posters on either side of the cashier's booth. The heroes in immaculate cowboy clothes and ten-gallon Stetsons rode noble horses. They were even-featured, rugged like Johnny Mack Brown, silk scarves tied around their necks; tall, strong-jawed, yet boyish like Gary Cooper, Stetson pulled over one eye; lithe ones like Tom Mix in snug black trousers pushed into high-heeled cowboy boots, his black horse Tony decorated with silver-tooled bridle and saddle. There were other heroes who arrived in the nick of time and in the background of the posters was a starlet with cupid-bow lips, straight-plucked eyebrows pulled downwards in anguish, wearing a gingham dress with low square collar, snug over her breasts, puffed sleeves. Invariably her hands were clasped pleading for help.

It was many years before I realized that those stunted, wiry men from the sagebrush land and Johnny Mack Brown, Gary Cooper, Tom Mix were supposed to be the same people—cowboys.

From Helen Zeese Papanikolas, unpublished reminiscenses.

Larry McMurtry

Cowboys, Movies, Myths, and Cadillacs

Hud, a twentieth-century westerner, is a gunfighter who lacks both guns and opponents. The land itself is the same—just as powerful, just as imprisoning—but the social context has changed so radically that Hud's impulse to violence has to turn inward on himself and his family. Hud Bannon is wild in a well-established tradition of western wildness that involves drinking, gambling, fighting, fast and reckless riding and/or driving (Hud has a Cadillac), and, of course, seducing. The tradition is not bogus; the character is pretty much in line with actuality. The cowboy, on screen and off, has generally been distinguished for his daring and his contempt of the middle-class way of life (he remains acutely conscious of the mores of his peers). Though nowadays most cowboys are solidly middle-class in their values, the values sit more lightly on them than on their white-collar cousins.

Hud, of course, is not simply a cowboy; if he were, he could never afford the Cadillac. It is his gun, in a sense, and he can afford it because he is the son of a well-to-do rancher, and a wheeler in his own right. Cowboys and ranchers differ primarily in their economic resources: a rancher is a cowboy who, through some combination of work, luck, judgment, or inheritance, has made good. To a rancher a Cadillac has a dual usefulness, just as the gunfighter's gun once had: it is an obvious and completely acceptable status symbol, and also it is capable of making the long, high-speed drives that are frequently necessary in cattle country; it will do the work. The cowboy proper could no more afford Hud's car than he could afford Hud's women, though granted the latter might vary considerably in expensiveness. In spite of his reputation for going on wild binges the cowboy has usually had to accustom himself to rather Spartan living conditions; indeed, there has always been an element of asceticism in the cowboy's makeup, though it is an asceticism that has tended to wither rather badly when faced with the continuous blasts of sensuality this century has provided. Even so the cowboy's life has not yet become lush; he still gets by with far fewer creature comforts than most Americans have. . . .

There will be a very poignant story to be told about the cowboy, should Hollywood care to tell it: the story of his gradual metamorphosis into a suburbanite. The story contains an element of paradox, for the bloated urbanism that makes the wild, free cowboy so very attractive to those already urbanized will eventually result in his being absorbed by his audience. In a sense he has been already: nobody watches TV westerns more avidly than cowboys. Of course in this respect legend and fact had long ago begun to intermingle; nature imitated art, to a degree, and the cowboy, however much he might profess to scorn Hollywood, was secretly delighted to believe the romantic things Hollywood told him about himself. Even in his most golden days the cowboy lived within the emotional limits of the western movie and the hillbilly song. Hud Bannon's West is a sort of new lost frontier, and Hud is one of the many people whose capacities no longer fit his situation. He needs more room and less company, and he is unlikely to get either. Someday the ranches of America will all be Southern California size, and all the cattle, perhaps, will be grown in the great feedlots of the Middle West. The descendants of the trail hands will be driving beer trucks in the suburbs of San Antonio, Dodge City, Cheyenne, and a hundred other towns whose names once held a different sort of promise. By that time Hollywood will have grown tired of parodying the gunfighter, the ironic mode may give way to the mythic and the Lone Ranger ride again. Romance will succeed realism, and Gary Cooper (as in *The Plainsman,* say) will be as remote and appealing a figure of romance as Roland or King Arthur. Hud Bannon, by that time, will have traded in his big pink Caddy and left the ranch forever, to become a secret agent, or an astronaut.

From Larry McMurtry, "Cowboys, Movies, Myths, and Cadillacs: Realism in the Western," in *Man and the Movies,* edited by W. R. Robinson with assistance from George Garrett (Baton Rouge: Louisiana State University Press, 1967), pp. 50–52 *passim.*

Robert Warshow

The Westerner

What does the Westerner fight for? We know he is on the side of justice and order, and of course it can be said he fights for these things. But such broad aims never correspond exactly to his real motives; they only offer him his opportunity. The Westerner himself, when an explanation is asked of him (usually by a woman), is likely to say that he does what he "has to do." If justice and order did not continually demand his protection, he would be without a calling. Indeed, we come upon him often in just that situation, as the reign of law settles over the West and he is forced to see that his day is over; those are the pictures which end with his death or with his departure for some more remote frontier. What he defends, at bottom, is the purity of his own image—in fact his honor. This is what makes him invulnerable. When the gangster is killed, his whole life is shown to have been a mistake, but the image the Westerner seeks to maintain can be presented as clearly in defeat as in victory: he fights not for advantage and not for the right, but to state what he is, and he must live in a world which permits that statement. The Westerner is the last gentleman, and the movies which over and over again tell his story are probably the last art form in which the concept of honor retains its strength.

Of course I do not mean to say that ideas of virtue and justice and courage have gone out of culture. Honor is more than these things: it is a style, concerned with harmonious appearances as much as with desirable consequences, and tending therefore toward the denial of life in favor of art. "Who hath it? he that died o' Wednesday." On the whole, a world that leans to Falstaff's view is a more civilized and even, finally, a more graceful world. It is just the march of civilization that forces the Westerner to move on; and if we actually had to confront the question it might turn out that the woman who refuses to understand him is right as often as she is wrong. But we do not confront the question. Where the Westerner lives it is always about 1870—not the real 1870, either, or the real West—and he is killed or goes away when

his position becomes problematical. The fact that he continues to hold our attention is evidence enough that, in his
proper frame, he presents an image of personal nobility that
is still real for us.

Clearly, this image easily becomes ridiculous: we need only
look at William S. Hart or Tom Mix, who in the wooden ab-
soluteness of their virtue represented little that an adult could
take seriously; and doubtless such figures as Gene Autry or
Roy Rogers are no better, though I confess I have seen none
of their movies. Some film enthusiasts claim to find in the
early, unsophisticated Westerns a "cinematic purity" that has
since been lost; this idea is as valid, and finally as misleading,
as T. S. Eliot's statement that *Everyman* is the only play in
English that stays within the limitations of art. The truth is
that the Westerner comes into the field of serious art only
when his moral code, without ceasing to be compelling, is
seen also to be imperfect. The Westerner at his best exhibits a
moral ambiguity which darkens his image and saves him
from absurdity; this ambiguity arises from the fact that,
whatever his justifications, he is a killer of men. . . .

. . . Why does the Western movie especially have such a
hold on our imagination?

Chiefly, I think, because if offers a serious orientation to
the problem of violence such as can be found almost nowhere
else in our culture. One of the well-known peculiarities of
modern civilized opinion is its refusal to acknowledge the
value of violence. This refusal is a virtue, but like many virtues it involves a certain willful blindness and it encourages
hypocrisy. We train ourselves to be shocked or bored by cultural images of violence, and our very concept of heroism
tends to be a passive one: we are less drawn to the brave
young men who kill large numbers of our enemies than to
the heroic prisoners who endure torture without capitulating.
In art, though we may still be able to understand and participate in the values of the Iliad, a modern writer like Ernest
Hemingway we find somewhat embarrassing: there is no
doubt that he stirs us, but we cannot help recognizing also
that he is a little childish. And in the criticism of popular culture, where the educated observer is usually under the illusion
that he has nothing at stake, the presence of images of violence is often assumed to be in itself a sufficient ground for
condemnation. . . .

. . . At its best, the war movie may represent a more civilized point of view than the Western, and if it were not con-

tinually marred by ideological sentimentality we might hope to find it developing into a higher form of drama. But it cannot supply the values we seek in the Western.

Those values are in the image of a single man who wears a gun on his thigh. The gun tells us that he lives in a world of violence, and even that he "believes in violence." But the drama is one of self-restraint: the moment of violence must come in its own time and according to its special laws, or else it is valueless. There is little cruelty in Western movies, and little sentimentality; our eyes are not focused on the sufferings of the defeated but on the deportment of the hero. Really, it is not violence at all which is the "point" of the Western movie, but a certain image of man, a style, which expresses itself most clearly in violence. Watch a child with his toy guns and you will see: what most interests him is not (as we so much fear) the fantasy of hurting others, but to work out how a man might look when he shoots or is shot. A hero is one who looks like a hero.

From Robert Warshow, "Movie Chronicle: The Westerner," in *The Immediate Experience: Movies, Comics, Theater and other Aspects of Popular Culture* (Garden City, N. Y.: Doubleday & Co., 1962), pp. 140–142, 151–154 *passim.*

Frank Bergon

The Marlboro Man

You already know his weathered face. You have seen him on billboards, in magazines, and in television commercials as one of the Marlboro Men. He stands an inch over six feet, and from the square jaw and straight, dry lips to the cold blue eyes, surrounded by razor-thin wrinkles, his features are those of the archetypal cowboy, etched in whang leather. Even when he rode across television screens, accompanied by music intended to excite everyone's Western blood, his unhurried movements and gestures suggested a man perpetually and wondrously relaxed. *Come to where the flavor is. Come to Marlboro Country.* The viewer's cynical smile is to be expected. Surely this man is anything but what he appears to be. In a time of pervasive phoniness, encouraged by advertis-

ing that caters to our most tenacious fantasies, we do not
even expect a television cowboy to *be* a cowboy. But the
name of this Marlboro Man is Darrell Winfield, and he lives
and works on a ranch in Wyoming—as a cowboy. . . .

How Darrell Winfield came to be [Marlboro Country's] symbol was mainly accidental. In the fall of 1968, camera crews
from the Leo Burnett Agency arrived at the Wyoming ranch
with some models, including a former professional football
quarterback. In search of a region with mountains, trees, and
water, they had been advised by the general manager of the
Four Sixes ranch in Texas to contact a Madera cattleman
who also ran stock in Wyoming. "The first time I saw Darrell
I thought he was the second-meanest-looking guy I had ever
seen," said Ken Krom, the executive art director of the Leo
Burnett Agency, "and that's only because I saw Sonny Clement first. Darrell was heavily bearded, and he and Clement
were bundled up, chipping ice to get water flowing. I'd heard
about the hospitality of the West, but after they introduced
themselves, those guys proved it. We took test shots of Darrell and later some 16mm footage, and the agency and Philip
Morris Company approved it. We like to keep our pictures
pure and have had several cowboys working for us. For one
thing, you don't have to tell a cowboy how to sit in a saddle."
(It also eliminates letters complaining that a model's spurs
are upside down or his rope is on the wrong side of the
saddle.) "Darrell has the kind of face we think depicts the
West, and when we first saw him he also had a mustache,
something else we'd always wanted. On the first shoot we
went out by his barn and let 'em rip until we thought we had
the right expression." Since that first photograph, called "The
Sheriff Picture" by the agency, Darrell has appeared, with or
without mustache, in more than [160] advertisements and
commercials. . . .

. . . There is a habit of mind and speech in cattle country.
Most of the morning's conversations were marked by bluffs,
indirection, and teasing which hid a strong sense of emotional
privacy and self-assurance. The result is a gap between
speech and feeling that often puzzles urban visitors used to
social encounters that are fashionably "open," "out-front"
and "sincere." It is a remnant of that culture that bred the
West's preposterous story-tellers as well as its tight-lipped, laconic actors, a code that is reduced to its essence at the card
table.

During a late summer night patio party, a California

woman assailed Darrell with her religious views. In an effort
to shake him of his apparent inability to see a divine order to
the universe, she pointed toward the sky. "Answer this," she
said. "Who put the moon up there?"

Darrell looked at her and sadly replied, "I honestly do not
know." . . .

Because words cannot and need not say everything where
assumptions and experience are shared, there seems to be
among cowboys no nervous urgency to fill the long pauses
and silences that would embarrass city people. One afternoon
Darrrell offered to sell a neighboring rancher some heifers to
supplement the stock in the man's feed pens. "I'd like to,
Darrell," the rancher said without inflection. Wind flapped
the brim of the old hat that matched his equally battered
face. Darrell nodded. The rancher felt no need to add, *but I
cain't.*

It's all a pose, you say; you have heard and seen all this
before. After all, cowboys and ranchers are aware of how we
expect them to act; they too watch movies and Marlboro
commercials. And yet, no satisfactory explanation can ignore
how naturally the working conditions and insular community
of the West breed such a style, how free the people are from
the daily bombardments of changing ideology and fact that
threaten the urban dweller's sense of self. . . .

I asked him why he'd left California. "Coming to Wyoming was the best thing I ever did," Darrell said, as the truck
followed the curving mountain road. "I could make more
money back in California in feedlots, but that was a twenty-
four-hour job, and like a factory. I'd never go back unless I
absolutely had to."

He works on a ranch because, he says, he could never see
himself living in a city, commuting to a job, or working in a
building. "It all depends on what you want to be," he ex-
plains, underscoring *be* rather than *do,* an indication of the
extent to which he considers his choice of work a way of life.
His earliest memories are of trying to spend as much time as
possible on a horse or work mule in the small town of Kansas, Oklahoma, where he was born, and in Hanford, California, where his family moved when he was six. But for a long
time roping and riding remained only pleasant diversions.
Until his senior year in high school he had planned to own a
dairy farm like his father's. But he grew tired of milking
cows, and ran away with a carnival with which he toured the

state from Bishop to Los Angeles, running the pony rides and setting up equipment. Eventually returning to Hanford, he "bummed around," married Lennie, and in 1950 began work on a large ranch outside Madera. Thirteen years' experience with cattle made him, according to a former Valley ranch hand, "one of the best cowmen around." A cattle partnership, formed with a rancher in 1962, collapsed when the bottom fell out of beef prices. Broke, Darrell went back to work as a foreman on a California ranch. For the next three years, Sonny Clement tried to talk Darrell into joining him in Wyoming, but it was not until the winter of 1968, after Darrell's boss shot himself, that he left California with no intention of returning. "I don't want to have to work all my life," he said, "but first I'd like to invest in some business, maybe in town." What about a ranch? "Oh, I'd like to have a ranch, but you have to have the outlay. Nowadays it has to be either an enormous one or a small one that you can work yourself. And that isn't much fun if you don't have something else to do. There's no in-between." But what's the future of ranching in the Wyoming hills? "Most of this land isn't much good for anything else except cattle. You can't farm it." But aren't cowboys almost extinct, irrelevant? Won't feedlots and more efficient operations replace grazing? "Oh, probably," said Darrell. "Someday. But it will be a long time coming." . . .

A week after returning to my home in Boston, I was watching a television program with some friends when Darrell appeared on the screen, driving horses across some timeless Western river. "There he is," said one of my friends, "Virile Winfield." We laughed. "I have to get out West one of these days," another said, and the others quietly agreed. Whatever thoughts each of us had, I believe we were all willing, at least for a moment, to see Marlboro Country as a possible retreat from our urban lives, privately aware that the West is still the West in only one way: it's still a place where few people can live. It helps to know, though, that in the Winfield living room there is a framed photograph used in a magazine advertisement. It is similar to the commercial we watched in Boston, a distant shot of Darrell splashing across a creek behind a herd of horses. One night at the dinner table his daughter, Debbie, asked, "Daddy, do you ever watch yourself on TV?"

"Sure," Darrell replied, "when they come on the screen."

"What do you think when you see 'em?"

"Why, I think how handsome that guy is," Darrell answered, "and how much I'd like to be like him."

From Frank Bergon, "West of California: A Visit with the Marlboro Man," *Audience* 1 (September–October 1971), pp, 42, 46, 47–48.

THE LOOK OF THE WEST

Robert M. Pirsig

Herreid, South Dakota

At Herreid . . . I find some shade in a park and try to rest. It isn't restful. A change has taken place and I don't know quite what it is. The streets of this town are broad, much broader than they need be, and there is a pallor of dust in the air. Empty lots here and there between the buildings have weeds growing in them. The sheet metal equipment sheds and water tower are like those of previous towns but more spread out. Everything is more run-down and mechanical-looking, and sort of randomly located. Gradually I see what it is. Nobody is concerned anymore about tidily conserving space. The land isn't valuable anymore. We are in a Western town.

From Robert M. Pirsig, *Zen and the Art of Motorcycle Maintenance* (New York: William Morrow & Co., 1974), pp. 55–56.

Ernest Hemingway

The Clark's Fork Valley, Wyoming

At the end of summer, the big trout would be out in the centre of the stream; they were leaving the pools along the upper part of the river and dropping down to spend the winter in the deep water of the canyon. It was wonderful fly-fishing then in the first weeks of September. The native trout were sleek, shining, and heavy, and nearly all of them leaped when they took the fly. If you fished two flies, you would often have two big trout and the need to handle them very delicately in that heavy current.

The nights were cold, and, if you woke in the night, you would hear the coyotes. But you did not want to get out on the stream too early in the day because the nights were so cold they chilled the water, and the sun had to be on the river until almost noon before the trout would start to feed.

You could ride in the morning, or sit in front of the cabin, lazy in the sun, and look across the valley where the hay was cut so the meadows were cropped brown and smooth to the line of quaking aspens along the river, now turning yellow in the fall. And on the hills rising beyond, the sage was silvery grey.

Up the river were the two peaks of Pilot and Index, where we would hunt mountain-sheep later in the month, and you sat in the sun and marvelled at the formal, clean-lined shape mountains can have at a distance, so that you remember them in the shapes they show from far away, and not as the broken rock-slides you crossed, the jagged edges you pulled up by, and the narrow shelves you sweated along, afraid to look down, to round that peak that looked so smooth and geometrical. You climbed around it to come out on a clear space to look down to where an old ram and three young rams were feeding in the juniper bushes in a high, grassy pocket cupped against the broken rock of the peak.

The old ram was purple-grey, his rump was white, and when he raised his head you saw the great heavy curl of his horns. It was the white of his rump that had betrayed him to you in the green of the junipers when you had lain in the lee of a rock, out of the wind, three miles away, looking carefully at every yard of the high country through a pair of good Zeiss glasses.

Now as you sat in front of the cabin, you remembered that down-hill shot and the young rams standing, their heads turned, staring at him, waiting for him to get up. They could not see you on that high ledge, nor wind you, and the shot made no more impression on them than a boulder falling.

You remembered the year we had built a cabin at the head of Timber Creek, and the big grizzly that tore it open every

time we were away. The snow came late that year, and this
bear would not hibernate, but spent his autumn tearing open
cabins and ruining a trap-line. But he was so smart you never
saw him in the day. Then you remembered coming on the
three grizzlies in the high country at the head of Crandall
Creek. You heard a crash of timber and thought it was a cow
elk bolting, and then there they were, in the broken shadow,
running with an easy, lurching smoothness, the afternoon sun
making their coats a soft, bristling silver.

You remembered elk bulging in the fall, the bull so close
you could see his chest muscles swell as he lifted his head,
and still not see his head in the thick timber; but hear that
deep, high mounting whistle and the answer from across another valley. You thought of all the heads you had turned
down and refused to shoot, and you were pleased about every
one of them.

You remembered the children learning to ride; how they
did with different horses; and how they loved the country.
You remembered how this country had looked when you first
came into it, and the year you had to stay four months after
you had brought the first car ever to come in for the swamp
roads to freeze solid enough to get the car out. You could
remember all the hunting and all the fishing and the riding in
the summer sun and the dust of the pack-train, the silent riding; in the hills in the sharp cold of fall going up after the
cattle on the high range, finding them wild as deer and as
quiet, only bawling noisily when they were all herded together being forced along down into the lower country.

Then there was the winter; the trees bare now, the snow
blowing so you could not see, the saddle wet, then frozen as
you came down-hill, breaking a trail through the snow, trying
to keep your legs moving, and the sharp, warming taste of
whiskey when you hit the ranch and changed your clothes in
front of the big open fireplace. It's a good country.

From Ernest Hemingway, *By-Line: Ernest Hemingway*, edited by
William White (New York: Charles Scribner's Sons, 1967), pp.
298–300.

Georgia O'Keeffe

A Painter's West

A red hill doesn't touch everyone's heart as it touches mine and I suppose there is no reason why it should. The red hill is a piece of the bad lands where even the grass is gone. Bad lands roll away outside my door—hill after hill—red hills of apparently the same sort of earth that you mix with oil to make paint. All the earth colors of the painter's palette are out there in the many miles of bad lands. The light naples yellow through the ochres—orange and red and purple earth—even the soft earth greens. You have no associations with those hills—our waste land—I think our most beautiful country—You may not have seen it, so you want me always to paint flowers.

I fancy this all hasn't much to do with painting.

I have wanted to paint the desert and I haven't known how. I always think that I can not stay with it long enough. So I brought home the bleached bones as my symbols of the desert. To me they are as beautiful as anything I know. To me they are strangely more living than the animals walking around—hair, eyes and all with their tails switching. The bones seem to cut sharply to the center of something that is keenly alive on the desert even tho' it is vast and empty and untouchable—and knows no kindness with all its beauty.

From "About Myself" in the catalogue to "Georgia O'Keeffe, Exhibition of Oils and Pastels," An American Place, New York January 22–March 17, 1939. [pp. 2–3.]

Edward Weston

A Photographer's West

I have several times noted that Eastern people do not at once see Western values: to them our values are not "correct." I have observed painters first coming to this coast and painting

463

here with Eastern eyes: and I have watched them change. I have had my work criticized as having false values. At times I do exaggerate, print with more contrast, with reason, but usually I feel my values are true.

This leads to furthur consideration of the difference between East and West: a difference which could easily lead an unacquainted Easterner to think my work "theatrical," though I think a more just observation would be to call it "dramatic." Everything is relative. To the New Yorker of fifty years ago the present startling architecture—now accepted as a matter of course—would be dramatic, maybe called "theatrical." So to one not used to the West, to the scale of things out here,—nature must seem very dramatic. But can nature ever be labeled "theatrical"? Of course not, or only by those not used to, or not big enough to feel a part of nature on a grand dimension. Only an inability to commune with, be on close terms with a given nature, can account for the label "theatrical." It is fear of a thing which makes it strange.

Everything in the West is on a grander scale, more intense, vital, dramatic. Forms are here which never occur in the East,—in fruits, flowers, vegetables, in mountains, rocks, trees. Go to Mexico, and there one finds an even greater drama, values more intense,—black and white, cutting contrasts, am I theatrical because I see important forms importantly?

All these forms,—trees, rocks, natural manifestations of Western vitality are my neighbors, my friends,—I understand and love them. I do not lie about them. After living here for ten years, I made a trip back East. Nature seemed soft there, poetic, tenderly lyrical, almost too sweet. Someone pointing out the sights to me from the train window said, "See the mountains." I looked and saw not!—then I realized they meant what, to me, were low rolling hills! But I must have had some apprehension that several of my prints would be misunderstood, probably because last year many did not know our Western kelp. I recall now laying aside one cypress, saying to myself, "I will not include this, no one would believe it true!"

From *The Daybooks of Edward Weston: California*, edited by Nancy Newhall (New York: Horizon Press, 1966, in collaboration with the George Eastman House), pp. 250–251.

Richard Hugo

Camas Prairie School

The schoolbell rings and dies before
the first clang can reach the nearest farm.
With land this open, wind is blowing
when there is no wind. The gym's so ugly
victory leaves you empty as defeat,
and following whatever game
you will remember lost, you run fast
slow miles home through grain,
knowing you'll arrive too late
to eat or find the lights on.

Flat and vast. Each farm beyond
a gunshot of the next. A friend
is one you love to walk to, 28 below.
A full moon makes this prairie moon
and horses in a thick night
sound like bears. When your sister's raped
help is out of range. Father's far
from Mother and a far bell's
always ringing you can't hear.

The teacher either must be new each year
or renewed forever. Old photos
show her just as gray beside the class
of '35. Indians rehearse
the Flag Salute, and tourists
on their way to Hot Springs wave.
The road beside the school goes either way.
The last bell rings. You run again,
the only man going your direction.

From Richard Hugo, *The Lady in Kicking Horse Reservoir, Poems*
(New York: W. W. Norton & Co., 1973), p. 68.

Thomas Wolfe

The West from a Car Window

The little, slaughtered wild things in the road—in Oregon, in California, across the desert, going up—through Utah, in Idaho, Wyoming, and Montana—the little crushed carcasses of the gophers, chipmunks, jackrabbits, birds—in the hot bright western light the black crows picking at some furry mangled little carcass on the hot road—rises and flaps slowly vauntingly away as the car approaches . . .

So all through the morning at good speed upon fine roads up through a great, enlarging, and constantly growing richer valley—at first mixed with some desert land—

bald, scrub dotted ridges on each side ascending into lovely timber then to granite tops, and desert land now semi-desert, semi-green—clumped now with sage and dry, but bursting marvellously into greenery when water is let in—and the river (the Sevier) refreshing it. Still semi desert with occasional flings into riper green—the cool dense green of trees

clustered densely round a little house, and the fields ripe with thick green, and the warm green of hay, and fat steers and cows and horses grazing, apparent men are Mormon Sickling reaping, mowing hay with reaping machines and fields strewn with cut mounds of green lemon hay, and water—the miraculousness of water in the west, the muddy viscousness of irrigation

ditches filled with water so incredibly wet—the miracle of water always in the west—the blazing whiteness of the sunlight now, the light hot blueness of the skies, the piled cumulousness of snowy clouds—and then the dusty little Mormon villages—blazing and blistered in that hot dry heat—and the forlorn little house—sometimes just little

cramped and warped wooden boxes, all unpainted, hidden under the merciful screenings of the dense and sudden trees—the blistered little storefronts, the wooden falsefronts of the little towns—sometimes the older

Mormon houses of red brick—sometimes still more ancient
ones of chinked log—sometimes strangely an old Mormon
house of stone—but all in that hot dry immensity
                                        of heat and light
so curiously warped and small and dusty and forlorn—just a
touch of strangeness maybe in the set of eaves, the placing of
the tag porch, the turn of the shop gables (temple-wise perhaps)—but of architecture graceless, all denuded, with the
curious sterility and coldness and frustration the religion
has—but the earth meanwhile
                            burgeoning into green and fat
fertility—the windbreaks of the virgin poplars, the dense cool
green of poplars in the hot bright light and the staunch cool
shade of cottonwoods—and the valley winding into Canaan
and the Promised land—the fields lush now with their green,
their planted trees, the great reap of their mowings—
strangely Canaan

now—hemmed by the desert peaks—the hackled ridges on
both sides—denuded and half barren, curiously thrilling in
their nakedness—and Canaan magical, the vale irriguous below—The marvellous freshness and fecundity of the great Sevier valley now and in the midst of the great plain of Canaan
the town of Richfield (so named because of the
                                        fat district)
—a stop here—so on steadily into growing fertilities—a
blessed land of Canaan irriguous—by L.D.S. made fertile,
promised, and 'This is the place'—Jacob, Levan, Nephi, Go-
shen—the names Biblical in Canaan—or Spanish Fork and
American Fork—names like the pioneers—but ever the towns
arising from the desert

now—the lightness of new brick—the stamped hard patterns of new bungalows—and in the bright hot light clear wide
streets, neat houses, an air of growing and of prosperous-
ness—but still a graceless lack of architectural taste—but
now a kind of cooler sterner magic in the scenery (impassion-
ate, granite, clearly barren in the
                        hackled ridges of the limestone peaks,
the austere blackness of the timber)—and the great valley
floor burgeoning with Canaan in between—the cool flat silver
of the lake at Provo and the full fat land of plenty now—
cherry orchards groaning with their fruit, fields thick with
grain and hay, and
    fertile tillages betwixt the granite semi-arid clearness of
the desert peaks—Provo—its thriving look—the immense

smelter plants—in hot bright air the hot bright sunlight of the business street, the ugly sparseness, stamped out smartness of the stamped brick bungalow—the marvellousness of populars and of cottonwoods, the

dazzling brightness, richness, fragrance of the rambler roses—and full fat land of Canaan all away—great canning plants now, and fine wide roads, and flashing and increasing traffic—and Brighams great vale irriguous of Canaan and of plenty is marching, marching Northward between hackled peaks, is sweeping, sweeping Northward through the backbone of the Promised Land, is sweeping onward, onward toward the Temple and the Lake—and by a rise approaching the barriers of the hackled peak, up, up, around the naked shoulder of a gravel mountain and down, down into the salt plain of Salt Lake—half-desert still, half burgeoning to riches and

the irriguous ripe of the sudden green, and walled immensely on three sides by the hackled grandeur of the massive hills—but to the West, the massive peaks also but desert openness and the saline flatness, the thin mist lemon of the Great Salt Lake—so now the houses thicken both sides—another town with hot bright

central street, and stores, and city hall and, like the others, a denuded absence of humanity—then down four miles away to Salt Lake City—the bungalows close-set now on both sides—suddenly—heat—heat-misty on its splendid rise and facing the approach backed by the naked molding of the hills—the Capitol—with its

dome—looking like a capital and dome always do—So into Salt Lake—skyscrapers, hotels, office buildings, an appearance of a City greater than its growth and in 4 directions the broad streets sweeping out and ending cleanly under massed dense green at the rises of the barren magic hills—so into town, past a fantastic dance hall, "the worlds

biggest"—stores, streets, blocks 600 feet in length and Sunday hotness, brightness, emptiness—the old feeling of Mormon coldness, desolation—the cruel, the devoted, the fanatic, and the warped and dead.

From Thomas Wolfe, *A Western Journal* (Pittsburgh: University of Pittsburgh Press, 1951), pp. 69, 32–37.

Gary Snyder

Northwest Lodgepole Pine

"Lodgepole Pine: the wonderful reproductive
power of this species on areas over which its
stand has been killed by fire is dependent upon
the ability of the closed cones to endure a fire
which kills the tree without injuring its seed.
After fire, the cones open and shed their seeds
on the bared ground and a new growth springs up ."

Stood straight
               holding the choker high
As the Cat swung back the arch
               piss-firs falling,
Limbs snapping on the tin hat
               bright D caught on
Swinging butt-hooks
               ringing against cold steel.
Hsü Fang lived on leeks and pumpkins.
Goosefoot,
          wild herbs,
                    fields lying fallow!

But it's hard to farm
Between the stumps:
The cows get thin, the milk tastes funny,
The kids grow up and go to college
They don't come back.
               the little fir-trees do

               Rocks the same blue as sky
Only icefields, a mile up,
               are the mountain
Hovering over ten thousand acres
Of young fir

From Gary Snyder, *Myths and Texts* (New York: Totem Press in association with Corinth Books, 1960), pp. 5–6.

J. B. Priestley
Boulder Dam

In order to see [Boulder Dam], we traveled for hours and hours along narrow dirt roads through the high emptiness of Nevada. Anybody who is under the impression that the world is becoming too crowded should move into Nevada. If the whole of Great Britain were inhabited by the people of Oxford, there would still be more folk about than there are in Nevada. A road there seems to lead endlessly from nothing to nothing. A solitary filling station soon gives the Nevada traveler a sense of a bustling urban life. When they do achieve a town there, they throw it wide open, probably feeling that any restriction would be intolerable at the end of such trails. Reno, with its divorcing, and Las Vegas, with its all-night gambling, are tiny oases in an immense mile-high desert. To meet a few other human beings in Nevada is to assist at a miracle. Here, like the young Mark Twain, they are roughing it still. Anything new that has been introduced since his time is lost in these vacant immensities.

Except Boulder Dam. And that is worth traveling weeks to see. . . . Here in this Western American wilderness, the new man, the man of the future, has done something, and what he has done takes your breath away. When you look down at that vast smooth wall, at its towers of concrete, its power stations, at the new lakes and cataracts it has created; and you see the men who have made it all moving far below like ants or swinging perilously in midair as if they were little spiders; and you note the majestic order and rhythm of the work— you are visited by emotions that are hard to describe, if only because some of them are as new as the great dam itself.

Compared with this piece of building, the recent skyscrapers seem like toys. The shining towers of New York merely express the new man in his initial playful mood. With Boulder Dam he has really set to work. This is what he can do when given a real job. This is a first glimpse of what chemistry and mathematics and engineering and large-scale organization can accomplish when collective planning unites and inspires them. Here is the soul of America under socialism.

This is the reply to the old heedless, wasteful individualism. . . .

. . . There is no doubt whatever that it is a thing of beauty, and that the impression it makes on any sensitive observer is not unlike that made by a massive work of art. But if you feel that language is being abused here, and hold that nothing so impersonal as a dam can be a genuine work of art, then you have to find some new way of accurately describing this new creation.

From J. B. Priestley, *Midnight on the Desert* (New York and London: Harper & Bros., 1937), pp. 109–112.

Joan Didion

The Great Central Valley of California

A hundred miles north of Los Angeles, at the moment when you drop from the Tehachapi Mountains into the outskirts of Bakersfield, you leave Southern California and enter the Valley. "You look up the highway and it is straight for miles, coming at you, with the black line down the center coming at you and at you . . . and the heat dazzles up from the white slab so that only the black line is clear, coming at you with the whine of the tires, and if you don't quit staring at that line and don't take a few deep breaths and slap yourself hard on the back of the neck you'll hypnotize yourself."

Robert Penn Warren wrote that about another road, but he might have been writing about the Valley road, U.S. 99, three hundred miles from Bakersfield to Sacramento, a highway so straight that when one flies on the most direct pattern from Los Angeles to Sacramento one never loses sight of U.S. 99. The landscape it runs through never, to the untrained eye, varies. The Valley eye can discern the point where miles of cotton seedlings fade into miles of tomato seedlings, or where the great corporation ranches—Kern County Land, what is left of DiGiorgio—give way to private operations (somewhere on the horizon, if the place is private, one sees a house and a stand of scrub oaks), but such distinctions are in the long view irrelevant. All day long, all that moves is the sun, and the big Rainbird sprinklers.

Every so often along 99 between Bakersfield and Sacramento, there is a town: Delano, Tulare, Fresno, Madera, Merced, Modesto, Stockton. Some of these towns are pretty big now, but they are all the same at heart, one- and two- and three-story buildings artlessly arranged, so that what appears to be the good dress shop stands beside a W.T. Grant store, so that the Bank of America faces a Mexican movie house. *Dos Peliculas, Bingo Bingo Bingo.* Beyond the downtown (pronounced *down*town, with the Okie accent that now pervades Valley speech patterns) lie blocks of old frame houses—paint peeling, sidewalks cracking, their occasional leaded amber windows overlooking a Foster's Freeze or a five-minute car wash or a State Farm Insurance office; beyond those spread the shopping centers and the miles of tract houses, pastel with redwood siding, the unmistakable signs of cheap building already blossoming on those houses which have survived the first rain. To a stranger driving 99 in an air-conditioned car (he would be on business, I suppose, any stranger driving 99, for 99 would never get a tourist to Big Sur or San Simeon, never get him to the California he came to see), these towns must seem so flat, so impoverished, as to drain the imagination. They hint at evenings spent hanging around gas stations, and suicide pacts sealed in drive-ins. . . .

U. S. 99 in fact passes through the richest and most intensely cultivated agricultural region in the world, a giant outdoor hothouse with a billion-dollar crop. It is when you remember the Valley's wealth that the monochromatic flatness of its towns takes on a curious meaning, suggests a habit of mind some would consider perverse. There is something in the Valley mind that reflects a real indifference to the stranger in his air-conditioned car, a failure to perceive even his presence, let alone his thoughts or wants. An implacable insularity is the seal of these towns. I once met a woman in Dallas, a most charming and attractive woman accustomed to the hospitality and social hypersensitivity of Texas, who told me that during the four war years her husband had been stationed in Modesto, she had never once been invited inside anyone's house. No one in Sacramento would find this story remarkable. ("She probably had no relatives there," said someone to whom I told it), for the Valley towns understand one another, share a peculiar spirit. They think alike and they look alike. I can tell Modesto from Merced, but I have visited there, gone to dances there; besides, there is over the main street of Modesto an arched sign which reads:

WATER—WEALTH
CONTENTMENT—HEALTH

There is no such sign in Merced.

From Joan Didion, *Slouching Towards Bethlehem* (New York: Farrar, Straus & Giroux, 1968), pp. 180–182.

Thomas Pynchon

San Narciso, California

San Narciso lay further south, near L. A. Like many named places in California it was less an identifiable city than a grouping of concepts—census tracts, special purpose bond-issue districts, shopping nuclei, all overlaid with access roads to its own freeway. . . . She drove into San Narciso on a Sunday, in a rented Impala. Nothing was happening. She looked down a slope, needing to squint for the sunlight, onto a vast sprawl of houses which had grown up all together, like a well-tended crop, from the dull brown earth; and she thought of the time she'd opened a transistor radio to replace a battery and seen her first printed circuit. The ordered swirl of houses and streets, from this high angle, sprang at her now with the same unexpected, astonishing clarity as the circuit card had. Though she knew even less about radios than about Southern Californians, there were to both outward patterns a hieroglyphic sense of concealed meaning, of an intent to communicate. There'd seemed no limit to what the printed circuit could have told her (if she had tried to find out); so in her first minute of San Narciso, a revelation also trembled just past the threshold of her understanding. Smog hung all round the horizon, the sun on the bright beige countryside was painful; she and the Chevy seemed parked at the centre of an odd, religious instant. As if, on some other frequency, or out of the eye of some whirlwind rotating too slow for her heated skin even to feel the centrifugal coolness of, words were being spoken. She suspected that much. She thought of Mucho, her husband, trying to believe in his job. Was it something like this he felt, looking through the soundproof glass at one of his colleagues with a headset clamped on and cueing the next record with movements stylized as the handling of chrism, censer, chalice might be for a holy man, yet really tuned in to the voice, voices, the music, its message, surrounded by it, digging it, as were all the faithful it went out to; did Mucho stand outside Studio A looking in, knowing that even if he could hear it he couldn't believe in it?

From Thomas Pynchon, *The Crying of Lot 49* (New York: J. B. Lippincott Co., 1966), pp. 24–25.

W. H. Auden

The West from the Air

It is an unforgettable experience for anyone born on the other side of the Atlantic to take a plane journey by night across the United States. Looking down he will see the lights of some town like a last outpost in a darkness stretching for hours ahead, and realize that, even if there is no longer an actual frontier, there is still a continent only partially settled and developed, where human activity seems a tiny thing in comparison to the magnitude of the earth, and the equality of men not some dogma of politics or jurisprudence but a self-evident fact. He will behold a wild nature, compared with which the landscapes of Salvator Rosa are as cosy as Arcadia and which cannot possibly be thought of in human or personal terms. . . .

. . . All European literature so far has presupposed two things: a nature which is humanized, mythologized, usually friendly, and a human society in which most men stay where they were born and do not move about much. Neither of these presuppositions was valid for America, where nature

was virgin, devoid of history, usually hostile; and society was
fluid, its groupings always changing as men moved on somewhere else. . . .

Many poets in the Old World have become disgusted with
human civilization but what the earth would be like if the human race became extinct they cannot imagine; an American
like Robinson Jeffers can quite easily, for he has seen with
his own eyes country as yet untouched by history.

From W. H. Auden, *The Dyer's Hand and Other Essays* (New York:
Random House, 1962), pp. 358, 363–64, 359.

Robinson Jeffers

November Surf

Some lucky day each November great waves awake and
     are drawn
Like smoking mountains bright from the west
And come and cover the cliff with white violent cleanness:
     then suddenly
The old granite forgets half a year's filth:
The orange-peel, eggshells, papers, pieces of clothing, the
     clots
Of dung in corners of the rock, and used
Sheaths that make light love safe in the evenings: all the
     droppings of the summer
Idlers washed off in a winter ecstasy:
I think this cumbered continent envies its cliff then. . . .
     But all seasons
The earth, in her childlike prophetic sleep,
Keeps dreaming of the bath of a storm that prepares up the
     long coast
Of the future to scour more than her sea-lines:
The cities gone down, the people fewer and the hawks more
     numerous
The rivers mouth to source pure; when the two-footed

Mammal, being someways one of the nobler animals, regains
The dignity of room, the value of rareness.

From Robinson Jeffers, *The Selected Poetry of Robinson Jeffers* (New York: Random House, 1938), p. 360.